Very good

Penny's Diner Love Stories

All the best!

Penny Burgess

Penny's Diner Love Stories

Penny Burgess

2948-BURG

Library of Congress Number:		00-192241
ISBN #:	Hardcover	0-7388-3855-1
	Softcover	1-59109-144-6

This book was printed in the United States of America.

Contents

A BROTHER'S LOVE

Returning For Love

A Safe Haven

To my family and especially my husband,
Bill, whose love and support keeps me going.

2948-BURG

Everyone has their own love story, and it's nice to know some things have a happy ending. These three stories show love can be found anywhere, any time, at any age.

Penny's Diner Love Stories is a set of three novels in one that involves couples who fall in love at different stages in life and under very different circumstances. What they all have in common is that they meet and fall in love at Penny's Diner.

The stories are, of course, not true and not based on any real person or group of people who have either worked at or even visited a Penny's Diner. However, perhaps if you hang around a Penny's Diner long enough, you too might find true love.

2948-BURG

A Brother's Love

by Penny Burgess

2948-BURG

Chapter One

Olivia Patterson drove up to the new "Penny's Diner" she'd noticed when she first moved to town. Cutting the motor, she lingered in her car for a few minutes, wondering once again if her plan would really work.

Ever since she'd left Chicago to move here, to a town where people did not know her, did not gravitate to her simply because of her position, family name, and money, she felt she'd done the right thing. In fact, she'd been so confident when she discovered this place, large enough, yet small enough for comfort, that she'd bought a house on the outskirts of town.

Her next line of business was a stop at the new 24-hour diner she'd driven by time and again, slowing but never stopping. As she pushed through the door of Penny's Diner, she wondered what drew her so much about the shiny new structure decorated in the 50's era motif. The thin neon at the top that scripted out Penny's Diner called to her somehow. It was time to make her move, but would they give her a chance? she questioned.

The only thing that built up her confidence in trying such a different job than any in her past was that the "waitress wanted" sign was still up after over two weeks.

Once inside, she glanced around at the lively restaurant and smiled. It was perfect, she decided, and a total change from her top executive job in Chicago. It made her quickly wonder what her parents or her friends in Chicago would think if they knew her plan. The image of their surprised faces amused her, and spurred her on even more, for Olivia was sure they'd all figured she'd now lounge around aimlessly, licking her wounds from the fiasco of the marriage that had caused her such dismay. Well, they were wrong, she thought. Whatever she decided to do long-term, she knew moving to a place where nobody knew her would be the very thing to get her head on straight.

As she edged up to the counter, a tall, attractive woman with blonde hair about fifty years old headed in her direction.

"You can just sit anywhere that suits your fancy," she called out.

"Actually, I was hoping to apply for the job," Olivia explained.

The waitress stopped in her tracks, and her eyes widened as she took in Olivia's well-dressed form. Olivia decided the cut of her rich suit and designer shoes might cause a little confusion. She now decided it had been the wrong choice of what to wear to this interview, for Olivia was certain a month's salary from the diner wouldn't cover the cost of this one outfit. But she had no interest in the money part of it. She had plenty of that. Olivia needed the job for her emotional well-being. She straightened her shoulders, still determined to put her best foot forward.

"The job?" Olivia reminded her.

"The waitress job?" the woman echoed uncertainly.

"Yes. Is it still open?"

The woman finally relaxed after a few awkward moments, then leaned against the counter in Olivia's direction.

"That job *is* still open. I'm the manager, and my best waitress, Sadie, is starting a new family. She got married, and I think the young couple wanted kids right off. Sadie's announcement a couple of weeks back proved me right."

"I see," Olivia answered. "So, I'm interested in the position," she managed. "What do I need to do to apply?"

"Well," she began slowly, "I do need help. As soon as possible. Do you have any references? Past experience?"

"I don't have any experience, I'll tell you that right off. But I'm a quick learner. I have a master's degree in marketing management," she added, certain as soon as the words escaped her that presenting this information for the job was also a mistake. Normally, for the positions she'd applied for, it was a selling point. Here it might be construed as making her "overly educated for the position." The waitress in charge would now decide Olivia was not the right person for the job since she might leave right away, Olivia quickly reasoned.

Sure enough, the woman's eyebrows drew together in a frown, and after a long pause she leaned back up.

"Ummm, I'll be right back," she promised. The waitress snatched a coffee pot from the burner and quickly refilled a customer's cup a few seats down. Olivia noted the confused look remained on the waitress' face as she refilled another customer's cup farther down the line. By the time she returned, Olivia decided she'd tried her best and would let the woman off easy, not making it any more uncomfortable a situation than it already was.

"I understand about the position," Olivia began. "You need a different kind of experience. Perhaps I'll just have a cup of coffee while I'm here," she added, placing her purse on the counter and sliding onto the stool.

A slow smile then formed across the waitress' face. She poured Olivia a cup of coffee, reached under the counter, and pulled out a piece of paper. She then extended her free hand in Olivia's direction.

"The name's Millie Holmes. If you're really interested in the job, why don't you fill out this application and if there're no holes in the information you give me, just show up tomorrow morning at 7:30 a.m. and we'll see how you like it. If you decide after a day or two it's not your cup of tea, then no hard feelings. Deal?" Millie asked cheerfully.

"I can't ask for better than that," Olivia answered, surprised at the generosity of the woman, as well as her not pressing Olivia for her personal reasons for being interested in this position—which were surely no one's business but her own.

As she busied herself with the application, she couldn't help but look up every time the door opened, which was frequently. This waitress certainly did need extra help, and from a snatch of conversation she now heard a few seats down, the waitress job wasn't the only position open.

Olivia took a quick peek over, then brought her focus back to her paperwork and listened as Millie busily explained to a man around his late-twenties, same as Olivia's age, that she also needed a cook. Olivia darted a look over again to the handsome man who appeared to be interested not for himself but for someone else. She also overheard Millie mentioning that she'd just filled the waitress' position, and Olivia caught sight out of the corner of her eye as she gestured in her direction.

Olivia paused as she held her pen suspended in mid-air. Millie had rushed off to help a new group of customers who'd come through the door, and she had the distinct impression the man was staring a hole through her. When she glanced up, he quickly looked away.

From then on, Olivia remained distracted from the task at hand. The stranger was tall, rugged, and handsome in a deeply masculine way. When their eyes met again, he smiled. His style and manner were refreshing, for he didn't seem to even notice her clothes, but focused on her face—and hair. This feature also got people's attention with its unusual, natural auburn color. She gave him a quick smile in return, then forced herself to look back at the half-finished application. Moments later he left, and she was able to concentrate once again.

After filling out the paperwork and finishing the cup of coffee, Olivia felt a weight already lifting off her shoulders. The place simply felt good, and the honest, down-to-earth customers she'd witnessed coming and going were exactly what she needed to re-establish her faith in the human race—especially after Millie Holmes. She'd given Olivia a chance to prove she could do something she'd never tried before, and it was time she started anew, no matter what the rest of her world thought.

* * *

Red Taylor came in the back door loaded down with groceries he'd gotten while in town. He'd had to double his efforts on this front since his younger brother had abruptly moved back home at the worst possible time. Not that he didn't want the best for his brother, but the young guy didn't seem to have a handle on the best direction to head at this time in life any more than Red did.

Jimmy assumed all was well when he'd shown up out of the blue. And he definitely wasn't aware of the problems that plagued Red, much less the decision hanging over his older brother's head—one that would affect them both. Now that Red had Jimmy to support again, he'd have to hang on a little longer, and wouldn't burden his younger brother with the family dilemma.

Poking his head down the hallway toward Jimmy's bedroom, he attempted to solicit his brother's help.

"Hey, waif? Get out here," Red said good-heartedly.

"Why do you call me that stupid name?" Jimmy Taylor called out defensively.

"Because it suits you," he teased, hoping to re-establish the banter they'd enjoyed as kids.

"Says who?" Jimmy challenged, now emerging from the bedroom and coming down the hall in Red's direction.

"Me, you little waif," he said, smiling. "So, go get the last grocery sack in the truck," he added, then headed back to the kitchen and shoved the bulging bags of groceries onto the counter.

"Get it yourself," Jimmy answered as he detoured into the adjoining den and tossed himself onto the sofa. With a quick push of the remote, the silence was replaced with the blaring of a sporting event Jimmy'd found on one of the satellite channels.

Red took in a deep breath, his good humor now leaving him.

"Look, Jimmy, you owe me to help out. It's the least you can do, don't you think?"

Jimmy remained silent while Red opened the fridge and pushed fresh produce into the bin.

"Well?" he asked again, as he closed the refrigerator door and crossed to the den, pushing his large, six-foot frame between the television and Jimmy's reclining form.

"I can't see," Jimmy complained.

"Yeah. That's the point," Red argued, now beginning to lose his cool. Taking care of his younger brother after his father had died sometimes seemed like a full-time job—one he thought he'd finished, much less caring for the family business. The fact that he worked so hard and Jimmy displayed the opposite behavior seemed to get under his skin even more. Jimmy remained obstinately on the couch, craning his neck around Red, determined to continue to watch the useless entertainment.

"You're gonna have to pull your weight if you continue to stay here, Jimmy," he warned.

"Yeah, well, this living arrangement is wearing a little thin," he put in.

"Nobody's keeping you here. Just move out," Red said, angry at the whole situation, and Jimmy's attitude making it worse.

"I can't," he said, pushing himself into a seated position. "Not 'til I get back on my feet financially. Get some cash put away."

Red took in a quick breath, ready to say his rehearsed line now that the stage was set and the timing was right.

"Well, they need help over at Penny's Diner. A cook, I think."

"That's not what I'm looking for," Jimmy answered, slumping down again.

"Well, that doesn't matter, kiddo. It's what's looking for you, 'cause like you just said, you need a job."

"I don't want to be a cook. You make me do enough of that around here."

"It doesn't have to be a long-term thing." Red paused in the awkward silence, seeing he was making no progress with his brother. It was time to pull out the big guns.

"Hey, I'm not gonna support you forever, bro. I'm doing all I can as it is," he pointed out.

"You just want the house back to yourself."

"Yeah. That's it, all right," Red answered sarcastically. "You're putting a crimp in my social life, being here all the time, after all."

"What social life?" Jimmy asked. "You haven't had a date since I moved back two months ago."

"Maybe that's cause you're here," he said, giving his brother a quick smile and moving back into the kitchen.

"I should have never come back to this stinking town," Jimmy shot back, as he turned off the television and followed on his brother's heels.

"So leave. You're the one who wanted to make it in the big city."

"I still do," Jimmy said, slumping down into a kitchen chair now.

Red turned around, giving his brother his full attention. They had a tendency to fight, had some tension and a brotherly competition thing going, but Jimmy was a full eight years younger and Red's responsibility since both their parents had died. He wanted to help his brother, he just didn't know how.

"Okay, Jimmy. I know small town living isn't for everybody. When Dad died that left me to run the business, but I can see you don't have any interest in farming, not that I blame you, but you've got to get *some* money together before heading back East. Why don't ya just go talk to Millie at the Diner. See what she says about a temporary position. But be honest with her, though. Don't let on that you're gonna stay forever. Just tell her your situation. She'll understand."

"What makes you think I'd lie to her?"

"You tend to skirt around the truth sometimes to get what you want, that's why. And Millie's a good friend. Now, are you gonna to be straight with her?"

"I'm not lying to her 'cause I'm not going over there," Jimmy taunted.

Red stormed out the back door to retrieve the last bag of groceries his brother had refused to get. He was literally at his wit's end and he had to put his foot down. Jimmy's mooching was not going to make things any easier. At twenty-eight years old, Red had other things on his mind—like fixing this present problem so he could think about normal things like starting a family of his own. Of course, Red would have to find the girl of his dreams first, and he wouldn't settle for just anyone. She'd have to be special—like the one he presently had his eye on.

As he moved back into the house, he found Jimmy had returned to the couch, the same show blaring through the house. He could take no more.

Dropping the sack onto the kitchen table, he moved back in front of Jimmy again, snapping the power off with the remote.

"Look, bro. I've got more work around here than I can stand. If you're planning to stretch out on the couch all day, you can forget it."

"I'm not working the farm. I didn't come back for that."

"Yeah, we've been through that, but I'm beginning to get the picture. You'd hoped I'd just hand over some cash and wish you well. Sorry, it just doesn't work that way."

"I've got money in the inheritance. Not that much, Dad saw to that, but enough to get started for a long time in a new town. Unless you're planning on using it for the farm, which isn't going to happen," he added, rising to his feet and facing Red.

Red told himself to take another steadying breath. His brother really knew his buttons and did everything he could to push them. He realized as he looked down at his brother, a good five inches shorter and light of frame, that Jimmy continued to balance a very large chip on his shoulder. The boy was hurting from a lot of things life had dealt him, and he hadn't found anything to build his confidence. Red understood the resentment his brother held, but he couldn't let him ruin both their lives.

"I wouldn't touch your money, Jimmy," Red finally answered. "You know that. But neither can you. Not until you turn twenty-one this winter."

"Six months away. Why not just give it to me now?"

"I can't. I promised Dad and it's in the will. So, you'll have to make money till then, and you'll have plenty to spend on the move and getting settled someplace else."

His brother remained with his hands on his hips, facing off his older brother.

"If you're not gonna try to find work over at the Diner, then I've got a list here that I've made up of places that might need help," Red continued.

Jimmy snatched the list from his brother's hand. He took a quick look, crumpled it into a ball, then tossed it onto the coffee table.

"That's the way it's gonna be?" Red asked, feeling the blood rise to his face.

"Just relax. You're too uptight," Jimmy said as he calmly walked across the room and grabbed the keys to the used compact car he'd bought for a song a year before.

"Where do you think you're going?" Red trailed after him.

"Penny's. Anything's better than sticking around here," Jimmy said, slamming the door behind him.

After his brother pulled out of the driveway, Red watched him from the picture window as he drove defensively up the dirt road that lead to the main highway. When the trail of dust disappeared and the sound of the car quieted into the distance, Red sank down into the kitchen chair.

He wasn't sure he'd done the right thing, setting Jimmy up like that. The boy did need a job, they needed the extra cash, and Red had to encourage him to get one or he'd spend the next six months waiting on the couch for his inheritance, getting madder and madder at Red for not forking it over. But he just couldn't give him the cash yet—for a lot of reasons. Still, he'd just manipulated his brother into getting a job where it would help out Red in another way—at Penny's Diner. And Red had an ulterior motive in doing so.

The new waitress he'd spotted who must have just moved to town worked the shift that Red knew held the opening. With Jimmy working there, it'd give him the opportunity he wanted to get close to her.

He needed an "in," somehow, because for the life of him, he couldn't understand why just the sight of the woman with the auburn hair and bright green eyes rendered Red speechless, and brought out the shy side he hadn't experienced since the third grade. If anyone were to know it, they'd never have believed it. But it was true.

Perhaps it was just that he'd never seen anyone like her. Perhaps it was because all his life he'd envisioned a beauty with such unusual looks and spell-binding charisma who could tie him to the oldest family institution in the book. If only she would realize Red was alive.

Chapter Two

"Hi, Jimmy. Heard you moved back to town," Millie Holmes said as he breezed through the door at Penny's Diner.

"Yeah. Heard you're looking for somebody to cook," he answered.

"Hmmm. How are you in the kitchen?"

"Red says I'm pretty good."

"What do you say?"

"I'm a good cook, but I don't really want to do it all day."

Millie grinned back.

"What's so funny," he asked finally as Millie leaned across the counter, her smile broadening.

"Just wondered why you came in for the cook's position yet you tell me you don't want to cook."

"You asked me if I *could* cook. Which I can. I said I didn't like to do it all day. Hours about 7 a.m. to 3 p.m., right? You offering okay money?"

"Pay's commensurate with what others are giving for this type of work," she informed him.

"I can take breaks? Get free food?"

"Yes—and no. Breaks, yes. Food? That's at a discount. Not free."

"Well, okay. I'll take it."

Millie broke out in contagious laughter. It made Jimmy smile despite his sour mood, lifting his spirits for the first time in a long time.

This lady kinda reminded him of how his mother used to be before she died. Most of what he could remember anyway.

"What's funny. You think I'm pretty funny, huh?"

"Seeing that you took over the interview, like I was the one asking to be your boss. Nobody offered you a job, you know."

"You're turning me down?" Jimmy asked incredulously.

"No. In fact, since you just accepted the position, the least I could do is give you a chance," she put in. "You ready to roll?"

"Now?" Jimmy felt reality hit him in the stomach. He'd just gotten used to the idea of doing this, but starting that minute was not in his plan. More TV was on his mind before settling into this work-a-day world.

"I'm short, and we could use an extra helping hand. I'll help train you as you go. Suit you?"

"I guess."

"Good. Be a good new employee and fill out these papers first. Then put on this apron here and get going before the lunch crowd builds up out of control."

Millie shoved an application and a set of legal-looking papers behind it onto the counter, then placed a pen on top.

"So, you don't have to check my references or anything?" Jimmy asked, feeling good about being around such a cheerful person as Millie Holmes.

"No, I don't believe that will be necessary," she told him.

"Why not?" Jimmy smiled back, sitting up taller and imagining that he looked like the honest and hard-working type.

"Simple. I know your brother, Red. That's enough reference for me," she explained, as she dashed off to help a customer at the end of the counter who wanted to pay.

Jimmy felt his smile fade. Red. Always Red. He wondered if he could stand it, being back in town again in his brother's shadow. At least at Penny's he could be his own man without Red hanging over him. He'd make a good impression here and Red had better keep his nose out of his business while he was at the Diner.

He then filled out the papers and donned the apron Millie had pushed in his direction. It already felt good being outside of Red's influence. People would now see Jimmy Taylor as his own man—not as Red's younger brother. Starting today.

* * *

Red forced himself to keep his concentration going on the work at hand. Harvesting the last of the forty acres was almost finished. Finally. As much as he liked the great outdoors, the hot August sun beating down on the back of his neck caused his muscles to ache and his body was tiring sooner than usual today.

Red knew why. It had been the argument he'd had with his brother earlier. At least he'd gotten him to see about the job at Penny's Diner. Since he hadn't returned, Red hoped that was a good sign.

In retrospect, he wished he'd gone over there with him—just to ensure that Jimmy went through with it, and to get to say a quick "hi" to the auburn-haired beauty he wished he had the nerve to speak to before.

Maybe Jimmy could fill him in on the details of her down the road. Perhaps he could find out if she was dating anybody before Red made a fool of himself. Yes, he thought, as he cut the motor of the massive harvester and climbed down to the earth he'd been working all afternoon, he should've gone. Still, as soon as the thought passed his mind, he realized he could no more have done that since the rigors of keeping up this business called for him to finish in a timely manner.

He looked out over the farm his father had so lovingly worked, bringing in an income to support his family, having to do so later on with no wife by his side and two sons to keep in line.

Red walked toward the house, trees now shading his path and giving some relief from the late afternoon sun and heat of the day. He hadn't chosen this life. It had chosen him, he decided. But then again, Red realized if he wanted his life to be any different, he'd have to be the one to make the changes. He only had to have the cash to do it, and that was building way too slowly, and leaving him so little time to go after his own dreams, or the love of a woman he had in mind to pursue.

When he made it to the back of the house and saw that Jimmy's car was still missing, he knew he'd gotten the job. He shrugged his shoulders around, stretching the sore shoulder muscles and smiled. At least this was going right, and now that he'd finished the rest of the harvesting that afternoon, he decided that tomorrow he'd surprise Jimmy by showing up at his new job and showing support.

Getting a cool drink of water from the kitchen faucet, he also admitted to himself the real reason for his visit. Not for Jimmy. For himself. As he began to consider the dream he had in mind, and the pretty waitress there, he felt a renewed sense of determination building. He was on a roll. And tomorrow was just the beginning.

*   *   *

"So, this is what it takes for you to get up and at 'em early in the morning?" Red teased as he brother came into the kitchen, pouring out a cup of coffee and taking a quick sip.

"Yep. Duty calls," Jimmy answered, not bothering to sit down or finish the cup. Three gulps later he was headed out the door.

"Hey, just a minute! You hardly talked about your new job at all last night," Red said, hoping to get a word about the waitress and see if she had already started and perhaps was working the early shift that day.

"What's to say? I'm the chief cook and bottle washer," he said, smiling. "And over at Penny's, they're paying me. Which is more than I can say for you."

"You've got free room and board. Free food."

"So what? This is my family home. And don't worry about the food. I'll be taking most of my meals at Penny's."

He nodded curtly then stepped out the door and slammed it behind him.

Red cringed. He could sure use his father's words of wisdom about now. Still, all he could do was keep trying. Later on he'd go over for lunch and brag on the new cook. Jimmy actually was highly talented in that area, and for the life of him Red didn't know where he'd picked it up. Just a knack, he imagined.

Just as he'd promised himself, by lunch time Red tied up the business he had begun and felt good about taking the break. As he moved through the glass door and checked around the Diner, he noticed a back table just freed up by an elderly couple.

Red nodded to them in passing, and positioned himself in the chair that allowed him a full view of Penny's. Jimmy was positioned at the grill, his back to the Diner. But as he glanced to the right, he discovered Olivia Patterson taking an order from a full table of customers.

At this, Red found himself catching his breath. She was just as beautiful as he'd remembered. Though not classical in her looks, her features were unusual and pretty as well. He felt a lurch in his stomach that did not speak of his hunger for the Diner's food, but of his need for a woman who could make him feel like this. A woman who could make him forget the burdens of the family business.

Moments later, Olivia came skirting over to his table, flashing him a receptive smile that lit up her whole face.

"What can I get you to drink? Or are you ready to order?" she asked in a voice smooth as silk with a light-hearted overtone.

Red had never seen the woman this close up. Only at a short distance. He felt his eyes widen as he tried to decide what to say.

"Iced tea to drink, please. But I'm not ready to order yet. I think I need a minute," he answered as she smiled, slipped the order pad into her skirt pocket, and breezed away.

Red wiped his hand over his face, trying to re-focus. What had he been thinking, he wondered, now realizing what a beauty the woman really was. She would never go out with him. She must have a thousand guys hanging around, doing the exact same thing as he was, coming in here trying to get a brief few moments of her time. No wonder Penny's was so crowded that day, he decided and smiled.

2948-BURG

Within seconds she was back. She placed the iced tea in front of him then began her spiel.

"So, let me tell you about our specials today," she said with a smile. "First, if you're a late breakfast eater, we've got a really unique Vegetarian omelet as a special. Packed *full* of veggies. Or if you're the meat-eater type, we have a smothered country steak special with mashed potatoes and gravy. Green beans, too."

"Wow. I'll have to come in here more often. Sounds great. You have specials like that all the time?"

"Well, we've got a great new cook. Cooking up both the tried and true, and some really different kinds of things too. So try one of his specials and you won't be disappointed," she promised.

"I'll take the country fried steak this time," he said.

"It'll be right up," Olivia said, rushing off.

Red watched the shapely legs beneath the rather short skirt she wore. Some of the waitresses wore pants, but not this spirited beauty. She was all woman, feminine through and through.

As she shoved the ticket in front Jimmy, Red got a glimpse of his brother in his element at the grill. At some level he felt a warmth of pride as he saw the lean boy who'd grown to be a man racing around the area energetically. He even thought he'd heard a distant whistling, characteristic of his brother's earlier years.

Jimmy was happy, Red realized. He was having fun in this creative venture, and perhaps he felt appreciated, not just expected to help out as Red had pushed him to do. The funny thing was, the more you pushed Jimmy, the quicker he was to dig in his heels and thumb his nose at you. So, this little plan had worked out well for both of them.

Millie came rushing by, stopping abruptly when she recognized Red.

"Well, well. If it isn't Red Taylor again," she exclaimed.

"Yes, ma'am. How are you today, Millie?"

"Doing great. Busy. But I sure have to thank you for steering Jimmy in our direction. That boy has just about turned our grill area upside down and set it straight again in record time. And can he cook! Gosh, did you teach him?"

"I'm afraid I can't take credit for that, Millie. About all I teach him is how to stay mad at me. I'm glad he's doing so well here with you."

"It's the age, Red, and the circumstances. Give yourself a break. You've done a good job stepping in when you should've been still being a kid yourself," Millie told him.

"True. But I'm glad you had that opening."

"Yes, me, too. Jimmy adds a freshness, and he's fun to be around. Most of the time."

"Most of the time?" Red interjected, his eyebrows rising. "He's not causing any trouble, now is he?"

"No, no. I can just tell he's trying hard to get people to like him."

"He's defensive at home."

"Here he'll earn his own money and own way. Earn his own reputation."

"That again?" Red said. "I can't help it that I was the oldest and both parents died before the kid was grown. He's resented me for something totally out of my control, and I've tried to be both brother and parent to him. He's never considered my perspective. Suddenly I had to deal with all that, the family business, and I had Jimmy to raise and support besides myself. Yet he resents me," he finished, glad he had a friend to finally get the heavy burden off his chest. He knew Millie well. Knew she'd understand.

"You done good, Red. Just let Jimmy fly. He's in his element," she answered.

"Yeah. Well, like I said, I'm glad there was an opening. Seems you had a couple there to fill right at once," Red added, glancing over at Olivia who was presenting the table down the aisle with overflowing plates of food.

Millie followed his line of vision then turned back to Red with a smirk.

"I should have known, Red Taylor."

"What?" he asked with innocence.

"It's the new waitress who moved to town, the one who took my little Sadie's place after she and her husband decided to start a family. That's why you sent Jimmy over, isn't it?"

"No. She was here, all right, filling out that application when I came in to see if you had something for him to do, but Jimmy needed the work, Millie."

"I don't doubt that, Red, but I imagine you pushed this job opening first before any others you might have discovered around town."

"So what if I did?" he smiled, knowing he'd been caught.

"And besides that, I can see through your coming in here again so soon. It wasn't to check up on Jimmy."

"I don't know what you're talking about," Red argued with good humor.

"Uh, huh. Well, all's I can say is 'good luck'."

"Oh. She's got a boyfriend?"

"Nope. Just good luck. You're gonna need it to get past 'go.' By the way, I'll tell Jimmy you stopped by—after you get your lunch, that is. I don't want to make him nervous. We want to keep him as long as he'll stay," Millie explained, glancing over at Olivia, then back to Red and shaking her head.

Olivia brushed past Millie on her way to the table with Red's lunch special. As she bent over to place the plate of food squarely in front of him, he caught the light, clean scent that followed her.

"Anything else I can get you?"

Red started at the creamy, smooth skin that needed very little make-up. It was such a match for the dark auburn hair that waved seductively around her heart-shaped face. He wanted to tell her she could get him a free evening to spend with him so he could see if this fantasy he'd visualized was real or not, if they had anything in common or not, but he just glanced down at the abundance of food and shook his head.

"Nope. Nothing at all," he answered.

As she gently laid the green ticket onto the table and rushed off to see to another customer, Red exhaled deeply. She'd rendered him speechless once again. The opportunity had come and gone and he was still sitting here just watching from afar. Just like he'd reacted in the third grade when he'd developed a crush on his teacher with the same auburn hair.

Maybe that's what this is about, he mused, digging into the tender meat and real mashed potatoes. Maybe that's why I can't seem to get my head on straight when I talk to her. The fact that Millie had warned him that he'd need a lot of luck did nothing to build his confidence. It probably set him back. But now that Jimmy was working here . . .

At that moment, the lanky boy showed up at his table, his hands placed defensively on his hips.

"Checking up on me? Didn't you believe I could do this job?" Jimmy demanded.

Red felt his face flush. It was one thing for Jimmy to start an argument at home, but in the middle of Penny's within earshot's distance to all around? Red knew his brother and how to diffuse the situation, though—and quickly.

"Well, you've done yourself proud, bro. This smothered steak is the best I've ever put in my mouth. I'm glad to pay for your cooking," he added. "You deserve it."

Jimmy's stance relaxed.

"Yeah?"

"Oh, yeah. I hear you're giving them new ideas, too. And I'm glad, Jimmy. Now all the town can enjoy your cooking talents," he added.

With this, Jimmy took a seat in the opposite chair. He looked sheepishly at his brother.

"I'm glad you pushed me to do it. To find a job. Especially this one. I need a kick in the pants sometimes. And you're always happy to oblige."

Red chuckled. It was one of the first real conversations they'd had in a while. He assumed it was because it took place here, on Jimmy's turf, where the kid was proud of what he could do that others couldn't.

"I'm not here to check up on you, Jimmy. I think I just wanted to get away from the house and give myself a treat. So, don't let me hold you up. We can talk at home any time," he added, not wanting to keep Jimmy from his job, and also wanting the waitress to come back again.

Jimmy rose and gave Red a quick smile before walking briskly back to the grill area. He read over a ticket and quickly went back to work.

Olivia came by two more times, refilling his tea glass without so much as a word, and shuffling off the dirty dishes the moment he was finished. He knew one thing about her, she was efficient, and yes, Millie was right. She'd be a tough nut to crack, but if he could get past his shyness he'd at least ask her out. He owed himself that much. Maybe next time, he promised himself rising to go.

Chapter Three

After Red paid Millie at the cash register and headed out, Olivia picked up his generous tip, then breezed up to the front. She found Millie gazing out the window as Red drove his almost new, bright red truck out of the parking lot.

"So, who's the tall guy? I saw him in here yesterday."

Millie's head swiveled around at Red's retreating truck, then back to Olivia.

"Oh, you mean Red?" Millie asked and smiled. Olivia knew her interest in him, which went further than curiosity, showed through. She quickly tried to think of an impersonal comment to throw in.

"Red? That's an odd name. What kind of name is that?" Olivia asked, now amused. "Don't tell me they call him that because of the color truck he drives?"

"No. It's short for his middle name. Redmond. His mother's maiden name."

"Oh," Olivia answered, absently clearing away a plate from the counter and dragging a damp dishcloth over the counter where a drop of syrup remained from a pancake order.

"So what's his first name?" she asked, hoping to get more information about him.

"Nobody knows, except his brother, I suppose, who's probably sworn to secrecy so you might as well not ask him. Since we all call him Red, I get the impression his first name is not something he wishes to share," she finished, turning away to check the coffee maker.

Olivia could see fishing for information about the handsome man who drew her attention would be of no use. Millie had closed up about him and she didn't know why. She told herself to leave it alone right then and there. Her instincts told her so. But she couldn't seem to stop herself from trying again.

"Is this guy's brother somebody I'm supposed to know?"

Millie cracked a small smile. She slid her a look then nodded her head toward the side. Olivia glanced in the direction Millie gestured. Jimmy stood in front of the grill, cooking up one of his special vegetarian omelets, whistling away. He reached toward the numerous bins of veggies, tossing a mixture on the griddle with style.

Getting the picture, Olivia suddenly knew why Millie clamed up so quickly. The man's brother stood two feet away and could easily overhear anything they discussed. No, the time was not right to find out about this "Red" person, but she would. She'd been instantly, strongly attracted to him from the first time she'd laid eyes on him—and she knew there was nothing she could do about it. It was like standing squarely on the middle of the tracks of an oncoming train, and she, already mesmerized, not doing a thing but watching it, helpless to move out of it's path.

Olivia had a feeling it was a trip that'd be rocky. She could sense it from deep within, and with her past, she didn't know if she could withstand it. She only knew she was about to fall headlong into Red's path anyway.

* * *

Red slammed the door of the truck behind him. He was so angry with himself for not taking the opportunity to at least talk to the woman. What was wrong with him, anyway?

He then turned toward the sound of a car coming onto his property. Moments later Gus Rigsby came barreling into his driveway. As if things couldn't get any worse, Red thought, as he watched the man climb out of his Lincoln.

"What can I do for you today, Gus?"

"What I always want," he said, smiling. "You can't put it off much longer," he told him.

"I might have to," Red answered.

"Sell the land, Red. It's your only choice. Before you're forced to," the man warned.

"This land is my father's legacy and I won't sell."

"You're no farmer. You barely make ends meet," the man argued without malice.

"I've done it for the past five years. I haven't lost the land, or gone broke. I've stayed just ahead of things," he said, bringing his height towering above the older man. Red hated pulling this stunt, but he'd gotten his dander up and he would not claim a failure to such things.

"You don't intimidate me with that stance, son. Your father used to pull the same thing. You musta picked it up from him, watching him all those years, looking up to him so," Gus said.

Red felt his shoulders relax as he glanced down at the ground. His hands remained on his hips, but the defensiveness was gone. He looked back at his neighbor whose face harbored no hard feelings, nor was he trying to take advantage. Red knew all of this. It just still felt bad.

"Want to come inside a minute?" he asked.

"Just for a few," Gus answered. He followed Red through his back door and situated himself at the kitchen table.

Red pulled out two glasses and filled them with iced tea. He glanced at the older man who'd been his father's friend and neighbor since the beginning. He was still a young man, though. Plenty of years of working the land was left inside him.

"Truth is, I don't know much about farming. Not really," Red confessed as he scooted a chair back and joined the man at the table, easing the iced tea in his direction.

"Actually, you do, son. I didn't mean to offend you. It's just that if you pulled in with me, joint effort or sold it completely, lock, stock and barrel, I'd be able to do what I've wanted for years. That extra acreage would mean the difference in making a living and making a profit. Besides, it'd be good for both of us."

"So why didn't my dad kick in with you if this was such a good idea for everybody?"

"You know the answer to that," Gus said sincerely.

"Why don't you explain it to me?" Red answered, not really ever sure the cause of the underlying tension that ran between the two men.

"I bought this land before he could. Competition. Just friendly competition. Selling the rest to me would be like selling his right arm. Never happen in a million years."

"So, I shouldn't sell to you, either," Red said. "For no other reason than for my father's memory."

"Oh, not that again. And your grandfather before that. Times have changed, Red. Farming's different now, but that's not even the point."

"What is the point, Gus? Why are you here again. I've said 'no' before. What? You wait a given number of years and keep asking?"

"The point is, you are not a farmer. You don't like farming. You're doing this for your father who is no longer alive, and trust me, he'd be terribly disappointed if you continued something that's not your calling."

"It runs in my family. Who says it's not my calling?"

"Is it?" Gus demanded.

Red felt the color rising to his face. He had no argument for that. The fact was, Gus was right. He understood the dynamics of this family. He lived close by and was a confidant of his father's, even if they were at odds with each other now and then. Gus did not wait for an answer. He already knew it.

"Funny you should ask about the timing," Gus continued.

"Yeah, want to explain that to me? At least I'd know when to expect you back to try again."

"You know Dale Bentley's Big Furniture Showcase down on Highway 98?"

"Sure," Red answered, having frequented the store many times.

"It's for sale," Gus answered flatly.

Red took in a quick breath. How did Gus Rigsby know of his dream? He'd told no one.

"What's that got to do with me?" Red asked slowly.

"I know you make furniture for them on the side. Right there in the empty part of the barn now that the animals are long gone. I've seen your work on the showroom floor, and if you recall, I've seen you in action before your father died, remember?"

Red bent his neck and took his head in his hands.

"It's one thing to build hand-crafted furniture. It's altogether different to sell it, along with such a huge warehousing operation. People from all over the tri-state area come to Dale's for everything from the run of the mill to the different—like my stuff."

"Exactly. I see your whole face light up just in that one sentence. Tell me you feel that way when you talk about soybeans and wheat."

Red sat still at the table. The impossible situation wore hard on his shoulders, especially taking Jimmy into account.

"I'd be lying if I said it wasn't tempting, but this property's been in my family for three generations. You think I could just waltz off and leave all that behind? Seeing what it meant to my dad?"

"It was his father's dream, and maybe his as well. But not yours. Face it, Red. Now, I know I'm pushing this for my own agenda, but I was friends with your father—not his enemy. I wouldn't take advantage of his oldest."

Red contemplated the top of the kitchen table. He heard himself sigh long and hard, but Gus was wrong. The timing was off. Way off."

Red pushed back his chair and rose to his feet.

"Gus, thanks but I've got a little brother to see after and a home here."

"I wouldn't take your house away. It's on the far edge of the property I want, anyway. The money from the sale is just about enough to invest in Dale's."

"I know. But it'd come up just short because the part I've got put away is for something special. I'll be needing it in six months. It's a promise I have to keep. If I used any part of it to do this thing, even that small amount that'd put me over the top, and wasn't able to deliver in six months, I couldn't sleep at night," he explained, moving toward the door.

Gus rose as well, heading out as Red held the door open.

"Just think about what I've offered, Red. Sleep on it. Isn't it time you went for what's important to you? Give other's their dreams as well? And think about this, too. This may be the last time I can offer to buy you out, so consider it carefully."

With this, Gus went on his way. As Red watched him leave, he contemplated the older man's last words. He was right, but he didn't realize how. Red did want to make other's dreams come true. Not so much as Gus' dream of picking up this land, but his brother Jimmy's dreams of being on his own with enough money to make it work. He'd have to make sure his brother was taken care of in the transaction. He had made a promise and he would keep it no matter what.

*   *   *

Olivia's shift was about over. She'd been distracted the rest of the afternoon after Red had left, and she was quite proud of herself for not pumping Millie or Jimmy about him. Still, it might be best to find out more so she could get a handle on these growing feelings in Red's direction before it was too late. If it wasn't already, she amended. What if Red were married? Just not wearing a ring, she mused.

With this last thought, she decided to give herself permission to do some investigating on the sly. Jimmy would be the right target, for he was the younger brother and showing interest in the new cook might prove to both make him feel welcome and answer her initial questions.

Deciding this was a little more honorable than her initial intent, she edged over in his direction. After all, she was already fond of the new cook who'd added an upbeat atmosphere around there.

"Hey, Jimmy. You're really good with your culinary skills," she began.

"My what?" Jimmy asked, his eyebrows rising as he cleaned the grill and back splash.

"Your cooking. You've got quite a knack for blending flavors and coming up with new things. Not to mention the timing of cooking things just right."

"Thanks," he answered, throwing her a big smile.

Olivia felt her stomach tighten. The smile ran in the family. Red had used it only once, she realized, but it stuck with her. Jimmy had the same broad smile that made the other person automatically smile in return.

"So, where'd you learn to cook like that?" she asked, thinking it would open a door.

"By myself. I moved off last year and just came back. It was just me, so I had to do something. Or starve," he explained, continuing with the tasks of cleaning the equipment for the next shift to take over.

"Most kids your age do the fast-food sort of thing. I'm impressed."

"Yeah," he answered.

Olivia realized she was getting nowhere. She decided to stop playing games and take the direct approach.

"So, I waited on your brother earlier."

"Un-huh."

"He seems nice. Do you live with him? Or have a place of your own."

"Why all the questions, as if I didn't know?" Jimmy asked, tossing the cloth to the side and facing Olivia. "You know, I thought you were pretty smart. Smarter than all the rest of his women. Now you're telling me you're interested in Red, too?"

"I, ah," Olivia felt her face flush. She didn't have a poker face nor did she have the ability to hide her real intent, as if anyone really did in the long run, she thought. She'd quit the games and let things happen as they would, she decided.

"I'm sorry. I shouldn't have pried—about you or your brother," she answered, turning away and reaching under the counter for her purse. "But I am glad you came to work here and certainly hope you like it," she added. "Otherwise, they might put me to work at the grill, and Penny's would lose business fast."

She gave Millie a wave good-bye, and gave Jimmy no other reason to suspect her slight dishonesty in the questioning. She certainly would not let him know again of her interest in his brother. And from here on out, she'd be straight with the young man who'd put her on the spot. The only thing she found out for sure was that Jimmy had a chip on his shoulder about his brother, and that other women had an interest in the man—and she'd never be willing to share her man with other women again. Her pride just couldn't take it.

* * *

Jimmy finished cleaning the equipment, handing over the cooking duties to the woman who worked the second shift. As he left, his last conversation with Olivia continued to bug him. Even here where he'd proved himself, Red seemed to take over again.

He could tell by the way Olivia was trying to pry information out of him about Red that she liked him. Not that Jimmy had any interest in an "older woman," cause he didn't. She must be about Red's age and to him that was way too old. But why did she have to pick his brother. He didn't want Red hanging around there. It was too much like being at home, being in with the crowd that knew only Red existed.

He wouldn't let Red get everything again. He'd done enough to mess with his life, not giving him his inheritance money early and making sure Jimmy was always in his big, old shadow. Well, he wouldn't let him get away with it here at Penny's. This was *his* work. The best place he'd ever worked in his life. He'd fix Red if he tried to muscle in on his territory at the Diner. Hanging out with Olivia just wasn't gonna happen. He'd make sure of it.

Chapter Four

Olivia quickly left the Diner and headed toward home. Thoughts of Red Taylor continued to play on her mind, as they had most of the day after he'd come in. His strength, his quiet demeanor, his sexy manner she knew he didn't mean to put across played on her mind. He was nothing like what she'd experienced in the past, or at least she hoped not. She'd been highly disappointed that she hadn't found out much about Red, and that which she had, she wondered about. Jimmy had implied there were lots of women interested in Red. She didn't want to be in a line-up of other women. She couldn't take that again.

Her ex-husband's meanderings from the first day they were married was masked in his activities of late night entertaining and frequent trips out of town required in his position as a top-notch corporate attorney. When Olivia discovered he'd never quit seeing the woman he'd been involved with before their wedding, Harrison had easily confessed he'd only married Olivia because of what he thought it would do for his career.

It looked good, he'd thought—especially to be married to one of the firm's major partner's only daughter. The fact that Olivia had also inherited funds from her grandfather's estate that would set her up for life was a selling point, too. Not that he'd gotten any of it, but he also knew if it didn't work out, Olivia wouldn't set out to get any of *his* money, either.

There were signs, of course. But she'd been trusting. Too trusting. It would never happen again, she'd promised herself. Now she wanted an honest, faithful man, and she certainly didn't want anyone to like her for her money or her parent's position in society ever again. That part had been taken care of by moving three hundred miles away where no one knew that part of her life. So anyone who fell for her here meant they were interested in the real Olivia Patterson, she reminded herself.

She also wanted the house she'd just bought to be a reflection of who she really was. She'd lost herself in Harrison's world before. After they'd married she'd moved into his house with his furnishings and his tastes—which were directly opposite of hers. He had to have things just so, elegant, stark, and perfect—like a museum, not a home. She wanted to choose for herself now.

With this in mind, Olivia turned the car around, deciding a trip to the large furniture showcase she'd noticed time and again was the right thing to do next to get her life in order. And maybe, just maybe, it would get her mind off Red Taylor, when she might see him again, learn more about him, and perhaps get to be alone with him in private, she thought and smiled.

Shaking her head free of these thoughts, she pulled into the parking lot and headed into the furniture store. From there she moved directly to the sofa, chairs and end tables that drew her from the road. Perched inside one of the front windows, made up as a whole suit of furniture, she admired the polished rugged wood left in it's natural state, hand-made and curved into a style that spoke of quality and unique design. Just the right reflection of the laid-back lifestyle she was looking for. It'd go in the den of her new home, stretched around the fireplace and arranged so that the room would be filled with this creative work of art, she decided.

Olivia's parents always said she had an eclectic taste in art and furnishings, yet put together so you felt right at home. This was the kind of home she wanted to make for herself, and she loved the house she'd bought on the outskirts of town. Yes, everything was going to be perfect now, she reminded herself, and I won't let someone like Red Taylor distract me, she decided.

At that moment an older man came rushing to her side.

"Good afternoon. I'm Dale Bentley. Sorry to keep you waiting, but a phone call had me tied up, and my two salespeople are in the back showing a couple of customers something we just got in."

"That's all right, Mr. Bentley," she said warmly.

"Dale. Just Dale. Miss?"

"Olivia. Just Olivia."

"Okay, Olivia. So good to have you stop in," he said, turning his attention to the grouping of furniture. "I see you're interested in one of our local artists. Most tourists who pass by get pulled in by his work. That's why I give it such a prominent spot in the window," he explained, giving a chuckle. "We can ship it anywhere in the country," he added.

"Do you deliver?"

"Certainly. But I don't recall your being a local. Never met you before," he began, absently touching his leather braided string tie with the silver clasp.

"I've just moved to town, Mr., I mean, Dale. And I need a whole house full of furniture. You think you can accommodate me?"

"Yes, indeedy. If you can't find it here, I don't know where in the world you could."

Olivia glanced around at the showroom in surprise. She knew from the outside that it was large, but what wasn't evident from the road was the different furniture groupings displayed for the varying tastes for such a small town.

"Are you the owner, Dale? You must be since it's named Dale's?"

"Yes. I am that. For now, anyway. And have been for the last twenty-five years."

"So how can you run a business like this for such a small town?" she asked, her marketing and business background taking over her brain.

2948-BURG

"Oh, it's not as small as you think. You being a newcomer and all, you don't realize how many states all around feed into this business. I've got hotel and other industry accounts, and I run a fair catalog order business for local artists and things other people can't afford to stock. So, it *is* quite lucrative—and busy. Too busy for me most days now."

"I see," she answered, now turning to the task at hand. "Well, I'd like to buy this set. It's got such a good feel to it, and it'll be perfect for where I have in mind. I have an informal den that leads to a screened-in porch. Lots of shade trees. Stone fireplace," she explained, getting excited about having this artist's work filling out that part of the house.

"You have fine taste. I'll work up the bill of sale while you take a look around at the rest of the showroom—just in case you want to come back at a later date for more."

"That I'll do," she promised, glancing around. After a quick perusal, she found herself back admiring her purchase still displayed in the front window, then went over to the counter where Dale Bentley waited for payment.

"So is tomorrow morning soon enough for delivery?" he asked as he pushed the approved credit card ticket toward her to sign.

"Make it after 3:30 p.m. That'll give me time to get off my shift at Penny's."

Dale Bailey's head tipped upwards. "Penny's Diner? You work there?"

"Yes. It's quite fun," she answered, finishing signing and placing her copy in her purse.

"Hmmm," was all he answered. She knew what he must be thinking. How could she afford such an expensive purchase as the handmade furniture grouping she'd bought without blinking an eye at the price. Still, he didn't venture down that road at all. Instead, he kept up his professional conversation.

"Well, you just write down that address and we'll load the whole package of the things in the window up and bring it over to your house by late tomorrow afternoon."

The fact that they would take the display furniture out of the window surprised her.

"I thought there'd be some packed up in the back you'd send. Is that the only one you have left?"

"Yes. It's hand-made, like you said, and we display all we have of that sort of thing in stock at the time of purchase. You're getting the last stick of what we've got."

"Oh. You say a local artist supplies it?"

"Yes. He's a farmer by trade. Does this on the side. I'll have to let him know I'm out. Already told him I was low, but he has his hands full trying to work the land left to him by his father and grandfather before that," he explained. "So, you're pretty lucky to have come in when you did. Don't have any idea when he'll get any more like it over to sell," he added.

"My timing must be good," Olivia commented, thinking her life was certainly falling into place. "I'm happy to be the new owner of something that really reflects my style."

"I'll put a 'sold' sign on it right now," he promised as he shook hands and saw her off.

Olivia strolled out into the warm afternoon. She felt a new lease on life now that she'd made the purchase. It was as if she were actually starting over, this time in the right direction.

* * *

Red came in exhausted and collapsed into the kitchen chair, wondering what he was going to pull together to make for dinner. He knew he'd be the one to do it. He didn't want Jimmy accusing him of forcing him to work night and day—even though that's exactly what Red did on an on-going basis. Still, having to turn around and cook after doing so all day would certainly start a fight, and Red wasn't ready for a fight. When the kitchen phone rang, he picked it up on the first ring.

"Hello. Red Taylor," he answered.

"Hi, Red. Dale Bentley."

Red heaved out an exasperated breath. He also didn't want to face this thing Gus brought up again, and figured he'd better tell Dale right off before he began working him down, too.

"Look, Dale, I'm grateful for the first option on your furniture business, but like I told Gus, I can't afford it and I don't want to sell the farm to do it. I've got a brother to put up for now and the land's been in the family for . . ."

"Now, hold on, Red. Nobody's trying to upset your apple cart there. I've called for a different reason entirely."

"Oh, I'm sorry, Dale, I just assumed . . ."

"Look, I've got good news. I've just sold the entire rest of my inventory of your furniture goods here. Nice lady with good taste just bought the whole Kit and Kaboodle of it. Have anything else on hand I can replace it with?"

Red stood up now, stunned by the turn of events. The profit from that purchase had come just in time since the harvest income was low. It'd give him some extra income the farm had little chance of producing before he had to face the facts.

"Well, I *have* been working on some extra pieces, but I can't say they make up a set. Well, actually they do, but one of a different kind. It's a bedroom grouping," he explained.

"Sounds great. I'll take anything. It goes like hotcakes. Especially with the folks from out of town."

"I see. A man is appreciated everywhere but in his own home town," Red chuckled.

"Oh, no. That's not true. I just meant that people from all over are looking for the uncommon. Things they haven't seen from where they're from. You know, the unusual catches their eye. And the handmade quality is certainly a rare find. Now, you just bring over what you've got ready, or I'll send Ben over with the truck after we've finished with tomorrow's delivery. How's that sound?"

"Super, Dale, and again, I'm sorry about the mix-up when I answered the phone. It's been a long day, and this good news kinda makes up for an earlier disappointment I had. Missed an opportunity I wish I hadn't, you know."

"Nothing major, I hope," Dale inquired.

"You never know. Like ships passing in the night. I read that somewhere," Red explained, with a chuckle.

"Well, let's not let the truck pass by the house in the middle of the afternoon. I need that extra furniture. It'll be a selling point to this business whenever I get an offer," he explained. "Need that unusual quality to round out the rest."

"Good deal, Dale. And thanks."

Red hung up the phone just as Jimmy came home, waltzing through without a word. Somehow Red had thought after the good day he'd seen Jimmy having at Penny's that his brother would have softened up towards him, and that he'd be willing to talk.

When his bedroom door slammed in the back, Red knew he was in for a disappointing night. He'd wanted to pump his brother for information about work—and the auburn-haired beauty, but he could now see that was totally out of the question.

The fastest and easiest solution to dinner was hamburgers, Red decided. He gathered together the ground meat, buns and salad fixings and went to work. Once the salad was made and the sizzling burgers were almost ready, Jimmy reappeared from the bedroom. He looked pleasantly surprised at the nice dinner Red was moving to the kitchen table.

"Hey, you cooked. And went to a lot of trouble," Jimmy said, looking over at the sizzling burgers.

Red heaved out a deep breath.

"Well, thought you'd like somebody else to cook for you since you've done that most of the day," he explained. "Besides, maybe you need a break now and then from getting supper together," he managed.

Jimmy's eyebrows raised as he moved toward the skillet.

"These are 'bout done. Want me to take 'em out?" Jimmy offered.

"Sure," Red said, getting the rest of the dinner onto the table.

After Jimmy had piled his hamburger with all the fixings and began taking a big bite, Red decided to try his luck at finding out how the day went.

"So, work at the Diner was good?" he asked lightly.

"Sure. You knew I'd wow them with my cooking."

"Yeah, I did. I figured you'd fit right in at Penny's."

"I do. They appreciate me," Jimmy answered, a little of the defensiveness returning to his tone.

Red ignored this. He didn't want to move the conversation into a fight about how Jimmy didn't much lift a finger around there. Besides, he was interested in more interesting topics—like Olivia.

"Guess that means you like the people you work with?" he threw in.

"Your friend, Millie, she's real nice. She gave me the job cause of you, right?" he asked.

"Not true. You got the job on your own."

"Yeah, but she said something about not needing references cause she knew you."

"She did? Well, I suppose she figured you must be a good cook and dependable or else I would've stopped you from applying. That's all."

"Huh. Well, she likes me for me now. Not cause of you."

"Of course," Red answered, wondering how he would now throw in any questions about Olivia without being obvious. His brother was pretty quick, didn't miss much. Still, it was now or never.

"You like the other people who work there, too?"

Jimmy stopped chewing in mid-bite. He slid his brother a look and rolled his eyes. He continued chewing until he swallowed, then laid his burger down onto the plate.

"So, that's what the hundred questions is about. You got your eye on that good-looker waitress. Yeah, she's nice. But I think she's taken," he said, picking up his burger again, analyzing which part of it he'd bite into next.

"Taken? Who's she dating?" Red asked, the disappointment rising.

"Oh, I don't know for sure. Just imagine she is," he answered, now chopping away at the burger.

Red sat silently for a minute. He knew his younger brother like the back of his hand, and was keenly aware of all his tricks—and this was one of them. The reason why, he didn't understand.

"Ummm, you weren't thinking of asking her out, were you Jimmy?" Red asked tentatively.

"Me?" Jimmy glanced at his brother, amusement filled his eyes. "She's got to be your age or a year or two older. She's way over the hill for me," he answered.

"Just wondered," Red answered. He'd already blown it, he realized, and his younger brother had just found a way to play with him. He would now be of no help to Red in this matter. He'd have to proceed on his own, and his little brother baiting him would not stop him from at least trying. The best way to handle it from here would be to drop the subject cold and feign disinterest, he decided. But that wouldn't stop him from asking her out.

Jimmy sat there grinning to himself as if he now had a new way to taunt Red. He now had something to hold over him. But it wasn't true. Red decided he'd go over to Penny's tomorrow, perhaps for a late breakfast before the crowds took over, and he'd ask Olivia out. All she could say was "no," he decided, and he'd rather find out her answer sooner than later. If Jimmy was telling the truth about her being taken, then he'd rather find that out before he spent any more time daydreaming about the plans he had for her and the perfect woman he thought he'd finally found.

* * *

Olivia felt her pulse race. Red had just walked in and had positioned himself at a booth in her station. She was extremely glad to see him back and her intense reaction surprised her. She wasn't sure if getting involved with him was the right thing or not, but she decided to at least let this thing play out. Because somehow, her emotions had already done so.

Losing no time in getting over to him, she felt her reactions heighten seeing his slow grin forming as she approached the table.

"Good morning," he said with a low voice that made her stomach flip. Did the man realize how sexy he was? she wondered.

"Good morning. What can I get you?"

"I'd like whatever special Jimmy's got going for breakfast," he answered.

"That'd be a Denver Omelet with a side of Hash Browns—and a biscuit."

"Sounds filling," Red answered.

Olivia decided he probably needed lots of food to sustain his large frame and muscular arms and chest.

"I imagine it is. So, do you still want the special?" she ventured.

"Sure. And coffee."

When Olivia turned in the order, she leaned over to Jimmy.

"Your brother's here again," she said.

Jimmy turned around slowly, managing a glimpse of Red sitting at the table.

"Oh, yeah. I see. The farm must be falling apart with him gone. Guess a farmer's hours are pretty short these days."

Olivia moved away surprised. There was something defensive in Jimmy's explanation. Something she hadn't seen in his usual upbeat manner when Red was not there. The farm reference also explained Red's well-developed muscular body beneath the short-sleeved shirt and jeans. The man worked with this muscles on a daily basis, she realized.

His occupation as a man used to hard labor in the many aspects of farm life didn't deter her growing feelings for him, as she imagined was Jimmy's ploy—to discourage her interest. Though Jimmy knew nothing of her past, he could have decided since she drove a fancy car she might not be interested in someone in Red's profession. Jimmy was wrong. In fact, it made Olivia believe Red might be more honest than those she'd known in a job behind a desk.

When she returned with his coffee, she couldn't help but feel a pull toward him. Was it physical? An emotional connection? Both? When he spoke up, she welcomed whatever bit of conversation would keep her there a moment longer than necessary.

"Olivia, I don't know how else to do this but to come right out with it," he began.

She felt her heart pick up speed as she paused at the table. Luckily the crowd was light at the moment, and no one was within ear shot's distance.

"What's that?" she asked.

"Will you go out with me? That is, unless you're 'taken'."

Olivia felt her mouth drop open. He certainly was direct.

"A date?" she asked, thrown off a tad by his quick move at asking her out.

"Yes."

"When?" she answered. She absolutely wanted to go any place, any time, with this man so different from any she'd ever met.

"Is that a 'yes'?" he asked, his voice lowering, making her pulse race faster.

"Maybe. I'll be right back. From the sound of the bell Jimmy's ringing away, your order is ready," she explained.

Jimmy gave her a look before she headed back with the plate of food. She wondered what it was about, but she wasn't going to let Jimmy stop her from dating his brother. By the time she arrived back at the table, she was ready with an answer.

"Okay," she told Red. "When did you want to get together?"

"Tonight. Where shall I pick you up? Your home?"

Olivia hesitated for a moment. She knew Red from only the Diner and, of course, she did work with his brother. Still, she wasn't comfortable letting him know where she lived quite yet—for more reasons than one. He was a complete stranger, and she also didn't want to give too much away from seeing the expensive house she'd bought outright. She wanted him to get to know her as a person first, not as a woman with means, she reminded herself.

"How about if I meet you at that seafood restaurant down the street, say about seven o'clock. Will that work?"

Red just smiled and nodded. "It's a date," he answered, He then turned away from her to dig into his food.

Olivia rushed off to wait on some other customers. Something about Red warmed her all over. She could hardly wait to see what it felt like for him to actually hold her, then she wondered how in the world her thoughts had turned to that. This piece of business established, she had only to refill his coffee once, and no other lengthy conversation came between them.

The day would pass quickly, and then Olivia would finally discover the secrets of Red Taylor and why she felt such a pull toward a man she had only just met.

* * *

At 6:48 p.m., Olivia arrived at Sam's Seafood Cafe up the highway from Penny's. A more causal place than she'd imagined, the tables were set up in a family style arena where you might find yourself seated at a long table with a group sandwiched next to you.

It was not what she'd hoped for in terms of privacy, and she glanced down at her silk pants outfit and clutched her soft leather purse tighter as she noticed most of the people in the place wore jeans or highly informal wear. She immediately felt ill-at-ease, thinking she needed to get a handle on the changes in this town compared to the downtown Chicago life she'd been used to. The last thing she wanted to do was stick out, but it was too late, as all eyes were now on her.

As Olivia stood awkwardly at the front, waiting to see if you simply seated yourself or if a hostess would arrive at any moment, she checked her watch, then realized she was a good ten minutes early. Still, Red should be along any time now, she told herself.

When a table that allowed only two people at the seating became available, she quickly walked over and claimed the more private spot.

As she took a seat and glanced back up, she saw Red entering the restaurant. His handsome form seemed to fill the room the moment he came in. Wearing a tasteful red plaid short-sleeve shirt and stylish tan Khaki pants, she exhaled a pent-up breath. He'd dressed up just enough to make her feel she hadn't been so out of line in her choice of fitting in after all. She wondered if he'd imagined she would, or if he were trying to impress her, for the restaurant clearly didn't warrant a dress code.

When he scanned the crowd, he spotted her and rushed right over.

"I'm sorry you beat me here," he said, giving her hand a squeeze when he reached across the table and sat down. Olivia felt the warmth creep up her arm from the contact and she felt her eyes widen in surprise. The man had charisma and style that was smooth, but not phony like some she'd know far too personally. It was natural and honest.

"That's perfectly all right. I'm one of the chronically early types," she explained.

"Oh? Well, I bet Millie at the Diner is happy about that."

"I guess," Olivia laughed. "I never imagined being late to work. Back in Chicago, they'd have my head if I even thought about being late, especially to a meeting with a client."

Red smiled in return. She wanted to swallow her words and suddenly wondered what she'd intended to talk with him about if she wanted to hide her real self.

"So, what brings you all the way here to this budding town from the big city of Chicago?" he asked.

"A change. I'm ready for a quieter, simpler lifestyle," she said.

"And you work at Penny's?" he laughed. "It's a pretty lively place. Hardly get a chance to think with all the activity over there."

"I suppose you're right," she said. "But I want to hear more about you, Red. Your brother hasn't told me too much."

"Jimmy? What has *he* told you? I can just imagine," he added.

A young, pretty waitress with a bouncy pony tail appeared by their table, jostling some iced tea onto the table.

"Figured you'd want tea. Red always drinks tea," she said, giving Red a broad smile. "Are you ready to order?" she asked, still giving an energetic smile in Red's direction.

"Give us a minute, Danielle?"

The young woman headed off, and Olivia imagined she saw a slight red color rise to Red's face, but she could be mistaken. She did, however, notice the way his reddish blond bangs strayed over his forehead, and how the light picked up the rusty tint. As she allowed herself to examine his thick head of hair it struck her about his nickname and how it fit his hair color as well. It was certainly blond but going on reddish-blond.

"That's why they call you Red, isn't it?" she said spontaneously. "Your hair color?"

Now she knew she saw him turn slightly red as he pushed his fingers back through his hair. It was endearing, as so much of what she'd seen in him so far, the way he was so up-front and natural.

"No, afraid not," he finally answered. "Red's short for Redmond. It's a family name. My middle name."

"Oh. That's right. I forgot. Millie *did* tell me that," she said, remembering about Millie saying his first name must be something he didn't want to be called.

"So, you and Millie have been discussing me? What else did she tell you?"

"That you must not like your first name."

Red paused, glancing outside at an unexpected rain shower that began to deluge the plate glass window. He then turned back to her. "Well, my first name is Charles—after my father. It was confusing to be called the same thing when I was young. Charles. And I didn't quite cater to 'little Charlie' after I'd reached the eighth grade. Sounded pretty stupid and I hadn't quite grown into Charles yet, either. So, my girlfriend at the time began calling me Red after she'd seen my full name printed on something or another. Now it's history," he explained. "But don't tell anybody that. It's a secret," he laughed.

Olivia felt a warmth pass through her. She watched the man across the table from her with a deepening respect. She just felt so good to be with him, experience the confidentiality of a stranger who trusted her enough to tell this fun "secret," and be able to just be himself.

The waitress returned. Olivia ordered the Grilled Salmon Special, Red opted for one of the fried fish platters. She soon disappeared, and Olivia observed the full restaurant, so relieved she'd found a spot that didn't require her to rub elbows with anyone else, nor have her attention pulled to anyone else but Red. He clasped his hands on top of the table and smiled at her.

"Well, Olivia. You know all about my full name, and the secret history behind it, and I don't even know your last name. Tell me about yourself," he urged.

Olivia exhaled. She knew she needed to start building a relationship with the people here, especially Red, in order to regain her trust in human nature. The only way to do it was to jump in and start swimming, she decided. A few facts at a time, though, she cautioned herself.

"Patterson. Olivia Patterson. I'm from Chicago, and like I said, I needed a change and decided to move to a nice spot like this to see if I liked it."

"So, you're here only temporarily?" Red threw in, disappointment lacing his tone.

"Not exactly. I've bought a house," she said, suddenly wishing she hadn't dropped that tidbit. If he knew where and which one, it would give away her financial status, and she couldn't let that happen. Not yet. It was too soon and she'd never know if he'd get to be close to her for herself alone.

"Oh?" he said. "That's good," he said in a more upbeat tone.

Olivia paused a moment, flabbergasted that he didn't question her further about the location or anything else. Most people would, either from curiosity or an ulterior motive—trying to size up more about her from the house she'd bought. But Red sat patiently, not asking more than she was willing to tell. It was a good sign, she decided.

"I have a permanent job at Penny's. And I've set up housekeeping. So I'm in it for the long-run, I suppose."

"How're you fitting in? I mean, it is working out well? Are you comfortable here in such a smaller town?"

"Well, it's not that small. Don't get me wrong, compared to Chicago, it's minuscule, but I'd never settle somewhere that didn't have plenty to offer in retail and restaurants and business and industry to sustain a fairly robust existence," she explained.

Red balanced his chin on his clasped hands, grinning from ear to ear.

"What? What's so funny?" she asked in surprise.

"You. The way you express yourself is definitely different. Besides, if you think you can come here so you can blend in without being noticed, you've got another thought coming," he told her.

Olivia was a little taken aback. Did the man read minds or was she that obvious. But how could she be? At that moment the waitress brought their dinners and placed them on the table front and center. After she left, Olivia found her voice again, now digesting his comment.

"All right. I'll bite. What makes you think I've come here to 'blend in'?"

Red ate his food heartily, his eyes focused to the side, as if he were studying the answer to her question. Then, as though he'd just seen the answer, he turned back to her.

"This is what I think, since you asked, mind you, so take no offense."

"Uh, oh," she put in before he continued.

"You've come here to escape Chicago and whatever hurt you so much there that you went to all this trouble to leave it behind. City and all. Like 'throwing out the baby with the bath water.'"

Olivia put down her fork and cleared her throat.

"Throwing out what?"

"The baby with the bath water. You've never heard that expression?"

"I guess not."

"The city itself is to blame as well as the people or circumstances that are in such close association that you felt to make your life better, you had to leave all of it. Throwing out all of it, not just the dirty bath water. But in this case, it might be warranted. I don't know. But my take on it is that you felt you had to start fresh somewhere totally different in order to get past it."

Olivia glanced down at her plate. He could see straight through her careful facade, and almost see straight into her soul. So much for trying to remain a mystery while getting to know each other.

"What else have you deduced about me, Red?" she asked, not sure she wanted to hear the answer, but afraid not to.

"Your manner of speech is so refined, I suspect you're highly educated and grew up around parents who were as well."

"You've talked to Millie," she put in suddenly.

"No, Millie's told me nothing about you, nor has Jimmy."

"So, you've decided this because of the way I talk?"

"Mostly the circumstances, your refined manner, the way you talk, dress. Hope you're not offended, it's certainly not meant that way. Just an observation."

Olivia decided hiding pertinent facts about herself would serve no purpose, so she admitted most of what he'd said. If she didn't, she imagined he'd see it written across her forehead as well.

"So, are you running away?"

"Yes. I'm not ready to talk about that, though."

"Educated, then? Is that a safe topic?"

"Masters Degree in Marketing. Does that surprise you?"

"No. Yes. Actually I took you to be a lawyer, the way you are with words."

"My father is an attorney," she supplied. "My mother a tenured professor at the university."

"I see. Well, that fits."

"How about you?" Olivia said, trying to turn the conversation away from herself.

"I've got a two-year college degree. I'm afraid the concerns of my family business has kept me totally busy for most of my life."

"That being?"

"Well, I have a farm and a few other ventures on the side," he answered.

2948-BURG

"Do you work side-by-side with your father?" she asked cheerily. The total opposite world from Olivia's suddenly intrigued her. The answer he gave, however, was a surprise.

"No, not for a long, long time. You see, my father died about six years ago. That left just me and Jimmy. Jimmy being eight years younger, I had to finish raising him the best I could. Luckily I was of age enough to do it, but it's been tough. Hard as it's been on me, it's been even rougher on Jimmy."

"I didn't realize," Olivia said quietly.

"Yeah, the kid always felt bad about me being older. Dad always sided with me, and my Mom always favored Jimmy, being her youngest, you know."

"Is she still in touch from afar? Did she leave or something?"

"Or something. She died of breast cancer. It came fast, took her quick. None of us had a chance to prepare for such a thing, especially Jimmy. He was a young tike, clung to her, and she was suddenly out of our lives forever. My Dad worked such long hours on the farm, though he had lots of help he'd take on at various times—and me," he answered, trailing off. "Jimmy felt totally abandoned and was then stuck with me, who my Dad liked better, I might as well admit it. I was the most like him in build and stamina. I felt responsible for the farming business, too, being that it's been in our family for three generations."

"So Jimmy's resented you because you were older, stronger and your father's favored son?"

"Partly. He also hates the farm. He thinks he's a failure because he didn't cater to it, not that I blame him. Besides that, he's always compared himself to me. I got my father's genes with my height and all. Jimmy's so slight of build and short, I think that's always bothered him too. Then to have to up and have to answer to me after both his parents died was more than he could take."

"But you get along now?" she ventured.

Red laughed. "Well, let's say this about that. Soon as Jimmy is able, he's gonna high-tail it out of here. Probably go to Chicago," he added in an amused tone and began eating his dinner again.

Olivia was dumbstruck. She hadn't meant to open up Pandora's Box. It was private and personal and this man told her without hesitation. She wondered at his candor.

"Red, does everybody in town know about this little feud and discord between you and your brother? Is it common knowledge, I mean?"

Red cleared his throat and took a quick peak around at the table next to him. He looked satisfied that no one was paying attention to them, then focused back on her.

"A precious few who know us well. That's all. It's not exactly the type of thing that looks good for Jimmy, so I'd appreciate it if you'd keep this under your hat. I'd never do anything to shed a bad light on him. He's a good kid, remember, just confused and still struggling. Fighting back at the circumstances life's handed him. Fighting me, in particular," he added. "But no. No one is aware of this 'feud' as you call it."

Olivia was still taken aback.

"Why tell me, then? I'm a complete stranger?"

Red finished the last bite of his food and pushed his plate slightly away. The waitress rushed up and whisked the dishes out of their way and hurried off, leaving the ticket behind.

"The answer to that question," he began, "is that you are not a complete stranger. You don't feel like one, anyway. It's like we connect. Comfortable, safe, seems like. I think you're hurting more from your problems than Jimmy," he added. "And if you need anyone to talk to, I'd sure be happy to listen. I'll be patient. Wait 'till you're ready," he promised.

He then picked up the ticket. "I'll be right back," he told her as he strolled over to the cash register. Olivia wondered what plans he had for them next in this small town. Would he offer to take her back to his home? She wasn't sure how the evening would go, but she really, really liked him and how well he treated her—something she hadn't been used to in a long time.

He came back to the table and laid a tip on the table. Red then escorted Olivia to the door and paused.

"I hope you brought an umbrella," he said, glancing out at the rain that had started once they'd begun their dinner and hadn't let up since.

"No," she answered, not really caring if she got wet or not. As long as she was with Red.

"Your outfit will be ruined," he said.

"I guess it can't be helped unless *you* have an umbrella, which I see you don't."

"No," he answered, glancing to the side at a few umbrellas a few customers had left at the front door. "But I think this umbrella belongs to the Smith's. Saw them bring it in. I'll just borrow it for a second and get you to your car. They won't mind."

With this, Red gestured to the couple, then he rushed Olivia into the rain, sheltering her with the overly spacious umbrella. When she was snug inside the car with the door closed, she rolled down the window to ask where they were going next.

"It's been a real nice evening, Olivia," he said, raising his voice a little to be heard over the pelting of the pouring rain. "Perhaps you'll agree to see me again. Here's my number if you decide to," he suggested, shoving a crinkled torn strip of notebook paper in the window.

Olivia parted her lips to answer, but Red pushed his head through the opening of the window and kissed her gently and quickly. Then he was off.

She watched him rush back into the restaurant, return the umbrella, then run to his truck. Olivia sat perfectly still, except for touching her lips. She could still feel the burning sensation he'd left in that quick, soft touch. The rain splattered continuously onto the car, echoing off her roof and leaving her mesmerized. She watched his truck's tail lights come on, then saw him wave to her and wait for her to pull out, making sure she was all right.

With this, Olivia started the car and headed out. Only then had Red found it proper to leave. He was more of a gentleman and honest human being than she'd ever met. After all that'd happened, her faith in mankind had returned in only a matter of hours.

Chapter Five

Red wore a smile all the way home. He couldn't help himself. This auburn-haired beauty with her stunning green eyes was everything he'd ever imagined the perfect woman could be. He knew he couldn't keep away from Penny's Diner now that she worked there. Though he didn't really have the time, he'd find some way, because she'd done a number on him with just one look. Now that he'd spent a little time with her, he was even more convinced.

He hoped she'd call, and felt that if she had a good enough time with him she would. He'd left it up to her for another date, but he wouldn't give up. He just had to discover all aspects of Olivia Patterson.

Red thoughts drifted away from the woman of his dreams and wanting to start a life for himself, a real life, and his mind unhappily returned to the dilemma that weighed him down. Money was getting more and more tight now that his farming business was growing more difficult.

It had certainly been a blessing when he got that call from Dale about his furniture, but it also made the dream of doing something like that more appealing. How in the world would Jimmy feel? Could Red consider the impossible? Getting out of this farming business for an industry he felt much more suited for interested him greatly, but switching over would take every penny—and more.

The decision to change had plagued Red for years. Though he'd gotten some pretty good offers, he'd elected not to sell—out of family loyalty and perhaps down-right stubbornness that he could make it work. Which was the greatest factor, he didn't know.

But now, having a business he'd love up for sale, dangled in front of him like a carrot in front of a hungry rabbit, was almost more temptation than he could take. The added incentive to sell his land and all the equipment to Gus danced before him, since he'd come to the conclusion that he just couldn't maintain the farm anymore.

Still, it felt like giving away his family heritage by selling. And he still wasn't sure what that would do to Jimmy. The kid had already had his whole world ripped out from under him, and even though he pretended not to like the farm, Red felt it gave him some sort of stability in life. If he took that away, too, it might really do damage to the boy who'd had to grow up much too fast. Besides that, if the sales exchange wasn't in Red's favor, between selling and investing in the furniture business, it might delay Red in being able to give Jimmy his inheritance money on time. That would really put him over the edge, he thought.

Red realized he just couldn't do it if it meant taking a penny away from the boy. He hadn't been done right the way the will was written as it was, giving Jimmy one more thing to resent about Red.

When he pulled up to the house and went inside, he found Jimmy stretched out on the sofa in the den, the volume to the TV turned up high.

"Where've you been?" Jimmy demanded. "I got home and there was no dinner," he called from the sofa.

"I would've explained before I left, but you weren't here by 6:20 and I had to go. I'll bet you were able to fend for yourself, though. Being a cook by trade," he added.

"I did all right. You figured I'd already eaten?"

"Didn't know. Since we normally eat at six, and you're nowhere in sight, didn't call or anything, I just went ahead and left."

"So, you still didn't say where you were," Jimmy continued.

Red didn't want a fight. He knew Jimmy wouldn't like the fact that he'd taken out Olivia. It was clear from their earlier conversations that he hadn't been keen on Red moving in on Jimmy's work place territory. Still, it didn't give the kid the right to stop him from pursuing Olivia. Jimmy raised up off the sofa, challenging the answer. This attitude of his was starting to get on Red's nerves.

"Look, Jimmy, I took out Olivia tonight. Okay? You'll just have to accept that I plan to date her. Even if she does work with you. That's the way it's gonna be."

"Hey," Jimmy broke in. "You don't have to be so defensive about it. I just wondered."

"Well, I figured you'd be upset. But who I date is personal."

"Who got your motor all running hot? As if I didn't know. And why are you in such an all-fire hurry to take her out right off? You never go out with anybody."

"That's changed starting tonight. I'll have to move on with my life, Jimmy. It's time," he stated, the meaning of his words covered more than just the date. Red knew he was about to start making decisions in his life that would affect both of them, and Jimmy never liked it when he made a move. Any move.

He plunged himself in the easy chair, ready for Jimmy's explosion about why he shouldn't take out Olivia. However, those words never came. Jimmy settled onto the sofa again, silent. After a few minutes, Red felt more at ease and turned to his brother, thinking perhaps the next set of news would be a safe topic.

"By the way, got good news from Dale Bentley," Red began.

"Oh, yeah?" Jimmy answered, focusing his full attention on the television.

"Yeah, it seems they've sold all the furniture I made. Wants all the pieces I've been working on lately."

"You gotta be kidding. Who buys stuff like that?" Jimmy asked, rising from the sofa.

"Customers," Red answered, upset that Jimmy had picked on the one thing he did that he was most proud of to criticize. "Paying customers. That money'll come in handy," Red answered.

"Now we're back to that," he spat. "Always about money and what you're bringing in," Jimmy said, storming out of the room. "Maybe you ought to just give me some of those proceeds toward my inheritance Dad left me in his will. All he gave me was just a bunch of savings you won't part with. Gave you the house and everything else. So, that's real good about your stupid furniture. Some people got it all, while I gotta cook for a living," he said.

Jimmy then disappeared down the hall and Red heard his bedroom door slam shut once again, then the muted sound of the smaller TV in his room came to life.

Red knew it had been too good to be true. Everywhere he stepped was a sink hole when it came to his brother. There was no good way out. It didn't really matter what he did with the family heritage. That was now clear. Especially after hearing his brother's last comments.

He'd hoped to wait until the last possible moment before turning his back on his family's heritage. If he'd been able to hold on six more months, then Jimmy would be on his own and away from the area when he sold out. He'd give him the money, and there would be no discussion on using the extra funds. It would just be a done deal.

But the impossible timing loomed before him, blocking out the momentary relief that his evening with Olivia had brought. He was facing the hardest times of his life, and he hoped she'd call, asking to see him again. He needed support from someone who cared, and after only one evening with her Red knew he needed Olivia in a way that went down deep in his soul. And he hoped she wasn't set on being a farmer's wife, for that legacy was about to come to an end.

* * *

Olivia sank down on the cushioned seats on her screened-in back porch. The rain had finally stopped, and the darkness of the evening overtook any remnants of the day, leaving her completely surrounded by the sounds of nature and the privacy of her thoughts.

It was hard to believe that just one year before on that very day she'd married Harrison Mobley, only to find out that he'd done so for her family name and reputation and how it'd further his career in the law firm where her father was in partnership. They'd managed to convince him that a wife and family front would also do wonders for moving ahead, and that's when he'd proposed to Olivia.

How naive she'd been, believing he'd wanted her because of what she had to offer as a person, as a woman. But all too soon she discovered the reason why he'd introduced himself at the company party, realizing she was none other than the daughter of Michael Patterson, the most prestigious attorney in the firm.

Harrison had movie-star good looks, tall and slender, and never did a thing to lift his finger beyond his desk or some expensive sporting activity that looked good to others. She had been taken in by his rapt attention, his whirlwind romance, and the elopement that sent her father into orbit. If she'd waited and listened to her father, perhaps she'd still be in her luxury apartment overlooking Lake Michigan right now, watching the twinkling of the city lights all around. Instead, she was miles and miles away with nothing but woods and lots of land that separated her from all of that.

She thought about Red and what a hard worker he must be. He'd have no time for other women, like Harrison had at every turn. Olivia unhappily recalled when her best friend told her that Harrison had been spotted with his old girlfriend, Marcia. Olivia then began to piece together all the signs and signals she'd been determined to ignore, but no longer could. It had been such a troubling time, and this particular day made the memories even worse.

Olivia jumped as the blaring of the mobile phone beside her startled her reminiscing. She groped around at the wicker table beside her. She'd forgotten she'd even brought the phone out there, and now wished she hadn't.

After answering, the unbidden voice of her past shattered her sheltered world.

"Happy Anniversary, sweetheart," her ex-husband chuckled.

"Harrison? How did you find me? How did you get this number?"

He laughed again.

"A good attorney has all sorts of connections," he boasted.

"What do you want?" she asked flatly. "You're out of my life. We're divorced. Have been for many moons now, remember?"

"Oh, my dear. Yes, indeed. I thought you'd like to know I've tied the knot with the love of my life. She waited for me, after all. Waited her turn even through the mistake I made in feeling I had to marry you to get ahead. Now, I'm happy, she's happy, and I don't have to hang my head about your quickie divorce. I'm the family man everyone always knew I could be. With the right woman, of course," he put in.

"So, you've called me on our 'would-be' anniversary to share this tidbit? Congratulations, Harrison. If you wanted to get a reaction, I'm afraid you'll be terribly disappointed. You see, I've moved on with my life, too. Found the man who'll do for me what 'what's her name' obviously does for you. So, good luck. And don't call here ever again," she demanded.

Why she didn't just depress the hang-up button right then and there Olivia didn't know. Instead, she was faced with one last insult to ruin the heels of her perfectly wonderful evening.

"Not to worry, my dear. I'm tearing up this little piece of paper with this number on it right now. Never to be used again. After all, why would I?" he asked, then hung up before she had a chance to beat him to it.

Olivia let the instrument slide into her lap. Why had he been so intent on making matters worse? she wondered. He hadn't suffered any consequences for his actions, still worked in the same law firm, now perfectly happy being married to that woman with the hour-glass figure and tight-fitting dresses that fit her like a glove. It didn't matter, she reminded herself. She'd found a man who was different, and somehow, since Harrison had called and thrown one last insulting piece of news her way, she found she could now put the past behind her. Actually, his calling couldn't have been timed any better, she decided, reaching over to turn on the soft light attached to the table next to her.

Olivia reached inside her pocket where she'd stuffed the number Red had given her in their quick parting. She eased the mobile phone from her lap then dialed.

* * *

The shrill burst of rings from the bedside phone roused Red from his slumber. After the long day he'd had, and since Jimmy had turned in as well, he'd dropped off to sleep the moment his head hit the pillow. He reached for the receiver, still so groggy that he couldn't imagine who'd be trying to call after bedtime.

"Hello?" he said, pulling the receiver to his ear and propping himself up on his elbow.

"Red? Is that you?"

"Yes," he answered, clearing his head enough to realize that Olivia was actually on the other end of the phone.

"It's Olivia. You don't sound like yourself."

"It's me," he said, trying to sound more alert. Normally, someone breaking up his sleep, especially when he'd first fallen off, would have been an irritation. But hearing the soothing sound of her voice made him smile. He sank down into the covers on his back, smiling up at the dark ceiling.

"You were asleep," she said. "I'm so sorry."

"What time is it?"

"Almost ten o'clock. Obviously, you go to bed early. I didn't realize."

"It's okay. I'm glad to hear from you."

"Well, I was going to wait a few days before calling you, but I needed to hear your voice," she explained.

This got Red's attention. He eased up to a seated position, swinging his legs over the bedside.

"What's wrong. Something's wrong. I can hear it in your tone," he urged.

"No. No. Not really . . ."

"I can come right over if something's the matter," he offered, now fully awake. "Just give me the address and I'm there," he added.

"No. It's fine. I appreciate it, but there's no need."

"So, what's wrong, Olivia?"

She paused ever so slightly. "It's just I got an unexpected, unpleasant call from the past, and you, well you bring me back to the now, so to speak. Where I want to be. It's why I called. I needed an anchor. You're pretty good about that. But now that I've touched base, perhaps I should let you go back off to sleep. I hope you can," she said.

"No problem. I'll sleep like a baby. Sure I can't do anything to help? Do you want to get together again soon?" he asked hopefully.

"How about tomorrow night?"

"Of course. Why don't I call you at Penny's tomorrow during your shift to make plans. I'm not sure I can be quite awake enough to get directions to your house or anything right at the moment."

"That's fine. And Red?"

"Yes?"

"Thanks," she said, then hung up the phone.

Red replaced the receiver and collapsed back under the covers. A smile crept over his face as he shut his eyes, hoping he hadn't been dreaming. He knew better, though. She'd called. She needed him as much as he needed her. And he suspected she felt the same attraction as well. He pulled the extra pillow in his arms and against his chest, wishing it were Olivia. With that thought in mind, he drifted off and slept more soundly than he had in weeks.

Chapter Six

"Gus? It's Red. Thought maybe I could swing by late morning and talk," Red said into the receiver right after Jimmy had left for work.

"You wising up, Red? It's about time," Gus Rigsby answered.

"Let's just say I'd like to talk it over. That's all. No promises." With this, Red hung up the phone. He'd now set up a meeting at the bank so he'd be clear on his options when he got to Gus' house, just one farm over. It was a milestone in his life, and he was just glad he had the promise of meeting with Olivia later that evening. She somehow gave him resolve to do the right thing—for all involved.

Later that morning he had his answers. He'd met with the bank, now he needed to hear what Gus had to say. The officer at the bank, Ginny Farlow, gave him a thumbnail sketch of what to expect, but she would draw up some figures that he could count on by the next day. They'd set up a meeting for 3:30 p.m. Friday afternoon. Now it was time to swing by their family's long-time neighbor.

Bringing his truck up the familiar drive, Red suddenly remembered occasions throughout his life when the two families helped each other out in times of crises. One needed help with tight harvest times, another when a family member was ill. And, of course, they'd brought food and support, like half the town, when his mother, then his father died. The sadness brought his mind to the business at hand. Yet another crisis, but this time both were helped out in the transaction.

The front door swung open before Red even reached it, and Gus' wife, Cora, ushered him in.

"Land sakes you've sure turned into a big man," she said, clipping through the hallway and taking him to Gus who sat at the kitchen table finishing an early lunch.

"Cora, you've seen me plenty before now. I've been grown for at least ten years."

"I know," she said, shaking her head. "But it always surprises me. You remind me so of your father, being so big and tall like he was, God rest his soul."

"Have you had lunch, Red? Cora's made plenty."

"Just a glass of water or iced tea would do. This won't take long."

"I'll get it," Cora said, turning to the task as Red sat down eye-to-eye with Gus. His wife removed the empty lunch plate from her husband and placed a large glass of iced tea in front of Red. She put the dirty dishes in the sink, then quietly left the room.

"I'll give you a fair price," Gus began without preamble as he pulled a folded piece of paper from his front pocket. He slid it over the smooth tabletop in front of Red. "All that extra land will allow me to do just what I need. I'll be needing to buy the equipment, too. Can't ask for better than that," he told him.

Red looked down at the paper Gus had shoved in front of him, unfolded it and inspected the long list he'd drawn up. Gus was right, Red decided. The price was good. Better than he'd expected.

"You make it hard to say 'no'," Red said sadly.

"No reason to say 'no.' You've done all of this for your father's memory, and your grandfather's before that, but farming is different now. And you're not cut out for this business, especially doing it the way you are. I'm not objecting to your methods, mind you, but you need help and things aren't looking too good out there unless you've got the type of operation I have. If you don't stop now, you'll find yourself deep in debt," Gus told him. "Now if I'm to be a help to your father's memory, I'll tell you straight without sugar coating it," he finished.

"I know, Gus. Seems I've dedicated myself to what somebody else threw in my lap. It wouldn't have been something I'd choose."

"Yep. Time you found a life of your own. You've got a good retailing kind of mind. One that's suited for that furniture operation. Making the kind of quality stuff you do in the barn is what made me put the whole thing together. Hope you don't mind me sticking my nose in about it, especially since you know I'd benefit from your decision."

Red shook his head in agreement. "Don't know if that'll work out, but it's certainly an option."

"Dale Bentley's ready to sell. Wants to retire and travel around in that new RV they bought. I think you can convince the daughter-in-law to stay on in sales, but she doesn't want any part of taking on the responsibility for it. So, they're anxious to sell—especially to someone they trust what they've built up all these years," he explained.

"I'll see about it, Gus. And I appreciate it. Now, back to this list. I don't see mention about the house."

Gus stared straight ahead for a second, not answering.

Finally he spoke. "Well, now, that's up in the air."

"Up in the air?"

"Depends. That price for the land includes the house. But if you're bound and determined to stay there, I'll have to knock off only a little. It's the land I want from this deal, not an extra house."

"Well, Gus. I'm not stuck on living there all my life, but there's Jimmy to consider. He's here only temporarily—he says. But to take that away from him too might not be something I have a choice in. This is hard enough as it is," he began.

"Son," he said, rising from his chair. "You deserve to get on with your life. You're the fortunate type, you know. Your father kept up with things, and the land is yours free and clear. House, too. Now get out before it kills you. You think I don't know, but I do. There comes a time in man's life when he has to move on, and I'm afraid if you don't take my offer this time, I'm gonna have to look into putting a few farms together to the east and south of me. This is the final deal," he told him.

Red rose from his seat, folded the piece of paper in his hands and headed out. Gus was on his heels.

"I'll let you know by tomorrow night," Red promised. He then drove off and headed back to the house he may have to say good-bye to forever. If he sold it along with the deal, he'd make more money. Money he needed badly.

The thought about his home where he'd been a son to his parents, a big brother, and a father figure to Jimmy haunted him when he walked into the kitchen. It was old, that was for sure, but he didn't want to face that it'd be abandoned or worse, bulldozed over. Surely somebody could use the comfortable older house. It had such character—and memories.

He glanced at the clock and decided to go ahead and call Olivia. She might not be able to talk long, seeing that it was just after the rush at lunch hour, but he suddenly couldn't wait to hear a friendly voice that would bring him out of this slump.

Sure enough, after he'd hung up the phone, all his problems seemed to dissipate for the time being. He'd just invited Olivia to come out there for dinner, and she'd accepted. It would be important to him for her to see his roots before he had to call it a day. Soon he'd have to tell her. Worse was what he was going to tell Jimmy. It would not be good. No matter what he did, Jimmy would not like it. He never did.

* * *

"So, this is where you live?" Olivia asked as she climbed out of her Mercedes Sedan.

"This is 'home sweet home,'" Red replied, holding her car door open for her. "What do you think?"

"I like it. I really do," she answered stepping onto the dirt driveway. "It's homey," she added, delighted to get to know the real Red

Taylor. Being able to see him in his home setting would tell more about him than words, she'd decided, and now that he was beside her, touching the small of her back as he lead her inside gave her such a feeling of warmth.

"Where's Jimmy?" she asked as she entered the spacious kitchen where delicious aromas filled the air.

"I can't rightly say," Red answered with a grimace. "He's taken to not telling me his plans, especially now that he has a job. He just shows up after he's through visiting friends or whatever he's doing. It's more of his attempt to rebel against me as the authority figure I suppose," he explained.

"You've set three plates," she ventured, glancing at the table.

"Yep. He might show up any minute, or he could drag in around ten o'clock or thereabouts. But if I don't add a plate, he'll be mad," he said.

Olivia found herself hoping that Jimmy would find something else to do that night, yet at the same time, she didn't trust herself with this man all alone at his home—he was far too attractive.

"You just take a seat here and I'll get dinner on the table," he said. Olivia sat as directed, enjoying the view. Red was certainly handsome, but not the kind of man you'd call movie-star good looking. And though also equipped with a fabulous, strong body, his appeal to her was mostly from what came from the inside. True honesty. A good sense of humor. A love of family, even when that family was not always good to him—like Jimmy. It spoke of character, and that, along with integrity, is what she'd so wanted to find in a man.

Her father was like that, and her mother'd told her not to settle for anything less. That in the long run she'd benefit from the kind of man you could count on. Trust. Red Taylor exemplified that and more. She knew it in her heart, and it made all the hurt of the past begin to heal.

She took in a deep breath and felt she'd finally arrived at home. A true home, she thought, as she watched Red bend over and pull a casserole from the oven and place it on the stove top. Next came out

2948-BURG

a pan of rolls, the store-bought kind. In fact, she saw the box discarded in the trash can that said the chicken dish they were about to enjoy had also been someone else's creation. Still, Red had gone to the trouble to fix her dinner. It was admirable. Endearing.

He swiveled around to look at her, then smiled.

"I see you noticed who really did the cooking?" he said, gesturing to the casserole box.

"I'm sure it will be delicious," she supplied.

He set everything on the table and Olivia could hardly believe the amount of pampering this man was able to give her. After a moment and a few bites into the meal, Olivia spoke up.

"Red, I want to thank you for all of this. It's lovely and everything tastes so good," she told him.

"Well, I figured you could use someone taking care of you for a change."

"For a change? What do you mean?"

"You live alone, you wait on others at the Diner, and you need some TLC after last night."

Olivia exhaled deeply. "Oh. That," she said, giving no further information at the moment.

"Care to tell me about it? You sounded pretty sad last night."

Olivia set down a roll she was placing a dab of real butter on at that moment and faced him. She'd need to know how he'd react right off, otherwise, she might be wasting her time, she decided.

"You might as well know, Red, that I've had a rough past with men. With one man in particular."

"Boyfriend troubles?" he ventured.

"Worse. I married him. We're now divorced. It lasted only three months, which was much longer than he deserved."

Olivia watched Red's face for his reaction, thinking he would render a judgment on what kind of person would be divorced after such a short period of time. Instead, a look of concern passed over his features.

"He didn't hurt you, did he?"

"Oh, not that way. He wasn't physically abusive if that's what you mean."

"Oh. Good," he answered, exhaling.

"Would it matter if he had?" she asked. "I mean, would that be something that would make you turn and run?"

"I'd turn and run, all right. Punching the guy's lights out."

Olivia laughed, imagining for a second Red actually confronting Harrison, perhaps in a fine restaurant with a crowd. Messing up his designer suit, causing him embarrassment.

"Well, there's no need for that. Not that it would do any good. He did hurt me, but in an emotionally abusive way. He belittled me, though in a way it was a compliment."

"A compliment?" he repeated.

"In a twisted way, yes," she answered.

"I don't understand."

"Okay. Harrison needed someone to marry who'd make him look good and further his career. My father is an attorney in a big firm. Harrison worked at that same firm, and he got it in his head that he'd be a notch higher on the ladder if he was perceived as a family man, and married to a fine lineage. The reputation of my father, my background, the fact that I am nice enough to look at and dress nicely, all added up to Harrison."

"So he married you but didn't love you. And you found out that wasn't enough? Had to get out of it?" he asked without judgment.

"Not that simple. No, he didn't love me. I loved him, or so I thought. It was all a plan. A carefully executed plan totally selfish on his part. Lies and deceit entered the scenario, and when I found he was still carrying on with his previous girlfriend, just as much as ever, the truth finally dawned."

"So, did they fire the guy?"

"No, they don't do that because you get divorced. But he did switch firms, and in that way, he got the promotion he was bucking for—a partnership. Now he's married to the woman he was seeing behind my back, and has the family life that looks good to the outside, as well as the woman of his desire. Just perfect."

Red remained quiet a moment. He looked pensive, compassionate. He reached over and squeezed her hand then edged his chair partly around the side of the table. He leaned over and Olivia thought her heart stopped beating for a second when she realized he was about to kiss her.

The gentleness of his lips against hers melted all the sadness. He'd wiped away all thoughts of her past life as he brushed his hand against her chin with a caress that spoke of a man who cared deeply.

He then released her and they focused on their dinner. Half-way through Red paused, looked up at her, and locked his gaze with hers. He blinked thoughtfully, then said the words she'd longed to hear from just someone, for she had blamed herself for not seeing through Harrison and had doubted her ability to judge after that.

"Olivia, the man's a fool," he said. "Not you. You aren't to blame for trusting him, for taking him at his word. But you've discovered the pattern of that type of man. Don't let anybody ever get away with that again. The man probably doesn't feel any better about it than you do," he finished.

Olivia paused. "Well, he didn't sound too sorry when he called to wish me a 'Happy Anniversary,'" she put in.

"Yesterday would have been your anniversary?"

"Yes."

"And he called you to rub your nose in it?"

"Yes. That and to tell me he'd remarried and didn't need me any more."

"Oh, I'll bet that went over great. No wonder you were upset."

"Look," Olivia began, pushing her empty plate away. "That's over and done with. I wanted to let you know of my past marital status, but let's not dwell on it any further."

"Okay," Red agreed. "What would you like to talk about next?"

"How about you? Have you been married?"

"No. I've never found the right woman. And, I must confess I haven't had the time—until now," he began. "But like you, there are some things I think you should be aware of. I wouldn't want you finding it out through Jimmy or through the grapevine," he started.

Olivia held her breath. "What's that?"

At that precise moment, the sound of Jimmy's car roared into the driveway, and within seconds Jimmy rushed in, slamming the door behind him. They both turned their focus to the doorway where Jimmy suddenly appeared.

"What are *you* doing here?" Jimmy huffed.

"She's my guest," Red answered incredulously. "Why would you be so rude?"

"Sorry," Jimmy sulked. "I didn't mean anything, Olivia. You just surprised me."

He then scraped an empty chair across the floor and fell into the seat. "What's for dinner?"

"Chicken Casserole."

"Hope you didn't make it. Olivia's likely to be poisoned and I'd have to wait on tables at the Diner, too," he said in a lighter tone.

Olivia was relieved at the change. Jimmy was normally so upbeat around Penny's, and this other side she'd just witnessed was strange and not so enjoyable.

After dinner Red offered to show Olivia around. She was greatly pleased to be alone with him again. Even though Jimmy'd put up a good front, there was tension there, making it uncomfortable. She decided it was a family thing and not her presence in his home that bothered Jimmy.

The tour of the house went quickly, then Red asked if she'd like to take a walk outside. The cooler evening air of late autumn spoke of changing seasons and change in her life. It had been the best decision of her life, she decided, to pick this town where someone like Red Taylor could come into her world and make everything right. Correction, she decided, she had been the one to do this. Choosing Red was also something she had elected to do on her own volition.

When their walk took them into a wide, spacious barn, she glanced around for any animals.

"Um, Red? I'm a big city girl. I don't know if any farm animals will take to me," she warned. Red chuckled and took her by the hand, leading her inside. Silence filled the darkened space and she wondered if something might jump out at her at any moment.

"Red, now, really . . ." she continued, pulling back.

"Relax, Miss Big City. I don't raise farm animals. Not anymore. That was something my father and grandfather were good at, but I've changed everything so much in the past few years my father's been gone, that this place is a mere shadow of the way things were. There's nothing in here alive that I know of. Save a few mice that might creep up on you."

With this, Olivia inched forward, glancing furiously through the darkness at the floor that showed nothing but remnants of old hay. Though Red remained close behind, her imagination continued to conjure up imagines she'd seen in movies and television, and a rustle from somewhere nearby sent her slamming backwards into Red's solid form.

His arms enveloped her and he held her tightly in his arms. Olivia felt herself instantly relax, totally at ease feeling him close and hearing the sound of his healthy heart though his chest.

She slipped around to face him, and the tiny bit of light coming from an outside pole light twinkled in his eyes. She watched his face as his eyes examined hers. His hands grasped her shoulders, then he pulled her closer and began to kiss her. Olivia answered his kiss. It felt so good to be in his arms, to be kissing him.

Moments later Red pulled away and led her over to a corner. He lifted her onto a tall bail of hay and stood before her. She was now head to head with him, and she looped her arms around his neck, taking in a deep breath. The lone light just outside the barn shed incredible shadowed light that outlined his features, sculpted his strong face, solid bone structure, with the contrast of his soft eyes sheltered by long, light-colored lashes.

He leaned forward, gently showering small kisses along her neck, then up to her mouth again. But just as one's worst nightmare interrupts a sound, peaceful sleep, her past marriage to Harrison suddenly broke into her thoughts. Harrison had no real feelings for her, and in retrospect, it showed. This man, concerned for her, respectful of her, was so gentle and loving.

Yes, Red was mesmerizing. Her thoughts returned to the here and now as Red held her in a spell that she'd yet to comprehend. Olivia leaned back on the pillow of hay and trailed her hands over his strong back. She knew she was in trouble, for she could not untangle herself from this emotional web she now found herself in. Still, her bad experience with Harrison was still fresh, she realized as she simultaneously fought with her emotional demons. Could she really trust herself with anyone again? she wondered, hesitating slightly.

Red stopped the passionate kiss, then held her lightly at arms-length distance. His eyes sparkled in the darkness as he studied her face. He then shook his head and eased away.

"Olivia, I think we'd better go back inside," he suggested, reaching out and lifting her off the bail of hay.

"What's wrong? Why are we going inside?" she asked.

"You have a past to work through that you're just not quite over yet."

"Why do you say that?"

"I can tell. A man knows these things. You just let me know when you're ready. Until then, we'll take it slow and easy. Besides, Jimmy will have something to say if we don't get back inside pretty soon. And believe me, you don't want to give him any ammunition."

Olivia's head was spinning as they made a quick trip back to the house. She wished she could stay longer with Red, but she realized he was right about everything. As she neared her car, she remembered she'd left her purse and keys on the coffee table.

She'd hoped to leave with no further conversation with Red's brother, but as luck would have it, Jimmy'd planted himself on the

2948-BURG

sofa to watch TV in the den instead of in the privacy of his own room. They came into the den and Jimmy looked up.

"You guys have sure been gone a long time," he pointed out.

"Nice evening for a walk," Red explained, reaching down to retrieve Olivia's purse and keys which lay squarely in front of Jimmy's feet now perched on the coffee table.

"Yes. Beautiful night," Olivia added. An awkward silence fell as Jimmy turned back to the TV. "Well, good-night," Olivia said to Jimmy, as they began to leave as quickly as possible.

"Oh, Olivia?" Jimmy called out, stopping her retreat.

"What, Jimmy?" she answered, swiveling back around.

"You've got hay in your hair," he said. She noted his focus remained on the TV and did not turn to look back at her. Still, she felt the color rise to her cheeks. She glanced at Red and both of them headed outside as quickly as possible.

Walking to her car, she breathed out.

"Well, this has certainly turned out to be some evening. More than I ever expected."

"There's more of that to come. I promise. I've got some things to work out in my life, and so do you," he supplied.

She moved into the front seat and started the car.

"That's right," she answered as she rolled down the window after he'd closed the door. "You were going to tell me something before Jimmy came home. Something you thought I needed to hear from you. What was that?" she asked, now remembering the earlier conversation.

"Another time," Red answered, leaning in and giving her a quick kiss on the cheek. It was just like him, she thought, moving down the drive. And he was right, she realized. How can he always be so right, she wondered. But more, she wondered where this road would take her, for if she had her way, it would be straight to a home like this where she could be totally at ease with the honest, loving, and compassionate man.

* * *

When Red came back in the house, Jimmy stood waiting for him, his fists pushed defiantly onto his hips.

"What's your problem, little bro?" Red asked wearily.

"You get a nice roll in the hay with the woman I work with?"

"That's none of your business. But we do need to talk, and I'm not sure how you're gonna take it."

"Oh, yeah? What other bomb you got to drop on me? Gonna take my inheritance money away or something?"

"No, at least I hope not. But Jimmy, you're on the right track. You have to understand, I'm gonna have to sell the farm."

Jimmy's mouth dropped open in shock.

"You gotta be kidding! You're actually gonna give up this place Dad and Grandpa built and worked at all their lives?"

"I don't have any extra help and it's starting to drain all the savings," Red explained.

"You mean my inheritance?" Jimmy boomed.

"Yes. It could if I try to hang on much longer," Red answered honestly.

"That does it!" Jimmy said slamming his fist against a nearby wall.

"Calm down, bro. I think I can swing the right kind of money so your part won't be touched."

"You'd better. What about the house?"

"Don't know," Red answered honestly.

"Look," Jimmy said flatly. "I don't care what you do with this farm. Just so you have enough to free up my inheritance money."

"Well, I'll know soon enough. I'm meeting with Ginny Farlow at the bank tomorrow at 3:00 p.m. After that, around 4:30, I'm signed up to meet with Dale Bentley, actually his wife and daughter-in-law since he's got to be out of town and I've already talked with him earlier in the week."

"Oh, so you've already decided to sell our house out from under us and the farm Daddy worked himself to death over for some furniture business? You'd better not take any of my money to do it," he warned.

"Jimmy, you've got a lot of nerve talking about the farm like it means a whit to you. You left me with this and now I've finally got to sell while I've got an offer on the table and a business I can make some money at."

"All's I've got to say is you'd better give me my share as soon as you sell it, cause then you'll have it freed up—it's rightfully mine from the will."

"There's still six months before I'm supposed to do that. Besides, I can make up more than your share in the furniture business once I'm in it, rather having the farm drain away any more."

"You don't have my money now, is that it?" he demanded.

"It's tied up," Red answered. "But Dad didn't want you to have it until you were twenty-one. When you were more mature than you clearly are right now. So, after this thing's settled, you'll still have to wait."

With this, Jimmy stormed back to his room. The slamming of his door echoed through the house. The next morning Jimmy wasn't speaking, but that wasn't going to stop Red from doing what he had to do. He could tell Jimmy had mixed feelings about the house, but not the farm. Red would now have to do what had to be done.

Besides, the only thing Jimmy really cared about was getting his inheritance as soon as possible. But he'd just have to wait for the money, and hopefully in having to do so, he'd grow up a little in the process. And sooner or later, perhaps Jimmy would back down from the fresh, new battle lines he'd now laid out with Red.

Chapter Seven

"Have a good time last night?" Jimmy taunted Olivia as they began the work day the following morning.

"Yes. Your brother is very nice," she replied, not wanting to discuss her personal life with Jimmy. Somehow it didn't seem right. Even though her two worlds blended now, she wanted to keep them separate. Jimmy had other ideas, however.

"He's nice, huh? Yeah, that's the way he likes all his women to think of him."

Olivia paused as she unloaded some dishes from the industrial washer. She wasn't going to let Jimmy get away with what he was implying. Nor did she think he wanted her to.

"His 'women'?"

"Yeah. Girlfriends. Lovers. Whatever you all call yourselves."

Olivia continued with her task, feeling her face burning from the implications. The memories of the night before with Red in the barn was all she had been able to think of ever since. Still, she needed to set Jimmy straight, set the tone right from the beginning.

She raised up and stepped in front of him, blocking his path to the opposite side of the work station.

"Listen, Jimmy. I don't like the inference to my dating your brother culminating into the term 'his lover.' Furthermore, what I do in my free time I'd like to be kept private and not the topic of conversation at work. Let's keep it professional here. Understand?"

The younger man nodded. He looked unmoved by her lecture, and slightly amused.

"Sure. I understand. It's better for Red that way too."

"I don't get your meaning?" she answered, unable to stop herself.

"Well, the less said about his carrying on's the more he can get away with. You know—with more women. I'll bet he asked you to keep your rendezvous secret," Jimmy added, skating around her. Olivia swiveled around, watching the younger man disappear into the confines of the storage area, leaving her with disturbing questions about Red. If anyone knew his normal behavior it was the brother who lived with him.

Olivia knew herself enough to count to ten—no, to twenty, before saying another word. She'd consider carefully how she put what she wanted to ask, so there'd be no question as to the answer. No confusion in interpretation—on either of their parts.

After she'd set up and began waiting on some of the early-bird customers, she found Jimmy busy at the grill. His whistling signaled a better mood, and a let-up in the diner activity gave Olivia the opportunity she'd been seeking for the last thirty minutes.

She sidled beside him. He faced the inside toward the grill area so there was no way anyone could overhear her question or the answer that Jimmy would give. She just held her breath, hoping it was one she'd be able to live with—one which would allow her to continue seeing Red.

"We've got some unfinished business left between us," she began.

"We do?" Jimmy asked with a flare of innocence.

"Are you trying to tell me Red has other girlfriends? Other women he sees and is, let's see, women who you claim are his 'lovers?'"

Jimmy sniffed and concentrated on the two eggs he'd just carefully placed on the hot grill. He then saw to the bacon also sizzling away.

"Jimmy? I want an answer. A straight one."

He then turned to face her eye to eye.

"Fine. You want to see Red? Your choice. But you're not the only fish in the sea. Why, he's seeing another woman this afternoon. Guess last night didn't satisfy him," he answered, quickly turning back to the grill and expertly handling the cooking breakfast special.

Olivia felt her face burn in anger. She sensed the problems between the brothers, but would Jimmy stoop so low as to spread lies about Red just to keep him from building a relationship with her? Was it that Jimmy didn't like his brother dating someone from his work? No, she thought, there was something much deeper that would lead him to this.

She turned away abruptly when she realized two customers at the counter had just breezed in and needed her attention. The moment she was through getting them coffee and letting them consider their food order more carefully for a few minutes, she stepped back to Jimmy. She just had to know.

"Well, I don't believe you. I know the type of man you're implying your brother is, and Red doesn't fit the description. I don't know why you'd lie to me about him, but I know it isn't true. Red isn't like that, and I know I couldn't be fooled by a liar and a cheat again."

"So, don't take my word for it," Jimmy said in a quieter tone. "If you want the truth, go lookin' for it. Try making a stop at the First National Bank around three—right when you get off your shift. Ginny Farlow is one of his women. Then go by that furniture store out on Highway 98, say around 4:30 p.m. I'll make you a dollar bet you'll find him carrying on with women at both places this very afternoon," he supplied.

"I'm not going to snoop around, Jimmy. It's not my style," she whispered in disgust.

"Suit yourself. Want to be blind to his charms, that's your business. But if you want the truth, you'll check out what I've told you at exactly the times I mentioned. I know his schedule and today, that's his pattern. He doesn't even care if they're married," he put in at the last moment, zipping by her to see to something in the back storage room.

"Coward," she said under her breath at his retreating form.

Olivia knew this couldn't be true, but with her past of putting on blinders, of being hit with something when all the signs were there, she knew she couldn't quite trust her instincts yet that screamed that Jimmy was doing this to spite his brother.

Much as she hated it, the only thing to do was to check up on him and follow the leads just as Jimmy had suggested. Then, if there were no truth to the matter, she'd warn Red of what his brother was doing to his reputation behind his back. He must be trying to sabotage his brother's happiness, simply from jealousy and a long-term struggle for power. By late that day, she'd have her answers.

* * *

Red felt like he was walking on cloud nine. He'd finally made the decision that'd weighed so heavily on his mind for years, and this last date with Olivia, which he'd dreamed about before she seemed to know of his existence, turned out better than he'd dared to hope.

His meeting with Ginny at the bank was quite promising, too. She'd been in touch with Gus, who gave her a verbal verification of the amount of money he was willing to pay Red for the land, equipment, and the house, or just the equipment and the land itself. It gave Red an idea of his options, which he would run by his brother before agreeing—even if he didn't deserve that chance. After all, the kid had moved back and needed a place to live.

He felt badly about not just sending Jimmy away with the amount of money his father had squirreled away for his youngest boy, but his father had also been very specific and made Red give him his word when it looked like he was not long for this world. Red would honor that promise, no matter what tricks and tantrums Jimmy pulled. He would also make sure that no matter what, in six months, he'd have the cash to let Jimmy start a life somewhere else if he wanted, and maybe try to make things right for him. But he couldn't do that now.

Still, he was in good spirits as he spoke with Ginny about the turn of events. They laughed and talked with renewed excitement about the possibility of the new career path Red had decided to take.

The only thing that didn't go exactly as he would've wanted was when he looked up through the glass windowed office and had seen Olivia standing in line at the bank. He'd tried to wave, get her attention, but as soon as he'd looked out, she'd quickly turned back toward the front of the line. Maybe she hadn't seen him, he decided as he finished up his meeting. When he went out to the parking lot, Olivia was gone.

With renewed conviction, he then turned toward Dale's Big Furniture Showcase, started by Dale Bentley's uncle years back. They, too, were turning over a long-standing, family tradition and handing over the reins to another to continue on.

After the short meeting he'd had with Dale's wife and daughter-in-law, he was escorted by their daughter-in-law, Sandi, through the showroom. She began filling him in on the manufacturers and their relationships with them all, how things were normally handled, and other tidbits.

Red realized she was a flirty, pretty woman, and decided that was one reason she made such a good salesperson. You felt good about the attention, and she knew her business. She could make any person, male or female, glad they'd come in. When Red asked if she would still stay on after he'd bought the business, she threw her arms around his neck in excitement, saying she was afraid he'd try to start with all new people of his own. Red awkwardly patted her back in the embrace.

It was at this exact moment when she'd startled him with the hug, that Red caught a glimpse of the familiar Mercedes parked out front. He checked to see if Olivia was in the showroom, but Sandi kept him in a neck-lock which he thought would last forever. When she finally released him, he glanced around again at the strolling customers, but Olivia was not among them.

When he left, promising to work out a deal with them within the next two weeks, her car, if it was Olivia's, was gone.

2948-BURG

It did make him start thinking about her, and wondered if she'd be available for a late dinner. First he'd fill Jimmy in on the facts, then he'd share them with her. After all, he planned for the events of his life to impact Olivia. For now that he realized his dream woman from Penny's Diner was real and even more enticing on the inside as well as the outside, he intended for her to be a part of his life permanently.

* * *

Olivia stared at the telephone, then broke down and dialed the familiar number.

"Hello?" the sing-song voice called out.

"Hi, Mom."

"Olivia?" her mother replied hopefully.

"Yes, it's me."

"Why, we've been worried sick. Where did you go? Are you in town?"

"No. I moved out of town."

"Whatever for, dear? Where are you?"

"Just in a small town I imagined would be better for me. A place I thought people would be different. Only to discover it's more of the same everywhere else."

"Tsk, tsk," her mother chided. "If you'd have come to your mother, you wouldn't be in such a state. I could have told you that. People are people no matter where you go. Where is it you said you went, dear?"

"I didn't. Needless to say, I've made another colossal mistake. Another inept understanding and judge of character," she explained. "What's wrong with me?" she asked.

"Oh, my. You haven't gotten involved with a man again, have you? We were all fooled by Harrison, dear. Now, if you've gravitated toward another of his nature, well, shame on you," her mother added.

"Great. Just great. This is what I get from my mother. The woman who gave me life, supposedly loves me more than anyone in the whole world. Is this your best attempt at support?" Olivia asked, whisking away a tear she hoped her mother hadn't detected on the other end.

"Really, now, Olivia. Do you always have to be so melodramatic?"

"No, mother. I don't," she added, realizing her mistake in making the call. "How's Dad?"

"He's fine. And doing quite well in the firm."

"Good. Give him a kiss for me? I've got to go," she said, ready to hang up.

"But dear! We don't even know where you are. Won't you give me a number or . . ."

"Yes, Mom. Now that I've got a permanent address, at least for a while, I'll send you all that in a note. Love, love," she added, then hung up.

Jimmy had been right, Olivia thought, feeling like she'd been sucker-punched in the stomach again, and she'd never felt so alone in all her life. It was too bad that she couldn't have her mother as a confidant, but she wasn't made that way, she reminded herself.

Olivia had told herself many years back that the woman just couldn't help the way she was put together emotionally so that she responded to her daughter in a distant, chastising way, rather than a loving, comforting one.

It doesn't matter, Olivia thought. It's never done any good to feel sorry for myself, either. I'll just have to get used to feeling men out before giving them my heart, body and soul, she told herself.

She'd been so sure Red was different, and in the short time they'd been together, she'd really, really thought that's why fate had brought her to this town. That she would live happily ever after with a man like Red—down-to-earth and forthright, honest, she thought with a derisive laugh.

Since a picture is worth a thousand words, seeing Red laughing so and carrying on with the girl at the bank, then turning around and going to the furniture store and seeing that woman flirting so openly with him, then watching them hug in such a prolonged embrace told

Olivia all she needed to know. Clearly there was much going on between them all, she thought sadly. But this time, Olivia was certain that she would not link herself with a man who was this smooth—maybe even more so than her ex-husband.

The shrill sound of the telephone startled her from her building resolve. After just hanging up from her mother, she wondered if her telephone number had been displayed on the other end and her mother had decided to show Olivia that she knew where she was. She wouldn't put it past her mother, but when she picked up, Red's low, enticing voice answered instead.

"Hello, Red," she answered coolly.

"Hi," he shot back with sexy enthusiasm. "I've done nothing but think of you all day," he said.

"Oh? Is that right? Stayed around the farm, working hard, all alone, thinking of nothing but me? Does that about sum it up?" she baited.

"Well, you have to admit, you've given me quite a bit to think on. Our escapades in the barn came to mind every time I turned around, getting me all disturbed at all times of the day."

"I imagine you didn't go anywhere today? All alone all day, right?" Olivia knew this wasn't quite fair, but it would certainly drive the last nail in his coffin if he pretended otherwise.

"Oh, I had a few things to do, people to see, but let's not talk about that right now," he suggested. "The reason I called was to see if you'd agree to a late dinner, say about seven thirty or eight o'clock? I've got a few more people I have to see late today, then I'd like you to be the last one. I can focus all my attention on the most beautiful woman this town has seen in years," he added.

Olivia's heart fell. Only yesterday, she'd have believed his sincerity. Only yesterday, she thought her luck had turned to a man who could not only bring out a passion within her that her ex-husband had certainly not done, but fill the emotional void he'd left as well. But her luck remained the same, and so had her pattern with men.

"Olivia? Are you still there?" Red asked in concern.

"Yes, but you'll have to let the person you're visiting next be the last one on your list. Count me out," she told him.

"Tonight's not good?" he asked, still upbeat about his day that Olivia knew had been filled with women friends at every turn.

"Tonight, tomorrow night, and every one after that. I won't allow a re-run of what I came here to escape, and from where I sit, you're the same song, different verse," Olivia said.

With this Olivia carefully laid the receiver back in it's cradle. Unplugging the instrument, it remained the last call she got that night as well.

Chapter Eight

"Jimmy, there are a few things I need to fill you in on," Red said to his brother as he strolled in at ten after six.

The younger man looked around the kitchen, focusing on the deli meat, bread, and sandwich makings on the counter.

"What? No home-cooked meal?"

"I've been pretty busy all day. Thought sandwiches would be enough for just the two of us," he explained.

"Hmmm. That mean Olivia's not coming back for seconds?" he asked with a smirk.

"Apparently not, though I don't know what I did to mess things up so fast. I'm so out of practice with women that I've managed to say or do something to upset her. She wouldn't even consider coming out. Tonight or ever again."

"Oh, that right?" Jimmy questioned, his smirk widening.

"She didn't say anything today at the Diner about me, did she? Something that would help me figure this out to help me get her back?"

"All I can say is the woman must not be interested in you. Farmer Red strikes out, I guess."

"I should have known you wouldn't be of any help," he said, leaning over the kitchen sink staring out the window.

Jimmy slid into a hardback chair at the table.

"And why should I help you? You've never done anything but hold me back all my life, not to mention keeping my money and probably spending it all before I can even get twenty-one," he blurted out.

Red turned and shifted to a standing position, eyeing his brother, wishing he understood. Soon the guy would move away, probably never to see him again—his only remaining family.

"Jimmy, I just don't understand how you could say that. I may have been only a couple of years older than you are now when Dad died, and I've been your caregiver ever since. If it weren't for me, you'd have been sent to a foster home or some other in-between place for a fourteen-year-old boy. If you think you'd have had a better time of it elsewhere, then I'm sorry. I did the best I could under the circumstances."

"I didn't need your help," Jimmy snapped back. "I coulda taken care of myself. You just started running my life and never gave me a choice. I would have done better on my own."

"Oh, sure. Who do you think would have given you a job? What about school? You couldn't support yourself that young in the first place, much less finished school. Besides, how was a kid that age supposed to deal with losing his other parent. Aren't you at least a little glad you had me for support?"

Jimmy's gaze dropped to the tabletop and he slumped down lower in the chair and crossed his arms over his chest.

"Yeah, well, you and Dad never believed in me. Not like Mom. And at least she loved me," he said finally.

Red felt his heart tighten.

"I'm sorry, Jimmy. I'm sorry we lost her. I'm sorry we lost Dad. And we all believed in you."

"Not after she died. It was all Red, Red, Red. Everybody likes Red. Red is so big and tough and can do all things. Nobody was left to love me—or give anything to me. Then Dad died and left you with everything—except this little bit of inheritance money, which you won't give me," he finished.

Jimmy's eyes turned upwards toward him. Red didn't know how to respond. He'd just thrown him a curve ball chocked full of long-held resentments he'd never told him before. It did appear Jimmy'd gotten the shaft as far as the will was concerned, but it was only because money was tied up in the farming business and their father knew Red would know what to do. Except he didn't.

The fact remained that he *did* love Jimmy, no matter how obnoxious or rebellious he tended to be. Red still loved him—unconditionally.

"What do you want me to say?" Red asked, wishing he could somehow make things right for Jimmy.

"Admit you felt stuck taking care of me?"

"I chose to, Jimmy. I wanted to. You're my brother."

"But you had to take care of the farm to support me," he said. "You never liked that and you blame me."

"No. Again, it was my choice. Good or bad. I can't blame anyone else for my choices. But now things are changing. It's time I found a career I'm suited for and time I settled down with the right woman and started a family of my own. This decision I've made that affects both our lives is the first step," he explained.

"Well, I'm outta your hair after you give me my money. So why don't ya. You *did* sell the farm today, didn't you?"

"Not yet. Things don't happen quite that fast, but I've made verbal commitments to all the parties involved."

"That's fine with me. I'll be in my room."

"But don't you want to hear the details? When it's all going to happen?"

"No. Just tell me when you're gonna boot me outta here. Getting rid of me," he put in defensively.

"What about dinner?" Red asked.

"I'll fix my own sandwich later. I'd rather not 'dine' with you tonight," he answered sarcastically.

"All right, Jimmy. I'll be in the barn," Red answered, turning to go, knowing he couldn't do anything with Jimmy when he was in this kind of mood.

"Don't tell me you've got another woman in there again tonight?" he challenged.

Red exhaled. "I'm working on my furniture, Jimmy. I need to restock a full set for Dale's."

"You're buying that place, aren't you?"

"Yes," he said simply.

"And that's why you won't give me my money. You need all you can scrape together to make your dream come true. And taking mine to do it. I'll never forgive you for this. You've always been the one. The only one. I've been in your shadow all my life. Big, tall Red with the big muscles and all the women falling all over him. Then comes along the one that took after his 'mother's side of the family.' Then you had all the say around here. And nobody in this town thinks I can do anything being your little brother. Calling me 'waif' and all that business. Well, now I got a place that appreciates me for me and what I can do. I'm a good cook and I plan to make a living at it. Maybe be a big chef at a fancy restaurant some day," he threw in. "One thing's for sure, they like me over there and they don't you. So for once in my life, I've won. So sell the farm and buy your stupid business with what our parents left you. I guess they forgot they had another son when they started dying off. Otherwise, we would've been equal partners. But no, who'd believe Jimmy could do anything anyway."

With this, Jimmy stormed down the hall. Instead of Red hearing the sound of the TV or stereo blaring, there was silence. It was the worst, most painful silence Red had ever heard in his life.

Chapter Nine

Red went to Penny's Diner three days after his fight with Jimmy and his unexpected break-up with Olivia. He was due at the bank in an hour for a meeting with Gus, his neighbor buying the adjacent land, and Dale, for the furniture business, and Ginny Farlow, who'd be able to tell him just what other funds were necessary to make the thing happen. Though Olivia had her phone unplugged or was just not answering it, he really needed to find out what he'd done or said in the short time they'd been together to mess things up. He'd gone over it a thousand times, and only wondered if the physical thing had been a mistake. They hadn't done much, and maybe she felt rejected, or maybe it brought back bad memories of her husband.

Red figured the way she'd been hurt in the past, she'd want a solid relationship before getting close like that. He was sure of it, but something had gone very wrong. And he hoped to straighten it out with her before he signed papers that changed his life forever. He simply needed the support, and hoped to get the woman of his dreams on his side before making this big step. He had no other family but his brother, and he wasn't speaking to him.

He eased in the doorway, wondering if pots and pans would fly between both Jimmy and Olivia's present disposition towards him. Instead, he found the place at a lull in traffic, at which he felt relieved. It'd give Olivia a chance to talk with him a little longer—

something he'd force her to do because he wouldn't let her go. Not without a fight, he decided.

Soon she strode over to his table cool as a cucumber.

"Good morning!" he said in his most upbeat tone.

"What do you want this morning?" she asked flatly as she stood focusing on the order pad with her pen perched, ready to write the food order.

Red reached up and pulled the order pan downward, causing Olivia to take in a quick breath and her eyes rivet onto his face.

"No touching," she said, pulling her fingers free of his hand.

"What is it, Olivia? What did I do? I thought we were really going somewhere together," he said quietly.

Olivia stared back at him and Red noticed she swallowed hard.

"Going somewhere together? What does that mean? Like taking me into your harem?" she challenged.

"What on earth?" Red laughed. "I'm not sure I get your drift," he added in question.

"Forget it, Red. The game's up. I've known all too well the type of man you are. This time I saw the signals early and did something about it. Before you messed with my mind, not to mention what you'd already done to my heart. I don't know how you can live with yourself, is all I can say."

Red frowned up at her.

"Look, I don't know what you're talking about, but I just came in to tell you, just in case you're interested in my life or my life plans, that I'm about to sell the farm. Jimmy's mad, for his own reasons, and now you're on my case too. For what, I can't imagine. Anyway, I'm about to meet with the bank again. Going to buy that furniture showcase place out on Highway 98 south of here. I'm already involved with the folks there. Now it'll be *my* business. Something I'm good at, and not trying to make my father's business my own. Something I'm clearly NOT good at, but I can say I gave it my best shot. So, if you're even vaguely interested, I just wanted to tell you," Red finished.

"Why would I care what you do?" Olivia shot back. "You've got women friends all over town who might be interested, but not me."

"Well," Red said, rising from the booth. "I guess that says it all. I thought you'd like to know what type of life you'd be in for, since you'd first thought of me as a farmer with lots of land. I'd hoped you'd be a part of this new life, but I guess I was wrong."

With this, Red brushed past Olivia, heading out the front door. He wouldn't be eating breakfast that day. He'd just lost his appetite.

* * *

"What was *that* all about?" Millie Holmes questioned as Olivia zipped back and flung her order pad down onto the counter.

"Nothing. Nothing that matters, anyway," she answered.

Millie smiled. "Hmmm. If it means that little, then why are you so upset?"

"I'm not upset. I just put that Red Taylor in his place. I'm not going to be the next notch he puts on his bed post."

"What?" Millie laughed good-heartedly.

"It's not funny," Olivia spat. "Men like that who two-time their women are a thing of my past—not my present and future."

"I see," Millie said. "You're still not over what your 'ex' did to you, are you?"

"Of course I am. I simply won't tolerate a man who claims to be making a relationship with me, while holding onto at least two other women at the same time. I'm so glad I hadn't fallen for him yet," Olivia answered, glancing back at the empty table Red had abandoned.

"Yes. So glad you hadn't fallen for him. Like you didn't do that at first glance," Millie prodded.

"What? I did not," she argued.

"Look, sweetie," Millie began, turning toward her. "Not much gets by me. You and Red have something special. Yes, it's early in this little union, but my bet is that the seed sown the moment you two met has grown into quite a healthy plant. One that promises to deliver a big harvest," she said. "You'll have to forgive my planting and harvest analogy. Red *is* a farmer, you know, or pretends to be. He won't make it much longer, though. That's the talk of the town," Millie added. "Not bad talk, mind you, but he's not cut out for it, and it's hard work trying to make a go of it under the circumstances."

"Yes, I know," Olivia answered quietly. "He's selling it this morning. At least he said so. Unless I can't believe *anything* he says," she added sadly.

Millie turned toward a new group of senior citizens coming through the door. A bus had pulled up and Olivia glanced out the window, still wishing Red had returned after he'd stormed out. Olivia knew she'd tried and convicted the man without even giving him a chance. But she guessed that was over anyway. She couldn't take any further risks if he had those tendencies. Tendencies she'd heard from his own brother, and seen with her own eyes—just as Jimmy had promised. Still, she couldn't help the hurt that pounded in her heart.

Why did she have to fall so quickly for this man, changing her life forever. Why did it have to be a man who wasn't satisfied with only one woman, she lamented. Even still, she knew these feelings continued to grow, and there didn't seem to be a thing she could do to stop them.

As Olivia drove home late that afternoon, she pulled into the tree-lined drive of her new home in the remote location. She still felt her decision to come here and settle down was a good one, even though it'd brought heartache right off. She also knew that working at Penny's, though so different from the career she'd had in Chicago, was ideal. It got her around honest, hard-working folks who made her feel special. Like Red Taylor, she thought sadly.

As she came inside, she wanted nothing more than to get a glass of iced tea and put her feet up. As she snuggled into the cushions that overlay the hand-carved furniture that reminded her of the essence of this community, she suddenly felt at ease. The hand-crafted furniture gave her contentment, and had the ability to make her troubles ease away. How this was possible, she didn't know. It must be the maker's personality that showed through and gave her a good feeling.

She wanted to meet this old farmer some day, the one who'd made such comforting, beautiful furniture, she decided. As she took in a deep breath and finally relaxed, she fell immediately to sleep in a long nap.

Chapter Ten

"So, is it a done deal? You sold the farm?" Jimmy demanded first thing upon Red entering the kitchen. His younger brother had avoided any contact with him the night before by being gone until late. Red realized there was no avoiding the firing squad he now faced.

"Yes, all the paperwork and legal work is behind me."

"So, you've sold everything that's been my whole life out from under me."

"Jimmy, you're being awfully hard on me. You don't want any part of the farm. You've got no emotional ties to it at all."

"Why do you say that?"

"From what you told me earlier. You don't want the farm, but you're resentful that I was given the funds to oversee everything."

"Yeah, what kind of deal was that? How'd you end up with the whole bundle and I get some lousy inheritance money Dad set aside, which doesn't equal half of squat. Now I figure you've lost it all and spent whatever was left to buy that furniture store so you can have everything you ever wanted."

"I don't have everything I ever wanted, Jimmy. You think I like living alone and working my fingers to the bone? And for what? You're not appreciative, and I can't even get the woman of my heart's desire to give me the time of day."

"You don't deserve her," Jimmy sniffed and plopped into the kitchen chair at this point.

Red considered him. "I don't deserve her? Why not? Is she too good for me? Or have you somehow decided I don't deserve a wife and family of my own since you don't like me anymore?"

"Oh, now you want to get married too? What else?"

Red exhaled. He wouldn't be drawn into this again.

"I'm getting my life in order, bro. By the way, one of my options was to keep the house, if I wanted. So, if you want, it's yours to keep."

"You mean yours, and I can be your boarder. Dad deeded the house and everything else to you. It's like I wasn't even a real son to him. I guess that figures. I was Momma's favorite and Dad had you. His big, strong, handsome son who was good at farming and building furniture and lifting heavy things—all in his image. So, why bother with a son who's little like me who likes to cook?"

"He was dying, Jimmy. You were so young. His mind wasn't right and he figured I'd do the right thing by you."

"Sure. Like keeping what he'd put aside for me. I'm through competing with you, Red. I've had it. If you'd just give me the cash, I'll get out of this town. I'm sick to death of everybody thinking I'm nothing but Red's brother."

"Now there's that thing again," Red huffed.

"Yeah, well, Penny's was my first real chance to show I could be somebody apart from you. I've proved myself, found what I really, really like. I want to be a cook and move up to some fancy restaurant someday. But you had to move in on that territory, too, didn't you? Well, ha, ha. I finally bested you on something," he finished.

Red shook his head and stared at the floor.

"Jimmy, I'm through arguing with you. I'll just leave these papers for you. It spells out everything."

Jimmy glanced down at the legal documents Red put on the kitchen table in front of him, then started to walk away.

"Oh, no you don't. You stay here and tell me what kind of bomb this is. Face me like an equal, Red. For once. Just once."

Red swiveled around.

"Fine, Jimmy. It says that the money Dad put aside for you will be forthcoming on your birthday this coming January. It also spells out the conditions of the money from the sale of the land and equipment of the farming business. For now, I've invested almost all of that in Dale's Big Furniture Showcase. When you reach thirty years old, I'll divert more, making up half the funds from the sale to you. I plan on making good money in this new investment, much more so than losing everything by me trying to make it in farming. I'm just no good at it, Jimmy, and I don't enjoy it. So, you'll receive half. Dad knew I'd take care of you, do you right. I think he knew how to make this thing work with the money tied up in the farm and all the equipment."

Jimmy looked up, stunned.

"What about the house?" he asked in a subdued tone completely out of character.

"Well, I managed to get Gus to agree to let us keep it. He'll work around the lands and has a way of dividing things so it will be profitable for him, without taking away the family legacy of this home."

"So, you didn't have to sell it. That money stays in the house. It's not divided half between us."

"There's no reason it ever has to be sold," Red stated.

Jimmy looked relieved, overly satisfied with the turn of events.

"So, in other words, I can still stay here 'till I get the money?"

"I see no reason why not. If you look on page two, you'll see I've deeded the other half of the house to you, Jimmy. You're a full brother, and when you sign on the dotted line in a meeting this afternoon at the bank, it'll be official."

Jimmy stared down at the paper. No further words came out. Red realized his brother would be late to work if he kept him in this conversation any longer. So in consideration of him, and the fact that Red also had lots to do to get things in order for the transfer of equipment and land, he needed to get going.

He opened the back door and let himself out, but not before noticing Jimmy glance up as he closed it behind him. His brother had tears in his eyes, something Red hadn't seen since his mother had died. Moments later, after he'd rounded the house and headed for the barn, he heard Jimmy's car start and watched it disappear down the drive.

* * *

Olivia raced around the Diner, handling the breakfast rush with ease. She felt better after a long night's rest, and a weight had somehow been lifted, though for the life of her she couldn't understand why. Everything remained the same—Red Taylor and the ache in her heart because of him being the number one problem.

When things died down and most of her customers finished and left, she eased over in Jimmy's direction. He seemed pretty down that morning for some reason, and she thought she'd try to cheer him up.

"You make a killer omelet, Jimmy. You've got some talent between that and the home-made lunch and dinner specials. You just can't find food this good even from the higher-priced places I was used to going to before moving here. And I know Millie is awfully glad you showed up when you did," she added.

Jimmy shrugged, continuing to focus on the grill which he began to clean after the last rush of food orders.

"Jimmy? Are you all right?"

"Yeah. And thanks. About the compliments, I mean. At least I do something right," he added.

"Don't be absurd," Olivia said, edging closer. "You do many things 'right.' Cooking is only one of them. I see how you brighten up the place being so friendly with the customers. You obviously care about other people."

"Oh?" Jimmy questioned, turning around to face her. "How do you figure that?"

Olivia hesitated, but only for a moment.

"I've seen you in action. You're nice to all the people who come in, and what about what you did for me? You let me in on your brother's activities with other women so I wouldn't get hurt. I think that deserves a medal, since it could have been a serious relationship on my part and if I'd gotten in any deeper, there would have been serious consequences—especially with my past, which you know nothing about. Still, to go against your own brother to let me know was admirable," she finished.

Jimmy frowned back at her.

"What's the matter with you? Does nothing I say help this bad mood of yours?"

"It's what you say that makes me so upset."

"Well, I'm terribly sorry. I didn't mean anything by it," she said, starting to turn away.

"No, wait," Jimmy began. "I might not be as admirable as you think. In fact, I've been a real jerk who hadn't really cared about anybody but myself. So much that I couldn't see what the real story was, and I made sure you didn't either," he answered.

"I don't understand," Olivia answered tentatively. Jimmy looked very upset and she wasn't sure she wanted to hear what he had to say.

"Yeah, that's right. A real jerk. Not my brother. Me," he said, jabbing his finger into his chest. "I'm the bad guy. Not Red. He never went out on you, whatever it is you two had going on. I just wanted to bust you up since I worked here, didn't want Red hanging around, and I didn't want him happy either. I blamed him for everything wrong in my life, and punished him with the one thing I thought I could. The place it would hurt the most. You," he finished.

"Jimmy, are you saying you lied about the other women?"

"Yeah."

"I'm sorry, but I don't buy it. I saw those two ladies. Red is obviously involved with them. You told me where to find them, and I caught him in the act."

Jimmy shook his head at the floor.

"I set that up pretty good, didn't I? Maybe I'll start using those smarts for something better than that. It was a really good trick."

Olivia could hardly believe her ears. She stared back at Jimmy not certain of the real truth.

"Trick? A good trick?," she echoed. "Playing with people's lives and emotions? Jimmy! Tell me you're making this up. I saw Red laughing and even hugging one of the women, the one at the furniture store—the married one you mentioned."

Jimmy ran a hand over his mouth, stifling a grin.

"You think this is funny?" she asked, knowing she should lower her voice but couldn't.

"Not really. That woman from the furniture store is like that. She'll hug anybody who comes through the door. She just flirts and hugs a lot of people. And the one at the bank is one of the top people there. She's not involved with him either. Just from business. He's just made some big deal with selling the farm and buying that furniture store. That's how I knew his routine that day. He was meeting with both of them and had filled me in on his plans."

"You mean he doesn't go to see them on a regular basis? Date them, or whatever you implied?"

"Nope. When would he have time to work the farm if he did? In fact, it's kept him so busy trying to make it make money and keep it in the family, that he hasn't had time for a woman. And I never lifted my finger to help him. So, I've been the jerk, not Red. So if you want to hate somebody, hate me. Red deserves better than that—from both of us," Jimmy finished.

Millie dashed past them, mentioning a group of customers looking like out-of-towners passing through were pulling up in the lot, and that they were in for another rush.

Jimmy and Olivia turned away, nothing else being said for the time. The things Jimmy had confessed to Olivia stayed on her mind the entire length of her shift as she wondered about her judgment. She'd given her "ex" the benefit of the doubt, while not giving Red a chance.

After considering it all day, Olivia decided to give herself a break. She'd been through a hard time and had overcompensated for the hurt she'd been dealt. But Red Taylor was not like that, and she would make sure she hung onto him. Now she wanted to gain *his* love and *his* trust, as he had so easily given her.

Before she left for the day, Olivia came back over to Jimmy. All day long the two of them had avoided any communication not totally directed to the Diner business. She felt she was finally able to say the words she knew she needed to for Jimmy's sake as well as her own. He looked both pleased and apprehensive when she approached him.

"Jimmy, about what you said about your brother, well, I just want you to know it's fine. I don't blame you. Not that it was right, what you did, but it's not all your fault."

"What do you mean? Of course it is," he argued. "I was a jerk."

"Yes, you were a jerk. You're probably saying terrible things to yourself about yourself, but stop it. If you apologize to your brother, then I'll forgive you, too," she said.

"Oh, man! Don't make me tell him. Why don't you get back with him and that'll be good enough. Okay? Then you don't even have to say what made you stop seeing him. I wouldn't have to say anything," he suggested hopefully.

Olivia gave him a sly smile. "Oh, no. That's not the way it works, Jimmy. You must confess to Red. He's the one you *really* hurt in desecrating his character . . ."

"Doing what?" Jimmy broke in.

Olivia put her hands on her hips, not going to be dissuaded by his tactics.

"Jimmy, it'll cause a rift between you if you don't, because you couldn't live easily with yourself. If that were the case, you'd have never told me. And don't think you're all to blame, like I said. I have to take responsibility for my part, too. I let you make me believe that because I was looking for it, being too sensitive to it in the first place. All I needed was something that felt like it, looked like it, and I was out the door. So, you'd better do it and do it quick, because I plan to see Red tonight if it's the last thing I do," she promised, as she reached for her purse and headed out the door.

CHAPTER ELEVEN

Late that afternoon Olivia felt drawn to visit the furniture showcase she'd loved going to since she'd arrived. If Jimmy were being straight with her now, which she believed he was, then Red had just bought the place.

As she drove into the spacious drive and parking lot, the store took on a new meaning. This was Red Taylor's new dream, the one he wanted to tell her about at the Diner that day. The news she would not let him get out. She had been so wrong, and had seen only that which she wanted to see.

Moving inside she glanced around, hoping Red was nearby. Instead she found the saleswoman she'd seen hugging Red that day—the one she'd gotten the wrong impression about. As Olivia looked on, her new insight about the woman Jimmy had supplied was now confirmed.

The attractive saleswoman was busy fussing over an elderly couple considering an oak kitchen table set. Within seconds, she'd bent over to hug the woman, then the man, all smiling and laughing as they moved toward the cash register with sales ticket in hand.

Olivia shook her head in amazement that she'd so easily believed and seen what was in her present mind-frame. She was so afraid Red would be like Harrison, that she'd been easily duped by Jimmy.

Since Red was clearly not there, she toured the showroom once more, ending up at the unusual hand-made furniture. This present grouping hadn't been there the last time she'd visited. Olivia marveled at the workmanship, and the vision this local furniture maker had that brought the raw wood product to a smooth finish with such graceful curves. It was clearly the same person who'd made the set she'd bought before, except these were different pieces. She decided she might have to get this as well, but only after she'd settled in completely.

The flirty saleswoman moved over in her direction.

"Hi, welcome to Dale's. I see you're admiring our most valued local's work," she began.

"Yes, I already bought one set for my den."

"Oh, you're the customer who snapped up the last one. Well, I guess you'd be drawn to this as well. His bedroom pieces are rare. In fact, I think this is the first time he's ventured into this area," she explained.

"The bedroom," Olivia echoed. "Yes, I might be ready for a new set in there. I'd have to move a few things around before I buy something else, though," she said, considering how beautiful the furniture would look in the most private place in her home.

"I don't blame you for wanting more. His is the best of the best," she added.

Olivia bent to trail her hand down the smooth finish of the chest of drawers. Rising up, she turned to the saleswoman again.

"I simply must meet this farmer who does such beautiful work," Olivia breathed out. "It'd be so much fun to put a face with the expert handiwork."

"That'll be easy," she replied. "He just bought the place, and after next week, he'll be a permanent fixture around here."

"Wait a minute. Who makes this furniture?" Olivia asked, thinking there *must* be some mistake.

"Red Taylor. After the paperwork goes through, he'll be the new owner. Guess he can keep an eye out for what he needs when his own brand sells out," she laughed.

Olivia stood speechless for a moment, stunned that she hadn't made the connection before. The day just continued to be filled with surprises, but it also explained why she'd been so drawn to the furniture—she was drawn to the man behind it. Like a magnet that held her tightly to him.

She then glanced back at the furniture before her.

"I've changed my mind. I don't need time to think about it. I'd like to buy all of this right now, and I want a king-sized mattress set to go along with it," she said. "Oh, and I want it delivered today. Is that possible?"

The saleswoman broke out in unrestrained laughter.

"Oh, yes, indeed it is. The truck and delivery people just got back. It can be yours today," she said. She then rushed forward, grabbed Olivia, and gave her a big hug.

Olivia just shook her head in understanding as the woman prolonged the hug. She then released her and Olivia followed the woman over to the cash register. Red was in for a big surprise.

* * *

"And that's the whole sordid story," Jimmy finished, raising his eyes to meet Red's glare.

"And Olivia knows the truth now? It wasn't something I said or did that made her drop me?"

"Nope. It was me. But she said she was going to call. I think she's fallen pretty hard for you. She said she forgives me. Made sure I told you about it, too."

Red smiled.

"Would you have told me anyway?" he asked.

"Yeah, I guess. Maybe not today, though. Not after you did what you did for me with that 'will' business. Giving me half the house and everything. I've been such a jerk. I'm really sorry, Red. I blamed you for a lot of things not your fault, but you really came through for me even though I was a jerk."

Red shook his head in agreement.

"You were just a kid when your world fell apart. You did the best you could. I think Dad put me in charge because I was older and able to handle it, and he knew I'd do right by you. He never meant to imply you were less of a child of his. He loved you every bit as much as Mom did. And as for people comparing you to me, just thinking you were nothing but my younger brother, that's nonsense. That's the way people do, but then after you're grown, you prove yourself. And you have. Especially today," Red finished.

Jimmy hung his head. After an awkward silence, he looked up again.

"So, you're not sore at me for what I did to you and Olivia?"

Red understood his brother and couldn't stay mad at him for long. He hesitated, trying not to let the smile that tugged at the corners of his mouth show. He let Jimmy twist in the wind for a minute more, then spoke up.

"Well, you really pulled quite a fast one on me this time, didn't you, waif."

"Oh, again with the name."

"You deserve it. It fits," he teased.

"Yeah, well I just wish you hadn't read that stupid story in high school that gave you that stupid name. Am I gonna be stuck with that for life?"

"Afraid so. Just like you're gonna be stuck with me. And if we're both really lucky, we'll be stuck with Olivia too. That is if that phone would ever ring and her be on the other end," Red put in.

As if on cue, the telephone burst into a series of rings. Both brothers gave each other a knowing smile.

Chapter Twelve

"Now this is what I call the 'royal treatment,' Red bragged as Olivia picked him up in her Mercedes and whisked him off.

"It's time I shared my life with you. What I'm about, where I live. You tried to do that with me, but I pushed you away at the most disastrous moment."

"Well, I'm glad we've straightened all that out," Red answered. "So, we've both already eaten diner, where is it you plan to take me on this excursion?"

"My home. My new home. I'm here permanently, Red. I've decided. In fact, I even made a clean slate of it and called my Mom and Dad after I talked to you. I gave them my phone number and new address in person—not in a note like I told them I would. I even explained why I was doing what I was doing, moving away like I did. Remarkably, it was a very nice chat, that is until Mother had to rush off to finish getting ready for a dinner party they'd been invited to by some of the top clients of the firm."

"Sounds like quite a change from what you'll get around here," Red put in.

"Their life is exciting and rush-rush, and oh, so appealing. But not to me. I'm ready for a quieter life-style. I just thought you'd like to see where I live and the furnishings I chose for inside the house. I think you'll be surprised," she added.

"Oh, I think I know. You look like a woman who surrounds herself with things she likes, things of beauty and unusual decorations that reflect her personality. So, no. I won't be surprised," he answered. "But I *am* curious. Especially since you let me show you all around my house and even the barn before letting on where you live."

She turned into her driveway and Red let out a low whistle.

"Whoa, I take that back. I *am* surprised. This is some set-up."

"It's home," Olivia answered, as she drove down the long, tree-lined path that lead to her spacious house.

Red chuckled to himself.

"What's funny?"

"Oh, I was just wondering what you must have been thinking when I showed off my family home to you. With my simple tastes, it must have really been a stark difference," he explained.

"Oh, I wouldn't say that," she answered. Red couldn't help but notice a small smile that had formed and tenaciously held on.

Parking in the garage, she let him in the side way through the utility room and into the kitchen. Red whistled again, marveling at the large area with all the modern conveniences that made his own kitchen pale in comparison.

"Good grief. Jimmy would have a fit in here cooking on all this fancy stuff. See? I told you our tastes would clash. The modern things in here I'm just not used to," he added. "But it's beautiful, don't get me wrong. I could get used to this in a heartbeat."

"Red? I'll be right back, okay?" Olivia said, disappearing down a hallway to the back. Red made his own tour in her absence, one room leading into another. When he made it to the den, his eyes widened. Olivia then joined him, wrapping her arms around him from behind.

"Where did you get this furniture?" Red asked in surprise.

"Where do you think? Dale's. Or will you call it Red's now?" she added, sliding around in front of him.

"Did you know I made this?" he asked, still confused, but delighted that a woman like Olivia would want his furniture in a house like this. No, that Olivia wanted *his* furniture. Appreciated it—and him. His work was a part of himself of which he was proud.

As she snuggled closer, he wrapped his arms around her, and he bent to kiss the lips he'd missed so much since they'd broken up. The good news was that Olivia seemed to be totally his, and had somehow gotten over the barriers of her past. She then pulled away, ever so slightly and her awesome green eyes, deep with emotion searched his face.

"You never answered my question," he whispered.

"What question?" she asked.

"About the furniture. Did you know I made this before you bought it?"

"No," she breathed. "Not *this* set."

She then tugged at his hand, leading him into a different area of the house until they were around the corner from what he believed was her bedroom.

"I've got something to show you," she promised.

When Red edged inside, he understood. He felt his jaw drop as he glanced around at the full set of bedroom furniture that he had just now gotten over to the furniture showcase to sell.

"When did you . . . ? How?" Red struggled, looking at how beautiful his hard work looked in this room. He marveled at the finished display with the antique lavender and beige bed coverings, matching pillow shams, the lavender throw across the rocker he'd built, the antique perfume bottle collection set up over the lace coverlet on the dressing table, and other feminine articles interspersed in the room.

His handiwork was perfectly complimented with that which was Olivia's personality, blended together, and highlighted by numerous lit candles shimmering around the room.

"I bought this set after I knew the identity of the talented artisan."

Red laughed. "Is that what I am?"

"Yes, it is. I would have been drawn to it even if I hadn't know you'd made it. But then again, I think that's why I was drawn to it in the first place. It's such an expression of you, Red. And I find it only fitting that you help me try it out," Olivia coached.

"Oh, wait a minute, now. You've still got to get your head together about some things. I'm not chancing losing you again," he said.

Olivia tugged him downward, as they both sank into the soft covers of the down comforter. Red eased up beside her, propped up on one elbow, brushing back her lovely auburn hair.

"Perhaps we *should* take it slow, Red. But one thing I know. I'm finally ready to get involved with a man like you. Harrison did me a favor. He showed me what the other side of mankind is like, and you represent the good side. I'll take you any day. Or night," she added, pulling him back into an embrace.

Red held the beautiful woman of his dreams in his arms, the woman he intended to make his own forever. No matter how long it took. For he knew in that instant—this woman would one day be his bride. He would make sure of that.

* * *

"Now what's everybody so chipper about this morning?" Millie asked in amazement. "First Jimmy's whistling up a storm, now you come skating around like you're on cloud nine. I mean, it's a fun place to work, but you and Jimmy are acting crazy."

Jimmy caught the comment as he whizzed by.

"Yeah, well it's a good idea to be nice to your future in-laws," Jimmy answered, sending Olivia a broad smile.

"What? You and Red?" Millie asked in surprise. "You've only been dating six months, and you do a pretty good job of keeping that a secret. I haven't seen him hanging around here lately."

"Oh, he's pretty busy at Taylor's Furniture Showcase," Olivia explained. "Besides, we see lots of each other at night," she answered smiling.

"Yup, I knew you two were in trouble the moment you laid eyes on each other, now you're up and getting married?" Millie asked.

"That's right," Jimmy breezed by again. "And it's all because of me," he said.

Millie swiveled around, watching Jimmy rush around, and Olivia began to hum.

"You two are something else. Well, congratulations and best wishes and I'm so happy for you," Millie said, then glanced at Jimmy. "But what's this nonsense about Jimmy taking credit for you two love birds. Any truth to that?" she asked.

"Well," Olivia began as Jimmy stood nearby, "I think you can give all the credit to a 'brother's love'," she answered. Jimmy turned a shade of red and looked sheepishly toward the floor then back up at Olivia. She smiled lovingly at him, then punched him lightly on the arm.

"Get back to work, waif," she whispered to him.

"The name again," Jimmy stated and shook his head. A broad smile widened across his face from the endearing name they shared since the turn of events that had changed all their lives. Olivia returned the smile, then all three of them quickly dispersed, getting back to work as an onslaught of tour bus customers piled in the door.

THE END

2948-BURG

Returning For Love

by Penny Burgess

2948-BURG

Chapter One

Robert O'Grady slipped around the back of the counter, taking over as the second shift manager and relieving Millie Holmes. A man in his late sixties, Robert always looked forward to coming to work at Penny's Diner, having discovered retirement was simply not for him.

He particularly took interest in the people who came in to have a bite to eat or just drop by to socialize. It kept a widower of his years in the thick of things and around people.

The afternoon grew more interesting as he glanced over the light 3 o'clock crowd. New faces always caught his attention, and this one especially so.

He studied the unfamiliar woman alone at the two-top table and stopped Millie before she headed out the door and called it a day.

"Say, Millie, ever seen that little lady before? The one in the back looking teary-eyed and upset?"

"You mean the one ripping the paper napkin into tiny pieces? She's never come in here, but I know who she is. She's Mrs. Hannibal's spinster sister who's come to town to help her with her recovery. You know, from heart surgery?"

"How do you know all of that? Including her marital status?" Robert asked in surprise.

"What do you do all day long, Robert? Keep your ears stuffed with cotton? A new person shows up in town and people talk. Story is, her sister married the man she always loved, and she never got over it. Moved away and didn't speak to the couple for years. She now lives in Arkansas, if I understand correctly," Millie explained.

"Well, I'm not privy to past history kind of things."

"That's because you're not from around here originally. Mrs. Hannibal's sister, Dora Thresher, made up with her later on. Now she's got to live with her to nurse her through this operation."

"Hmmm. Doesn't seem like a very happy lady," Robert said.

"Give her a break, Robert O'Grady. She's having to live in the very house where her true love lived with her own sister as husband and wife, and she has to be reminded of it at every turn. It must be really rough," Millie finished.

"I'll betcha you're way off base. From her tender years of sixty or so, the woman is long over such a thing. Especially since Mrs. Hannibal's husband died over five years ago," Robert declared.

"She might be over the man, but the hurt's still there. Count on it. Anyway, I gotta go. Make sure her coffee is freshened up in a minute. She just lets it sit there, getting cold, staring out the window, wallowing in her sorrows," Millie said.

"I can think of a mite more appropriate drink to drown her sorrows," Robert commented.

"We don't serve alcohol here, Robert. Now, don't you go over there and say anything unkind after I'm not here to supervise you," she warned him.

"Hey, you don't supervise me! I'm the second-shift manager, Miss Know-It-All. Besides, do I ever upset the customers?" he teased.

"I'm not even going to answer that. See you tomorrow," Millie promised as she whisked out the front door.

Robert removed any remaining dishes on the countertop and wiped it down, checked all the details surrounding the shift change, then poured out a fresh cup of coffee and headed in the direction of Dora Thresher. He cleared his throat then approached the table slowly.

"Good afternoon," Robert beckoned.

Dora Thresher looked up in surprise.

"Thought I'd bring you a fresh cup," he explained, removing the old one and putting the piping hot liquid in front of Dora.

"Thank you so much," she said, wiping the torn napkin into a pile and pushing it aside.

"See you've made short work of that," he said, smiling down at her.

Robert didn't know what had gotten into him. He never stood idly by the customers hoping for an invitation to join them, yet here he was like an awkward teenager trying to make a date or something.

Never one to be tongue-tied, Robert decided on a different approach, because clearly, an invitation to sit down would not be forthcoming.

"I'm Robert O'Grady. The second shift manager. Mind if I join you?" he said.

"That would be fine. Guess the Diner isn't busy this time of day," she answered.

"About the only time it's not. Normally, I've got my hands full. Too much so to sit and chat, but seeing that you're the only customer in the place right now . . ." Robert trailed off, noting the woman had gone back to staring into her coffee cup.

"So, what brings you to town?" be began again, hoping to ease her out of the clearly upset state. "I take it you're not from around here?"

"I suspect you already know that," she answered. "I might be getting on in years, but I still don't need a pair of glasses to see what's what. Like the fact that you were discussing me with that Millie person before she left for the day. She probably told you who I am and what I'm doing here," she said.

Robert chuckled, running his hand over his mouth to keep from laughing outright. He liked this spunky woman already. "Guess I'm caught," he said. "Can't fool a woman who knows 'what's what,'" he added in a teasing tone.

Dora's eyes flashed up at him, a small smile twinkled there, giving Robert a little more encouragement.

"All right. I'm Dora Thresher," she said, extending her hand over the table top.

"Yes, ma'am. And I'm Robert O'Grady," he added, squeezing the soft, petite hand in his. He liked the feel of her skin, wished he could prolong the contact, but knew better. Especially with a woman who showed this kind of spunk from the get-go.

"So, you're here in town nursing your sister back to health?" he continued, releasing her hand and shifting in his seat.

"Betty. That's right," she said, sniffing.

"Pretty upset about her heart condition, huh?"

"Betty will be just fine. She always has been, always will be," she snipped. "Operation was a success."

"That's good to hear," he said. "Nice of you to come all the way over from Arkansas," he added. "To care for her, that is."

"She's got no one else. Now that Laird's gone."

"That would be her husband," Robert supplied.

"Her husband." Dora raised the coffee cup to her lips and sipped. Her eyes darted away, as her whole demeanor changed. The woman before him became suddenly reclusive and unresponsive again.

Robert then glanced outside at the parking lot as two cars pulled up and several teenagers began unloading and heading inside.

"High school musta just let out," Robert explained. "They'll be wanting our sundaes and malts and such. It was right nice to meet you, Dora. I'd sure like it if you came around again about this time of day for a cup of coffee and a quick snatch of friendly conversation. Taking care of a recuperating sick person, you must need a break from time to time. I'll be here from 3 o'clock on, if you need me," he added as he raised up and waved a friendly hello to the incoming crowd of regulars.

*　*　*

Dora Thresher placed a dollar bill on the table. She was in no mood to be around loud teenagers with all their laughing and cutting up, and she'd stayed gone from Betty far too long. The "cheerful" man who'd come around the table was nice enough company, though, she decided.

It had lifted her spirits, talking to Robert O'Grady. It wasn't every day a man paid such attention to a woman her age, not that early sixties was "old" by any stretch of the imagination, she thought as she pulled herself to her full 5'2" height and breezed through the restaurant. On the contrary, she still turned heads. Wasted, she thought.

As the bitter thoughts returned to harden her heart again, she totally ignored Robert's upraised hand she noticed from the corner of her eye as she made her way out of the "too lively" diner.

Those people in there could just be happy, she thought. They didn't have to walk back into that house—the one where her sister spent her entire married years with Laird, the man who was supposed to be hers. Dora's one true love.

She'd made up with her sister for taking him away. She could hardly be to blame. Betty never really knew what had passed between them, nor the love Dora had harbored all these years. Dora had just up and moved off, explaining she didn't have time to visit at Christmas and such. Now Dora had to face the truth and nurse her only sister back to health—when at one point and time in Dora's life, she had wished her sister had never been born.

2948-BURG

Chapter Two

"Hey, Mr. O'Grady, what's gotten into you today?" Wes Stanford pressed.

"What do you mean, son?" Robert asked the teenage boy who seemed like one of his own. They all did to Robert. All the kids who piled in here. But especially Jim.

"You know, Jim," Robert began. "No two days are alike. You think it'll be business as usual, then something happens to change your whole life around, you know what I mean?"

"Not really. What happened to you today?"

Robert contemplated the woman who'd just sailed out of Penny's smooth as silk, but understood that troubled waters rumbled underneath her carefully constructed exterior.

"Soon as you think you have life figured out, somebody comes along to turn it upside down," he answered.

Jim grinned, pulling his straw up and down in his chocolate malt.

"I get it. That woman who was in here. Nice looking lady, Mr. O'Grady. Are you gonna make a move on her?" Jim inquired with a smile.

"Watch your mouth, son," he answered, returning the smile.

"So, are you?" he urged.

Robert chuckled. "To tell you the truth, I'd like to. Haven't thought about dating again until she showed up. But I'm afraid if I did the least little thing to imply a romantic interest, that woman would . . ." Robert stopped, shaking his head, leaning against the counter and laughing at the mere possibility of her reaction.

"What? Whack you over the head?" Jim suggested, laughing too and joining in with the older man's humor.

"More like punch me in the stomach. That one's a fireball, son. A real fireball. And the very kind that can light a fire in a man after he'd thought the pilot light was long extinguished," he answered, walking away to clear away a few glasses and dishes left on the counter.

* * *

Dora glanced through the etched glass that made up the middle of the front door. Finding no movement within, she unlocked the door and walked back inside the Victorian house that had been one of the finest of its kind in all of the town. Should've been *my* house, Dora thought for the millionth time, making herself miserable once again.

"Dora? Is that you?" her older sister called out from the back bedroom area.

"Yes, Betty," she answered, grimacing. "It's me."

"Where've you been? I needed to get to the bathroom and I had such a time of it," she explained, still speaking just loudly enough to be heard in the front living room area.

"Had some errands to run," Dora explained, hoping her sister's recuperation would proceed at a faster pace than it had so far. Dora secretly thought Betty was prolonging the time she needed help, making her stay longer, getting extra attention. She knew her sister had been lonely since Laird died, and missed him terribly, but so what, she thought. Dora'd had to do without the man her entire life. Betty would have to adjust, she told herself, marching back into the woman's bedroom where she sat laid up with extra pillows stuffed behind her.

"So, where'd you go?" Betty persisted.

"Had a few things to pick up at the store," Dora said, wishing she hadn't just told the lie.

"I thought you went there this morning," Betty answered. "Fluff these pillows, will you, please? It's still hard for me to reach over with this tightness in these muscles across my chest," she said in a pitiful voice.

Dora reached over, shifting a pillow, wondering how much difference it could actually make to her sister's comfort level.

"Oh, my! That's much better."

Dora took a seat next to her sister's bedside. She wondered about the large, comfortable rocker placed in this corner. Had Laird made the indentations in the worn cushion where Dora now positioned herself? she asked herself.

Taking to the rocking motion the chair provided, she closed her eyes and thought of the man whom she'd loved all of her adult life without letting up. It hadn't seemed to matter to her emotions that the man chose her sister instead. It didn't matter that other suitors came and went. Yet none could fill the empty space that man had left when he abruptly dropped his relationship with her. The next thing Dora knew, her older sister, the one the family sent to college, came home and boasted of the new beau—her Laird. Then, suddenly, they were married. And that was that.

"Dora, it's so kind of you to come here," Betty supplied, interrupting her thoughts. "I guess it took a life-threatening illness to bring us back, face-to-face, after all this time," she said.

"Yes, Betty, I guess it did."

"I suspect if Laird was still alive, you wouldn't be here now. You'd figure he could take care of me."

"He would have. He always took care of you," Dora answered sharply.

An awkward silence hung in the air for a moment. Betty played with her hands. Dora glanced over at her sister's once model-like quality in her hands with her long fingers and perfectly proportioned nails. The porcelain-like skin was now marred with age spots and large veins interrupted the smooth skin. Her sister, almost six years older had begun to show her age with more than just this heart condition. It softened Dora's hostility towards her, but not much.

"Well," Betty began again. "I'm so sorry you had to come out here like this. I don't want to be a bother. I could have someone come in soon. You won't have to stay. I know it must not be easy to give up your own life to wait on me hand and foot. If you find you need to get out and take a break sometimes, just get out of this house and the four walls that must be suffocating for someone like you, used to being out and about, I surely will understand."

Dora let out a pent-up breath. Maybe Betty understood more than she expressed, she thought.

"I went to Penny's Diner this afternoon. Not to the store. I had to have a moment to myself, Betty. And a cup of coffee that I didn't have to make. Have someone wait on me for a short time."

Betty smiled. "Good for you. Why don't you make a habit of it. I think you need to let off the steam that must build in taking on such a thing as looking after me. Take a break every afternoon. I normally have a nap that time of day anyway, and I can get along just fine. How about it?"

"Yes," Dora answered, stilling the rocker. "That might be a good idea at that."

* * *

"Your lady is back," Millie informed Robert when he eased into the front door at Penny's. His head swiveled around, spotting Dora at the same back corner table, sipping on a cup of coffee.

"So she is," he answered.

"That's it? So she is? You don't fool me, Robert O'Grady," Millie began. "You've got eyes for our little out-of-town visitor."

"And what's that to you? Don't you have a life to go to?" Robert asked with a grin.

"So I'm right! You *are* interested in her. Can't say I blame you. She's very attractive, and it's about time you found someone after all this time of being alone."

"Well, it doesn't harm a man to look," he answered. "But she is from out of town, and I don't think she has any plans of putting down roots again here. Left a long time ago, didn't she?"

"Oh, yes. But if you want to know any more about this Dora Thresher, you can find out yourself. As you so adequately put it, I do have a life outside of here, and my shift was up five minutes ago," Millie said. "So, good luck," she added. Millie winked at Robert then headed out the front door.

"Yeah, I'm gonna need it," Robert mumbled to himself as he went about rinsing some dishes and loading them into the industrial dishwasher. He took a few more minutes before picking up the coffee pot and heading over to Dora. He didn't want to seem too eager, he decided as he took in a deep breath, pushing out his chest and walking over to her table.

"Can I freshen that up for you?"

"Just a half a cup more," she answered. "I can't be too jittery taking care of my sister."

"How is Betty?" Robert asked, hovering over her.

"Betty is getting along."

"That's good," he said, hesitating then moving slightly away from the table.

"Wait, Robert? It is Robert, right?" she asked, glancing at his name tag that told his name and his manager position at the Diner.

"It is, indeed," he answered, edging closer.

"Well, since I'm the only customer in the Diner right now, how about joining me for a few," she suggested.

"Yes, ma'am, I'd like that," Robert answered as he eased into the chair opposite her. A renewed excitement washed over him as he did so.

"So, you came back for an afternoon break, huh?"

"Yes. It's a good idea. Penny's is bright and cheery. Besides that, the coffee's good," she said.

"You ought to taste some of the food sometime. Let me bring you a malt or something."

"Oh, no. I mustn't. I have to watch my girlish figure," she explained grinning down at her coffee cup.

"You sound like my wife, now," Robert said, chuckling.

Dora's head snapped back up.

"Oh? I didn't realize you were married. You're one of those who doesn't wear a ring," she said flatly.

"No, ma'am. I'm not married now, exactly."

"What's that mean?" Dora demanded.

"Well, I guess I often speak of Margaret as though she were still alive. Seems that way for me at times, but when I pass through that door at home, it's clear no one is there waiting."

"You're a widower, then," Dora commented, backing down. "So, how long has it been since you lost your wife?" Dora asked more quietly.

"Five years. I'm pretty much used to the fact, but it's still painful when I allow my mind to dwell on Margaret."

"I understand. Sometimes one never gets over one you loved and lost," Dora commented.

"True. But life goes on. I'd retired by then, but I figured I didn't need to be sitting around the house after all that had happened. Besides, I've got lots left to give, and when they built this diner last year, I signed right up. Working here at Penny's has made all the difference," he explained.

Dora just nodded in response. The conversation died down a bit. Robert realized he always had something to say to the customers passing in and out of Penny's, but found he was out of practice when it came to being with a woman—especially one he wished he could get to know better.

"So, you were brought up around here, I understand."

"Yes. That's right. Millie tell you that too?"

"That's about all Millie knows, if that concerns you. She's not one to gossip," he explained.

"No, I suppose that's common knowledge anyhow. A stranger returning to town."

"Bet you've got a few old friendships you've renewed since being back," he suggested.

"No. Nothing I've decided to pursue as yet."

"I see," Robert answered, not really understanding at all.

"Except my for my sister, I've not been in touch with anyone," she continued as a her lips formed a thin stern line. "I just packed up my suitcase and left."

Robert didn't know how to respond to this. The woman was filled with a past that was clearly not all smooth sailing. He turned a moment and checked the Diner, making sure no one had come in and the other employees weren't in need of his assistance. Confident all was taken care of for the moment, he swiveled back around to converse with Dora.

"So, your sister is getting along fairly well. Think you'll be staying around much longer after she's up and around and back in good health?"

"Not if I can help it," she stated flatly, giving no further explanation.

Robert cleared his throat, giving this thing one more try. "I guess caring for an invalid isn't an easy thing," he suggested.

"Betty's no invalid. She's had heart surgery. She'll be back to her old self soon," she snipped.

"Hmmm. I sense a little tension between the sisters," Robert added.

"Sisters are like that, aren't they?" she asked.

"Not always. I know many who are like best friends, others that don't speak at all," he answered.

Dora laughed derisively. "Well, Betty and I will never be best friends, but at least we speak now. That wasn't the case for many years. Been rather awkward in the years in-between, and now I'm here in town, living in her house, being in the same town I grew up in, and having to deal with all that again."

"Something tore you apart way back when, did it?"

Dora's eyes shifted from her coffee cup and riveted to Robert's face. "You're pretty blunt, aren't you, Robert O'Grady?"

"That's what people say. I get right to the heart of a matter, I guess."

"Even things that aren't any of your business?"

"That seems to be my specialty," Robert answered with a laugh. "I don't mean to tread where I'm not wanted, though," he added. "I guess that question really isn't any of my never-mind, unless you want to talk about it."

"I don't," she snapped. "But to answer your previous question, as soon as Betty is able to get along on her own, it's back to Arkansas for me. Hard as I'm trying, I can't seem to make the ghosts go away," she added. "By the way, you've got some new customers," she said, pointing to the usual car full of teenagers crowding into the parking lot.

"That I do. Didn't mean to offend," Robert added as he eased up and walked away. As he waved to his younger friends coming in the door, Robert turned to his business duties, shaking his head at this last encounter. Dora Thresher was a woman with a lot of pain, and he didn't see that she was making any progress dealing with it. He decided that meant any romance with this woman was certainly a lost cause.

* * *

Dora lingered in the Diner just short of a quarter hour longer. She watched Robert in action as he interacted with the teenagers. They seemed to be inspired by the older man, laughing and cutting up, then mingling among themselves.

Robert busied himself with making one ice cream treat after another, wiping down the counters, checking and making fresh coffee, and other duties behind the counter she couldn't see. What she could see was that she had been just rude enough to Robert to alienate herself from the man. He didn't even attempt to offer her more coffee. Though it wasn't warranted within the small time period she remained, she'd hoped she hadn't scared him away completely. But she had. She could feel it. It was always the same, she realized. She knew when a man was trying to get close to her, and Dora pushed them away every time. Residuals from a long-lost love yanked her back into a bitterness that hardened her, allowing no man to enter.

Dora walked out into the parking lot. Robert was totally engaged in a conversation with a young man at the counter when she left, preventing any further communication with her. Dora's sense of disappointment overwhelmed her as she got into the car and drove away. She didn't know whether it was because she was heading back to her sister's house, a constant reminder of her pain, or that she felt she'd pushed away a man trying to be her friend—or maybe more and she'd sabotaged it once again.

Perhaps it was time to move past this thing. Way past time, she decided. As she started the car, Dora realized she would now make the first move toward recovery, toward healing for herself. And as she drove out of the parking lot in the opposite direction from her sister's home, Dora knew she was about to take that step right now.

Chapter Three

Twenty-five years hadn't changed the outside exterior to the home that stood before her. Only a crumbling of the driveway and the overgrowth of trees that hadn't even been there the last time she'd laid eyes on the place made the appearance any different.

Dora pulled up to the curb and cut the motor. She clutched the steering wheel as though holding on for dear life. During the three weeks she'd been in town, she hadn't been able to force herself down this street. But now, here she was.

Just then a tall, thin older man with a white shirt and tan pants made his way out onto the porch. He ran a hand through whatever was left of his white hair and leaned over, trying to get a glimpse of who was inside the car parked in front of his house. Dora recognized him immediately. It was Laird's cousin, Charles.

As he swung back around, digging his hands deep in his pockets, he began to whistle. Dora could hear him even with the windows rolled up. The song from a different era lilted through the air.

Dora knew in that moment she was caught, for Charles had remembered her song—that song. There was nothing left to do but get out of the car now. Face what she'd avoided most all of her life.

Dora heard her own footsteps clipping up the stone walkway up to the expansive front porch where Charles now edged gently back and forth on the porch swing. She moved up the stairs and stood before him, ramrod straight and poised with confidence.

"You haven't changed a bit," Charles said easily.

"Nor have you," Dora answered.

"That's not true and you know it. I've lost half my hair and the rest of it has turned white. Prematurely, I might add."

"Age is kind to men, Charles. Most of them. They grow more handsome. Women become frumpy—unless they work very hard," she said.

"Well, now. I suppose that means you've been quite a hard worker bee for the last forty years of your life. Since I last got a glimpse of that pretty little thing that scooted out of here without so much as a word of explanation."

Dora considered the gray painted wooden slats on the porch floor. He wasn't going to make this easy, she decided.

"Come on, now, Dora. You've come the distance, why don't you take a seat beside me here. Let's talk. That is why you've shown up at the front of the house, isn't it?"

Dora edged over, taking a seat. The swing jostled in trying to balance another person. Then they began a smooth, swaying back and forth motion that put her at ease.

"I've been in town for three weeks."

"I know it," he told her.

"You didn't try to come by or anything," she ventured.

"Your call to make."

"It's been hard enough."

"Yep, I imagine so. You ready to talk about it?"

"No. Yes. I don't know, Charles. I've never been able to put the past behind me. But I suspect you realize that. I've been perfectly aware that you've kept up with me."

"Sarah was concerned when you left. I married her. You *did* know that," he stated.

"Of course. How is Sarah? Is she here?"

"Nope. Runs an antique store over in Cloverdale. She likes the past. Turns a pretty good profit at it, too," he added.

"That's nice."

"Look, Dora, if you've come here looking for answers, I've got a few, but I'm not sure you're gonna like it."

"Then keep it to yourself," Dora said, coming to her feet.

Charles chuckled. "You really haven't changed, have you? Never wanted to know the truth if it hurt your ears. That's one of the problems that happened between you and Laird, you know."

"Now you're going to blame me for your cousin walking out on me and picking up with my sister? Was it for spite?"

"That wasn't it, Dora."

"I think it was," she pressed.

"Tit for tat, huh?"

"Yes, in a manner of speaking. Laird made me mad and you and I were attracted to each other, then he found us out and took out Betty. His cousin, my sister. What better thing to do to show me how much I'd hurt him. But to marry her?"

Dora picked up a quick pace back and forth across the porch. She felt her anger rising as if the forty-year-old incident was fresh news. Charles shook his head and rose to his feet as well, placing his hands behind his back.

"Whenever you're ready to hear the truth, Dora. Just whenever you're ready," he said, making a path toward the front door. "It's too hot out here to rehash old news that didn't have the facts right then either."

"Fine, Charles. You see it your way, I'll see it mine," she said. "I don't know why I even came by here today. I should have known it was a waste of time."

Charles paused as he held the doorknob, glancing back at her.

"Why did you come back? To this house, I mean? To see me? To argue about what a rotten scoundrel Laird was to you? Or was there something more?"

"Like what?" Dora said, stepping quickly down the front stairs. "To hear some convoluted truth you think I should hear?"

"Would that not put things to rest for you, Dora? Or do you want to cling onto your bitterness and resentment all your life?" Charles asked.

Without waiting for a response, Charles made his way inside the house and closed the door behind him. Dora wanted to pick up a large rock from a row that lined the bushes next to the walk and toss it at the wooden barrier Charles had just passed through.

The decorative granite called to her as she remembered as a young woman of twenty years old, she'd actually done that very thing to the house in front of her. But that time, she'd hit her target. Funny, she thought, the door didn't seem to have the chink she'd wanted to put there then either.

* * *

"Dora? Is that you?" Betty called out when Dora came through the front door.

"Yes, Betty," she answered impatiently. "Who else would come in with a key?"

"Well, I was just wondering," Betty said.

Dora still fumed from her outrageous interchange with Charles. She didn't know what had gotten into her thinking he could fill in the blanks and make her feel better about this thing. No one could, she decided as she flung her keys onto the coffee table.

To Dora's surprise, Betty shuffled down the hallway in her direction.

"Betty? Have you lost your mind? Aren't you suppose to stay in bed? And look at you. You said just two days ago you could hardly make it to the bathroom on your own."

Dora watched as Betty clutched pieces of furniture as she went along, desperate to make it without anyone's help.

"I've decided I must begin to stand on my own two feet," she chirped. "This recuperation period must be so maddening for you, the least I can do is try to help," she said, collapsing in the nearest chair at the end of her walk.

"Oh, Betty. You're not going to do either of us any good trying to do too much too soon," she said.

"The doctor says I need to get around as soon as I can. I haven't been trying very hard, I must admit. I have ulterior motives, you know."

"How's that?" Dora asked, easing into a nearby wing-back chair.

"Surely you're aware, Dora. You're the 'smart' one in the family," she added. "You don't miss a trick."

"Well, I've missed this one."

"Land's sakes, Dora. Don't you realize how much I want you to stay? I figured if I took longer to get better, why, then you'd be kind of used to being around here. Maybe starting to like it. This was your hometown once. Where you grew up. I want you to be close to me," she added with a smile belying the physical pain from the exertion Dora knew Betty must have felt.

Dora leaned up in the chair, making sure her sister heard and understood her every word.

"Betty, I will never make this town my home. It has too many ghosts and unpleasant memories. There is nothing here to hold me. Now, I'm sorry, but that's the way it is."

Betty let out a little whimper and Dora cringed inwardly. Not only did Dora have the reputation of the "smart" one in the family, she also realized she'd also just lived up to the other name. The "blunt" one in the family.

"I understand," Betty allowed as her eyes swept across the room. "There's nothing much here to hold me either now that Laird has passed. I had just hoped we could rebuild what was left of our sister friendship before he came between us."

The words were out in the open now. But it hadn't been the "smart" one who had spoken the words of wisdom, but Dora's sister. Up until that point, Dora had no idea Betty had even the vaguest understanding. Now she wondered just what Betty knew.

"You think I left all those years ago because of Laird?"

"Well," she began sweetly. "I didn't have a clue at first. You know, being away at college, the rules of not letting us come home for long periods of time. I'd missed out on so many things happening in my absence."

"We kept in touch," Dora put in with little conviction.

"As you recall, you weren't much of a letter writer," Betty reminded her. "And if you had been, it wouldn't have mattered. You never thought of me as a sister in whom you'd confide," she added. "Letters or no letters. So, I could hardly be to blame for going out with Laird. He'd grown up so handsome, being a few years behind me, and a few in front of you, I suppose he was anyone's game. But I didn't realize what had gone on between you until it was too late."

"What does that mean? Too late?"

"Just that. Now, since we've cleared the air, I'm beginning to tire greatly being on this sofa. Could you please help me back to the bedroom? I don't think I'm up for it, dear," Betty answered.

Dora rushed to her feet. Regardless of the circumstances with Laird, when Dora saw her sister in pain, there was nothing in the world she wouldn't do for her. But there was still lots of ground to be covered in this town before she could find any peace, she decided, and she was willing to give it a try.

* * *

Robert eased into bed that night exhausted. His shift ended at 11 o'clock every weekday night, but this particular day it seemed like he'd worked 24 hours straight. Even so, he found himself tossing and turning. It was at times like this that the darkness would close in, almost suffocating him with loneliness. He'd normally think of his wife and the place she'd been on the other side of the bed.

To his surprise, it wasn't his wife's memory that nudged him and kept his mind working and his body aching for the company of a woman's body close to his. No, it was Dora Thresher that kept him awake. He pictured her smile when he'd break through the barrier of her sorrow, and could visualize her face when her temper would immediately surface—making sure he didn't get away with a thing. It was this strong trait in Dora that challenged him.

Not being one to give up on something so easily, Robert decided not to let up on Dora Thresher. From his estimation, he had approximately three weeks to convince her that the town she'd left all those many years ago could become home once more. He wanted to be a part of her life, and for whatever romantic bones were left in him, he would put up a fight to win the attentions and perhaps even love of Dora Thresher.

With this commitment made, he fell off to sleep like a baby.

Chapter Four

Dora found herself anxious for her afternoon coffee break the next day. She knew she'd been down-right rotten to everyone the day before. Robert, Charles, her sister. It had been a banner day as her most painful memories had come to the surface. Many confrontations marred the day, and Dora decided she needed to mend a few bridges. However, when she discovered Betty had a doctor's appointment around the same time she normally went to Penny's for coffee, she realized her heart-felt apologies to Robert would have to wait.

She escorted her sister back inside late that afternoon and it surprised Dora how much she missed Robert's easy conversation. He hadn't meant to pry the day before, after all, and somehow she longed to tell him what was on her mind. A desire she rarely felt for a man, for she'd never trusted that many men before. Somehow, Robert was different, being so up-front and putting it all out there on the line.

"I'll be all right, now, Dora," Betty said as she eased into bed. "In fact, I think you should splurge and get yourself something at Penny's Diner. I made you miss your regular outing with my appointment," she lamented.

Dora felt herself softening toward her sister with every passing day. How could she hate someone this generous, this caring and understanding? Dora almost hated to see her walls against her sister lowering. It had been easy to blame Betty for making her lose her true love. Now, for the first time in her life, she was having to face the truth. Something she was barely ready for. However, going over to Penny's sounded like the best idea yet. Robert would still be on his shift, and he had suggested she try the food.

An hour later, Dora snuggled into the back table at Penny's Diner once more. She watched when Robert turned from his duties and noticed her sitting there. The pleased look that passed over his face was a relief. At least they were still friends, and when he came over right away, she realized they were still "speaking" friends.

"Well, now I wondered what happened when you didn't show this afternoon. Thought maybe I'd scared you away with too personal of a question."

"Nonsense. I don't scare that easily."

"No," Robert chuckled. "I guess you wouldn't."

"But I will take a sample of this food. I see your special is all the ribs you can eat."

"Yes, ma'am. Comes with our own special baked beans and from-scratch potato salad. However, I've got to warn you, I have a feeling we might make a little profit off of you. A woman as petite as you won't finish the first set, much less take us for a second."

"Don't bet on it," Dora warned. "I'm capable of a lot more than you give me credit for," she added.

"Oh, not so," Robert chimed in. "Iced tea or coffee?"

"Just water. Don't want to be up all night," she added.

"Course not," Robert answered. "I'll get right on that."

Dora enjoyed the gentle man, six feet tall with the large hands that spoke of kindness not force. She wondered what had taken her so long in discovering Penny's Diner, and the man who came with it. For that matter, what had taken her so long in discovering the feelings that were coming alive within her. Ones this widower seemed to elicit where few other men ever had—except for that Laird who'd ruined her life, she decided.

Moments later, Robert was back with a large platter with certainly more than she could eat.

"How's that for a serving of food."

"Well, I've got my work cut out for me," she answered. "Wish you could join me but I see this is hardly the quiet time of day at Penny's."

"You've got that right. Got my hands full right now, but I do have an idea. Since you didn't mind the last session of personal questions, wondered if you could stand one more."

"Don't know. What is it?" Dora asked frowning.

"Tomorrow's Saturday. I'm not on duty on the weekends and I just wondered if you might join me for dinner. Not here, perhaps, but somewhere that's not work for me the rest of the week. That is, if you're interested," he added, looking somehow confident yet ready to rush off if her answer was "no."

Dora surprised herself when her answer of acceptance was forthcoming without blinking an eye.

"I think I'd like that. Uninterrupted time where you're not having to run off with the coffee pot in somebody else's direction."

"You jot down the address of your sister's and I'll pick you up at 6:30 p.m.," he said, heading off to take care of matters behind the counter.

Dora felt her face flush as an unfamiliar excitement coursed through her. It surprised her even more that she cared about such a thing.

"This just can't be happening," she heard herself whisper under her breath. "Not now. Not after all these years," she added. But it was, and it was time she enjoyed it, she thought, as she began working away at the full plate of food before her.

* * *

"A date! Imagine that," Betty chirped.

"It's not a date. I'm just having dinner with the man, and I won't be gone too long. You've got the telephone numbers right by the phone by the bed if you need help while I'm away."

"Don't you worry your head a bit about me. I'll doze off after that show I like. So, don't rush. I'll be fine."

"Take care, Betty," Dora answered, shuffling a selection of magazines onto the rumpled covers of her sister's bed before leaving the room and taking a watchful perch beside the front window.

When a long car pulled up into the drive, Dora realized it could only be Robert O'Grady. The make might be a few years old, but it was a nice, luxury type that she liked. She found herself smiling at her previous thoughts. She'd wondered how she'd react if he'd come up in a clunker of a car with dented sides and perhaps a wrecked door panel replaced by one with the wrong color or something of that nature. Well, at least she'd go out in style this evening, she thought, relieved she wouldn't be riding around in a vehicle that might break down at any given moment.

Dora opened the door as Robert scaled the front steps, closed it, and immediately locked it behind her.

"Well, no doorbell necessary for you," he chuckled.

"No. I'm prompt and organized," she answered. "I watched for you through the front window."

"Well. I see you're not a woman who keeps her date waiting," he answered, offering his arm.

"And I don't need assistance down the steps. I'm not an invalid at sixty-five years old, my present age, in case you're wondering, and I'm not interested in chivalrous gestures at this stage in my life," she told him, as she marched down the steps and flung open the passenger side of the car.

"Yes, ma'am," Robert said, a look of surprise evident on his face.

"My name's Dora. I'm not a ma'am," she added as he slid into the car and started the motor.

Robert paused, his hands resting on top of the steering wheel. He considered the front of Dora's sister's house, making no movement to pull out.

"Well? What's the matter?" Dora pushed.

"Dora, you'll have to excuse me. Even though I enjoy your headstrong nature, I'm not used to being given a list of do's and don'ts at the beginning of a first date."

"This isn't a date," she snapped. "Now, let's go. I don't like leaving Betty alone as it is without dawdling like this."

Robert made no attempt to leave.

"Dora, you seem so defensive. Like an animal caught in a trap. Perhaps you've changed your mind. Maybe you wish you hadn't accepted my invitation. I'll let you out of it, if that's the case."

Dora released a tightly held breath, her shoulders relaxing. Perhaps she had been more upset than she'd let herself believe. Under the circumstances, anyone would be, she thought. But Robert O'Grady wasn't privy to those reasons, nor anyone else in the whole wide world in on the pain she'd endured and the impossibility of the situation at hand.

She sighed, then spoke in a more kindly tone.

"Robert, forgive me. I'm under pressure here, and you've been unfortunately in the way of my temper. More than once already. Perhaps it's more of a compliment, me going off on you, than you realize."

"How do you figure that?" he quipped.

"Well, I must feel safe around you for me to let you in on my feelings—even bad ones. Besides that, I haven't been out on a date in over five years. I'm quite out of practice as far as people skills and dating," she added.

"Just let me know if you still want to go," he said quietly.

"I do," Dora answered, relieved when Robert began backing out of the driveway.

Her mind worked furiously as he drove in silence toward the upscale restaurant he'd suggested. She tried to think of safe topics, any topics, but as the car glided through various streets and thoroughfares, she couldn't help but be reminded of a past that would not let her go.

"My, my, how this town has changed," she finally said. "Do you know that shopping mall is where a drive-in once stood?" she asked, then wished she hadn't thought of that memory.

"That so?" Robert asked with interest.

At least he's feeling a bit better, Dora told herself. She decided she'd have to be extra nice that evening to make up for her unnecessary roughness in the beginning.

"Yes, as teenagers it was quite the hot spot. That and the ice-cream joint afterwards. Now look at it. What could anyone need at that mall, what with all the shopping around everywhere you look."

"Sure enough, that's true. Now the teenagers congregate in the mall, I guess."

"Couldn't be as romantic," Dora put in, thinking of the times she and Laird had half-way watched a move at the drive-in. She'd be just barely aware of the wide screen that loomed in front of them, or of the speaker that stood beside the window of his borrowed parent's car. Perhaps a mall would've been better after what she'd gone through, she thought.

"Romantic," Robert piped up, bringing her back to the present. "Drive-in's were that. But the quality of the theater conditions can't compare these days. Besides, if I want a romantic movie, I don't want a sea of cars around and anything interfering with my conversation with a lovely lady," he said. "I'd rent something like that at home."

With this, they pulled into the parking lot of the restaurant. It was a fairly new addition to the area, which meant no extra memories would be flooding her head and making her crazy.

"Before I step on my own two feet again, do you like me to get the door, or shall I wait and let you do it all yourself," he asked tentatively.

Dora smiled at his forthrightness.

"I'll get my own car door. You get the restaurant door," she said. "How does that sound?"

"I can live with it if you can," he answered. His familiar grin returned, making a tingle of interest course through Dora once again. Now they were back on track, she decided.

After being seated, Dora and Robert considered the menu. He made suggestions to Dora, pointing out the more expensive entrees as ones he was sure she'd like. It pleased her more than she'd imagined. She'd been rotten, set out rules of all kinds, and he still insisted on treating her like a queen. The man was all class, she decided.

"I'll have the roasted chicken," she told the waiter, "and just one glass of that wine you told us about at the beginning," she explained. "Just one, mind you," she added.

"The lady knows what she wants, and doesn't hesitate to tell you about it," Robert chuckled to the waiter.

He ordered the same and then focused all his attention on Dora. She felt herself flush under the close inspection. She shifted nervously in her seat, and she remembered what it had been like when she'd fallen for Laird. Sitting across from this man began stirring up old, similar feelings which she could hardly believe.

"So, here we are, you've ordered your food, and I'm not rushing off trying to get it for you. Feels a little strange, doesn't it?" Robert said as he gazed intently at Dora.

"Strange is the right description," she admitted. "But not because of that."

"Oh?"

"Well, you know. A date with a man I hardly know, for one thing."

"I can fix that," he answered. "I'll tell you about myself. I'm a widower for over five years now, miss my wife still, but I appreciate the time we did have together. I can't say I've dated much since, and haven't asked anyone out in the past year and a half, if my calculations serve me correctly."

"Not a man about town?" Dora asked, more interested in the answer than making a joke.

"I'm a man about town, all right, but not with a lady on my arm. In fact, the last one I offered my arm, say a half hour ago, wouldn't even take it."

Dora flushed again. "I'm sorry. I'm out of practice and don't want to be condescended to."

"To me it means respect. An endearment. Guess my wife was fond of the gesture and it's habit."

Dora nodded, duly straightened out as the waiter returned with their glasses of wine.

"Shall we make a toast?" Robert asked, holding his in the air.

"You do it," Dora agreed.

"To a lovely woman who has graced this quiet town long ago, and has now returned to do so again. Even if it is for a short time."

Dora touched her glass to his, then sipped. Robert scooted his chair closer to the table, then resumed the conversation.

"So, back to the man you hardly know, I can tell you more if you like."

"Sure," Dora answered.

"Well, I've been here for many years, but certainly not from way back like you. But I've made my home here. I retired from working at the same company for the entire time I've lived here, but found having lots of free time was not what I expected."

"You don't strike me as a man who wants to sit and rock his days away on a porch somewhere," Dora put in.

"No, but I'm not opposed to doing such on my off hours. A man needs a balanced life," he added. "But anyway, Penny's Diner fits the bill for me just fine. Gets me around people, makes me feel valuable, and gives me an outlet for all this energy the Good Lord blessed me with in such abundance. And believe me, Penny's keeps you hopping."

"It must."

"What about friends?" Dora asked.

"Friends? I feel like everybody in the whole dang town are my friends. From some of the teenage boys that come in the afternoon wanting to talk, to some of the real old-timers, couples, and men and women alike who stroll in for dinner and like a friendly face and kind word for somebody outside the four walls of their homes."

Dora felt the hardness of her heart melting away as she listened to the genuine and generous nature of this man. She hadn't met anyone quite like him. Perhaps she'd never allowed anyone close enough to find out, she decided.

"So, Dora. How's your sister?" he asked, quickly switching gears. "I don't want to monopolize the conversation with talk about me," he added.

"Betty is doing some better," she answered, taking another sip of wine. "She might make more rapid improvements if she'd get it out of her head I'm not going to always be around to wait on her."

"Your sister is your opposite, isn't she?"

Dora's gaze shifted to Robert's kind face.

"What do you mean?" she asked, wondering which character traits he'd picked up on between them.

"Well, you're such the independent type. Don't need anybody. Don't seem to even be interested in keeping company with much of anybody. Which is fine, mind you, I'm not finding fault with that. It's a good thing, especially when you consider Betty is now alone and probably having a whale of a time handling it. She's as dependent on someone else being with her as you are in the other direction."

"I guess that's so. Never thought about it much."

"Now don't get me wrong, I don't know your sister well enough to make a statement like that, but from what I've heard, after Laird died, she wouldn't go outside the house unless one of her friends went with her."

"I didn't realize," Dora said slowly, thinking she hadn't had a clue of her sister's traits or needs after Laird was gone.

"No, she wouldn't dare peak out of that house without a friend from over at the church pulling her into some function, or someone taking her to dinner at Penny's. Always with a woman friend or two, though. Never, never by herself. Not at all like you," he added.

Dora fell silent. She wondered about her sister's life with Laird. The strong man who seemed to have it all. Dora had worshipped him, but she hadn't needed him. She had herself to depend on. Even after they'd gotten close and she couldn't imagine life without him, she'd done so, and without batting an eye. Betty would never have had the strength to move off and have a career. Especially in those days.

"You're mighty quiet. Have I managed to hit a nerve again?" Robert asked.

"I was just thinking about what you were saying. I guess I don't know my sister at all," she allowed. "We had a long period of silence that gathered from a falling out."

"A sister's spat?"

"Not exactly. Good old Betty had no clue of the dispute. But it was enough to send me packing and to go start a new life elsewhere. It would have been the death of me to stay here and watch idly as Betty and Laird made their life together."

The food came blessfully at that moment, shifting Dora's focus to the excellently prepared dish before her. The chicken had been laid out just so, and the vegetables were elegant and dainty, making an artist's creation on the china plate.

"This is certainly more cosmopolitan than I'd have dreamed this town could offer," Dora said, picking up her fork.

"I hope that means you like it," Robert put in.

"Yes, indeed," Dora answered, taking a bite and relaxing even more.

It was over dessert that Robert brought up the long-forgotten conversation about Betty and Laird. However, the underlying meaning hadn't been lost on Robert O'Grady, and Dora realized the man was very sharp and an expert on the study of people.

"So, may I be so uncouth and blunt to ask if Laird, your sister's husband, was somehow a suitor of yours before you let him go to Betty?"

Dora froze. Of course, he'd gather that from her earlier comments, but the very thought had her unglued.

"Laird choose Betty. What can I say," she answered flatly.

"There must have been more to it than that, but if you don't want to remember such things, I can certainly understand."

"Remember? How can I forget?" she snapped.

"Oh, I believe I've found the source of that raw nerve."

"Perhaps you have. You've just walked into a mine field, just to warn you."

"You don't have to say another word. No explanation is needed. It's none of my business, anyway," Robert answered.

The waiter came up again at the best possible time, and Robert took care of the bill quickly.

When they were both secured in the car, Robert spoke up again.

"I was going to suggest we take advantage of this pretty night and go rock on my porch or sit in the swing, but I guess I've dug up too many unpleasant memories for that now," Robert ventured.

Dora sat, glancing out at the twilight. She couldn't face going back into Betty and Laird's house just yet—now that she'd finally let out the words she'd so carefully kept inside for all these years. She felt as though she were a dam about to break, and if she didn't get the rest of it off her chest, she felt the bitterness inside would, in fact, break her.

"I'd love to see your house and sit on the porch," Dora answered. "There's unfinished business here and it's time I got a head start on it," she answered.

"Yes," Robert put in. "I've got some things I want to say to you as well," he answered, turning his car out of the parking lot.

Chapter Five

As Robert pulled into his driveway, he glanced up at his wrap-around porch, presently lit by a single light at the front door. With the fallen twilight and darkness that had followed, this meant the porch swing and rockers were shrouded in the comfort of a soft light.

He escorted Dora onto his property and up the few steps that led to the luxury of the evening. Crickets chirped in rhythmic fashion, and the out-of-the-way street where he lived was not one normally traveled by any but those who resided at the very end.

Robert had always prided himself on his selection of older, stately homes. This one he'd bought many years ago, and progress had bypassed this area of town. This meant the homey feel he'd so loved at the beginning remained. He also enjoyed the large trees that gave shade and privacy from the two vacant lots he'd scarfed up at the time he'd bought the home many years before.

Now he had a woman to entertain on the porch he'd forgotten was such a lovely place to be. Dora had been right. He was not a man who normally spent much time out here, but as he steadied the swing for Dora to sit and he eased beside her, he wondered why he didn't take advantage of the private comfortable place more often. His expansive yard, which he now paid someone else to care for, and his neighbor's well-groomed yard across the cul-de-sac allowed a very pretty view.

"This is really quite lovely," Dora said, breaking the silence. "If I had a porch like this, I probably would be out here most of my free time," she said, as her body relaxed back into the gentle motion of the swing and she molded herself next to Robert's form.

Robert eased his arm around her shoulders, realizing he was taking his life in his hands at that gesture. Still, Dora snuggled slightly closer to him. With the soft air swirling around them with every sway, Robert believed he'd put Dora completely at ease. Then her next words came out, startling him into reality.

"I could never live here," she announced.

Robert cleared his throat.

"Here as in this neighborhood? Or this house, you mean?"

"This town. I made a big mistake here years ago, and I've been paying for it ever since. That's what makes me so irritable, I think."

Robert felt his throat tighten. If he'd been unsure of how to proceed before, he certainly had no idea now.

"Oh?" he managed, thinking that the only safe utterance he could emit.

"Yes, Robert. You were right about Laird and me. He was mine and I threw him away without even realizing the impact of my actions. But that's how it is, you know. You're careless, and you lose."

"I see," Robert answered, obviously not seeing at all, but not wanting to stop the flow of what Dora clearly wanted to talk about.

"But you don't see, do you?" Dora pressed.

Robert smiled. At least the same Dora came through even in her pain.

"Always call me on things, don't you, Dora?"

"Well, don't say what you don't mean."

"Yes, ma'am. I mean, yes, Dora."

"Okay. Here's what happened. My Laird and I became an item back when my sister, Betty, went off to college. Mother and Father felt an education was important to a girl, even if Betty never had such aspirations. Her only thought was to find a man there on campus while she was at school, marry, and settle down with children and set up housekeeping. It was my sister's only drive, I tell you."

"Again, opposite of you, right?"

"True, but that's beside the point."

"Sorry, please continue," Robert urged, squeezing her shoulder. He liked the hint of Dora's light floral scent. He liked the stylish fashion of her sleeveless dress, and softness of her skin under his grasp. It'd been a long time since he'd felt the warmth of a woman close to him in this way and he liked it. He had to push his attentions away from the unexpected pleasure of her closeness to pay heed to her words. Words very important to Dora.

"Laird went away to that same college mid-year. By then, Betty had been there for three years, but Laird and I hadn't dated except starting that fall. I wasn't close to Betty, and Laird's family took off for Christmas that year. It was not her fault that she knew nothing of our involvement."

"So, they were re-acquainted at school. Not here."

"That's right."

"Laird knew he was dating you and your sister, Betty, at the same time? Even though he was away at school and separated from you for awhile?"

"I guess that's true. He knew Betty and I were sisters."

"So, I'd say you're not to blame for any of it. When people are dating they sometimes drift apart, meet another and fall in love. I hate to say it, Dora, but it seems to me that Laird was never yours at all. All this hurt about who he chose is more a matter of Laird not staying with one person until he met your sister—rather than it being your sister's fault."

"I never said it was Betty's fault. Betty was the innocent," Dora snapped, jumping from the swing and going to stand beside one of the white posts intermittently spaced down the porch.

"Now, calm down, Dora. I seem to have a negative effect on you when I tell it like I see it," he said, coming to stand next to her.

"You don't know all the facts," she spat, anger flashing in her eyes. "I got involved with that no-good cousin of his over the Christmas break. If Laird's family had only stayed put, then I would've never been in that predicament, never gotten mixed up with Charles, and Laird wouldn't have retaliated by dating my sister—and marrying her, for goodness' sakes! How could he have done it? I know I was in the wrong, but my life has never been the same. It should've been me in that house of Betty's. Not her, and besides that . . ."

Robert pinned Dora against the railing that ran the length of the porch to the posts on either side of the front steps. Without warning he captured her into his arms and quieted her lips with his. He felt Dora's body, almost trembling with anger, begin to relax as he showed her the passion she'd stirred within him.

When she slipped her arms around his waist, he felt he had the go-ahead to continue, pulling her closer and holding her tightly against him. He felt Dora's breathing begin a depth and security that matched his as they kissed in the softness of the porch light and moonlight.

Robert hadn't felt this good since a time long past. He'd never rushed a woman into his arms like this in forever, either. Something about Dora's fire, her fierce independence and intensity made him want to tame her and make all her troubles melt away. He was also surprised at the quickness of her passion, yet, it matched the way she responded to life. Again, with intensity. He then had the sudden desire to discover all her attributes as they pertained to this intimate direction.

He felt his desire pulsing through his body, coming alive for the first time in quite a while. It was at this moment that Dora pulled away. Embarrassment flooded his entire being, realizing she'd discovered his thoughts and rejected any further embrace.

"Robert, I must go," she said quietly. "Betty said she'd fall off to sleep, but I know she's keeping vigil. She needs to have the security of me back inside the house before she can rest quietly."

Robert nodded in agreement and led Dora to the car. His body shuddered with the passion he wished he could share with a woman again. Dora had now reminded him of one more thing he missed in losing his wife, losing a companion, a confidant, a lover. But Dora was a slippery one with fire, and now she slid into the front seat, ready to be taken home. Robert just hoped he'd be able to convince her to see him again. Have another try at it. But after what had just transpired, he wondered if that would indeed be possible.

* * *

"Oh, I'm so grateful you're back," Betty called out as Dora unlocked the door and stood inside, watching Robert's headlights as he pulled out of her driveway and into the street.

"Yes, Betty. I'm back," Dora answered, still hovering in the doorway and looking through the front window as the dark silhouette of Robert's car disappeared around the corner.

"Did you have a nice time?" she questioned, her soft voice wavering at the exertion.

Dora headed to the bedroom finding Betty propped up against a mound of pillows. She'd put the TV on mute and the magazines Dora had left her were scattered across the bedspread.

"I thought you were calling it an early night. Going off to sleep after that first show that's been over for what, an hour at least," Dora began.

"I couldn't sleep. Not with you out with a strange man."

"Betty, the man's lived here in this town for some time."

"Well, I know that, but I'm not that familiar with him or his family. He used to be married, didn't he?"

"He's a widower, Betty. Now, can I get you anything to make you comfortable? I'm ready to call it a night myself."

"No, no. Having you back in the house safe and sound is all the comfort I need."

"Fine. Good night, Betty. Ring the bell if you need me," Dora said, closing the woman's door behind her.

As Dora made her way down the hall, mixed emotions raged through her. Everything from picking at the sore of the past by telling

Robert all about the Laird business, to the suffocating way her sister had in needing to have somebody in order to put a sense of purpose back in her life. Laird was her sister's main focus, and her only child, Kathy, had one of those high-faluting jobs in San Francisco that kept her traveling non-stop.

As Dora closed the door to the guest bedroom, she stared at her reflection in the mirror. She pushed a section of hair back into place, realizing it had gotten a little off kilter in her embrace with Robert. It was this fact that disturbed her the most. The man had gone and stirred up something inside her that had laid dormant all this time—as she'd willed it to. Dora had forced herself to stay away from men for good portions of her life, comparing them to Laird and sending them away.

Now here was this high spirited man who met her nose to nose on matters, not holding back his opinion or his words. Just like her in that way. Except he was more humane in the way he went about it. Dora knew she could be simply rude and abrupt. He didn't seem to have a thin skin though, she thought. He might be just the type of person who'd be able to stand up to her. Except that wasn't the way she was thinking of him at the moment.

She found a glow emanated from her face. A tingle remained. For heaven's sakes, she thought. I cannot be falling for someone like I did with Laird. But with all the years under her belt, she knew it was different. More mature. More certain of the package she was getting. In some ways she realized she'd hardly known Laird. Just been dreadfully in love with him. Until she ruined it.

With this, she forced her thoughts off the subject, determining that protective measures would be necessary with this Robert O'Grady. Yet she hadn't a clue what to do next. Or what not to do.

The next day Dora couldn't avoid the questions her sister obviously had about her "date." But she'd determined she would not share a thing with her. Not one little bit. Still the conversation would not drop no matter how true to form Dora was in her abrupt answers.

"You might stick around if there's romance in the air," Betty pressed again.

"You've been watching too many of those day-time love stories, Betty."

"Well, perhaps you're right, but I see a look in your eyes and a new spring in your step that says I'm right."

"You're grasping at straws, Betty. I'm leaving this town as soon as you're up and around."

Betty sighed. "I know, Dora. You've got a life elsewhere, just like my Kathy, and I wouldn't stop either of you from your happiness. I suppose I'm just a little down with this empty house after this ordeal with my heart. It brings back the sorrow of losing a partner in life when he's no longer there to pamper you, bring you things when you need them," she added.

Dora fumed. She did not want to hear of the many tender things that Laird had done for her sister, but as though on cue, her sister rambled on about just that.

"He was especially good about bringing me things when were watching TV in the den, you know what I mean?" she asked.

Dora managed a nod which sent Betty into that nonsense tangent even further.

"Like if I wanted a glass of iced tea, or a cup of ice cream right before we retired for the night. We both liked a little dessert late at night. Made me sleep better. Or he'd bring a blanket over if I was chilly and he'd turned the heat down. He liked it hot and I was always cold. Ah, what a gentleman he was," she expounded.

Dora felt her stomach turn. She wouldn't have made Laird bring her anything. In fact, if she remembered correctly, Dora was the one doing all the work in their relationship. She didn't like to be waited on. Liked things to flow in unison. Equals. Clearly theirs was of a different nature. At any rate, she certainly wanted to hear no more of her sister's "Life with Laird" stories.

"Well, can I bring you anything now, Betty?" she asked. "Are you still comfortable sitting up in the front room like this?"

"Actually, could you help me out to the back porch? A little sunshine might do me good," Betty said.

Dora helped her out onto the back patio under the large dark green and white striped verandah overhang they'd added in the last few years. It gave shade to the intense overhead sun, but the light was plentiful nevertheless. As she settled her there, Betty chimed in again about Laird's activities.

"If there was a game or sporting event on any of the channels within the scope of our cable stations, Laird would find it. He was such a sports fanatic. Loved to have that TV blaring with football games, basketball games, baseball—oh, he just loved baseball. Our home was filled with the sound of some kind of sports year-round," she explained.

"How horrid," Dora exclaimed before realizing the insult.

"What?" Betty chirped.

"Oh, I mean that it's simply noise to me. I detest those things blaring away. That would've driven me crazy."

"I didn't mind. I just loved to watch his face, getting all excited and telling the players or referees what to do."

Dora grimaced. "Sounds heavenly."

"Then he'd like to debate on politics. Always mad about somebody doing something. He just loved to bring up the latest with his friends, Carl and John Davis. You like politics, don't you, Dora? After all, you were always the 'smart' one in the family."

"Hmmm. Smart enough to stay away from the topic of politics. No, not for me," Dora answered.

"Yes," Betty continued as they both considered a little bird that lighted on the bird feeder on the comfortable late summer, almost into fall afternoon. "Even his cousin, Charles, would come over once a week for a deep discussion of the world's state of affairs," she added lightly, the intent barely noticeable.

"All right, Betty. I see what you're up to."

"What?"

"Don't put on that innocent act with me. Charles is *not* a person I want to speak of. Not now, not ever."

"But Dora, he was Laird's cousin. He's family."

"He's *your* family, Betty. Not mine."

"Well, by marriage . . ." she stressed.

"No, he is *not*. He ruined my life."

After the words escaped her lips, Dora brought her hand over her mouth, a few sentences too late. The look of amazement across Betty's face indicated the woman's total lack of knowledge of the events past. A long past so tender that it still smarted.

"Charles ruined your life? But how? When did this happen? When I was away at school? Tell me, Dora, please. Is it why you left town so abruptly and never looked back until now?"

"No, Betty. It wasn't because of Charles," she answered.

Dora rose to her feet. The sound of her shoes echoed against the brick patio as she took a few steps back and forth.

"Listen, Betty, I'd like to run out for my normal visit to Penny's for a little outing. You've had enough sunshine for now. I don't want you getting too hot, either. Let me help you inside before I go."

To Dora's surprise, Betty held up a warning hand.

"No, no. I can get back into the house when I'm ready. You go on."

"Betty, don't be upset. This really isn't something I'm willing to discuss, and I don't want you getting hurt being out here without being close to the phone."

"I can get back on my own," she insisted flatly.

"But if you were to fall on this hard surface . . ."

"Dora, if you don't mind, I'd like to be left alone now. I want to stay out here to think. Being in the fresh air is the best place I know how. It's suffocating in that house and I want to just sit here. If I'm still out here when you return, come and get me. Otherwise, please, just leave me alone to my thoughts," she said, the subject clearly not up for debate.

As Dora hesitantly went inside, she wondered what spark of knowledge her sister chewed on. What about Charles set her mind to reeling like it obviously had, she wondered.

Well, she hadn't said anything unkind about her sister, and whatever Betty had on her mind, she would do well at considering it in the back there amongst the birds and nature and all, she thought. Dora had other things to consider for the moment, like a certain gentleman who'd suspect the wrong thing if she didn't show up at Penny's that afternoon.

As she pulled up, she noticed several other cars filled the parking lot of Penny's beside the usual crowd of teenagers. When she went inside, she smiled at Robert who was busy making a malt or some other ice cream concoction for the regular boy she'd seen him talking to many times.

She positioned herself into the same table near the back, not even scanning the crowd of others sitting nearby. As Robert made eye contact with her, waving in her direction, she then noticed the couple a few tables in front of her.

Dora froze in anger as Charles turned around in his seat, and he and his wife, Sarah, waved a greeting. She felt trapped in a time warp at that very moment, but escape was not an option, for Robert was already heading her way.

Chapter Six

"Wasn't sure you'd show up today," he began quietly as he placed a fresh cup of coffee onto her table.

"Why wouldn't I?" she asked a little shakily.

"Last night I may have taken too many liberties."

Dora glanced nervously over at Charles' table, noting he'd turned around again. She grabbed the coffee cup and raised it to her lips. The steaming liquid was too hot to drink, so she put it down again with a clunk.

"I can see I'm making you uncomfortable," Robert put in. "I'll leave you to your thoughts. I've got my hands full with these added customers anyway," he said, turning to his duties.

Dora wished she'd found the words to tell Robert that her discomfort had little to do with the night before. In fact, in bed that night she'd tossed and turned thinking of him. Reliving the embrace, the kiss . . . She wondered how he'd gotten through the hard bitterness she'd carried with her as a protective shield against any permanent relationship all these years.

Now, Laird's cousin, the man who'd been instrumental in helping her whole world crash permanently before her, sat only a few feet away. To her horror she watched as Charles and his wife, Sarah, eased out of the booth and headed her way, toting their ice cream dishes with them.

"Mind if we join you, Dora?" Charles asked, smiling broadly as if they were indeed old friends with no unpleasantness between them.

At that moment, Dora wished she'd seated herself at a two-top table instead of the spacious booth she'd chosen. Sarah smiled sweetly back at her. There was no way out, Dora knew as she nodded in response.

"I'd like that," Dora lied.

"Good, good," Charles agreed, indicating to his wife to slide in first over the seat.

"It's so good to see you again, Dora, dear," Sarah added after they were completely settled and Charles had fetched the accompanying water glasses from the other table as well.

"Yes, thank you," Dora answered. She would not further the exaggerated lie with saying how happy she was to see the two of them. No sir, one stretch was enough already, Dora decided.

"Sarah and I come over here from time to time for an ice cream sundae—chocolate, of course," Charles explained.

"Of course," Dora said.

"Aren't you having anything other than that coffee?" Sarah asked. "It'd be such a shame what with all those delicious milkshakes and malts, not to mention these sundaes. They're our favorites. Penny's has such good food, 24 hours a day."

"Just coffee."

"Betty doing okay?" Charles asked.

"Fine. Just fine."

An awkward silence hung in the air. Robert came by, splashing some new coffee in her empty cup.

"I see you know our Dora?" Robert asked, glancing at Charles and Sarah.

"Oh, from way back," Charles supplied.

"Way back," Sarah echoed.

"Way back," Dora ground out, startling everyone. Robert drew his eyebrows together as he made quick eye contact with Dora, but she decided she couldn't very well indicate that this was the man she'd been talking about the night before without giving away something.

He quickly retreated. Dora didn't know whether it was to take care of other customers and duties or to get away from the icy atmosphere that had crept over their table. If she could've she certainly would have rushed away at that moment.

Charles spoke up, breaking the silence.

"Look, Dora, we didn't mean to cause you any harm by coming over. We just thought you'd like some company. Must be difficult caring for someone night and day while they recuperate from surgery. Betty tends to need quite a lot these days, too. Even before the heart trouble. Guess it all falls on you," he finished.

Dora felt her own eyebrows draw together in concern.

"What do you mean she needs a lot these days?"

"Since Laird died," he explained.

"Oh, mercy. If I hear one more word about poor Betty because of Laird's passing," she began. "It's been long enough for her to get on with her life. I've always depended on myself. I can't have too much more pity on a person if they don't help themselves and stand on their own two feet."

"Betty's different from you, dear," Sarah put in. "Her whole life revolved around Laird. Taking care of his home, his needs. Her outside activities were few. She's been quite at a loss afterwards. You don't spend that kind of time with a person without feeling you've somehow lost your right arm. I know if anything happened to Charles, that's how I'd feel."

Dora hated it that she could see Sarah's point, and hated it even more that she felt a pang of concern and understanding for her sister. Still, being in Charles' presence and speaking of Laird and their long marriage settled unpleasantly in a knot in her stomach. She could take no more of this conversation at the moment.

"Well, speaking of Betty, I need to go on back to the house. See how she's doing," Dora said, rising from her seat. "Nice to see you again, Sarah, Charles," she finished.

She began pulling a couple of bills from her purse.

"No, Dora. Let us take care of the coffee," Charles insisted.

"Fine. Thank you very much," she added, as Dora strode purposefully out of the Diner without glancing at Robert as she did so.

Driving out she felt her resolve rush through her rapidly, dissolving like a puddle around her as the tears cascaded down her cheeks. She couldn't face Robert right now, not until the rest of this past was finished, and that would not take place in the middle of Penny's Diner for all possible on-lookers to see. No, she'd pay a visit to Charles later that week when she'd let herself ask the questions that remained lodged within the secret places of her heart for so many years. The answers would be the key out of this secluded world she'd built around herself, and she would get them soon.

* * *

When the afternoon crowd began to clear, Robert strolled over to Charles and Sarah's table.

"Want some coffee or iced tea to top off that ice cream I see you made short work of?" he asked, chuckling.

"No, my," Sarah began. "I'm so full I can't eat or drink another thing. It was wonderful once again, Robert.

"Yes, so good. So good," Charles said, pausing, then giving Robert a sideways glance.

"Say, Robert, what do you think of our Dora?"

"Nice lady," Robert answered, wondering where this was leading.

"Too bad about all that mess with me and Laird and that history and such. He was my cousin, you know," Charles said.

"Laird's cousin?" Robert asked, nodding in understanding. In fact, he'd just made the connection as the man explained it.

"Yes, dog-gone-it. I'd thought she'd snapped out of it. Way I figured it, whenever she met "Mr. Right" that business with me and her and that cousin of mine would be a thing of the past. Though, I swear, I never understood it. But I can see from the couple of times I've been around Dora since her return, she hasn't found love. Not the real 'stickin' kind. But then again, I guess old grudges die hard."

"Charles, should you be telling Mr. O'Grady such things?" Sarah advised him, poking him gently in the ribs.

"It's okay, Sarah. I'm very fond of Dora myself. If there was anything I could do to ease her pain, I'd do it in a heartbeat," Robert promised.

"How about sweeping her off her feet. Show her love that counts. Make her forget all this nonsense," Charles suggested.

"Charles!" Sarah said. "That isn't proper for you to match-make with Mr. O'Grady like that. He may not have gotten past his own loss."

"It's been five years, dear," Charles argued, turning in her direction.

"Perfectly all right, Sarah. It's been tough, but I'm ready to move on with my life."

"And I recognize the look a man has in his eyes when he's got something for a woman. And Robert, you've got that hunger in yours for our Dora."

Robert felt a smile creep over his face and an unexpected flush. "Yes, Charles, you have me hand over fist. But Dora isn't interested in any romantic involvement, I'm afraid."

"I've know her since we were teens, Robert, and I can still read her like a book. You push this one, Robert, and you'll get your prize. I have a feeling you're just the type of man who could bring her the love she's missed out on all these years. The type who can show her a better way than the track she's chosen all this time. She's a treasure. Just dig."

Robert pushed his shoulders back, bringing himself to his full height. Armed with new knowledge, he had a new resolve, and he'd take the advice of Laird's cousin, Charles. He'd set his cap for Dora, and now that he had extra encouragement, he wouldn't stop until he'd given it all he had. Dora Thresher was in for a surprise, he decided.

* * *

"You're mighty quiet. Did you get hot out on the patio?" Dora asked as she entered the house to find Betty stretched out on the sofa watching a TV show.

"It got a bit warm," Betty murmured.

"I see you were able to get back in on your own. I wasn't gone that long."

"No, you weren't. And you're right. I was able to make my way inside just fine. I suspect I'm gaining strength and it feels good," she answered.

"Betty, you're acting differently," Dora said straight-away. She took a seat on the easy chair next to the sofa and immediately wondered if this was where Laird always sat while the two of them watched TV together.

"Yes, I suppose with my new insight I can't very well help it," she answered.

"You didn't like it that I bad-mouthed your precious Laird's cousin, Charles. Is that about the size of it?" Dora asked, feeling her day couldn't get any worse. That is, until Betty spoke again.

"Not so. It's the intent and the meaning that I'm just now getting," she began.

Dora sat in silence, afraid of what was to come. She was right. It was only one of her worst nightmares played out before her.

"I guess since you're the 'smart one' in the family, I lived up to the opposite all these years. I never figured it out, why you left in such a huff—leaving all your family behind. I'd thought it had something to do with Charles, but Lord knows I never dreamed it had anything to do with Laird. But I guess that's the difference in us, once again."

"Where are you going with this, Betty?" Dora asked, hedging.

"You were in love with that man and never let on to a soul. Yes, I understand there was talk after you left, but I never paid it any mind. Gossip is full of lies and I refused to consider any of the town's theories. Even Charles' ideas."

"I never loved Charles. If that's what he led everyone to believe, I'll kill him with my bare hands," Dora stormed.

"No, Dora. Not Charles. Laird. Maybe your trip has opened my eyes. Maybe that's why you left. You didn't want either of us to know it but you resented our marrying. Well, I'm sorry for you, Dora, but it was life at the time and we made the best of it."

"I guess there's no sense in me denying it at this juncture," Dora said quietly. "I never wanted you to know. I was afraid I'd let on how I felt if I stayed past a day or two."

"Best that I finally understand at least some of your actions, Dora. But why didn't you come to me?"

"You were married. Came home married. Remember?"

Betty hung her head. The sadness in her entire demeanor crushed Dora. She hated to see what this news had done to her sweet sister who'd never harm a flea.

Betty remained quiet for an interminably long moment, then spoke up again.

"Why didn't you come off to school, too, Dora. I urged you to join me after you'd graduated. Mother and Father begged you to get an education."

"What does that have to do with a dad-blamed thing? I didn't want to go to college. Laird either. He held his ground for two years, until his family insisted. I guess they twisted his arm over that long Christmas break when he took off from work. Next thing I know, he's going off to college where you were and then several months later, the two of you are married. Married!"

"If you'd been there on campus, maybe this whole thing wouldn't have happened."

"What are you saying, Betty? That you'd have given me Laird?"

"Well, I guess I'm dumb, but he said you'd dated each other, but that you'd fallen for his cousin over the Christmas holidays. He figured it was completely kaput with the two of you. I had no idea it was something serious within your heart. You never seemed to need anybody, such the independent type and all," she added. "I just never dreamed, until it all fell into place earlier today."

Dora eased to her feet, brushing off a piece of lint on her jersey knit outfit.

"I'd say this is all water under the bridge, Betty. The man's dead. So is this subject."

"No, I don't think it is. Next you're going to tell me I've ruined your life by marrying Laird."

"I don't blame you, Betty. I never have. Not later on, after I'd gotten past some of the initial hurt."

"Well, you should. Laird would have never gotten married so quickly except for me."

"Except for you? What do you mean?"

Betty paused, glancing up at her sister and wearing a sad face.

"A girl just didn't do that sort of thing back then, you know."

"You're talking in riddles and I've run out of patience on this topic, Betty. Spit it out, whatever it is."

"I guess I sort of made Laird marry me. I felt so guilty for how we got carried away one night, then I believed no man would have me since I'd gone that far. He agreed it would be best. He didn't have to marry me, I suppose. I know he cared for me and liked me a lot right off—and I fell in love with him from the first date. I felt we were made for each other, and he grew to love me deeply as time went on. A good solid marriage and I'll miss him to my dying day," she said. "So hate me if you must, but that's the whole story. Now, I'm glad I've gotten it out in the open and off my chest. I never had anybody to confess that to before."

Dora felt her head spinning and her stomach turning. She wished she'd never found out the facts before her own dying day. She quickly excused herself and went to sit out on the back patio. The late afternoon sun streamed through the large branches of the trees with their plentiful leaves as though nothing earth-shattering had just occurred. But the meaning behind Betty's words left her stunned and heartbroken once again. How could Laird have had intimate relations with another woman, let alone her sister, after the two of them were an item—even if he thought she'd started dating Charles.

Dora could not stop the images that flooded her mind. He had been with her sister before the marriage. Laird and Dora'd had no such relations. Dora wondered if Laird had really been in love with her at all, now that she'd discovered he'd been with Betty in such a way.

The answer became painfully obvious. Laird had never loved her, never returned her feelings. It had been a fantasy love affair in her own head all these years, and the false memories had made Dora keep all men she'd dated at arm's length's distance. What a waste, she thought unhappily as she watched a bird on the feeder a few feet away feasting away.

Dora's mind shifted to Robert O'Grady and the feelings he'd inspired within her so quickly. He was quite taken with her, Dora knew that for sure. She just wondered if he'd ever be able to break through the barriers she'd so carefully erected all these years. If he did, he'd be the only man who'd ever been able to do it.

Chapter Seven

"Why, land's sakes. Who could that be?" Betty asked in surprise as her doorbell rang out over the house. "You expecting anyone, Dora?"

"Who would I be expecting, Betty, really! Must be a package or something," she answered, rising from the kitchen table where Betty had agreed to try and sit up for a while. They'd finished breakfast an hour before, but Betty felt staying up longer would help her regain her strength more quickly.

When Dora swung open the door and saw Robert standing there with a fresh flower arrangement in his hand, she felt a warmth flood through her.

"Hello, Dora. I hope I'm not interrupting anything."

"No, Betty and I are just sitting in the kitchen looking out the sliding glass doors at the bird feeder," she explained. Her feet remained planted firmly in the doorway, still unable to believe this man would continue to be so kind to her after she'd run so hot and cold.

"Are you going to invite me in?" Robert asked hopefully. "I knew if I called first, you'd say 'no,' but I thought if I showed up you'd at least let me in to talk a spell," he explained.

"Sure," she answered, raising her hand to her chest. "You caught me so off-guard that I forgot my manners."

Robert stepped inside as Dora began closing the door. "Your manners?" he questioned with a half-concealed smile.

"All right. Perhaps I do forget them most of the time," she agreed. "I'm more of a 'what you see is what you get' kind of gal."

Robert pushed the flowers he held tightly in his grip in her direction.

"Well, I like what *I* see, as far as that matters," he answered.

"Let me get a vase for those," she said, admiring the bouquet. "Would you like to come in the kitchen to speak to Betty?"

"Sure," he agreed, as the two of them walked back together.

"Betty, you know Robert O'Grady?"

"Yes, from afar, I suppose," Betty answered. "I'm so glad to see you."

"And you as well, Betty. Dora tells me you're making progress and it looks to be that way from here," he added. "You're the vision of good health."

Betty smiled brightly. "Why, thank you."

Dora busied herself with the flowers, arranging them loosely in a crystal vase then poured in just enough water to keep them fresh.

"See what Robert gave us?" Dora asked as she set the vase in the middle of the table.

"My, you've brought Dora flowers!" Betty exclaimed. "Perhaps I should go back to my bedroom so you two can have some privacy. Or, on second thought, perhaps you'd be kind enough to take Dora out of the house, Robert. I know it must be suffocating for her," Betty added. "I'm getting to where I'm perfectly fine alone for a few hours at a time."

"Dora?" Robert questioned.

Dora didn't have to weigh her decision. She wanted to be with Robert. She was more sure of that every day. And an invitation out of the house sounded like just what the doctor ordered for Dora.

"I suppose that would be all right. You sure, Betty?"

"Go ahead. I've got a few calls to return and that show I like is about to come on," she answered.

Dora couldn't help but enjoy the feel of Robert close to her side, the warmth of his hand on the small of her back as he gently led her to his car. He did hesitate when he tried to round the corner to the passenger side with her.

"Oh, I keep forgetting not to get your door. It's hard for me to ignore the manners my wife ingrained in me," he explained.

Dora smiled. She appreciated his not forcing his way on her—or his previous wife's way. It showed he wasn't trying to replace her, but took Dora just the way she was.

"What shall we do? Where would you like to go?" Robert asked.

"Let's take a tour around town again. The times I've done it have been in such a rush, or with trepidation at being back. Maybe this swing around will be better with you driving me."

Robert nodded, reached over and gave her hand a squeeze, then started the car and headed off. As they began touring around, Dora began to see the town in a different way. The easy way of life compared to the bigger city calmed her, and she was aware of a new appreciation she saw in the older neighborhoods with well-kept yards, along with the convenience of the easy drive to the most needed things in town—the grocery store, cleaners, several choice places to eat, and even a branch of the insurance company where she worked so many years of her life. She wondered about the people inside, having a sudden twinge to go back to work again herself.

"It's easy to misjudge a place when you first see it, or when you first return," Robert suggested. "Don't you think?"

"Perhaps," Dora answered without giving away too much. She decided if Robert wanted her, she'd let him go completely out on a limb before she'd let on that the feelings were mutual.

She also noticed he'd turned down the street where he lived.

"Take my situation in life, for example," Robert began. "I have the most wonderful, supportive neighbors on earth. That house there? The Wilson's live there. Salt of the earth kind of people. Retired, too. He plays golf in the next county over most every day. And that house there," he continued, pointing to the next one on the block in close proximity to his, "young couple with three little kids. Schools here are pretty good. And next door and across the street are some of my best friends. They'd do anything in the world for me. Anything. Used to look after our cat when my wife was still alive. Cat's no longer living either," he added pensively.

When he pulled into his driveway, Dora looked at him suspiciously.

"You haven't brought me over here for any funny business, have you?" she asked sternly, yet inside almost hoping he had.

Robert cut the motor and laughed heartily. Dora found she loved the sound of his laughter. It melted all her unhappiness and she found herself smiling in return.

"What's so funny?" she demanded.

"I value my life, Dora Thresher. I wouldn't dare try anything that might result in a blow to my head that would mean instant death—or to any part of my body that I value the use of either."

Dora continued to smile as she let herself out of the car and followed Robert to the front. He fiddled with the keys, then went on inside.

"No, Dora," he finally answered as he closed the door behind her and they stood in his foyer. "I'll be totally honest with you. I want you to stay here after Betty's recuperation. I want a relationship with you and I want you to give us a try. So I'm pulling out all the stops and showing you everything about myself and what I am as a person so you can make up your mind. Now, are you ready for a tour of my home? It'll tell you volumes about me," he put in.

Dora found herself speechless. She'd never met a more down-to-earth and up-front kind of person in all her days. He'd laid it on the line, and she decided she'd like nothing better than to find out more. She stepped forward and discovered in doing so, she'd passed the point of no return. She was in this now, and she'd have to see what came next.

The formal dining room, furnished in antiques, looked as though it hadn't seen any changes for many years. This room felt more like his former wife's territory. But when he led Dora to the den, she immediately sensed Robert's influence—not even a hint of his previous wife's decorating touches.

"So this is one of the places I spend most of my time. It's got my leather easy chair, the big-screen TV, my fishing trophies . . . Sometimes I go fishing and just sit there for hours not caring if I catch anything or not. I just contemplate life, loving being surrounded by nature," he explained.

Moving into the back, Dora found even more surprises as she walked into the modern, fully-equipped kitchen where an array of copper cookware hung spotlessly from a center island. The latest in black appliances appeared almost new, and shelves of cookbooks surrounded much of the back walls in tasteful fashion. Plentiful windows letting in lots of morning light finished off the dazzling effect.

"Your wife must have been some cook," Dora ventured. "I don't cook much. Frozen dinners. You should know that," Dora warned.

Robert smiled down at her as they paused in the beautiful space.

"Actually, I'm the cook in the family. It's like therapy for me. One reason I like to be around Penny's, surrounded by people enjoying the times and luxury of being served good food."

"This whole back area looks new," Dora said, running her hand over the latest in counter design.

"I had the kitchen remodeled last year. Just to my liking. And the sun room off to the left there on the opposite site of this eating area all take advantage of the morning sun. Afternoon's bring in good light, too, but not so intense. Then the deck area that leads around from just off here to the corner of the house is new."

Dora considered all the renovated areas and drew in an appreciative breath. After this part of the tour, she turned around and considered Robert as he leaned against the center work station in the kitchen with his arms crossed.

"So, you did all of this after your wife died? Not before?"

"That's right."

"But why? Who's it for?"

"Well, myself, of course," Robert answered uncrossing his arms and standing upright, placing his hands on his hips.

"My wife passed away, but I'm still very much alive," he countered.

Dora smiled to herself as she recalled the other night and her close proximity to Robert when he'd gotten excited about her.

At this, Robert took two steps forward and circled Dora in his embrace.

"Dora Thresher, I find you quite an exciting and alluring woman, and I won't rest until I've convinced you that this is the place for you to be. Return to this town and I promise you won't be sorry," he said, bringing her closer.

Dora expected the kiss, but the passion underneath it sent her senses reeling. She realized as her heart melted and her boundaries dropped that she was still very much alive herself. It felt good to be this close Robert in this way, she thought.

He placed loving kisses down her neck, and Dora took in a quick breath, loving the feeling, but feeling her boundaries snap back in place.

She pulled away and out of his reach. Robert took a step backward.

"Oh, Dora," Robert began sadly. "I go out this morning fully intending to win you over, and now here I go again, ruining things, pushing you when you clearly aren't ready. I promise you I'm not normally like this. I feel like I'm eighteen again," he explained. "There's no disrespect to it, though, I assure you. But you're just a very alluring woman," Robert explained.

Dora looked at him uncertainly. The battle warring within her had nothing to do with an inappropriate move on his part—if you could even call it that. She'd been so out of the loop that she wouldn't know anything—except that sort of thing always seemed to mess things up. She always found herself pulling away from relationships when they went too far. It always spelled commitment and coupled itself with a past hurt in her mind.

Dora smiled. "I'm sixty-five years old, Robert. Not a young beauty I was forty years ago."

"You're a young beauty to me."

"But I'm not ready for something like this . . . this passion."

"I can wait."

"You might have a long wait, Robert," Dora answered.

"Guess that means you don't want to see the upper floor to the house?" he asked, a smile tugging at the corners of his mouth.

"Oh, no, you don't."

Robert laughed.

"How about I run you by Penny's and pick up lunch to go for you and Betty instead. She'd like that, wouldn't she?"

"Good idea," Dora answered, tipping her chin upwards and marching out of the house, her dignity still completely in-tact, which now that they'd discussed it all, it was. Robert O'Grady would have to go WAY out on a limb before she gave into that final step. That is, if she even decided to stay in town and give it a try.

WAY out, she decided again, as they picked up lunch and headed home.

* * *

"So, you must be making headway with your lady friend, bringing her in and buying lunch to go for the woman AND her sister," Millie said when Robert came in to Penny's to relieve her as shift manager.

"I knew that little trip over with Dora wouldn't get past you, Millie," Robert answered.

"Nothing much does," Millie laughed. "I also saw the smitten look on your face when you were with our little out-of-town visitor."

"Well, then, perhaps you could help me out a bit and give your take on how you think Dora feels about me?" Robert suggested as he rounded the counter and got down to the work at hand.

"Hmmm. You're asking a lot for just a few glances over at a woman I don't even know. Much less tell you what your chances are."

"I thought you were the one who knew everything," Robert teased.

"Okay," Millie answered, shoving a fist onto her hip. "I'll give it my best shot. Let's see," she continued. "First of all, if she wasn't at least a little interested she'd never have gone off with you—even if just to Penny's."

"We've gone out on a dinner date, too. Not just the afternoon rendezvous," he explained.

"So, there you go. She's agreed to more than one time alone with you. She must enjoy your company. Secondly, she drew rather close to you at one point. I saw that. Like she was comfortable with that element of the relationship."

"Uh, huh," Robert said, whisking a few dishes off the counter and into the rising sink to begin the cleaning process.

"Yes, the body language suggested she's attracted to you. I know if the opposite were true, she'd stand way back. Need lots of personal space, you know?"

"Personal space?" Robert questioned, his eyebrows drawing together as he raised upright to get more information.

"Yes, the distance someone wants to keep between themselves and others in their world. As for you, Dora doesn't mind letting you in closer. Touched you on the arm when she wanted to change her order real quick."

"That's cause she wanted to make it a turkey sandwich instead of a burger."

"She could've just said the words instead of the touching."

"I don't know about that."

"What? You're gonna disagree with me on my impressions? Don't you want her to be comfortable with you in that way?"

"Of course. I'm just trying to understand your logic."

"So, finally, the eye contact was flirtatious, in a Dora kind of way."

To this, Robert laughed heartily. "What is a 'Dora' kind of way? Didn't realize you knew her well enough to categorize her manner as 'Dora' like."

"The way I see it, Dora Thresher keeps things close to the vest. Especially her feelings. If you think she's not interested, perhaps you'd better look a little closer. She might need a little extra prodding, not too hard, but enough to show her what you're made of Robert O'Grady. You'd be a fine catch for any woman, and Dora Thresher would be darned lucky to land you," she answered, reaching under the counter for her purse.

"Now, with that said, I'm outta here," Millie announced, giving him a smile and a wink before exiting the front door of Penny's.

Robert busied himself with the current customers. He knew Dora wouldn't be back that afternoon. They'd discussed since she'd been away from Betty for several hours earlier, then she wouldn't be taking her regular break for coffee.

It would make for a long day, he decided, for although he normally enjoyed his work and the people who came in and out during his shift, he could think of nothing at the moment but Dora Thresher and her decision to stay or not stay and whether to give him a chance at this final play at love. Betty was clearly getting better, too. He hoped Dora would give him an answer soon, for his heart had already fallen hard for the lady, and if she up and left with no explanation, like she did so many years ago, he knew his rapidly growing feelings for her would take a beating.

Chapter Eight

Dora began to wonder if the afternoon would ever pass. Normally broken up with a trip to the Diner, she watched the long afternoon sun rays reach across the hardwood floor of her sister's front living room as she tried with little success to get into the book she'd bought at the drug store earlier in the week.

Unfortunately, Dora had picked one with heavy romantic elements in it, and every time the couple in the book would have an intimate exchange, Dora would become even more flustered. Thoughts of Robert O'Grady stayed in the forefront of her brain, driving her crazy.

She finally gave up on the book and picked up a framed picture of Betty, Laird and their daughter Kathy, with her husband and little girl. Dora imagined it must have been taken only a few years before Laird's death, based on the age of Betty's granddaughter, that is.

She looked into Laird's smiling face and grimaced. She felt not even a pang of desire for the man. She saw how even in the staged shot he catered to Betty's need to have someone hover so close. She thought of the lifestyle Betty had described, and realized there would have been quite an incompatibility problem between Dora and Laird if they had been the ones to make a life together.

Dora replaced the frame and took in a deep breath. Coming here had truly been an eye-opener and she wondered what paths her life would have taken if she'd come for a visit years and years before—

instead of just making obligatory phone calls to her sister on major holidays. She may have discovered the truth in what she really wanted and let go of the past sooner. But she also decided her life was not over and it was never too late to straighten out old mistakes and begin to live again.

Her sister had been so quiet that afternoon as well, lending to the boredom Dora felt. She raised up from the wing-back chair and made her way down the hall. Peaking in on Betty, she found her sister fully awake and clearing out a drawer.

"What in the world, Betty? I thought you were asleep."

"My strength is returning, dear. I'm just going stir-crazy doing nothing at all. I figured this old drawer could use a good cleaning. Throwing out things that no longer matter. Like this wrapper from a pair of hose. Who knows how it got in here, and even this crayon! Where did that come from? I'd say this drawer is long overdue for a straightening out. Will you hand me that trash can?" she asked.

Dora placed a wicker waste basket beside Betty. She then plopped down on the bed to join her.

"I was going crazy in there myself. Trying to read, but my mind keeps tossing and turning, keeping straight somebody else's life on the pages even more impossible than trying to figure out my own," Dora said.

"You need to go back to work," Betty proclaimed. "You're much younger than me with so much stamina and willpower. I bet you were a crackerjack manager."

"I am pretty good at bossing people around," Dora chuckled.

Betty laughed and continued to dig through her top dresser drawer.

"Actually," Dora started up, "I didn't do that at all. Bossing people, you know. I'm a pretty good organizer and I always enjoyed explaining things to people, managing the department. My work is what got me through life. It WAS my life. It's too bad they moved the main headquarters half-way across the U.S."

"You could get another job. I wouldn't let this age thing get you down, either. You've got more energy than a team of horses. I've watched you. And you're the 'smart' one. Still just as sharp as you were when you were twenty."

"I don't know about that, but I have a wealth of experience to add to it now," Dora considered.

"See? You might decide to make all kinds of changes," Betty put in, taking her focus off the drawer for a moment.

Dora sat contemplating her words. She added them to her consideration of moving there, and seeing what a relationship with Robert might develop into.

"He's very nice, Dora. Your man friend," Betty said, pitching a wad of trash into the waiting wicker basket.

"Yes, I suppose I'll have to agree with you there," Dora answered.

"He's in love with you."

"What? That's ridiculous. We've barely just met," Dora argued.

"Perhaps you have, but I do know people, and Robert does have a certain look of admiration in his eyes, the way he watches you and all."

"But 'in love', Betty? Isn't that a bit strong?"

"Love has to grow. But the seed is there, Dora. It has to have a seed in the beginning or it will come to nothing. I've spotted the seed. It's taken root and beginning to grow. I've also seen it in you."

"You seem pretty sure of yourself, Betty, especially since you have no idea of my type or anything. All you know is Laird and your relationship with him. That's all in the world you know."

"Not true," Betty said, rising to her feet and walking securely over to a nearby chair. "I've watched people all my life. Certain ones seem like opposites, yet fit so nicely together. Others gravitate to ones with similar interests and such and feed on that. But the characteristics must compliment each other," Betty finished as she eased into the chair and faced Dora.

Dora leaned on the bed post in a more comfortable stance.

"You might have something there," Dora conceded.

Betty paused, glancing down at her hands in her lap a moment, then looked back up at her sister.

"Dora, tell me about your past boyfriends. Surely you haven't shunned all men since your early years."

"There's not that much to tell, Betty. I had plenty of my share of men friends. Some more serious than others. Some lasting for many years. But I wasn't interested in making them my life, and they all wanted more. I just felt I'd be sick to death of them if I had to see any of them every day and every night for the rest of my life."

"Were they all about the same in looks, in what they liked and their interests?"

"Well, most of them were tall with blondish kind of hair, angular features, you know, high cheek bones, light blue eyes, slender. Most were pretty conservative in their dress and not big talkers. Most preferred to let me have my way rather than have a conflict," she explained.

Dora considered her answer a moment and reality hit. It did for her sister as well.

"Dora, you've just described Laird to a 'T.'"

Dora dropped her gaze to the material in the floral bedspread. Nothing was said for a few minutes until Betty spoke up again.

"What was Charles like when you dated him over that Christmas break?"

"Betty, that was so long ago. I just don't know. What difference does it make?" she said sourly.

"Humor me."

Dora paused, making a huffy noise, then gave in.

"Okay, fine. He was lively, full of ideas of his own, knew what he wanted, where he was going. Not that tall, just medium height with more muscle to his chest, I guess. He always teased me and wouldn't let me get away with anything. We had fun. But that was all. I didn't love him. I was just attracted to him. His personality too, I suppose," Dora answered, surprising herself. It was the first time she'd ever admitted even to herself that she had been attracted to Charles in the beginning.

"And he was your own age, too, wasn't he? Completely available while Laird was somewhat unattainable for you. A man you hardly even knew, it seems to me. Were you truly attracted to Laird like you think you were?"

Dora considered her sister, then finally answered.

"At this stage, I really don't know much of anything anymore," Dora admitted. "Perhaps I fantasized about a dream man that never really existed. Being 'in love' at such an early age can fool you."

"It wasn't based on reality, now, was it, Dora? I think if you go see Charles sometime, you'd see that if you were really so in love with Laird, you'd never have given Charles a second look, much less go out with him while Laird and his family were away on Christmas vacation. Now would you? And I have one more thing to suggest to you, Dora, dear."

Dora gave a snort. "What is that?" she demanded.

"Well, consider your attraction to Robert O'Grady. I suspect he's much more like Charles than Laird. He probably speaks what's on his mind, knows what he wants and isn't afraid to ask for it, has a good life, lively with plenty of conversation for the customers at Penny's. About the same build as Charles, and probably the type that is really what would make you happy."

"No relationship with my suitors has made me happy so far, why would I think Robert could do so?"

"These are my thoughts on this. I suspect you've been trying to re-create a Laird of your own all these years by being drawn to men who look like and act like Laird, but they're not Laird. There's not even a Laird that you would've liked. My Laird loved to be depended on, waited on me, revolved his life around me. I made him feel needed. You're too independent for such a union to have made for a good fit—for either of you. So, stop looking in the wrong direction and give Robert O'Grady the time of day, Dora. I believe you'll be pleasantly surprised," she added.

Dora stared at her sister for a moment. Here Betty was looking kindly back at her when clearly Dora had coveted her husband all these years. No one had ever suggested the theories Betty had just laid out for her to consider, either. Finally Dora said the only words that made any sense to her at all.

"Well, Betty, maybe the world has had it wrong all this time. Seems to me, *you're* the real 'smart one' in the family."

* * *

Dora took a walk around the block after her conversation with her sister, contemplating all the information that seemed to have come in tidal waves, threatening to overtake her. The outing seemed to have cleared her head a little, with only bits and pieces left to work through.

When she went back inside, she was surprised to find Betty in the kitchen sorting through the array of frozen entrees Dora had bought at the store.

"Just what are you doing on your feet again?" Dora boomed entering the room.

"I'm looking to see what I want for dinner," Betty explained.

"Well, it's not quite time yet," she said.

"Busy bossing me around, are you?" Betty laughed.

"Somebody needs to monitor your activities since you've taken this sudden urge to get well in an all-fire hurry."

"I am getting well. I've also got some people coming over in an hour and I have a suggestion."

"What's that?"

"Go to Penny's for dinner. I can stick this tray in the microwave with the best of them, and I think you need to go boss around somebody else," her sister said, turning around wearing a broad smile.

Dora gave out a hoot. "If you mean bossing around Robert O'Grady, I can tell you he wouldn't stand for that for more than two seconds."

"Yes, dear. I know that. It's just the kind of man you need. Now go put on a dress or something extra pretty. Show him you're warming up to him for once."

"I'll keep on this pants suit, thank you. I won't start trying to dress up for anybody. But I will make my way over there. Since you've got company coming. Anybody special?"

"My company?" Betty chirped.

"Yes, what's the big secret?"

"I'll tell you when you get back. Now scoot," Betty said.

Chapter Nine

As Dora made her way into Penny's, she noted that many of the tables were filled with early bird diners. Dora'd had to get used to eating sooner in the day than she'd been used to before coming to suit Betty's needs, but she had no idea so many people were on the same schedule.

Dora found herself having to choose the one of the two remaining stools at the counter if she wanted to be waited on at all. Glancing behind her, she also saw that a pretty, young waitress she'd never seen before was handling most of the tables and booths on the floor, leaving Robert and one other cook to take care of the back of the counter area.

Robert did a double-take when he saw her seated at the end of the counter and flashed her a big smile. He began humming a tune right after, causing the cook to glance back at Dora to see what had made the change in Robert's happy demeanor.

"I'll be right with you," he promised, as he whizzed by with two meat loaf specials in tow. She saw the way the middle aged couple joked and laughed with him as he placed the platters in front of them. He then turned and juggled several other duties, seemingly simultaneously, between setting another coffee pot to brew, picking up and delivering another order, and refilling a young woman's glass of iced tea. He then positioned himself in front of Dora, bringing her a glass of water.

"To what do I owe this honor, Dora Thresher? Two times in one day!"

"I was hungry," Dora said flatly, giving in to a small smile that made its way across her face.

"Then what can I bring you. Meat loaf special? Or some other treat on our menu?"

"Well, if you say it's good, then I believe you. Especially after getting a peak at that gourmet kitchen of yours. I'll concede to your expertise in food."

"It's the best. All our specials are—all the food. Trust me."

Dora gave him a reproving look. "I'll trust you on the meat loaf recommendation," she answered. "Other things may take longer," she said.

"I can wait. But I'll put in your order for the meat loaf straightaway—so you won't have to wait," he said with a grin and zipped off.

Dora watched Robert, thinking about what her sister had said. She did enjoy his high energy level, his broad chest, easy laugh and ready smile. He was a gregarious type, making everyone happy just to be there. She admired it. It wasn't in her character make-up to be like that, but she liked others who had the talent. He was a genuine person who loved people. Not a bad catch at that, Dora reminded herself.

Within minutes Robert had whisked a full plate of food in front of her.

"Well, there goes my girlish figure," she argued.

"I bet you don't have to worry about what you eat at all, do you Dora?"

"Eating like this I would," she boasted.

"Be back a little later," he said, and he was off again, working away.

Robert had a confidence and a strength that Laird never had, she realized. Laird did need someone who needed him. Robert appeared to be perfectly aware that he had so much to offer the world that he wasn't dependent on someone like her sister, Betty. He'd be just right for her sternly independent manner—especially after all these years of being on her own, making her own decisions and choices.

Which reminded her that she had a decision to make very soon. Betty was getting better every day, and the choice was Dora's to leave or stay. Watching Robert began to give her new resolve and understanding of the past.

Suddenly he was before her again, leaning close so those nearby couldn't eavesdrop so easily.

"Got a few errands I've got to run tomorrow morning before my shift, but would you be available the day after for another lunch date?" he asked.

Dora nodded in agreement. She also noticed the older gentleman next to her give her a quick sideways glance. He appeared to be the only one who'd overheard the invitation, and he staunchly took a sip of coffee and then looked straight ahead, letting them know their secret was safe with him.

There was only one last bit of business she needed to take care of before making that final choice. And she would put that off no longer. Tomorrow morning she would go see Charles. She had to do it, or else she may never be able to make that final move.

*   *   *

Dora scaled the familiar front steps with trepidation. Her nerve had suddenly left her as though a gust of wind had come upon her, leaving her speechless as the door swung wide to reveal Charles' manly statue.

"Guess I was the last person you were expecting to see this morning," Dora began.

"Actually, I was hoping you'd show up sooner than later. Won't you come in?" Charles ventured.

"No. Out here on the porch is better. What I've got to say is private. No offense to your wife, but it *is* personal all the same."

"I understand perfectly. Let me just let her know and bring you out a glass of iced tea. It's a little warmer today than usual," he added, returning through the front door.

Dora found herself sinking into the soft cushion of a white wicker chair and taking in the view. A sameness filled the place, even though progress had brought some changes. Charles had inherited the family home, and it was here many years ago in the middle of winter, late at night, that the two of them had sat enjoying each other's company. Christmas lights had formed a line around the houses the last time, she remembered.

Charles appeared again this time carrying two glasses of iced tea; one with lemon, one without.

"This one with the lemon's for you. With just a touch of sugar."

Dora took the chilled glass that tinkled with ice surrounded by the deep color of tea. Sipping a little, she turned to him shaking her head.

"You must have a memory like an elephant. Over forty-five years and the man remembers how I take my iced tea. Actually, I'm more of a coffee drinker now, but this sure brings back memories," she added.

Charles smiled and nodded. "Sarah said to take our time. That she totally understood what came before her marriage to her husband was none of her never mind."

"You've got an understanding wife. I think I'd march right out and plant myself between the two of us, if it were my husband and a former girlfriend—if you could even call me that."

"Yes, Dora. I consider you that. But I certainly wish you'd explain a few things to me. It'd sort-of ease my conscious."

"Ease your conscious? Whatever about? We only saw one another for a few months. Never got serious," Dora demanded.

"Let's get right to it, shall we?" Charles suggested. "What made you up and leave town the way you did—without so much as a word of warning?"

"Laird and Betty, of course," Dora spat.

"I never thought you and Laird were an item and that was over anyway, Dora. Besides that, you may never have been serious about me, but I was under the impression we had something going. Something we could've maybe built a future on," he explained.

"What in tarnation gave you that idea?"

"You seemed to enjoy my company. We got along well. Had a group of friends we both liked to socialize with from high school and the church group, of course. Where did Laird fit in, will you tell me? You didn't see him nearly as long as you saw me."

"Well, after Laird went off to school, I got one measly friendly-type letter. Then nothing. Next thing I knew I had a new brother-in-law. The true love of my life," Dora ground out.

"Laird was the love of your life?" Charles echoed flatly.

"Well, yes. He was. So, there's your answer. That's why I left."

"Was I just someone you chose only to pass the time away with?"

"I suppose I gravitated to you because you were Laird's cousin. If I couldn't be close to him, then you were the next best thing," Dora declared.

"I don't believe that, Dora. Not for one second. Why, Laird and I were complete opposites. And if you were so in love with Laird, why'd you even agree to a date with me? His own cousin," he argued.

"You told him, didn't you? That's what I figured," Dora put in. "You went behind my back and sabotaged my future with Laird. He got even and took out my sister. Well, thank you all very much. I missed out on the one man who was right for me—at least I've always thought so," Dora complained. "And I'd wondered if you were behind it all these years. Now I have my answer. I can't live in the same town with you or Betty now that I know the truth."

Charles rose to his feet. His statue did remind her of Robert O'Grady somehow, same build and manner of standing with his shoulders pushed back in a way that showed the world he meant business. After he'd taken this stance, Dora felt a little less sure of her self—normally so in control. Now she imagined a lecture or scolding was about to take place. She was right, too, she realized, as Charles began a no-nonsense speech that she believed he'd rehearsed for many years.

"See here. I'll tell you what happened way back then, but now that it's perfectly clear where you're coming from, I'm gonna put the truth out there where you can't miss it."

"Go ahead," Dora challenged. "Take your best shot. You couldn't do more damage than you did years ago. I should've never buddied around with all of you. You made Laird think there was something to us, didn't you?"

"Oh, Dora. Laird took you out a time or two, but no one, including Laird, gave it a serious thought. Especially Betty. Had she known you had eyes for the man, she'd have never agreed to go out with him. Sweetest woman I know, save my Sarah. Only you had such delusions."

"Delusions, now is it?"

"Yes, my dear, I'm afraid so. Laird and I were confidants, you see."

"And you led him to believe you and I . . ."

"Oh, snap it shut for a minute, Dora. Do you want the real information or do you want to just keep on harboring your own, made-up reality you've believed for all these years. Yes or no?"

"Go on," Dora answered, placing her iced tea onto the wicker table.

"Thing is, Laird began talking about your sister, Betty, as soon as he realized she would give him the time of day. He always imagined she was out of reach, being a couple of years older, you know. So, he goes off to school and suddenly there Betty is on campus and they're on equal footing. It was then he had enough confidence to ask her out. Laird was in love with Betty from the beginning. But not with you, Dora. With your sister."

Dora felt the pinch of the truth and tears threatened to surface. However, she would not under any circumstances let Charles see her cry over such a thing that happened over forty plus years ago. In fact, this little tidbit had been eating at her for all those years as well. She'd simply lost out on her true judgment and harbored a grudge for most of her adult life.

"I suppose I'd rather have thought the other scenario than admit to myself that he didn't love me."

"They call that sort of thing 'denial' these days, Dora. That means you were . . ."

"I know what denial means, for heaven's sake," Dora hurled back.

"So that's the truth of it," Charles finished.

Dora sat contemplating his words.

"So if Laird was confiding to you all that time about Betty, why didn't you talk to him about me?" Dora inquired.

"Who said I didn't?"

"There you have it! That's where the rubber meets the road. You gave him the idea we were an item and he had a clear conscious to pursue my sister," Dora announced.

"Blessed be. Are you dense? Didn't your parents always say you were the 'smart one' in the . . ."

"Oh, I don't want to hear it," Dora broke in. She suddenly remembered telling Betty less than 24 hours before that she could gain that title since her words on this same subject were so insightful.

Charles crossed his arms over his chest.

"What do you want to hear, Dora? You came over this morning for some reason. I'm the one who began my barrage of questions right off. Now, what can I do for you?"

He was right, Dora thought. I haven't gotten all the answers I need. Not to make a clear decision. The right decision. She needed to make the past smooth out so she could leave it behind for the first time in her life.

"Well, all I wanted to know is mixed up in what we've been talking about. I figured all this was a misunderstanding between me and Laird, and revenge, and your sticking your nose in it and telling Laird we were dating, making him ask out Betty—all of that. Then things snowballing with them . . . I've heard pieces of the answers, but what is it you told Laird that made him ask out Betty?"

Dora put the questions right out there. She'd gotten Betty's take on things. Found out more than she'd wanted, at least at the time. But these things had to come out. They just had to.

"Dora, I didn't get in that much talking with Laird. Long-distance calls cost money, especially back then when there wasn't much to go around for a college man. And I went up to see him only once. Your name came up just a time or two. First time he'd asked if I'd seen you around. I told him I was interested in you romantically. He seemed pleased, told me you were a nice girl."

"It was an act. Surely he was sore at you," Dora began.

"Let me finish. He also said he'd never gotten to know you too well, but from what he had, if you turned out to be anywhere near as nice as your sister, then I'd be a lucky man to get you. You see? Laird never considered that you had a romance together. Only a light friendship."

"He kissed me!" Dora spoke up.

"So what? A good night kiss?"

Dora opened her mouth to protest but shut it. Truly, there was very little that had transpired.

"Dora, he wasn't concerned about my seeing you. And he didn't appear that interested—nor felt it interfered whatsoever with his own love of his life. That's what he called Betty, you know. After the first date."

"Okay. That's the end of it then," Dora answered, jumping to her feet. "I've been living in a dream world that kept me from finding happiness with a true, committed man all this time because of my own stupidity."

Charles chuckled and shook his head.

Dora jerked up her purse and stared at him.

"You find something humorous, Charles?" she demanded.

"Dora, you can't fool me for a second. Never could. Except for making me believe something was between us, but I have finally figured that out right here and now."

"Oh, boy. I didn't know I was coming to see a 'Mr. Know-It-All,'" Dora said sarcastically.

"Well, it all just clicked into view like one of those old-fashioned kaleidoscopes that you twist and find a picture that falls together?"

"Hmmm. Why do I get the feeling I'm not gonna like this?"

"I can't control your feelings, Dora, I can only tell it like I see it."

"You sound like Robert now."

"Robert O'Grady? Yes. We are a bit alike in that manner," he said, pausing.

"But back to this subject, Dora. I think with your independent streak, you used your imagined injustice of Laird marrying your sister, thinking I'd busted the two of you up, that allowed you to keep all other men at a safe distance. Why, you didn't want to settle down with Laird, or me, for that matter. You wanted your freedom. You enjoyed making it on your own. You were like your father more than your mother in that regard. Now, Betty took after your mother. She reveled in making Laird the center of her universe. She waited on him and him on her. They were like two peas in a pod."

"Spare me," Dora broke in.

"No, you're gonna hear me out, Dora. Now, you've been seeing other men all this time, I imagine?"

"Of course. What do you take me for?"

"Oh, quit with the ruffled feathers attitude. Another ploy to get me off the subject."

Dora smiled. Charles was the type that didn't let her get away with anything. Just like Robert.

"And you've fooled yourself all this time in thinking Laird was the very man you wanted. Probably went so far as to see men you thought fit his description. Sort of a substitute, but it didn't do it for you. You know why?"

Dora put her palm up to her brow. "You're going to tell me that, too?"

"Because you'd never have been satisfied with Laird or anyone like him. That's why you dated me. You were already bored with Laird. But he was Betty's cup of tea. So, drop this nonsense with the past once and for all, Dora. This bitterness doesn't become you, and it hasn't gotten you anywhere."

Dora let out a long sigh. "Oh, Charles. Perhaps you're right. I enjoyed being on my own. I didn't want to share my 'space' as they call it now, with anybody. So I had long relationships with men who didn't want any more than I did. When they got that notion in their heads, I let them loose."

"And since you'd saddle yourself with men who didn't give any zing to life for you, it was easy. So drop the act, Dora, and get on with what you want."

"What makes you think I want something different now, Charles?" Dora asked, now interested in every theory her old friend had. He'd been on target so far.

"Robert is what you want now, Dora. Robert O'Grady."

Dora grunted. "What makes you think that? Just because he's an available widower in town not too far from my age?" she said with a huff, crossing her arms.

Charles chuckled. "I saw the way the two of you looked at each other over at the Diner. You've been out with him, haven't you?"

"So what if I have?" Dora boomed.

"Well, you couldn't be interested in a finer man. I'd say he's just right for you. He's gentle, yet straightforward and honest. He'll say what's on his mind and won't let you get away with any more than I would," Charles added. "He won't let the word games get in the way of a relationship with you."

"I don't play games."

"Only with yourself, Dora. Only in your thinking, as we've discussed for the past half-hour."

Dora tilted her chin upward, not going to be pressed into admitting the obvious.

"What else do you think of Robert?"

"Besides being one of impeccable character, he's an interesting guy. Likes people. Gets along with everybody. A man who didn't fall apart when his wife died. Has plenty of personal reserve, you know, having so many interests on the side. He's just independent enough to be a great match for you, Dora. He'd give you plenty of room."

"Not like Laird?"

"Nope. Not a bit, except that he's a man of honor and integrity, like Laird was. But that's about where the similarities end."

"You sure have high praise for this Robert O'Grady."

"Most everybody in town would tell you the same. So, you do like him, don't you?"

"Yes," she snapped. "More than I'd like to, actually."

"Enough to stick around town to see how it works out?"

Dora pushed herself out of the chair and stood by the railing of the porch, looking out at the neighborhood.

"I don't know, Charles. I'd go crazy living with Betty. She's so needy. I'm sorry, but that's the blame truth."

"Let Betty figure out her own life, Dora. She's about to a point in her recuperation that she can do that without you."

"But I'd have to live someplace else than with her. And what would I do here? Sit around and look out at the trees?"

"I've been thinking about both those things, Dora. Just a suggestion, but I happen to know they're looking for a new office manager for that insurance company branch down the street. With your background, they'd love to have you."

"Oh, I'm too old to get a position like that. They don't seem to trust you once you start getting a few gray hairs," Dora argued.

"Not so. Already talked to them. The job's yours, if you'll take it."

"Charles! Behind my back, fooling with my life? You've gone too far this time."

"Put a sock in it, Dora. A simple conversation with a friend of mine I see regularly. Don't make a federal case out of it."

Dora smiled. Though she'd imagined him to be the enemy, Charles had been a good friend all these years. He still was.

"Okey-dokey. I gotta go," she said suddenly. "I'll think about what you've said," Dora announced, making her way down the front steps.

"Give my best to Sarah," she added before clipping down the walkway and stepping into her car. Charles had shed a whole new light on many things, and Dora's mind was racing.

Chapter Ten

Later that afternoon Dora watched Robert intently. She'd made a trip over to the insurance company, and sure enough, they wanted to hire her on the spot. Seemed the last office manager left them in a lurch, through no fault of her own. Her husband was transferred out of the area, and they had to pack up and leave pretty quick to take advantage of the opportunity.

Dora discovered there was much work to be done at the office, and it stirred up a sense of excitement in her to consider going back to work. If she *did* stay, and if she *did* take the job, then with Robert on the second shift at Penny's they'd only see each other on the weekends and at scattered times during the day.

Dora quickly decided that would suit her just fine. She'd been used to having her time as her own, and she could adjust to that type of arrangement easily.

"More coffee?" Robert asked, pausing at her table during a short break in activity.

"No thanks. I don't want to be too jittery. I'm already a little on edge today."

"Oh?" Robert asked, sliding into the seat opposite her. "How so?"

Dora considered his face, handsome in a rugged kind of way. Not the pretty type of features that Laird had. Laird. She would no longer think on the man, she decided at that moment. Not then, not ever.

"I've done some soul-searching about my sister and the past, that's all," she answered. "Think I've straightened out a lot of years, all in a day's work," she added with a smile.

"Now, look at that. A genuine smile across that pretty face."

At this Dora found herself blush. It felt good, and the baggage of the past seemed to have been left somewhere on the road between Charles' house and hers. That felt good, too.

"Are you still up for my coming by late tomorrow morning?" Robert asked.

"Yes. I'll be expecting you," Dora said.

"Good. Guess I need to see to Mrs. Smithers over there. She's looking all around the counter for something. Probably wants more napkins," he said, giving Dora's arm a squeeze before heading off.

As Dora left Penny's she still enjoyed the warmth of the small touch. She'd look forward to the next outing with Robert. She'd be ready. She was finally ready for Robert O'Grady to come into her life.

* * *

"Dora, I have something to tell you," Betty began over dinner.

"Hmmm. I don't like the tone of this. Is something wrong?"

"I hope you won't see it that way."

"I think I'm getting even worse vibes by the minute. What is it, Betty?"

"There's no other way to say it than to come right out with it," she answered, pausing indefinitely.

"So?" Dora urged. "What?"

"Well, you see, I've asked a woman from the church and her teenage daughter to move in with me. They're a little strapped for income and I've got so much room here. The full basement we finished out for Kathy when she was a teenager is of no use now, except for that small storage area which isn't in the way anyway . . ."

"You expect me to live here with another woman and a teen-age girl? Land's sakes!" Dora said. "No wonder you were afraid to tell me."

"No, I didn't think you'd like that sort of living arrangement, but I'm used to people being around, and she's a nurse by day, and can lend me extra support if I ever need it, and I'll lend a stabilizing factor to the girl by being here when she gets home from school. I really like them both, and we've always gotten along famously during church functions. It'll be perfect, don't you see?" Betty chirped.

"You don't need anybody now that I'm around," Dora added uneasily.

"You won't be here forever, Dora. You have a life of your own. You'd go crazy cooped up here with me day after day, besides."

Dora sat a moment, taking in the news.

"Yes, Betty," Dora conceded. "It does sound right for you. You'll have a live-in family to care for and to care for you—be of help to a growing girl during a troubled time in life."

"I knew you'd understand," Betty said, finishing off the rest of the baby carrots on her plate.

Dora considered her sister's solution, remembering Charles' prediction that Betty would find a way of taking care of herself. She realized all of her remaining arguments for staying had all dissolved before her and Dora knew there was no other answer but to claim a life here. Return for love's sake and a happiness she'd never found in that town before. Knowing she'd just made her decision for sure, she spoke up.

"Ah, Betty, I suppose I have a little news myself," she began.

"Yes?" her sister asked cheerily.

"Yeah, I've decided to sell my house and move here again."

"Oh, my!" her sister exclaimed, clapping her hands together. "What marvelous news! Have you told Robert?"

"No," Dora snapped. "And don't you say a word to a soul. I'll tell him in my own good time."

"When might that be?" Betty asked, trying to stifle her broad smile.

"He's picking me up tomorrow late morning. Maybe then," she added.

"You won't be able to keep that news to yourself. Once you make up your mind about something, you go for it."

"Maybe it's him that's going for me," Dora put in.

"It won't take long for him to round you up for good."

"I'm no pushover," Dora announced.

"No, but you want Robert O'Grady in your life. You're just going to make him think it is his idea at running after you. I may not have been very close to you in our early years, but I'm beginning to get to know you better now," Betty said, pausing. "And I'm looking forward to getting even closer now that we'll be together again," she said, her focus turning to her empty plate.

Dora noticed the sheen to her sister's eyes before she'd averted her gaze. She tentatively raised her hand to the tabletop, reached over, and gave Betty's hand a quick squeeze. The two of them smiled knowingly at each other, then Dora jumped up to do the dishes.

* * *

"Missed you this afternoon after school," Robert said to his young teenage friend, Wes.

"Had to do some errands for my Dad," he explained, munching on some fries. "What do you think of my date?" he whispered, as the pretty girl Wes had brought to the Diner disappeared into the ladies room.

"Very nice. First date?"

"Second, actually. How about you and that new woman in town. Dora, right?"

"Seeing her as regularly as she'll let me," Robert explained with a wink. "She's a tough filly to break, let me tell you."

Wes laughed easily. "Guess you'll be sad after she leaves town," he added.

Robert leaned in his direction. "Hoping I can convince her not to. That there's something here to stay for, if you know what I mean."

"Oh, sure. I know. You want her."

"Well, that's one way to put it."

"Guess you're gonna have to move pretty fast, though, huh?"

"How so?" Robert asked.

"My date, Shirley? She and her mom are moving in with Betty, Dora's sister, next Monday. Her mom's a nurse and she'll take care of Betty from then on. In case she needs something, that is. Shirley is excited. She never has had much family and thinks she's getting a new grandmother when they move in with Betty. She's always been real nice to her."

At that moment, his date, Shirley, swiveled back onto the high stool at the counter and smiled brightly at Robert.

"Oh, I didn't realize our food had arrived," she said sweetly. "You shouldn't have waited," she cooed to Wes.

"Just ate a fry or two," he said, smiling brightly back at her.

"Shirley, I'm a friend of Dora's. I hear you and your mom are moving in with them all next week," Robert began uncertainly.

"That's right. We were only renting where we were and it wasn't that great. Now we'll have a really nice house with a built-in grandmother. Betty's so nice," the girl added.

"But won't you have two new grandmothers?" Robert asked.

The girl looked up from her plate, wide-eyed with a french fry perched in her hand.

"Whatever do you mean, Mr. O'Grady?"

"Dora's living there right now, too. With her sister, Betty."

"Oh, yes. Her sister. Mom says she's moving out next week, probably. Guess Betty is getting along well enough to stay by herself during the day. I get home in the afternoon, and Mom will be making diners and things. It's all part of the arrangement."

"Your mom said Dora is moving out next week? When did she tell you that?" Robert asked, hoping his alarm wasn't apparent.

"Oh, tonight before Wes picked me up. She thinks Dora might even decide to leave by this Sunday since we're moving in Monday."

After she answered that last question, the girl bit into her cheeseburger and turned her focus to Wes. Robert gave the couple a wink and headed off to wait on and visit with other customers.

It would be a long night of tossing and turning, he realized. He figured Dora was going to drop the bomb on him the next morning when he picked her up. He decided he'd spend the rest of his thinking hours coming up with the best strategies for making Dora stay. He didn't know quite yet what magic words he'd use, but he had to come up with something. At this stage he just couldn't let Dora go. Not now. Not ever.

* * *

Dora found she took more time than usual to select an outfit for the day. It aggravated her to realize she was doing the very thing Betty advised her to the day before—get all fixed up for the man. She'd protested greatly not 24 hours before, now she found herself taking extra pains in her appearance. She argued with herself as to why, though. Robert accepted her just "as is."

Still, she found it rather fun putting on make-up with care, and she smoothed down the front of her handsome dark purple pants outfit.

When the doorbell rang, she checked her hair once more, then turned to go let Robert in. To her surprise, she heard Betty answering the door.

"Why, come on in, Robert," Betty said in an upbeat tone.

"Good morning, Betty. It's good to see you on your feet."

"Yes, I'm making remarkable progress. I suppose it happens that way. Slow at first and in the middle, then all of the sudden I'm racing down the track full speed."

Dora rounded the corner at that moment. "Now, Betty, I don't believe the doctor would permit you to go full trot anywhere. Take it easy and go sit back down or you'll have a set-back," she warned.

Betty just laughed in response and obeyed Dora's directives.

"I have your lunch all set out for you. I know it's only 11 a.m., but whenever you're ready, it's there for you."

"Thank you, Dora. You've been so kind all these weeks of taking care of me. But don't let me keep you two. Go on and have a good time," she said, shooing them both away with a wave of her hand.

Dora winked at her sister and headed out the front door. She noticed Robert looked particularly handsome that morning in dress pants and a nice knit shirt that showed off his broad chest. She wondered if he'd put the same thought into what to wear to impress her as she had him. Realizing he didn't normally wear pants that nice to work, what with getting food on them or something, that he probably had.

"Thought we'd swing by that fancy restaurant I took you to for diner on our first date," Robert suggested.

Dora eased into the front seat. She had other plans.

"Say, Robert, I appreciate that and all, but I'd rather have a sandwich at that place on Broad Street.

"You mean Hal's in the business district?"

"Yes, it's the one near that insurance agency?"

"Oh, okay. If that's where you want to go."

Robert turned the car in that direction and Dora noted he acted much more nervous that ever before. He kept clearing his throat and opening his mouth to speak, but stopped. After several times of this, Dora wondered what was up.

"Something on your mind, Robert?"

"Me? Oh, I don't know. How about you. Anything you want to talk about, Dora?"

For a brief moment Dora wondered if Betty had secretly picked up the phone and called Robert, letting him in on the fact that she was moving to town permanently. She considered the possibility, then shook her head. No, Betty would not do that to her. It was her news to tell, but she wasn't quite ready to just blurt it out right there in the car.

"No, nothing in particular," she answered.

They drove in an awkward silence the short distance over to the sandwich shop. As they passed the one-story insurance agency building, Dora smiled knowingly to herself. By next week, she'd be sitting behind the desk of the front office, making sense of the chaos that had been left in the wake of no one being at the helm for so long.

"You're smiling. Does it have anything to do with me?" Robert asked, breaking the quiet.

"No, I was thinking of something that, well . . ." Dora trailed off. Telling him this tidbit would be giving away the full news of her staying and working at the job. Instead, she decided to go off on the tangent that was at least related to it. Betty's fast recovery was making Dora's working again possible.

"Well, what?" Robert urged as he pulled into the small parking lot and quickly found a space.

"I was thinking how good it is that Betty is finally getting well. She's almost totally functional, if she takes it easy and doesn't try to do too much too fast. She'll have to monitor herself, though. The patient is the only one who can keep themselves well by following the doctor's orders. But Betty's almost back to normal and I'm really glad," Dora finished as they opened the glass door to the small restaurant.

Dora had been drawn to the little sandwich shop because it was within walking distance to her new workplace. She wanted to check it out with Robert the first time around. Maybe he'd be able to come eat lunch with her once she'd started to work, she'd thought.

She'd also imagined this restaurant would be a great place to let him in on her decision. But once inside, Dora realized by the close proximity of all the tables, that it wouldn't be the proper place to tell Robert her news. She didn't want to tell the whole town, after all, seeing the gathering crowd of early lunch-goers already seated and munching on their meals.

"Guess that table in the back is the only one. Since you're fond of turkey, I think they've got a turkey club that's one of their specialties," Robert suggested as he headed toward the counter to place their orders.

"Fine. I'll get the table. Get me some iced tea. With lemon, and a little sugar," she added, heading to claim the available space before someone else did.

When Dora sat down, she went over her speech again of how she'd tell Robert and what to say. She knew he'd be pleased, but she didn't want to give him the impression that he was the only reason she was staying. Though her sister and the new job being other factors, if Robert wasn't in the picture, she would definitely not have even considered it. Still, she wasn't going to play easy-to-get, so she'd have to phrase it just right, she reminded herself.

Dora watched him, seeing how nice he looked in his black dress slacks. She imagined he must have been an athlete in his early years, and had definitely kept up with physical activity from then on. For a man any age, Robert O'Grady was a catch, she decided.

When he turned back with the tray, she quickly diverted her gaze to a laminated insert propped on the table advertising their sandwich selections. She picked it up as though she'd been giving it her full attention since he'd been up at the counter.

"Here's lunch," Robert announced as he began placing the plastic trays of food onto the table.

"That was fast," Dora answered.

Lunch went rather silently, making Dora wonder what was troubling Robert. Usually positive and full of talk to anyone close, Dora noted he was rather reserved.

"Anything wrong, Robert?" she finally asked.

"No, I suppose not. I'm just glad to be spending time with you, Dora, wishing I'd gotten to know you when you first moved in with Betty, instead of half-way through her recovery."

"Betty was in no shape for me to even take a break in the beginning," she explained. "To Penny's Diner or anywhere but the grocery store. Even then, I'd get the next door neighbor to come in for the short time I was gone."

"I suppose even if I had met you earlier, you were all wrapped up with caring for Betty. Didn't have the time or energy to devote to much else, but, well, I was just thinking it would have been so nice to have spent more time with you. Now it seems Betty is on the mend," he added.

Normally this would have been the ideal time for Dora to tell him her news. However, with the four businessmen seated so close to them that Dora felt they were practically in her lap, she wasn't about to let Robert in on the fact that she was staying in town even though Betty was almost well. Much less give away the more personal information of telling Robert part of the reason she was staying had to do with her growing feelings for him.

Instead Dora just nodded in response.

This seemed to make Robert go even more into himself, and Dora re-thought her news. Perhaps Charles had gone over and opened his big mouth to Robert, suggesting Dora might stay in town because of him. Charles knew that she was heading in that direction, and he probably got wind from his friend that she'd accepted the insurance company job.

That was it, Dora realized. And now Robert felt ill-at-ease that she'd made a life's choice to return, all become she was falling in love with him. Obviously he wasn't that pleased with her decision, she decided. Yes, it would be just like Charles, who never could keep his mouth shut, she thought. Once again, Charles had messed up her life.

At this, Dora crumpled up the thin paper wrapper from the sandwich into a tight ball, then rose to put away her tray.

Robert looked surprised, having just popped the last bite of his sandwich into his mouth.

"I'll get that," he mumbled through his full mouth.

"No need. I can care for myself," Dora answered as she returned the tray to the proper place.

Robert was on her heels, struggling to get out the door in time to hold it open just a hair before she'd scrambled out on her own. As she hurried to open the passenger door, Robert rounded the car and placed his large hand over the frame, closing it back before she could open it wide.

"What's wrong?" Dora snapped.

"I'd like to ask you the same thing. You're doing it again," Robert said.

"Doing what?"

"Getting all bossy on me for no apparent reason. You get your dander up and heaven help anyone who gets in your way."

"I can take care of myself. I explained that to you early on. Don't need anyone to carry my tray, open my door . . ."

"I know what this is about, Dora, but I don't want to discuss it here in this parking lot with all these people coming and going. Get in."

"Where are we going?" she asked, sliding in.

"To the park."

"I don't want to go to the park."

"Well, that's where you're going nevertheless."

Dora folded her arms over her chest, giving out a put-upon huff. The man always knew how to tame her, she thought. No one else ever had, but the way he did it was endearing, somehow. It would make it even harder to bear if he had, in fact, heard the news and didn't want to take the responsibility of her staying.

Moments later Robert pulled into a shaded parking space and cut the motor.

"My dear, we're going for a walk, and I have a few things to say and you're going to listen."

"Yes, sir!" she called out, as he rounded the car standing with his hands behind his back, waiting for her to open her own car door.

Dora scooted out and slammed the door behind her.

"I didn't want to offend you by opening it," he explained.

Dora couldn't help the smile that crept onto her face. Robert was so much fun, even in a maddening kind of way.

They made their way down the sidewalk underneath the shade of the many expansive oaks that filled the city park. Dora realized the trees must be very old to have such a large base and expand so high in the sky. She took in a deep breath, wondering when Robert would speak up about what he knew.

She had envisioned telling him in the restaurant when they were relaxed, face-to-face. She imagined that once outside the structure he would hug her close and tell her it's what he'd been hoping for every minute of every day. But from the look of concern he wore as they slowly walked down the worn paths of the park sidewalk, she realized things weren't as she'd imagined. Again. She'd returned for love, and this happened again.

"Dora?" Robert ventured.

"Yes?" she asked, continuing to walk slowly forward.

"Look, can we go over to that park bench to talk? I'd like to discuss this where we can look at each other instead of where we're going."

Dora agreed compliantly and sat on the wooden bench. She would let Robert do all the talking, for she was not going to put her feelings on the line here. If he wanted her . . .

"Dora, look. I've been talking to someone who told me your plans, and I must say it bothers me a lot. There. I've said it. It upsets me, what you've decided, and I've spent every minute since I found out last night trying to figure out what to say to you. But I find I'm now speechless, except for telling you that you should have consulted me first before making such a decision—especially when it involves me. You should have found out what I wanted, and it's not this. It displeases me greatly and I don't know what to do than what I've already done," he finished.

Dora raised up from the park bench.

"Well! I guess you've had your say, though I don't know how we got our signals crossed so badly. But don't take my decision on yourself," she warned. "I'm an adult and can make my choices of where is best for me to live. Clearly it isn't any of your concern," she added, turning on her heels and marching off toward the car.

"Wait just a minute, Dora. We're not finished."

"Yes, we are!" she answered, not daring to turn around. Angry tears began to threatened to surface, and that's the last thing Dora was going to do—and never to let Robert O'Grady see it. Why, everybody in town trying to match-make the two of them together, trying to

2948-BURG

talk Dora into giving Robert a chance. She realized in that moment than they should have found out if Robert was serious before pushing Dora so hard. Dora continued walking at a fast clip. She could hear Robert catching up. Moments later, he swung her around by the arm.

"Please!" he said. In that moment, Robert pulled her to him, pressing his lips down hard against her with an intensity that made Dora's head swim. For only the briefest of seconds she wondered what kind of audience they may have, but she quickly forgot that as she felt her body slowly melt against his. Why if he didn't like her decision to stay was he making it that much harder? A consolation kiss?

At this thought, she broke away. Robert only held her closer, hugging her tightly to him.

"Why are you doing this?" Dora asked.

"I suppose what I couldn't say in words, I could show you in my actions," he explained.

Dora tore herself away, pushing him to arm's length.

"But you didn't like my decision. What Charles told you about? Or was it Betty?" Dora inquired, trying to get a hold on her feelings before she showed herself too much.

"No, I've spoken to neither of them, except to say hello to Betty this morning. It was Shirley that let me know your plans."

"Shirley?" Dora asked, her eyes widening. "Who in the world is Shirley?"

"The teenage girl who's moving in with Betty on Monday. With her mom—the nurse who'll be taking care of your sister now that you're leaving town."

Dora blinked. "What'd give her that idea? I haven't told anybody my plans except Betty."

"Well, obviously they understand the implications. They're practically taking your place in caring for Betty. I guess you needed to go ahead and leave, but Dora, I've tried every way I know to make you feel there's something in this town to return to."

"Yes?" Dora urged, now getting a better view of the misunderstanding. She ventured back on the sidewalk, heading slowly toward the park again. Her back now turned to Robert, she could get away with allowing the small smile to form across her face. "And?"

"And, I've wined and dined you. Tried to show you what kind of man I am. Showed you what a good time we have together. We obviously have a physical attraction for each other to boot, and, and . . . doesn't all that mean anything to you, Dora? Or was I in this all by myself and just didn't know it?"

Robert caught up with her, as the two of them walked side-by-side. Dora let her hands remain folded behind her back as she contemplated the sidewalk and let Robert sweat a moment longer.

Dora started to speak up about then, to let Robert know he'd heard the wrong news, the wrong decision, and that she had planned a whole life there and wasn't moving away at all, but several people in business clothes began to pass by, vying for the small space on the sidewalk.

Dora kept her gaze downward as they all tried to scoot around one another in passing.

"Dora? Is that you?" one of the businessmen spoke up.

Dora snapped her head up, facing the group from the insurance agency.

"It is you! Good! I'd like you to meet some of the other people in the office. Jill, Barney, Craig, Jennifer, this is Dora Thresher. She's our new office manager I told you about."

All the group took turns shaking her hand as the man who'd stopped her rattled on. "Dora's going to make some sense of that mess Carolyn left. We're so fortunate to have found her," he continued.

"Imagine running into you here. We often take a quick walk through the park at lunch time and get a quick bite. Guess we'd better be moseying along," he said. "Look forward to seeing you on Monday, right?"

"Right," Dora answered as the group made it's way onward.

Robert stood ramrod stiff, crossed his arms over his chest, then glared at Dora as the group disappeared across the street and around the corner.

"Staring work Monday?"

"I was going to tell you, but you jumped to the wrong conclusion."

"I'd say you wanted me to show my hand before you did yours. You were having a good old time letting me wear my heart on my sleeve, letting you know how much you've meant in my life, making some commitments on my feelings, while you led me to believe you were out of my life for good."

"Wait just a minute. I'd made my decision to stay. You were the one who'd said my 'decision' bothered you. Upset you."

"Well, I thought you'd leaned in the opposite direction."

"Okay. So now you know the truth. I'm staying."

"Is it because of the job?"

"Partly."

"Mostly?"

"No."

"Your sister?"

"Partly."

"Not this again," Robert breathed out. "Look, Dora. You know how I feel."

"Actually, I don't," she said, making her way the park bench. "Since I've clearly gotten so much wrong all my life, it seems, when it comes to reading relationships, that is, then I think it'd be a grand idea for you to lay it on the line," she said, parking herself on the bench once more.

Robert stood before her, his hands on his hips. He glanced down to the sidewalk directly in front.

"I'm not gonna get down on a bended knee onto this hard cement surface, which I know you aren't ready for—probably scare you so bad you'd high-tail it back home, job or not. But, Dora, I think we owe it to ourselves to give love a second chance. I'm willing if you are."

Robert waited for a response. Dora finally glanced up at him. A grin played across her face as she stood up to him.

"All right, Mister. Let's see how far out on that limb you climb. You might get the brass ring after all. Time will tell," she promised.

* * *

When Robert came into work at Penny's Diner that afternoon he found himself whistling a tune and felt he was walking ten feet tall. Millie, of course, noticed right off.

"Another date with Dora, I take it?" Millie asked as he rounded the back of the counter energetically.

"How'd you know?" he smiled.

"Oh, let's just say you appear to be on 'Cloud Nine' at the present moment. What are you ever going to do when the lady moves back home? That's the only thing that worries me about this, Robert."

"Worry no more," he assured her.

"Why is that? You've fallen for this lady, it's clear to everybody."

"She knows it, too," he answered. "So, that makes everybody indeed."

"So, what are you going to do when she leaves? Write? Have a long-distance romance?" Millie pressed.

"No, it'll be a local call. Our Dora is returning for good," Robert told her.

"Oh? Returning for Love?"

"You might say that."

Millie smiled, clearly pleased with his new-found happiness.

"Convinced her to stay, did you? Are you planning to talk her into a long-term commitment with you as well?" Millie asked in a sing-song manner. "Are wedding bells ringing in the air?"

"Don't you dare mention such a thing to Dora," he warned.

"Well, what do you plan to do about it, Robert?"

"One step at a time, Millie. We're not kids. The lady is selling her place back home and renting a little house not too far from me. It'll give her time to let this thing grow on her."

"Think you can get her to fall all the way?"

"I've made it this far with her, Millie. I don't plan to give up now. All I have to do is climb out on that limb a little farther, then who knows? Only time will tell!"

"You'll have her in no time, Robert. Who could resist a man like you?" Millie said.

Chapter Eleven

"Is this the last box?" Robert breathed, heaving the large cardboard box onto the kitchen counter. "You've sure accumulated a lot of things over the years," he added.

"Of course. My life didn't stop just because I wasn't tied to anyone. I've lived a full life and these are my things. You should have seen what I put in the garage sale," Dora said.

"I would've helped you, if you had let me."

"No need. I've always been able to take care of myself."

Robert turned around, gathering Dora in his arms.

"Dora, will you ever get past that? That you can take care of yourself? Will you ever let me start doing my share of 'taking care of Dora?'"

"Maybe," she answered, easing her hands around his waist.

"Well, I've been thinking about this, and I gotta ask you, Dora. Does your moving into this house mean you want to keep our living quarters separate forever?"

Dora chuckled lightly.

"You always are right out in the open, aren't you, Robert?"

"Keeps there from being too many misunderstandings," he explained.

"You've got a point there."

"You haven't answered my question."

"Let me see," Dora paused. "Let me put this two ways," she answered. "First, this way."

Dora nuzzled up to Robert. She then kissed him like she really meant business, then pulled away.

"That's promise number one. But you'll have to wait until things are totally in place before you cash in on that one," she said.

Robert ran a hand through his full set of graying hair.

"Just remember, I'm not getting any younger. I'd like that lifetime commitment as soon as you're ready. What's the second promise?"

"It's not a promise, actually. More like a strong indication to the answer to your question."

Robert drew her to him again. "What was the question? I've forgotten already."

"You asked if our having separate living arrangements was a permanent situation or was there hope for a commitment from me sometime in the future that would change that."

"Oh, yeah. I would like to know that. I've spent most of my adult life being married, and I have to say I like that a whole lot better. Moving you in here makes me feel like you have no intentions of what I really want," Robert pressed. "Especially signing a year's lease, which is customary, I understand."

Dora smiled. "I guess that brings me to my point number two."

"Right," Robert said. "What is point number two?"

"I made a deal with the landlord. I signed a 'month-to-month' lease," she answered.

"Does that mean I have once a month, every month, to convince you that living alone and taking care of yourself all by yourself is a status you'd be willing to change? One that could change to a lifetime commitment of marriage?"

"I'd have to have some pretty good proof that something like that could work for me. But I guess you might be the man to do that. You've already done the impossible—made me return to this town. Return for a real chance at love," Dora answered, a smile forming.

To this Robert pulled Dora back into a long embrace. He'd win her over no matter what. And sooner than later. After all, he wasn't getting any younger.

THE END

2948-BURG

A Safe Haven

by Penny Burgess

Chapter One

Claris Pemberton struggled to keep the car on the road, to keep awake, and to keep driving through the darkest of nights. In the distance the faint light of the next town neared. A lone billboard announced a 24-hour eating establishment—Penny's Diner. Only two more miles off the next exit, it said. That's what she needed, Claris decided. A cup of coffee to give her the added caffeine rush to help her continue to drive farther and farther away from the nightmare that threatened to overtake her.

As she turned her car off the exit, now loaded with what belongings she could cram in her mid-sized Honda, she immediately spotted the tasteful neon lights of the shiny structure of the 24-hour eatery. Claris blinked back the blurry tears, and stared at the sign that read, "Penny's Diner."

It shined out to her, calling from the darkness of her storm to a safe haven. Perhaps someone there might even help her get an idea in which direction she should head next, she thought.

Claris had to find a quiet town where she could take refuge until she could figure a way out of the mess Nathan had put her in, and to escape the unexpected threats that had followed when she'd discovered and confronted him with his illegal schemes with the company funds.

The recent memory throbbed through her head as she remembered his steely cold blue eyes that meant every word of cutting her life short if she opened her mouth to the company president about what she'd discovered. Either she'd end up in jail, since it was Claris who was the office manager and had inadvertently put the forms through that allowed a steady flow of unsubstantiated funds in Nathan's direction, or he'd see to it that she never spoke a word about anything to anyone else again. His debonair smile punctuated the promise of ruining or ending her life, either way. How could she have trusted such a man and gotten personally involved with him as well, she wondered as her weary brain went over the facts one more time.

Claris eased out of her car into the night, and as she walked through the glass doors to the restaurant, she felt her legs grow weak, and her body ached with the weariness and emotional toil this trip had cost her so far. It was almost all she could do to carry herself over to one of the booths, and she wanted nothing better than to drop her head onto the table and sleep.

A wiry man in his late forties came over immediately.

"What can I do for you?" he asked cheerily.

Claris wondered how he could be so upbeat at 3 a.m. in the morning.

"Bacon and eggs?" he suggested.

Claris hadn't eaten since lunch, since she'd found the paperwork that cinched what she'd been afraid to face about the man she'd agreed to see on a social basis for the last six months.

"Ma'am? Are you all right?" he asked, interrupting her wandering thoughts.

Claris read the man's name tag. She saw his name was Fred and that he was the manager of that shift. That was all her mind seemed to register.

"I'm a bit tired. How about a cup of coffee?" she asked him.

The night manager shifted his weight to his other foot. He balanced one hand against the back of the booth and the other on his hip, clutching a wet dish towel in his hand.

"You look like you could use a good night's sleep better than a cup of coffee," he put in, not making a move toward serving her.

Claris gazed into his kind eyes. She couldn't think straight anymore. Not at this hour, anyway.

"Listen," he continued. "There's a nice, affordable hotel just across the street. Why don't you settle in for the night and come back for that cup of coffee in the morning? I can't in good conscious send you back on the road in the shape you're in," he finished.

"Okay," Claris agreed, rising to her feet and glancing at the hotel he mentioned right across the way. "Maybe you're right."

"There's always somebody on duty, so come on back after you're rested. Then you can get to wherever you're trying to drive to. You'll have the light of day to help you out too," he said.

Claris did as the kind man suggested. It was as though she'd needed someone, somewhere, to tell her what to do next, for her mind was a blur and her emotions were shot—not to mention not having any lingering physical energy to see her through.

She checked into the hotel and fell under the covers. It was the first time she'd been able to really relax since the fact that something wasn't exactly right about Nathan's activities had begun to prey on her mind. At least she was far, far away from him now. At least that, she told herself as she fell into a deep, sound sleep.

* * *

"What's wrong, Fred? You look worried," Millie Holmes asked the night manager when she came in that morning to take over the shift.

"Well, I'm just a thinkin' about this woman who came in here last night. I sent her away to get some sleep. I see her car's still parked in the lot in front of the hotel. Glad she took my advice," he added, rubbing his chin and staring out the plate glass window.

"Who is she?" Millie asked, pinning her name tag to her "Penny's Diner" T-shirt and gearing up for the early breakfast crowd.

"Don't know. Out-of-towner passing through. This one's in a big hurry, but she couldn't take any more travel for the night. Wanted a cup of coffee but I talked her out of it. Told her to go across the street and get a room instead," Fred explained, rounding the counter to leave.

"You've done a good deed, Fred," Millie answered, turning away.

Fred lingered for a moment longer.

"What is it now?" Millie asked, frowning. Fred normally wasn't this way. He was known to be good to the people who came through in the night, those who worked odd shift hours, or people who wanted food in the early morning when others were asleep, but she'd never seen him this concerned about one of his customers.

"Fred?"

"What?" he snapped, pulling his attention from the view across the street back to Millie.

"What's eating at you?"

"That woman. I'm worried about her. I can't say why, exactly, and maybe it was just that she was just so tired. Real tired. But I saw something in her eyes. Scared, I'd say. Running from something."

"You can't save the world, Fred."

"No, but I can be good to folks in trouble."

"Do you know she's in trouble for a fact?" Millie pressed.

"I don't. But if she comes in for that cup of coffee I promised her, make sure she's well taken care of. I think she could use a friend no matter what."

"I will. You've got my word on it," Millie promised.

"She's about mid-thirties, might be pretty without the dark circles under her blue eyes, slender, and drives a light colored Honda. Watch for her, will you?"

"Yes, Fred. I told you I would. Now go home," Millie answered, pushing him out the door so she could get to work.

Two hours later the Diner was in full swing with a local retired men's group holding a breakfast meeting taking up most of the back half of tables, and an unexpected tour group passing through taking up much of the rest. Regulars filled all the counter space and the sprinkling of tables.

Even Philip Barnett, the local middle-aged bachelor who, by just being himself, managed to attract most of the ladies' attention after moving into town almost a year back, had come in for a Saturday breakfast change of pace. Millie had to admit that Phil had turned into a real nice person after her first run-in with him over getting in the way of his son's and one of her former waitress' romance. Now that the couple was happily married, Phil had settled in and was a down-right nice, decent person, Millie reminded herself.

Her quick detour in thoughts of her history with Philip Barnett was short lived. She and the other waitress on duty had to move fast to handle the extra customers the best way they could, but no one was getting as much personal attention as normal. That's when Millie noticed a slender woman, about thirty-five years old, standing just inside the door. She was unfamiliar, but Millie's eyes darted outside at the front row parking place that had vacated a moment before, and now had a light compact car that could be a Honda, she thought, squinting through the sunlight ricocheting off the front window.

"That must be the woman Fred was talking about," she whispered to herself as she balanced two plates of food in her hands. She quickly delivered them, then rushed over.

"Hello. Welcome to Penny's Diner. I'd tell you to sit anywhere, but seems like everybody else had the same idea this morning," she said, glancing frantically around.

"That's okay. I'll just take a cup of coffee to go," the woman answered quietly. "I need to get back on the road anyway."

Millie studied her face. Her blue eyes were filled with a depth of sadness that the woman's forced smile could not hide. There was no question now that this was the right woman, and Millie would not send her on her way.

"Why don't you wait just a second. Surely someone is about to finish up here, and I'll bet you could use a good meal before getting back to your driving," Millie suggested, looking around and realizing no one was close to leaving. She then caught sight of one empty chair at Philip Barnett's table. Surely he wouldn't mind. He *is* a nice person, he's proved that, Millie reminded herself.

"Wait just a sec," she said, then darted over to Phil. Moments later, she ushered the woman over to his table and left the two of them in light conversation. As Millie glanced toward them a few minutes later, a thought occurred to her which she quickly shooed away. That just couldn't be possible, she decided. Millie's inclination always headed toward match-making in this town and especially in the Diner. But at fifty years old, Phil Barnett was clearly a good fifteen years older than the sad woman she'd just introduced him to, and she clearly had problems and would not be in the mood for romance. Still, as she looked at the two of them, they seemed to have an instant connectivity, a relaxed, comfort in being together.

The other waitress on duty took care of her order immediately, but Millie continued to watch them throughout breakfast. There was something to her theory, for as she watched them, she could just feel the attraction, the bond. There was something that would not let the two of them separate after a short breakfast together—regardless of whatever plans this woman previously had, she decided. Millie could just feel it in her bones and would bet her last nickel on it.

* * *

"So, you say you're just passing through?" Philip Barnett pressed after giving Claris a chance to take a few bites of food.

"Yes. I'm on the way to . . ." Claris trailed off, having no destination to tell. What would be the answer to that question? When a town looked "right?" When she felt she'd driven long enough? Far enough to be away from Nathan's reach?

"Way to where?" Philip spoke up, breaking her train of thought.

"I don't know, exactly," she heard herself say. The handsome man's eyebrows raised. He twisted his mouth in a half-smile, showing a deep dimple in his cheek. The soft look in his eyes put her at ease. Warmed her. With his friendly manner, he was just what the doctor ordered, she decided, and she was now glad there were no available seats left in the place except the one sitting opposite him.

"If you don't know where you're going, how will you know when you get there?" he questioned with a lilt of humor.

Claris lowered her coffee cup.

"Well, you tell me and we'll both know," she answered, finding a laugh making its way to the surface for the first time in a long, long time.

"I'll tell you this much," he said, his eyes twinkling. "If you let me take you on a tour of our fine town, you can see if this is it!" he suggested.

"What is 'it'?" she asked.

"Why, your final destination," he supplied, wiping his mouth of a droplet of syrup that remained from his now finished high stack of pancakes. Claris wondered where the man put it all. He seemed a bit older than herself, maybe fifteen years older than her thirty-five years, but his body was in superb shape, she decided, admiring what she could see so far.

"So, what do you say? Finish those eggs and let me take you around," he tried again.

Claris felt a lightness in her heart.

"I see no harm in that," she answered, surprising herself that she felt safe enough to stop her journey long enough to spend a few hours with this man.

A few minutes later, he'd paid for his breakfast—and hers, and Claris found herself being ushered into his large, luxury car and being taken on a first-class tour of the small- to medium-sized town. She didn't know why she trusted this stranger, except that she trusted the manager of Penny's Diner. Millie Holmes, as the name tag read, was as honest as the day was long. That was easy to tell. And so, she suspected, was this older man who'd clearly taken a shine to her.

The drive and Philip's easy companionship took her mind off her troubles, giving her perspective. And with every passing house, business, and retail establishment in town, she felt more and more at ease from the panic and sadness that had most recently held her in its grip.

"This town is much bigger than I originally thought," Claris told him.

"Oh, you'd be surprised at the way this town seems to fit the bill. It's big enough to give you choices, and small enough to supply the feeling of family," he added.

"You have family here?" Claris asked, now wondering even more about the man who she'd eagerly jumped in the car with without question.

"My son, Chad, and his new wife, Sadie. They're having a baby. My first grandchild. That's the full extent of my family."

"Does your wife live here, too?" she asked, fishing to see if he'd tell the truth about the absent wedding ring. Claris decided it didn't matter how blunt her query. She'd gotten in trouble by NOT asking questions. From here on out, things would be different.

"My *ex*-wife and no, she does NOT live here," he added with a forcefulness.

"Oh," Claris answered, a small laugh escaping her. "That kind of thing," she said.

"Yes. That kind of thing. She lives flirtatiously in a place far, far from here, and whatever communication that goes on between her and my son have been sparse, but that's their business," he added.

As he pointed out another restaurant on the outskirts of town that featured Mexican food, Claris took the opportunity to steal a few glances at Philip's flat stomach and strong chest underneath his polo shirt. He must work out, she decided, wondering the pull she felt toward him. He was definitely attractive, in a regular sort of way, but his manner had a way of taking you in without your being able to stop it. Still, she had other things to consider in her life, and unfortunately, Philip Barnett would not be part of it. If only they'd met at a different time and place, she thought.

"I suppose you should take me back now," she put in, as her escape from reality loomed before her mind again. Being with Philip had been a great diversion, but it was time to head off. The question remained, however, where that final destination would be. And what it would take to make her stop. What it would take to feel safe enough to settle in while she got a plan together to solve the problems she'd left behind in St. Louis.

Philip turned his car around in a parking lot and dutifully returned Claris back to Penny's Diner. As the restaurant that beckoned to her the night before, perhaps saving her from driving off the road, having an accident, and giving her a warm, safe haven, came back into view, she had second thoughts. There was a reason she was here, and as she glanced back at Philip Barnett, her heart warmed and she relaxed.

It was almost unbelievable that she could feel this safe, this soon, after her ordeal. Could it be that this town was where she'd been going all along? Would any other be any better than a place where she already had a few people looking out for her? And perhaps the hotel would have a weekly rate until she devised a plan to dig herself out of the trouble she'd narrowly escaped from only days before, she decided.

"So, it's off you go, huh? There's nothing I can do to keep you here? An offer to get you settled? I'll help however I can," he suggested.

Claris turned in her seat. She wondered why this man was so eager to help her. After all, she thought, as she trailed her hand through her hair she knew had not been properly styled, and her eye makeup could not cover the dark circles and the haunted look her eyes must still hold, if he found her this attractive in this state, just imagine . . . she thought, wondering what seeing a man fifteen years her senior might be like. The image brought a faint smile to her lips.

"Well?" he urged.

"Why are you doing this? The helpless, damsel in distress theme?"

"No. You're a fine woman, capable of taking care of whatever problems drove you through the night to our town. I can sense that. You could just as well keep on driving. I'm simply offering you a chance to stop here. And, yes, besides that, you're not hard on the eyes. Is that what you want to hear?" he questioned.

"I'm not sure," Claris answered. "But it's not a bad start." She felt herself smile and Philip's returning grin brought on an excitement from deep within. Claris knew she wanted to see him again. Not drive off forever without him.

"Well, I'll walk you to your car," he said, parking in the first available space. "If you want to stay, stay. If you're determined to go, I've tried my best selling job," he answered, easing out of his car.

Claris wondered if he had been selling the town or himself in this little jaunt. She eased out of the passenger's seat and found Philip by her side immediately, ushering her to her car. She couldn't help but notice him looking over the load of boxes and personal items that were stuffed in every available inch of space in her small car. He gave her a smile, opened her door, but didn't press. He had done his best, and Claris had now made a decision.

"Philip, thank you for breakfast, the tour, the nice company . . ."

"But you have to hit the road. I understand," he interrupted.

"As I was going to say," she began. "I think I'll take a room for the week at the hotel across the street. If things make sense after that, I'll stay indefinitely. But I'll give it a try," she said.

"Would you mind me giving you a call?"

"I wouldn't mind, no," she answered.

"Well, you might tell me your last name, Claris. The hotel might not know how to connect me without it."

"Pemberton. Claris Pemberton. And thank you again," she put in, easing in her car and starting the motor. She then pulled out of the parking space and headed toward the exit.

She glanced in her rear view mirror at the rugged man who seemed to have an extra spring to his step as he headed back to his car and jumped inside. Yes, Claris thought, this town might be just the place—as long as Nathan doesn't find me.

Chapter Two

"Hi, Dad. You were mighty chipper today at work. Especially for a Monday," Chad Barnett said as he moved through the sliding glass door off the deck of his father's home.

"Come in, son. What a nice surprise. Have a seat," Philip Barnett called out as his son breezed into the den and collapsed onto the sofa.

"Tired?" Philip asked casually. "Let me get you a pop or something wet to drink," he continued, rising from his easy chair and heading off into the kitchen.

"What in the world's gotten into you?" Chad called from his seat. "First I see you all smiles at work, and now you're offering to wait on me? Have you won the lottery or something? You're not your usual sour self."

"Ha . . . Ha . . . Very funny," his father put in sarcastically, handing Chad a cold can of Coke.

"No, really, Dad. What's up? You're too happy," Chad tried again.

"Oh, all right," Philip answered, taking his seat back into his dark burgundy easy chair. "I've met someone."

Chad made motions in mid-sip of his coke like he was about to spew the liquid across the room. He took a big swallow, then clunked the can onto the coaster on the coffee table.

"Has the world just come to an end? I never thought I'd see the day," he added, clearly stunned.

"Well, you've seen it now. I've met someone nice. A woman I think I could be interested in."

"I'd say you're already interested in her. Who is she? Do I know her?" Chad wore an amused smile, making his father happy to share everything he knew.

"Well, she's just come into town."

"Oh," Chad said, less enthusiastically. "Where is she from?"

"Can't say. She's relocating. Had most of her things with her in the car when she showed up at Penny's Diner. So, I've only had a breakfast date with her. Oh, and I took her on a tour of the town. That convinced her to stay—either the looks of the town, or maybe because of me," he added with a self-satisfied grin.

"So, what do you know about this woman, Dad?"

Philip noted his son's smile had faded, making his smile disappear as well.

"Who cares? You fell in love with Sadie from her looks alone," he challenged. "Now look at you. Happy, married, in a home of your own, expecting a baby . . ."

"It was more than her looks that got me, Dad," Chad said.

"It was a starting point. You knew very little when you went after that filly. And look were it got you? Don't you wish your old Dad a little of the same?"

"Sure, but for one thing, Sadie had lived here all her life. This woman is a vagabond."

"A what?" he asked incredulously.

"You know, a drifter for all we know. What about her past? Does she have a family? A husband? Really, Dad. I think you shouldn't get your hopes up about this woman until you're able to tell what you're getting into."

Philip felt his face redden. His temper threatened to surface. He'd been so happy. So relieved that he could think in that direction again after his ex-wife had left him like she had.

"Look, son. What's your point? Why are you throwing a wet blanket on my finally being drawn to someone again? Finally being able to put the past behind me and move on. Is it some misplaced loyalty to your mother?"

"No, no, Dad. You deserve love, and Mom's remarried."

"She is?" Philip asked in surprise.

"Oh, I guess I shouldn't have let that come out like that," he supplied.

"It doesn't matter, Chad. That hurt is finally long gone. In fact, the future is looking better and better. And Claris Pemberton is going to be a part of it."

Chad rose from the sofa, taking his can of Coke with him.

"Well, just be careful, Dad. You've been through enough in your lifetime with what Mom did. I don't want you to get hurt by somebody again. And until we know this Claris Pemberton better, I think you'd do well in keeping your expectations low," he finished, walking toward the back.

Philip rose from his chair.

"Seems Sadie hasn't even delivered that new baby of yours and you've taken on an overly protective, fatherly role already—but with me."

"Just be careful, Dad," Chad finished. "I'll tell Sadie you said 'hello'."

"Yeah, do that," Philip answered as he watched his son disappear out the sliding glass door.

As much as he loved his son, and was pleased with his visits to keep in touch after he'd gotten married, he somehow wished today Chad had stayed away. It would have allowed Philip to fantasize about being happily married and settled down with the company of a good woman. Oh, he knew it was a stretch, putting Claris in that role. For one thing, she was much younger than himself. For another, Chad was right. He knew literally nothing about her. She could have baggage that was not safe under his current circumstances. He couldn't afford to have a woman break his heart again, and from the way he'd reacted to Claris that morning, she'd have the capability of getting into his heart real fast—and able to break it as well. Still, his heart wouldn't let him give up until he'd given it a good try.

*   *   *

"Brad? It's Claris."

"Claris? Where are you?" Brad Freemont asked in a frantic tone. "Nancy? It's Claris!" he called out over the muffled receiver in his hand.

"Brad, I'm sorry I had to disappear like this," she began.

"Nancy and I have been worried sick. You haven't shown up at work all week, you don't answer your telephone, and none of your neighbors have seen you."

"You've gone to talk to my neighbors?"

"Well, yes. After you missed work for two days, Nancy and I used the spare house key you gave us when you're on vacation to look after your plants and took a quick peek inside. Nancy was scared to death we'd find you on the floor, hurt or worse. But luckily there was no foul play. Still, if you didn't show up at the office by tomorrow, we were going to call the police," he explained.

"The police? Brad! Don't get the police involved."

"I didn't, yet. But Nathan wants to. He's worried about you."

"Yeah, I'll just bet," she ground out. "What's the word around the office, by the way?" she asked.

"Just that you didn't show. They've got a temp in for the week—until they figure out what happened. But your job isn't an easy one to fill in. So, Claris, this isn't like you at all. What's up?"

"I had to leave for a while, Brad. That's all I want you to know, for now."

"Well, at least tell me where you are. This Caller ID just says 'unavailable.'" Brad said.

"That's exactly what I am. Unavailable."

"Look, Claris, Nancy and I have been good friends with you for years. Not to mention how well we work together at the office. Hey, does this have anything to do with Nathan? Did you two have a lover's spat and you hit the road? Trying to avoid him?"

"Don't get involved in this, Brad. You and Nancy deserve to live without this disaster."

"What disaster? Why'd you up and leave? I'll ask this again. Was it because of Nathan? He's looking for you, you know," he added.

Claris felt her blood run cold. She still needed to get her head on straight, figure out what to do. She didn't want Nathan finding her before she had her ducks in a row.

"Look, Brad, please don't tell anybody I called. Except Nancy which you obviously already have," she began.

"Are you all right? Tell me you're all right."

"I'm fine. That's all you need to know."

"No, Claris. I won't leave it like this. What happened?" he demanded. "And don't give me this, 'I'm fine' business, because you'd never do such a thing. Everybody in the office is worried. Are you in some sort of trouble?"

Claris paused. She had no one else to confide in. Brad would believe her. He and Nancy knew her through and through.

"Claris? Tell me," he urged.

"Okay. Yes. But it's not *my* trouble," she blurted out. "Only I think they won't believe that if things start coming out. Don't you let Nathan Beecham get away with anything, either," she added.

"He's who's driven you away? I'll strangle that womanizer."

"Womanizer? I could care less about his activities in that arena."

"Everyone knows you've been seeing each other. We even had you both to dinner, if you recall."

"Of course, I recall."

"So, what's wrong? What's he done?"

"He's an evil man, capable of who knows what, and he's managed to make something there at the office appear that I've been dishonest with the books. But it's not me, Brad. It's him. He's been skimming company funds and making it look like I'm to blame. I can't figure out how to get out of this mess, and he's also a very dangerous man. So

I ran. That might have been a stupid move, now that I think about it, but I'd rather be sitting in this hotel room trying to figure out what to do than in a jail cell or funeral home."

"A what? Don't be ridiculous, Claris. Whatever this is, we'll help you. My friend, Mark, is a great attorney. He'll straighten it out. He's a fanatic about such things."

"Great. But I know Nathan and what he's capable of. I'm onto him and I confronted him. He's threatened me. He's shown me how he's set it up from the beginning to look like I'm the one doing it all and like he was an innocent. Like I was using his name but taking the money all myself. So there was no way out. I had to take off for a while. Don't you see?"

"No, I don't see," Brad argued. "If things are as you say, this will only make you look more guilty."

"Well, I've got to protect myself somehow."

"You'll have to come back."

"Why? There isn't even anything to tell if I stay away. Nathan will keep quiet to make sure he's not put in any danger, and at least I'll still be alive if I keep my distance."

"Claris, come back. I'll give Mark a call."

"No, Brad. I'm sorry. You don't know that man. The things he's threatened. He's a madman. Crazy. And capable of far more than anyone in that office can imagine."

"Then it's up to you to let the top guns know."

"I'm telling you, Brad. He brought some paperwork home that he'd put through for me to see. I inspected it. It looks really bad on me. He's fixed it so I'd take the rap if I opened my mouth about his skimming off the top."

"Claris. Listen to me. It's your moral duty to expose him."

"That might be true, but it won't do any good from the corner he's painted me into. So, I'm laying low for a while until he feels like I'm out of the picture. Then I'll be able to figure out what I want to do next."

"What about your job? Your home?"

"All right. Look. Tell Judy in Personnel I called and that I had a family emergency and don't know when I'll be back. That I'm sorry I had to leave them in a lurch. Then if you want, you can go get my plants and take them home with you. Make sure the house is okay from time to time."

"Your prized plants? Claris, you really think you might not come back?" he asked in surprise.

"I don't know, Brad. If I don't I'll eventually sell the house, I guess. But unless I find a way to stop Nathan, I'm dead meat."

"That's it. I'm hiring a private detective and calling Mark," Brad said. "I won't let you go through this alone."

"I'm not alone. Not exactly," she answered, thinking of Philip Barnett, the kind stranger who she hoped she'd spend more time with in the future.

"Well, give me a number to reach you, at least."

"No," she answered sternly. "I won't have you that involved. Nothing they can trace back. Nathan is a professional con man. He's done this before, I can just bet on it. In the two years he's been at the company, he knew exactly how to work things—including dating me. So, he's dangerous and ruthless. Stay out of his way and whatever you do, don't let on you've talked to me at any length, and especially don't give away what I've told you about him. Just play like it was a short conversation about my family emergency and leave it at that."

"Okay. We'll play it your way, Claris. But you'd better keep in touch. When will we hear from you again?"

"Give me a week. By then, I'll know what I'm going to do," she answered then hung up the phone before Brad could talk her into changing her mind. She had to stay away for now. Otherwise, she'd either be in deep trouble with her office and the police, or worse, Nathan could get his hands on her.

Chapter Three

Claris held her head in her hands after she'd hung up the phone. She missed her friends, her co-workers, her home. This hotel room was very nice with its recliner and spacious enough room to feel comfortable, but she was used to home—her home. Nathan had thrust her from it in a most unfair way. She just couldn't see herself returning under the circumstances, yet what were her options?

When the phone rang, she jumped to her feet, staring at the instrument. It signaled a few more rings before she picked up the receiver. Somehow she imagined that they'd already found her. That Brad and Nancy's phone had been tapped and they didn't know it.

Claris put the receiver to her ear but said nothing.

"Claris? Is this the room for Claris Pemberton?" she heard a man's voice question. Her mind searched her memory banks. No one from home.

"Philip?" she asked hopefully.

"Yes. It's Philip. Why didn't you speak when you picked up?"

"I'm sorry. I was preoccupied with something I was doing," she explained, trying to sound normal.

"I got off work, came to my empty house, and figured, 'why am I sitting here all alone when Claris might be doing the same thing.' Thought you might want some company, being new in town," he explained.

Claris exhaled slowly. It wasn't her past trying to catch up with her. It was Philip Barnett trying to be friendly.

"It's good to hear from you," she finally answered.

"Does that mean you're available for a quick dinner at Penny's and maybe something afterwards? A movie perhaps?"

"Tonight?"

"Well, yes, I know it's short notice. Should have asked ahead, being a Friday night, but there's not much time at work to make personal calls," he explained.

"No. That's fine, Philip. I'm game," she answered.

"If I come by now, we can eat and have time for the seven-thirty movie across town," he suggested.

"Okay. Come on over," she said, then hung up the phone, delighted to have Philip take her out and get her mind off things—if only for an evening, she thought.

* * *

Fifteen minutes later, Philip pulled into the hotel parking lot. He glanced up at the second floor, and noted Claris had come out before he could come to the door. They then drove across the street to Penny's Diner and entered the 24-hour restaurant where Philip's world had instantly changed the moment he'd met Claris.

They took the booth the waitress suggested and Claris busied herself with the menu. She had been rather quiet on the short trip over, and Philip found he was very out of practice in dating. He even wondered if the young woman seated across from him considered this to be a "date." After all, she was a much younger woman. He worried that she took him up on this offer because he was the only person she knew in town. Knew that to be the case, in fact. But he was strongly drawn to this woman in a way he couldn't quite figure out. Still, that's the way it was, he thought as he glanced at her dark hair that spilled across her shoulders. He wanted to reach out and touch the silky strands, then caught himself and cleared his throat.

"Uh, everything is good here. Depends on what you like, but really, you can't go wrong no matter what you order," he told her.

Claris let out an agreeing murmur of sorts and kept her gaze to the laminated menu. Philip shifted in his seat, and pushed his closed menu into the folder at the end of the table. Claris then followed suit and they sat face-to-face for the first time that evening.

"Decided have you?" he asked.

"I'm a woman who makes up her mind quickly."

"So I see. Are you that way with everything? Or just ordering food?" he smiled.

"Everything. Maybe I tend to be a little impulsive too, at times. Then I have to rethink my actions later," she explained. Her gaze then shifted to the tabletop and Philip thought he heard a sigh escape as she turned to reflect outside.

Philip wondered if she were referring to her most recent actions. He knew it was personal, but he decided to go for it.

"So, do you feel you were too impulsive in leaving town? Are you thinking about going back now?" he asked.

The waitress found that moment to come take their orders, then hurried away. An awkward silence remained after she left. Philip hoped he hadn't been too aggressive in asking Claris such a question, but his hopes were building that she would stay in town, and that he could start a relationship with this mysterious, interesting woman. Still, he didn't want to pressure her to talk about it if she didn't want to.

"Well," she began after a long pause. "To answer your question, it's too soon to tell. I did what I had to at the time, so, no, I don't regret that. But where I go from here is still up in the air," she answered.

The waitress then returned with the chocolate malts. Claris turned her attention to the tall, frosty glass in front of her, pulled the straw up and down, then took in a long sip. Her smile immediately returned as her focus shifted back to Philip.

"Isn't it great to order a malt with your meal? Like getting to have your dessert first," she added.

Philip nodded. He got the hint. She didn't want to talk about why she'd come to town in the middle of the night, or discuss her future plans either.

"So, how long has it been since you relocated here?" she asked, turning the conversation around.

"Oh, it's been most of a year and a half, maybe almost two years, I guess."

"And you've found it to be a good place to call home?"

"Yes. People are friendly here. Like I said the other day, it's big enough to have things to do, but small enough to have the feel of family. Like here at the Diner. And like a family, the people aren't afraid of telling you how it really is.

"Let me give you an example. When I first came here, I had a pretty bitter attitude over what my ex-wife had done, and I'd yet to regain my trust in women. So, I made a mistake in judgment when it came to Sadie, one of the waitresses here—my future daughter-in-law as it turned out. But when Millie Holmes, the day manager here, found out I was turning my son, Chad, against Sadie, Millie let me have it with both barrels. Told me 'what was what' and set me straight. I try not to do that anymore. Millie Holmes might get on me," he laughed.

Claris smiled in return, but her smile seemed to fade as she glanced outside the plate window. Philip wasn't sure what he'd said, but it brought some unhappy thought to the pretty face across from him.

"You jumped to the wrong conclusion about that waitress before finding out the facts?"

"Oh, yeah. A big mix-up. But she was set up, you see. I believed the worst without trying to get to the bottom of it—without giving her the benefit of the doubt. And I convinced my son to do the same. But I'm a changed man now."

"So, next time something comes up about someone you know is not capable of doing whatever you think, you'll dig deeper until you know the truth? You'll give them a break?" she asked.

2948-BURG

"Sure. In fact, it's helped me in the workplace. I'm in management where all kinds of grievances are brought to my attention. I don't take it at face value anymore—even if the person in question appears to be the type to do whatever. I find out the truth. It's saved lots of trouble by me having an open mind," he explained.

Claris seemed to relax with this, he noted, making him feel more confident, yet he remained unsure of how to carry on with a woman these days. He'd just have to learn, he decided as the waitress brought them their dinners.

After a brief time, Philip decided to break the silence again. Claris seemed to have shrugged off the earlier change in mood, and had warmed considerably to him.

"Tell me about yourself," Claris urged, watching him from across the table. Philip noted the deep blue eyes that held such mystery in her gaze. The dark circles had disappeared, and her skin was so beautiful, giving her a fresh, youthful look.

"Me?" be started. "There's not much to tell."

"Sure there is. Everybody's got a story. What's yours?"

He swallowed hard. Dating conversations. He wasn't prepared.

"Oh, mine is an ordinary life. I'm plant manager at the Hennessey Company. Came here from Cleveland. I live alone, now that my only son is married. And that's about it," he finished.

"Cleveland," she said, pulling the straw from the chocolate malt out from the glass and trailing her tongue over dripping liquid. "That's a long way," she added when she was through.

Philip felt his stomach tighten at the alluring sight. He knew he was attracted to the woman, but seeing her enjoying each drop of ice cream in the malt to the fullest made his mind wander into areas he'd kept at bay for a long, long time.

"Are you all right?" Claris asked him.

Philip wondered what his face had given away. He hoped not what he'd been thinking.

"What was the question?" he asked quietly, hurriedly focusing on the food on his plate.

"Cleveland. What brought you all the way here from Cleveland? Your business?"

"Yes. The job opening was exactly what I wanted from here on out. I'll be retiring from this company, I suspect. The last place I want to go. I've got my home, my boy is here with his wife and a new baby on the way," he added, knowing he was repeating himself, but now safely away from the sensuous feelings he'd avoided for the moment.

"Is that the only reason you came?" she asked again.

Philip raised his head. Her deep blue eyes seemed to look directly into his soul. There'd be no keeping secrets or hiding his feelings from this woman. She was direct and insistent in telling it like it is. And somehow, she was able to read him like a book.

"No, it isn't," he confessed. "I wanted to get away from bad memories. From my ex-wife specifically. I needed to start afresh."

"She must have done some number on you to make you and your son high-tail it this far away," she suggested.

"Yes, ma'am. She did. At least in my book. She took off with another man, abandoning me and my son. Somehow it took moving far away to heal. So, relocating to such a pleasant, kind town has allowed me to do just that," he finished.

Claris just smiled. He felt his chest swell with a warmth for the woman. He'd been able to confide in her, she pushed him to do so, yet she stopped at just the right amount of information. She then pushed a strand of shoulder-length brown hair behind her ear. The motion caused yet another stir within him. Every movement seemed to be done with a sensuousness hard to describe. He couldn't believe she was doing it on purpose, but it made sitting there across the booth from her, not touching or being close enough to respond, very, very difficult.

"Have you ever been married?" he asked suddenly, wondering how he'd managed to get something so personal out there without thinking.

Claris smiled lightly, stirring her malt again with the straw. She moved the tip to the bottom where a sizable amount remained, and begin twirling it into her mouth again. Not this again, he thought to himself. She was driving him crazy, did she know it?

"I guess that's too personal a question to ask?" he said, clearing his throat and trying to focus on anything other than her mouth.

"No. Not too. But, no. I've never agreed to that institution. I've had long-term relationships, but none I'd consider a life-time commitment type."

"You like it that way?" Philip continued, wishing he could stop asking questions that clearly showed his intense interest in the woman he'd just met.

"So far. That could change, but I don't see it happening soon," she answered.

Philip then supplied light conversation during the meal the best way he knew how, but Claris wasn't making it any easier for him. She remained quiet and subdued, but *did* show interest in him, to his relief. After they were finished he checked his watch, realizing there was just enough time to make it to the theater. He then slid out of the booth.

"Guess I'd better go pay right quick. Be right back."

Going to the cash register, he glanced back at Claris. After spending a little time with her, he now wondered even more what to make of Claris Pemberton, and hated that he'd fallen so hard for her and was so intensely drawn to her this fast.

As he paid the check, he turned and stole another look at her. She had risen from the table, smoothing down the short skirt she'd worn. Since her back was turned, he slowly took in the full length of her long, shapely legs and shook his head. He then turned back, getting his change.

After all the time of healing from his previous wife's indiscretions and her abandoning them, why had he fallen for this complete stranger, at least a decade or more younger than his fifty years, who might move off any day. Why hadn't it been one of the many local women who'd showed interest in him since he'd moved here. Had it previously been just too soon to let anybody in? Was it the challenge of this woman? Or was it simply something about Claris that had awakened the man in him who wanted the love of a woman back in his life again?

He quickly laid his tip on the table, and ushered Claris out the door. Whatever this relationship would bring, he was ready to give it his best shot, and he hoped Claris would stick around long enough to give it a chance.

* * *

Claris felt Philip's hand on the small of her back as he ushered her out the door of Penny's and into his car. He was such a gentleman, an art she thought had been long forgotten. She also liked his touch, warm yet not threatening. Not demanding. It gave her room. Space. Yet, as she rode along side of him the short drive to the theater, she found she needed less and less of that 'space' and wished to be closer to him.

It was a dangerous game she was playing, she decided, for she had big problems threatening her life and she couldn't afford to let her heart be pulled into something she couldn't finish. Still, she found herself flirting with Philip. She couldn't help herself. She liked the way he responded, too. His eyes and facial expressions were so easy to read.

"So, Claris," Phil began, "Have you decided to stay here with us for a while, anyway?" he asked hopefully.

Claris felt her chest tighten at the very thought. She wished she could stick around, if only just temporarily while she figured everything out. But after looking around that week, she'd discovered the job openings she'd called about were already taken. As much in demand as her administrative skills were in a big city, this town seemed to be all filled up job-wise. She hadn't fixed the problems back home, and she was running out of cash reserves. The thought brought her back to reality.

"I have to be honest with you, Philip. I'm in limbo right now, but I can't hang out here forever. In fact, I plan to leave day after tomorrow," she admitted sadly.

"I thought you liked it here? You've made new friends here. Like me," he urged.

"This is a nice town, and I really like you, Philip, I really do, but I need to go someplace bigger so I can find a job. I can't stay at a hotel forever with no job and no money. My savings will drain—like real soon. So, you see, I'm in no position to stay."

"Well, what kind of work do you do?"

"I was an office manager at a sales and distribution center for a company that makes specialty clothes, but I've also been an administrative assistant to people in some pretty high-up positions at other places, too. But this place is a little smaller than I thought when it comes to employment opportunities."

"Now, isn't this your lucky day?" Philip began. "My son, Chad, works at the Hennessey Company too, and they've just promoted him to an executive position. And guess what? He's looking for an administrative assistant to help with his and a few other people's workload in the department. I'd say it's a perfect match. Especially seeing they've been totally unsuccessful at finding a replacement for the gal who left when her husband was transferred out of town."

Claris' mind began working frantically in this new direction. It might be just the thing, except that a company that size would call for references, alerting her work, as well as Nathan Beecham, of her whereabouts. She hadn't thought of that before. No, it simply wouldn't work to take a job that would call her office for references. She'd have to think of something else.

"Thanks, Philip, but I really can't let you do that for me. I appreciate the offer, though."

"Nonsense. You could use a job, and our company needs you."

When they pulled up into the parking lot and found a space, Philip cut the motor and turned in his seat to face her. Claris saw the kind, searching dark brown eyes and couldn't be dishonest with him.

"Look, Philip. I did a good job at my work, and wouldn't have left for the world, except for a man I was seeing on the job. Things got sticky, and I chose to leave without notice. I'm afraid my references wouldn't stack up, and frankly, I wouldn't want my 'ex' boyfriend to find me. Do you understand?"

Philip considered her words for a moment. He took in a deep breath and drummed his fingers on the steering wheel.

"Okay, here's what we'll do. Seeing I'm the plant manager, supervising the entire department I'm speaking of, I can override personnel and ask them to make an exception. You might have to give the name of where you worked before, but I'll make them promise not to call. I'll explain without giving out any details."

"They'd do that? Just hire me without knowing a thing about me except what I tell them? Take me on my word?"

"No. But they'd take me on *my* word, and mine's all they need."

Claris shook her head in disbelief. "Philip Barnett, why do you trust me so much?"

"I see it in your eyes. And I see it in your character. I know people, Claris. I've learned the hard way. You're an honest person who's obviously stuck in a bad situation. I'm giving you a break. Are you willing to take me up on it?"

Claris said nothing, but nodded in agreement. With the weightiness of her situation, she couldn't bear so much kindness and total trusting which she needed at a time like this. Things might be all right after all, she realized. Philip was a Godsend, and the more she was around him, the more she wanted to stay close by his side.

As they situated themselves into the seats of the theater, Claris was glad it wasn't overly crowded. Though a weekend night, they had a little corner all to themselves. Throughout the show she wondered if Philip would make any moves that would change their dating status from 'just friends' to something over the line.

When half the movie had passed with not even a touch, except for her hand brushing up against his in the shared carton of popcorn, Claris found herself taking action herself. She slid her hand around his arm, clasping it comfortably. The muscle was strong, solid, and she noticed he shifted slightly in his seat and took a quick breath when she did so.

Claris glanced at his face, and he slid her a quick look, then focused back at the movie screen. It was a telling look, however, and Claris knew just what was going on in this man's brain.

From then on out, Claris was unable to concentrate on the second half of the feature. She was more interested in the good part—the part that would happen once the movie had ended and Claris was alone with Philip Barnett.

Chapter Four

"Well, that was a good movie, don't you think?" Philip asked as they moved into the parking lot.

"I think so," Claris answered walking dangerously close to his side. Philip felt himself breathe deeply, taking in her light scent that was all woman. He wanted to be alone with Claris, not just in a darkened movie theater, but didn't quite know how to proceed. If he moved too quickly, she'd think he wanted one thing from a stranger passing through, and that just wasn't so. With this in mind, he decided to leave the next move to Claris.

He turned his car into the direction of her hotel, and when he pulled into the parking lot he found a space and cut the motor.

"Well, I'd suggest something else, Claris, but there's not much night life here. At least not something I'd be interested in," he put in.

"No staying up all night for you," she laughed.

"Afraid not. I mean, not in a smoky bar or nightclub, that is," he answered. Philip noticed how she gave him a sly glance.

"I guess I could ask you 'in,' but all I have in the little fridge I've got in my kitchenette is pop," she explained. "That and TV are about all I've got to offer," she added.

"That's fine with me," Philip said, thinking she had far more to offer than those two things. He made a promise to himself, however, as they walked inside, that he'd remain a perfect gentleman. He didn't want to scare off Claris, or give her another reason to keep trucking. He planned to keep Claris here if there were any way possible.

When they came inside, Claris shut the door behind them and offered Philip the easy chair. She then went into the kitchenette area and retrieved two cans of pop.

His taking the recliner left only the bed or a hard-back chair for Claris.

"Look, why don't you take this comfortable chair here," he offered, beginning to rise.

"No, no. I'm fine," she promised.

An awkward silence filled the quiet room. Philip glanced at Claris, his eyes took in the king-sized bed, which seemed to dominate the room. She eased down on it and opened her can of pop.

"So, what did you do today?" he asked, hoping this was a safe question and wanting to distract his thoughts from the sexy woman sitting in front of him.

Claris watched him, a little mischievous grin passed over her features.

"Oh, I cleaned up the old homestead most of the day," she answered.

"You did? Don't they have maid service here at the hotel?" Philip questioned in surprise.

"Yes, of course they do. I was just kidding, Phil," Claris answered. "Can I call you Phil? Philip seems so stodgy," she added.

Philip felt the color rise to his face. It had been a long time since a woman had called him Phil. Long before he'd gotten married. His ex-wife seemed to revel in pronouncing his name in a formal, condescending fashion. Snapping the "p" at the end like a criticism. How different this woman seemed to be. He wanted to get to know her better, but felt awkward sitting so far away. Did he dare move closer?

"How about we see if there's a movie on? The hotel has HBO," she suggested, suddenly bringing the sound of the TV on at low volume.

Claris strolled to the desk, checking the listings from the magazine supplied for just that purpose.

Philip watched the way her skirt hugged her slim hips, making him crazy. That's how he felt. Crazy. In a hotel room with a stranger having feelings that he'd buried along with his heart for several years. Now it appeared it had all surfaced again.

"Well, we're in luck. One's just starting, but I have to warn you. It's a love story, and a pretty steamy one at that," she told him, flicking on the beginnings of the movie.

Claris moved back onto the bed, slipping off her shoes. She then fluffed the pillows so that she could lean against them and Philip noticed she slid a glance in his direction. The next thing he knew Claris was patting the seat next to her on the bed.

"Come on up here with me. I don't want to watch this alone," she said.

Did the woman know she was driving him crazy with her sexy allure that seemed so much a part of her nature?

"But only if you promise to behave," she added, abruptly stopping his thoughts. "I didn't invite you here for any funny business."

Philip chuckled and moved to the other side of the bed, removed his shoes, then slid next to her, barely allowing his thigh to touch hers. He glanced down at her and realized how all-woman she was. Yes, it had been a while.

"Phil, you're not watching the movie," she began, crossing her arms over her chest.

"I'm sorry, Claris, but you're quite a distraction being such a good-looking woman."

"Well, thank you. But I knew you'd keep your hands to yourself," she said.

"Why are you so sure of that," Philip asked, a chuckle rising in his chest.

"Because you're too much of a gentleman. And you're no boy. You're a man. A mature man."

"I don't think I like the sound of that somehow," Philip put in.

"Aren't you?"

"In number of years, I suppose, but I'm not THAT old."

"How old are you anyway?" she asked.

"Does it matter?"

Claris glanced down at her crossed arms, a contemplation overtaking the friendly banter. "Well," she said finally. "I guess not. I mean, what am I thinking even going out with you, Phil? I'm in a . . . a predicament, shall I say, right now. Certainly not in any position to start up a relationship other than a friendship."

"We're dealing with that situation. I can help you, Claris."

"But why would you want to, Phil?"

"I don't know. Let's say you put a spell over me the moment Millie brought you over to my table. It's like my whole perspective in life changed in an instant."

"Because of me?" she asked flatly.

"Well, maybe things had been healing under the surface. Then you came along at the right time and things clicked into place for me. So, naturally I'd like to help, and how can I get to know you better if you leave? So, you'll be in close contact with me at the same place of work and we'll see where this leads," he answered.

"Hmmm. I got into a lot of trouble by dating a man from work. Much less working for your son. How old is he?"

"Twenty-five. No, wait, he's twenty-six now," he answered. "I can't keep up anymore."

"No, I'll bet not. You're getting some age on you and you can't do all you used to, right?" she challenged.

"Just how old do you think I am?"

"You tell me. I'm thirty-five. Can you top that by a couple of decades?" she laughed.

"I'm only fifty, thank you," he huffed.

"Okay. You're five years younger than I thought. You'll have to show me you can keep up," she said, a flirtatious look coming over her face. She then glanced at the television and her eyes widened.

"Hey! We're missing quite a show," she said, gesturing toward the screen where the two main people in the movie had landed in bed.

"On second thought, you'd better not watch. A man your age might not be up for such things," she put in playfully.

Philip could take no more kidding, and no more waiting. His years of missing the company of a woman overtook him.

"Lady, I'll show you who's an old man," he promised.

* * *

She had taunted him. Claris knew this, but she couldn't seem to help herself. Phil Barnett was a man, plain and simple, and put together in a way that surprised her. She knew good and well that fifty was not old. Not even close. But she loved to tease him about it, and had previously wondered if the age difference wasn't a little too much for her younger years. She now had no question about that as Phil took her in his arms.

His mouth came down hard against hers. She could feel the slight roughness of his face, probably shaved early that morning and now showing a slight, but not uncomfortable, edge to his strong jaw. He reached around her neck, holding her head gently, yet showing her with his mouth that he meant business.

He then abruptly broke the kiss, gazing down into her eyes.

"How was that for an old man?" he questioned softly.

"The jury's still out," she teased, not wanting him to stop with only the one kiss. Phil Barnett had put her in a world all their own, and she was ready for something good to finally happen in her life. Especially with a man this strong, this mature and honorable.

"Then let me convince the lady further," he said, pulling Claris close to his side. He then began soft kisses on her mouth, her jaw, the crook of her neck, then up to her mouth again, showing her a tenderness of spirit and soul.

Her world had taken such a different turn, being in the arms of man who was so tender and caring. But it did not last. Her thoughts immediately turned again to Nathan Beecham, the man she was running from, and the icy fear she'd felt when she'd left in the middle of the night came crashing down in the arms of Phil Barnett.

As if Phil could sense her hesitation, he broke the kiss and glanced down into her face. What he saw now was an uncertainty.

She then shifted upwards and Phil eased away, giving her space.

"Phil, this is probably my fault, I started this, but I can't finish it," she explained.

Philip sat on the edge of the bed.

"No, no. That's not why I came in, Claris. You must believe that. I never thought we'd do anything but kiss, if I was *that* lucky."

"I *am* attracted to you, Phil. You should know that."

"I should never have come in," he said, rising to his feet.

"Stop being so hard on yourself, Phil. Everything's fine. It's just I started thinking, that's all."

"You won't want to go out with me again, thinking I've got an agenda."

Claris rose to meet him.

"We didn't even do anything, Phil. You're far too much of a gentleman. So, relax. I've just got too much on my mind and too much going on in my life to do get involved with you—yet," she explained.

Philip wrapped his arms around her in a hug. Claris appreciated the warmth, the caring, the understanding.

"Are you still planning to come to work at Hennessey's? I'll set it up for Monday morning. Just show up and ask for Mary Beth. She's head of personnel. Then you'll probably meet my son, Chad."

Claris smiled gratefully. "All right. What do I have to lose?" she asked, as she showed Phil out.

He placed a kiss lightly on her forehead, then disappeared into the night.

Claris came back in and sank down on the bed. The place where Phil had sat next to her was still warm. She thought about her last comment to him, asking 'what did she have to lose' and sighed deeply. The more she had gotten to know him, the higher the stakes. For at this point, after spending this last evening with Phil, she had even more to lose. Because the stirrings of her heart and her soul caused her to believe she had more to lose now than ever before in her whole life. And she wasn't about to let that happen. Her decision was now made. She'd stay here, take the job, and let herself fall into Phil Barnett's life—and never look back.

After the affirmation was made, she didn't have a feeling of joy or elation. Instead a sinking feeling in the pit of her stomach told her that her troubles were far from over, and hiding out and running from doing the right thing—no matter what the consequences—would remain like a dark cloud over her world until it came to a head. But she couldn't face that possibility now that she'd found someone she'd looked for all her life. Could she? Otherwise, she might lose her life, and her reputation in a work setting because Nathan Beecham had framed her. With this last thought, she undressed and crawled under the covers, hoping her night-time thoughts would erase all the bad she had on her mind, and she would wake with the nightmares gone and only the world of Phil Barnett remain.

* * *

"Hi, Dad," Chad called out.

"I'm over here," Philip answered, coming around the side of the house holding the clippers he'd been using to prune some overgrown hedges.

"I see you're hard at work even on a Saturday," his son told him.

"Yes, you see, I lost my son to some sweet gal. Now instead of having an extra pair of helping hands, he's busy with 'honey-do's," his father put in with a smile.

"Very funny, Dad. But you're right. I've got a long list of those, some I put there myself, some Sadie added," he grinned. "There's never a spare moment when you've got an older house like mine to renovate and fix up."

"Wait till that baby shows up. You think you've got no time now," Philip teased.

"I'm so happy, Dad. I'm just glad you moved us both here. You've been able to start a new life away from the memories of Mom leaving us back when, and I found Sadie. We've both been the winners here," Chad said with both contentment and enthusiasm.

Phil set the clippers down next to another bush, then beckoned his son over to the deck.

"Come sit a minute," he suggested.

"Uh, oh. I know that tone. Something serious is on your mind."

Philip grinned in response, but continued in that direction. When they were both comfortably seated on the deck, Philip bent over and clasped his hands, glancing up into his son's face.

"What is it, Dad?"

"Well, you've been lucky, Son. You found Sadie right off and it's worked out that you're happy. You'll be pleased to know I think I've found my 'Sadie' too. Only her name is Claris," he explained.

Chad jumped to his feet.

"Not that woman you met that was breezing through town? The one you met at Penny's Diner?"

"Yes, Son. Now, what's the problem?"

"Like I said before. You hardly know her."

"I'm remedying that," he put in.

"It doesn't matter. Where does she come from? Who is she? How long is she going to stay in town before taking off again to parts unknown? Probably just long enough to break your heart and send you even further into a state where you'll never let another woman close again."

"Chad, sit back down, will you?"

With this, his son eased back down, though his face had become a bright red.

"You're going on circumstantial evidence only. Just because she relocated here doesn't mean she's all bad. After all, we did the same thing. In fact, I was running away from past troubles in coming here. If that happens to be the same thing for Claris, are you going to judge her on that? Would you have done that with me?"

"No, your case is different."

"Well, what's her case, Chad? I mean, you've never even met her and you're going off the deep end. Don't you think your dear old dad has a modicum of sense? Or did my mistake in trusting your mother ruin your opinion of me in my judgment about women. And let me give you one more thing to chew on. I didn't trust Sadie and see how wrong I was about her?" he asked rising to his feet.

"Okay. Okay. I'll settle down. But you talk like you're going to marry her."

"Maybe somewhere out there I will. Still, there's no other way of finding out than to get to know the woman. I admit I've got a thing for her right off, but that won't stop me from using my head."

"Now I do feel better. I'm sorry, Dad. Didn't mean to rain on your parade like that, but just be careful."

A quiet truce hung in the air for a brief moment, then Philip cleared his throat.

"So, Son, I've got a favor to ask," he began.

"Which is?"

"I want you to give Claris Pemberton a chance. A real chance. Can you do that?"

"Of course. I'll try my best," Chad answered.

"Good. I'm glad to hear that since she's your new administrative assistant—both to you and a few others in the department."

Chad's eyes widened.

"And what kind of experience does she have?"

"Plenty."

"References?"

Philip remained quiet.

"Dad? References?"

"That's for personnel to handle," he answered.

"She doesn't have any, does she?"

"Of course. But you keep your nose out of it. She doesn't need you digging up something from her past. Let her have a clean beginning and give her a chance."

Chad stood. His father could sense the tension, but his son began walking away toward the driveway. "I'll give her a try, Dad. But I don't like this. Let me go on record in saying that," he answered, then shot his arm in the air for a backwards wave as he kept walking and didn't look back until he was situated in his truck and drove away.

Philip was glad he'd had an opportunity to tell his son before springing it on him at work. It was fairer this way, and it gave his son a chance to let off steam in private. He *did* seem to calm down slightly, but he knew his son, and hoped beyond hope he didn't try to cause any trouble. Perhaps in time he'd lose his reservations about Claris, but Chad was not the type to let things drop. That was the only thing that scared Philip about the situation. For both himself and Claris.

CHAPTER FIVE

"Welcome aboard," a well-wisher said in passing by Claris' desk without stopping to introduce herself. That's how it'd been all day. Busy, busy, busy, and a steady stream of employees who had to pass by the main thoroughfare in the office. Everyone had been so nice, so friendly—except Chad Barnett. Claris imagined it was because he'd had his own administrative assistant picked for him, and by his father, no less. She could see how that might not go over very well, but she would prove herself in time, she decided.

It wasn't as though Chad were rude, just cool and detached. She focused on the correspondence at hand and began working at her computer. He couldn't say anything if she were doing a bang-up job for him and the rest of the group, and she was very efficient at this type of work.

"Got that report done yet?" Chad asked, coming up from behind and surprising her.

"Sure. It's right here," she answered, swiveling around in her a chair.

Chad flipped through the thick report he'd produced early that morning and Claris had finished in record time and gave it a quick once-over. His cool demeanor held fast, and she imagined this proof of her competence would melt that away in a hurry. Instead he simply walked away, then stopped and turned back. Claris readied herself for his praise, which wasn't forthcoming.

"Next time bring something you know I'm waiting for to my office as soon as it's finished," he said, turning on his heels. After that, he walked into his office a few feet away and closed the door, what Claris believed was a bit too hard for normalcy.

She drummed her fingers on her desk a moment, staring at the barrier Phil's son had just erected between them. Claris believed no one could have finished that report sooner, especially being the first day. His attitude was now bordering on rude and she wouldn't stand for it.

Phil then appeared at her desk, quite unexpectedly. It was the first time she'd seen him since she'd arrived.

"I've been in meetings all day," he explained. "How's it going?"

"Great," she said, then frowned.

"Your words don't match your face, Claris. Is there a problem?" he urged quietly.

"No. It's just I think your son resents that you've put me in this position without his interviewing me or anything. I wouldn't like it either."

Phil turned toward his son's office. "I see he's got the door closed. Not like him," he put in. "I'll go talk to him," he suggested.

"No," Claris said, jumping to her feet. "That's my job. He's my boss, and I never got anywhere keeping my mouth shut at the first sign of trouble. This time, I'll do it myself," she answered.

Someone caught Philip by the arm and ushered him away, speaking of some emergency elsewhere. Claris was pleased Phil had come by when he had. His presence somehow gave her the courage to do the right thing at the right time. And now was the perfect time to have a little chat with Chad.

Claris knocked at the door, then came in when he answered. She then shut it behind her and took a seat opposite him. Chad tried to appear overly busy at some paperwork he was hunched over, yet Claris knew what all he had to do, and it could wait.

"Is there something we need to discuss?" Chad asked.

"You tell me," Claris asked lightly. "No matter how well I've fit in, finishing that report in record time, getting the hang of things quickly, it seems that you have a problem with me. I know what that problem is," she added.

Chad took in a quick breath.

"There's a problem?" he echoed uncomfortably.

"Seems to be. Shall I spell it out for you, or do you want to get the ball rolling?" Claris asked in respect.

Chad laid down his pen and clasped his hands over the paperwork.

"Claris," he began. "I'll be totally honest with you. I'm sorry if I seemed a bit cool earlier, but I don't like it that you're here and I don't want you in my father's life the way you are."

"In what way am I in your father's life exactly?" she asked after a moment's hesitation.

"You know very well. He's infatuated with you, but you can't afford to hurt him. My Mom did enough of that."

"Chad, I'm not trying to hurt your father. He's a good man. So is that the only problem you have with me?"

"Like you're now working for me but you have a mysterious background and I'm not allowed to ask any questions or check references?"

"Well, I can assure you, I've got a solid background in office management and plenty of time spent in administrative assistant work. Doesn't my work prove that?"

Chad glanced quickly at the report to the side that she'd just finished. He nodded in response.

"Besides that, I'm certainly sorry if you wanted to handle the interviews and hiring for your own position without your father's interference. I guess it just worked out that I arrived at the right time, that's all. And as far as your father is concerned, let that business stay between your father and me. But in the office, I promise I'll handle even the most confidential of correspondence with professionalism and discretion. I've had plenty of experience with that," she promised.

Chad's earlier easing up disappeared as a frown took its place. She had meant to ease the tension between them, but what she'd just said caused a reaction she didn't expect. Deciding saying any more would only make matters worse, she rose to her feet.

"I'll be right out here if you need me," she said, and left.

Claris tried to remain focused on her work, but her conversation with Chad still troubled her. What was it that turned the tides like that, she asked herself again. As she made a back-up copy of the financial report she'd finished that morning the answer came. Instead of inspiring trust, she gave Chad a reason to feel ill-at-ease. The information on the Hennessey Company outlined in that report, and their marketing and retail plans for the future were quite confidential. If it got into the wrong hands, it would spell disaster for Chad and the company. He could have interpreted her comments in one of two ways. Either he could have decided she threw it out as a manipulative threat—as in, if you don't leave me and your father alone, I have a way to mess you up already. Or, he could now suspect the reason she was not giving out but the bare minimum on her background that she might be truly working for one of the competitors and just happened to rope her father in on this, cinching the deal for the job. In either case, Chad was now worried. He confirmed that as he raced by her desk without a glance. She would have to try even harder to gain his trust. But somehow, she didn't think he would simply take her word on that. On anything, in fact—and that scared her.

* * *

"It's only a cabin-sized place, not a big house, but a friend of mine has it up for sale," Philip explained excitedly over the phone to Claris late that week. "I was thinking of buying it, you see. Being on the lake and just a two-hour drive away, it'd be a great place to get away and relax. Fish."

"That's nice, Phil," Claris answered, tired from a full week of work yet still feeling in limbo with her present circumstances. She imagined the setting Phil had just described. How nice it would be for him to have such a place. How nice it would be to be able to relax again herself, she thought wistfully as Phil continued.

"He's offering the place for me to stay for the weekend. To check it out to see if I'm interested in making the investment," Philip went on. "So that's what I'm going to do. Spend the weekend there."

Claris stared at the door of her lonely hotel room and clutched the phone receiver in her hand. She'd almost memorized the hotel rules and regulations outlined on the framed list on the inside of the door that led to the outside world, and the four walls had become suffocating. She found herself murmuring a response to Phil's energetic explanation of his plans for the weekend. Claris imagined he wanted to let her know why he wasn't spending the next few days with her, and she found she was definitely disappointed that even a day would pass without seeing him.

"You think I'm being too presumptuous in coming up with this, but let me put your mind at ease. The place may be small, but it does have two separate sleeping quarters," he added.

"You're inviting me along?" she asked, the obvious meaning now dawning on her.

"Of course. But I understand your not wanting to go away with me. I'm overstepping my boundaries. It might be a bit too close quarters for you," he said more in a question that a final statement.

"No, it's not that," she answered quickly. She wanted to scream 'yes' right away, but she hesitated. She had already fallen so unexpectedly for this man, but he didn't know her. Not the real her. Not the baggage she carried along with her besides that which he noted in her car. The unfinished business and threats on her life she ran away from hung over her like a dark cloud—no matter how great this new life was shaping up. And putting herself, her heart, her life and his in as close a contact as this weekend trip would certainly complicate things. She just had to give herself a moment to think.

"Phil? Can I call you back in five minutes? I'll have an answer by then," she promised.

"Okay. But I'd like to get there before it gets dark—seeing that I've never been to the place. So, if I don't answer the phone, call right back. I'll just be back and forth loading the car."

"Five minutes," she said and gently laid the receiver back in its cradle.

Claris took in a deep breath. Suddenly the hotel room looked even smaller, closing in on her. Just like her world. How could she venture forth into a relationship, a life, when Nathan's white-collar crimes remained an issue she'd have to eventually deal with. Would he really just leave her alone? Or would he come after her the moment he knew of her whereabouts? Besides that, could she live with herself if she neglected to tell the president of the company of his schemes? Wouldn't he continue to simply move on to the next unsuspecting company and do the same thing, over and over, as was his pattern if she did not stop him?

She then wondered how many women were left in his wake. Some with broken hearts as well as broken lives from his cons. Nathan was born with good looks, high intelligence, great creativity, and winning ways with people—yet he used it for illegal and immoral purposes. These gifts could be shared with mankind in such a higher purpose, she lamented, thinking the man had redeeming qualities, but had never headed in that direction.

Claris glanced at the curtains in her room, closed up tight, sheltering herself from the outside world. It felt bad, she decided. She had to get out. Had to make a change but wasn't sure how. A weekend at a lake with Phil Barnett would be just the thing to give her the answers she sought. It would clear her head, she decided.

When she called Phil back, he answered on the first ring. He sounded so relieved, so excited when she told him her decision. She would gather something up to take along and would be ready in fifteen minutes. She just wondered what would happen during this important weekend, what decisions she'd make. As the reality of spending this kind of uninterrupted time, alone with Phil, blocking out the rest of the world and letting their relationship go in whatever direction it would take, she wondered most of all what would happen to her heart.

Chapter Six

"It's truly beautiful," Claris breathed out as she emerged from Phil's car and took a look at the quiet lake and wooded scenery.

"I think the cabin must be just down the hill where the steps begin," he gestured.

Claris reached for her duffel bag and purse, while Phil took the bulk of the weekend's supplies and his own bags in his hands and nestled under his arms. They made their way down the steps and Claris took in the crisp air, and noted through the approaching darkness, the falling leaves, now losing their brilliant color and falling to the ground, as well as a scattering of acorns along the path.

When they approached the side door, Phil propped a box load of food supplies against the wooden railing of the wrap-around deck and fumbled with the keys. Claris stood nearby, taking in Phil's strong muscles moving and showing themselves through his flannel work shirt at something as simple as reaching to open a door. When they both moved inside, Claris felt her life just took a turn in the road, and there was no turning back now.

"A little musty, but not bad," Phil commented, pushing the box onto the kitchen counter and moving over to the side to the thermostat.

"Mitch said I'd need to turn up the heat. Gets a little cooler here in the mountain area and by the water. I think winter's around the corner," he supplied, turning to face Claris.

She lingered by the door, placing her duffel bag next to it.

"Oh," Philip interjected. "I guess you're wondering where to put that." Philip picked up her luggage and turned away. "Let's see," he began, heading down the hall. "Yep. Your bedroom's back here. Bathroom is off of that."

Claris followed in his footsteps. The cabin was a little smaller than she'd expected. They would know each other's every movement in such tight quarters. The idea both intrigued and scared her. She came in the room and sat on the bed, glancing up at Phil, wondering his next move.

"There's just one bedroom," she said, almost more in a question than a statement of fact. "I thought you said . . ."

Phil eased down next to her, taking her hand.

"I know. But that's a sleeper sofa in the den," he explained. "I won't get carried away and overstep my boundaries this time," he promised. Claris felt her throat constrict, not allowing any words to escape. Phil patted her hand and rose, walking swiftly out of the room.

"Gotta go get the rest of the stuff," he said. "Sandwiches for dinner. I'm afraid I'm not much of a show-off cook," he said, leaving her with a moment of quiet to herself.

When Claris heard the door close behind Phil, she smoothed her hand over the covers of the large bed. It was so large that it dwarfed the size of the room itself. She swallowed hard. It was becoming increasingly difficult to keep her distance from Phil. She had to tell him about her past. Later that night she would, and she would have to face whatever consequences would come from that. It was a decision she had to make, for in doing so she would also be choosing to let him further into her heart, for both decisions were intertwined and could not be separated.

*   *   *

After eating dinner, they got the lay of the land with a long stroll, and now they sat cozily in a glider on the expansive deck which had a great view of the quiet lake below. The night air nipped at them as they sat admiring the stars, and Philip pulled a blanket around Claris and around himself as well.

"You're cold too?" Claris questioned softly.

"Not anymore," he answered edging closer to her under the cover.

In the darkness Philip could still make out the peaceful and contented look on her beautiful face. Gone were the worry lines and unsettled disturbance below the surface that she'd grappled with from the moment he'd met her. In only a matter of hours after settling in here she'd seemed finally at ease. The transformation had been remarkable, actually. He wondered if it was from being alone with him, or the peacefulness of the surroundings. Either way, Philip was happy too. He wanted to erase any bad thing that had happened in her past, or whatever it was that made her rush out in the night in search of happiness. For being with Claris had done that for him. His long time of being upset with the circumstances of his ex-wife leaving him with a son to raise all alone were now a thing of the past. He wasn't sure how she did it, but it just happened.

"So, you think you'll invest in this cabin?" Claris asked as she looked upward into the star filled sky.

"I might. It's certainly a good place to help ease the tension from everyday life," he answered.

"You got that right," she agreed. Claris then laid her head on Philip's shoulder and let out a barely audible sigh. He felt a warmth inside as she did, moving his arm around her yet keeping it still under the blanket. It also felt good to be needed for once. His ex-wife never had in any way, it seemed. But even as independent as Claris was, she did need him. The funny thing was, Philip believed he needed Claris even more that she did him. It was something he just now admitted to himself. He wanted to share his life with her, and every part of himself as well. It was no surprise when he found himself telling her his deepest feelings, finally letting her in the rest of the way.

"It was the darkest of my nights when I discovered my wife had chosen another man over me. It shouldn't have come as a surprise, really. But it did. Like a monster that comes through that door when you're a kid and imagine all kinds of horrible creatures in the shadows. This one was real. I knew that side of her when I married her, but I figured if she committed to me, it would be a thing of the past."

"But it didn't happen that way," Claris put in. "She didn't change."

"I guess people can change, but it was a restlessness she never lost," he answered. "For a while she made me think she was satisfied, but there were signs to the contrary. I choose to ignore them. Don't know how many others there were, but after the fact, you let your imagination really run wild. All I know for sure is that this last boyfriend of hers, passing through town on business, must have offered her something I couldn't."

"I don't see how that's possible," Claris said, squeezing his arm. "You're more than any woman could ever ask for," she added.

Philip took in a quick breath. In one sentence Claris had conquered the fears and insecurities that had haunted him ever since his ex-wife had left him for another man.

"Thank you for that," he answered.

"It's true. You're an attractive man who's honest, trustworthy, giving—trusting . . . I know because you gave me a chance with no questions asked."

"I'm a good judge of character—now. My past mistakes with women made me that way."

"She's the one who made the mistake. But I'm not certain why you feel you can trust me so much. You brought me into your life and your business—making me a key administrative person in your son's office. What if I wasn't what I appeared to be. Like your ex-wife?"

Philip stole a glance at her upturned face. If his instincts were right, she'd taken this conversation to a point where she could walk into some confession of sorts. Perhaps she needed to get something off her chest. He leaned down and gave her full lips a soft kiss, then raised back up, focusing out at the lake below. An owl hooted from high up in a tree, his deep voice echoing over the water.

He wasn't sure he wanted her to tell him anything bad that might spoil the perfect world he'd built around them. It had been such a blessing, her coming into his life.

"Phil?" she questioned.

He glanced back. Her face now turned in despair in the soft moonlight.

"Something is wrong?"

"Yes. I'm afraid it would be wrong of me not to tell you. Not to level with you about my past. It doesn't seem right to keep secrets from you—not if what you want is to progress past this point in our friendship. And that's what you want, isn't it?" she asked.

Philip nodded his head slowly. It felt ever so much like the time his ex-wife dropped a bomb on him, saying it was something she needed to level with him about. The possibilities that now rushed through his brain couldn't be as bad as the truth, but he had to ask before she could tell him.

"You're married. Aren't you? That's the trouble you were running from in the middle of the night. Perhaps you've decided you made a mistake in leaving him and you're going back?"

Claris turned her face toward the lake and drew into herself. Philip was certain he'd hit the target with full force and he also felt a crashing disappointment surrounding him where Claris' warmth had just been.

"No," she whispered finally. "It's nothing like that."

Philip exhaled slowly then inched Claris closer again.

"I'm sorry. I won't play a guessing game. I'll let you tell me in your own way, and whatever it is I promise it'll be okay," he said, wondering in what direction it would take their relationship.

"Phil, I've done something I'm not proud of," she began. "But I didn't see any other way out. There *is* a man, and I was involved with him, but not seriously. The problem is, he was not what *he* appeared to be. He was dishonest and a professional con man. He used me, and I have done nothing to stop him. I ran because I was scared of what he might do to me. That's what drove me into the night with only my bare personal belongings in the car."

"That night when you found Penny's Diner."

"That's right. Then the next day, I had intended on running away even farther."

"Why didn't you?"

"Because I found you. You and this town seemed like such a safe haven, and believe me, I needed one more than I've needed one in my entire life."

Phil pulled her closer, placing a kiss on the top of her head.

"You're safe with me," he promised.

"Phil, you're such a nice guy, but I'm not entirely certain I can pull this off, and I don't want you to come down with me."

"Did he get you to do something illegal, Claris? Something the law will catch you for eventually?"

Claris tore herself gently from Philip's embrace and went to stand at the railing of the deck. He could see her silhouetted as the moon's soft light angled against her form against the wooden slats in the deck. The owl hooted again and he watched from his seat as Claris covered her face in her sorrow. He rose to his feet.

"What do you want from me, Claris? Do you want to bare your soul, your mistakes, but you're afraid I'll call in the police? Or is it you care enough about me not to want to get me into that kind of trouble?"

Claris turned around, giving Philip the impression that she wanted him to come to her. He took the few steps over and wrapped his arms around her. She then buried her face in his chest and he could feel the jerking motion of her sadness as tears found their way onto his shirt. He held her tightly, placing his chin on top of her head.

He let her get the sorrow, which he imagined had been pent up for some time, to play out as he quietly held her against him. Though he hated that some terrible sadness racked her, plagued her for so long, Philip felt like the protector and confidant his ex-wife had never needed or wanted. He felt for the first time a woman appreciated all that he had to offer, and he wouldn't let Claris down. When her sobs subsided into a quiet calm, Philip spoke up.

"Whatever it is, Claris, I'm here for you. Trust me. I'll help you through this," he promised. "You only have to tell me."

She swiped at her eyes and sniffed, then glanced down at the lake.

"Can we go down to the dock to the lake? I think better when I'm near water, and I can gather up enough courage to tell you my story if I do," she said.

"Let me get a flashlight," he suggested, as he ducked into the house a moment, then came right back out, also carrying an extra couple of blankets.

Claris wore the one they'd had out on the deck around her like a shawl, and Philip took another, layering it around her shoulders. Philip showered each step to the dock with the flashlight's beam, carrying them safely to the bottom of the hill.

Their footsteps echoed as they made their way onto the small, covered deck that enclosed a ski boat and gave only a small amount of room in which to move around. She marched in front of him toward the end of the space, gazing out at the peaceful waters that lapped ever so slightly against the boat.

Claris leaned against the side of the boat, which had a canvass covering all around with only an elastic edging that kept it in place.

"I think we can sit in the boat, if you like," Philip suggested as he raised the covering and checked the inside out with his large flashlight.

Soon, they were both situated in the back of the boat, huddling against one another once again, pulled together with the blankets. Her voice came out softly over the moonlit lake.

"Nathan Beecham is an evil man who uses his high intellect to extract money illegally from unsuspecting companies. In my case, I was the one processing the expense reports, reimbursing him for airline tickets for trips he'd canceled and cashed in the tickets, only I didn't realize the discrepancies at first since he traveled so much. Then there was the new computer systems he told me his satellite division needed—except that wasn't the case, they never received the PC's, and other things like that.

"He was very smooth and it took me six months before he slipped up on another airline scheme when his expense report showed his being out of town at a time when we had a date. When he put it through, I started matching up some dates and investigating what I should have from the beginning. He's a pro, let me tell you, and I thought I was pretty smart. But he was something else. I'm convinced he began dating me so I'd be less likely to check up on things, trusting him as I did. But there's no excuse. I should have checked out my suspicions earlier. When missing funds became part of his deal, I confronted him with everything. Well, the joke was then on me because the way he'd maneuvered it, it would appear to anyone looking on that it was me that had done the illegal paperwork, receiving the funds myself, and him the innocent party. He'd put my name on all kind of invoices and paperwork. Turning him in would be pure suicide on my part."

"So, you let him leave the company without telling on him," Philip finished for her.

"No. He's still there. I'm the one who left."

Philip studied her face. No wonder she was in such turmoil, he realized.

"But Claris, the man is probably still extorting funds, making you look worse and worse. It's only a matter of time before someone else finds the discrepancy, especially since you're gone and another person has taken over the books," he said in alarm.

Claris turned to him.

"I hadn't thought of that. I figured he'd just stop since I was gone, would leave me alone and not hurt me, and if I just kept quiet only a small crime would be committed and at least I wouldn't be put in jail for something I didn't do."

"Claris, I hate to break it to you, but you're committing a crime now since you know of this and you're aiding him in covering it up.

Besides, don't you feel you owe your previous employer this knowledge? Wouldn't they believe you?"

Claris let out an exasperated sigh.

"I haven't a clue if they'd believe me. I just know that I can't live with this as it is any longer and I don't want to lose you, or my new job, or this new life I'm building here. It really has been a safe haven for me. Could I really face going back—perhaps going to prison? Or face his threats of worse?" she asked incredulously.

"It won't come to that. I'll keep you safe," he answered. "We'll work out all the facts, type them up, send them to the police and your employer, then go back to testify. I'll be with you every step of the way. The truth is on your side, Claris. Remember that," he finished.

"I do have the truth on my side. And I have you on my side, too, don't I, Phil? What more could I ask in life than that?"

"Oh, you have me, Claris. Hook, line and sinker. And after telling me your darkest secrets, there isn't anything that could keep me apart from you. I won't let it," he promised.

Philip saw her eyes moist with a shade of gratitude shining in the moonlight. He bent to kiss the lips of the woman he would make his own. The woman who could stand on her own two feet, yet could need him in her life all at the same time.

It was what he'd missed, wanted, all his married life, and now he had the promise of this kind of relationship. He would never let her go, and would guard her dignity and integrity. He held her to him, drawing the blankets more tightly over her.

Phil Barnett was a happy man, content, and more in love than he'd ever been in his entire life. And he would do whatever it took to keep Claris safe and make her his own.

CHAPTER SEVEN

Claris listened to Phil's rapid heartbeat finally adjusting itself to normalcy. She nuzzled her head against his chest and wished she never had to move or leave his side ever again. She smiled to herself as her mind played over the non-judgmental belief he had for her. He was certain of her honesty and never questioned the facts she'd just laid before him. Phil Barnett was like no other man she'd ever known, and he had everything it took to make her happy.

Not only in his physical command, but in his integrity and patience. He'd obviously learned some things in the extra years he had on her, and put them into perspective for her. The most important of all was the way he'd handled the news she felt would send them apart. Instead, he'd sided with her, offered her help, cleared her thoughts and lessened her fears. She knew she'd have to do the right thing now. Not just for her previous employer, but those businesses that might be effected in the future from Nathan's schemes—and most of all, for the integrity of her own life. A life she hoped to spend with Phil Barnett. Who'd a thought it, she imagined and smiled. She'd come to find an escape, and ran smack into a man who could finally take her heart. She'd do the right thing, and now, Phil would be beside her when she did, backing her up, giving her courage, making sure Nathan was stopped in his tracks.

* * *

Claris woke slowly and felt the unfamiliar warmth of another human being next to her. She cracked one eye open, taking in the morning light easing across Phil's sleeping form. The blankets continued to surround them as Claris realized that they had fallen asleep in the boat.

The sound of soft water lapping against the gently swaying motion of the boat made her feel peaceful and at ease. They had fallen asleep talking, and she now woke to his loving arms. She could get used to a thing like that, she realized.

The memory of the night before came immediately to mind and she then snuggled closer to Phil. She loved being able to take him all in as he slept. She noticed the peaceful look on his face, the way his normally well-kept hair was tossed in disarray, the unshaven, strong jaw, and strong lips. There was one thing she knew for sure. She'd finally found her man.

* * *

Later that day they were deep into a plan that Claris felt could actually be the answer to her problems.

"So, you really think this could work?" Claris asked as she and Phil hunched over the kitchen table and went over the detailed list of how to resolve her problems with Nathan and the illegal company dealings he'd wrangled her good name into.

"Absolutely. I'll give this information to Dave Powers as soon as we get back. He'll dig up anything in the man's past, which I can assure you is tainted with other schemes of this nature, and you need to level with your friend at your old job."

"I'm sure he'll help. I've been friends with Brad and his wife, Nancy, for years. They'll know I'm innocent."

Phil pushed the loose-leaf notebook away and rose to his feet.

"Let's go for a boat ride," he suggested.

"You know how to drive that?"

"Sure, and it comes with the sale of the property. We need to check it out. See how powerful it is," he said, still grinning.

Claris just shook her head. She loved being with this man. Not only did she feel alive once again, but her burdens had fallen gently off her shoulders after Phil had agreed to help her and outlined a plan that made her face her fears and go for it.

Finding the boat in great running order, they relaxed with the cool afternoon as they took the speed boat at a snail's pace around each cove nearby. The late autumn weather kept the lake traffic down to a minimum.

"It's as though we have this whole place to ourselves," Claris supplied, enjoying the experience immensely.

"You're right. The summer tourists are gone, leaving only those who live here year-round. Which isn't very many, looks like. In fact," he said, pulling into a quiet cove where it looked as though no houses graced the upper areas of the treed lots, "we can just park the boat right in here and relax."

Cutting the motor, Phil let the boat just drift into the quiet cove. They both took in the sound of the birds singing in the nearby tall trees and the gentle, cool breeze nipped at their faces while the sun warmed them. Claris realized they had something special, for they sat together, feeling a bond together, yet not having to say a word for long periods of time.

The afternoon eased into the early evening hours before they had to leave. Phil needed to be back that night in order to get things done over the weekend. Claris hated leaving this world behind, though, because when she got back, all the peacefulness she found here and with Phil would soon turn into facing the nightmare she'd given up everything to run away from. But the water, the trees, the surroundings, and Phil, gave her the stamina to face the impossible.

Chapter Eight

Claris fell into the hotel lounge chair and reached for the remote to the television. After spending Friday night and all Saturday with Phil, they'd even managed to get in a few hours together on Sunday afternoon. She inhaled deeply as she thought about the past weekend with Phil, and tomorrow was going to be a big day as the events unfolded to get her out of trouble.

She hated to even think about that at the moment, but she had work to do—starting tonight. She would put Nathan in his place, and with their plan and Phil at her side, she'd make sure he didn't pull her down with him. He had to be stopped.

She reached for the telephone and dialed Brad and Nancy's number. After only one ring, Brad was on the line.

"Brad. It's good to hear your voice," she said into the receiver.

"Claris! I've been waiting for your call," he said a little too urgently for comfort.

"Why? Has Nathan messed up my reputation already?"

"No, but there's talk around the office. Seems some discrepancies have been discovered in the petty cash fund," he said uncertainly. "They're saying you took it."

"I didn't," she answered, her feet hitting the floor. "I promise, I didn't. You do believe me, don't you, Brad?"

"Yes, of course I do. But you see, I think it's only the beginning. Nathan's setting you up with the company books, just like you said. First, the petty cash deal makes it look like you're capable of stealing. Especially since you took off without a word. Who knows what's next."

"It doesn't look good," Claris put in. "He figures it makes sense that if I was going to skip town that it'd be easy money. He also has access. He knows where I kept the keys," she added. "But why mess with small potatoes? Why not just go for it and say since he knew me personally that I confided that I was doing other things to get extra cash?" she questioned uncertainly.

"Perhaps he's afraid the other will come to light, his skimming off the top, but it hasn't happened yet. Why stir it up until it comes up. Then when it does, and you've still not reappeared, he'll make sure the evidence points to you. You've got to come back to prove your innocence, Claris. And that's not just my own opinion. That's what Mark said too."

"The lawyer friend of yours? You've talked to him about me?"

"Well, no names were mentioned, but you need some legal advice, Claris. You're in big trouble, and running away won't solve anything. I went to check on your house yesterday," he added, changing his tone to a more matter-of-fact attitude. "All's well, and I went at the crack of dawn when I figured no one would be watching."

"Why not just go after midnight. You're the late night owl?"

"That would be a more obvious time you'd slip in, don't you think? That is, if anyone is even interested in watching your house . . ."

"Nathan would be. No signs of him coming in?"

"Not a thing out of place. I've got all your plants, like you asked. Oh, and I didn't realize you were such a computer fanatic. I went in your spare bedroom where you have your desk and noticed you've got some new equipment. I mean, how can you work on three new computers at the same time, Claris? But anyway, don't hang out wherever you are too much longer."

"Oh, that's just great!" she added incredulously.

"What is?"

"Now Nathan's planting computers he stole with company funds from his expense report and put them in *my* house. So, of course everyone will think I'm behind that and all the rest. Brad, really, things are moving way out of control way too quickly. I need your help in the worst kind of way."

"You got it."

"Good. You'll have to sneak to do this, but can you get me copies of a few files? Nathan's expense accounts from the last six months, and the books from last month, say around the 15th? As well as July's. It should be right there on my desk in a blue loose-leaf folder. It's not locked up or anything. Oh, and in the file cabinet to the right are the expense accounts. If I'm going to come back, I'll have to be armed with the truth. I'll be able to show just where I found his mistakes when I first became aware of it. Make me copies and then fax them to me."

"I'll give it my best shot. Where are you having me fax these, anyway?"

"To my new office, but directly to a certain person's office—not the main number, please, because this certain person is on my side and he's helping me get this all straight."

"He?"

"Yes. He's a wonderful man, Brad. You and Nancy are going to really love him."

"Hmmm. Do you? Love him?"

"I'll take the fifth on that right now, old pal. Let's just say if there's a silver lining to this disaster, Phil is it. I couldn't have found a better friend or whatever I should call him if I'd gone looking all over the world. But I have to straighten all this out first, Brad. Then my love life can take off," she said.

When Claris' head hit the pillow that night, she felt completely at ease. Phil had an airtight plan that would fix everything. She only needed to keep it quiet and between only her closest confidants. Brad would help her with this part and no one would be the wiser. The timing had to be just right, and from what Brad had said, she'd be just in time before Nathan got too suspicious. He would be caught off guard and Claris could win this game and put him away for his crimes. Yes, there was no one who would get wind of it in this tight group of friends. Now nothing could go wrong, she decided then fell peacefully off to sleep.

* * *

The next morning, Phil wasn't ready to explain his long weekend with Claris to his son, but when he arrived at his office, Chad had planted himself firmly in the chair opposite his desk.

"You're certainly the early bird. Did Sadie kick you out of the house without breakfast?" his father asked lightheartedly.

"No. She didn't. Actually, I fixed myself some toast. Sadie's stomach is pretty upset during the breakfast hour," he explained.

"Morning sickness, huh?"

"Yeah. I told her I'd take care of myself with cereal or toast. I don't want her to have to smell eggs or bacon cooking or anything to make matters worse."

"Right," Philip answered, sitting down at his desk and pulling out a few stacks of papers from his briefcase. He noted Chad watched him intently.

"What is it, Chad?" he asked, giving his paperwork more attention than it actually needed. He was afraid his disappearance over Friday night and most of Saturday had been discovered. Chad didn't always keep so in touch, but if he had and there had been no answer to the phone, he'd gotten either worried or suspicious that he was off with Claris.

"You take all that work home with you this weekend?" he asked lightly.

"Yes, I did. But I can't say I got much done on it," he admitted.

"Oh? Claris take up all your time?"

Philip glanced up. His son sat solemnly with his hands clasped in front of him.

"In a word, yes," Phil answered. "And I don't want to hear this business of me not getting involved with her because I don't really know who she is and what's she's about."

"Well, you don't, Dad."

"Yes, I do. More than you would guess."

Chad's face fell. He leaned up in the chair over his father's desk and lowered his voice.

"You waited all this time to start a relationship with the right woman, and now you're going to get close to this stranger? Don't fall in love with this chick or anything, Dad."

"Chad, I'm fifty years old and who I choose to fall in love with is none of your business," he answered, slamming the file folders down onto his desk.

"Oh, you're sunk now. I can see it on your face. Dad, how could you? Were you with her all this weekend? I tried to call. Even came over there but you weren't home."

"That's because I was down at the lake trying out Mitch's place he's trying to sell. A nice cabin with a ski boat and the works. I'm truly considering making the investment. You and Sadie and your new little one would love it."

"Don't try to change the subject on me, Dad. Was she with you? This Claris person?"

"Look, Chad. This 'Claris person' is a very nice woman who I'd appreciate your giving a chance. She also happens to be your administrative assistant. If for no other reason, give her some respect for the company's sake."

"I'll give her a chance once I see what she's really made of," Chad answered, leaning back in his chair as though he would be there permanently.

Philip let out a long sigh. "Look, Son, don't make the same mistakes your dear old Dad did when I stuck my nose in your business. I didn't give Sadie a chance at first. In fact, I came between you. It's a miracle you two worked through it and ended up husband and wife."

"Well, that's different. It was a simple misunderstanding. This woman may have murdered somebody and run off with all her stuff. You wouldn't even let me check on her references," he argued.

"Does she do a good job?"

"Excellent at her work, Dad, but . . ."

"That's it. I'm through with this discussion. You've managed to waste all the time I had to prepare for this meeting. I can't be late, either. You can sit here all day long if you wish, but I wouldn't recommend it. I'll be tied up for at least the next two hours," Philip informed him. He then gathered his papers, looked backwards at his fax machine and frowned. "Dad-gum distributor was supposed to fax me a list I needed for this meeting. I see that didn't come through either," he finished.

"I'm sorry, Dad. I didn't mean to ruin your Monday morning, but I still have reservations about Claris and I just want to help."

"If you really want to help, I'm expecting that fax to come through. Stick around a few minutes and if that distributor sends it, pass it through to me at the meeting?"

"Fine. I'll hang out another couple of minutes," he assured him.

Philip headed for the door, and at that second the fax machine came to life.

"Hey, I'll check it out, Dad. If it's what you're looking for, I'll bring it to you. Promise," Chad said.

Philip went straight to the meeting, and was surprised Chad never interrupted with the fax, but once the meeting was underway he found the list wasn't as important as he'd thought. However, when he returned to his office, Philip was a little surprised that the fax had disappeared. He decided the incoming material must not have been from the distributor and perhaps even for someone else and Chad must have delivered it to them. So often his number was given out instead of the main fax number. It happened all the time. He'd just call the distributor and have him send it again. No big deal, he thought and picked up the phone.

48-BURG

* * *

Claris wondered why Chad was acting so funny that morning. She'd delivered everything in perfect order when she placed the reports she'd typed that he'd left over the weekend. It could only be one thing, she decided. He'd found out about her rendezvous with his father at the cabin.

She imagined Chad had too much tact than to mention it to her. It was none of his business, after all. But he walked around very subdued, contemplative. She decided it would do her no good to speculate. It could be anything, and she had her own problems to deal with anyway. Starting with why Brad hadn't faxed the info she wanted to her yet. She'd checked Phil's office earlier in his absence. No fax material lay in the tray, and later that morning, she clued him in on what to look for. She then decided Brad might be having more problems getting the data together without anyone watching. She'd just have to be patient a little while longer. If it hadn't come by lunch time, though, she'd go use a pay phone and make the call to Brad directly to the office. She'd have to. She was losing valuable time.

Chapter Nine

"I finally got this," Philip explained as Claris walked in his door at the close of the business day.

"Good. It took him long enough. After I called at lunch time, he said he'd thought that was taken care of. We couldn't talk, you know. Just a quick call. Boy was he surprised when I called at the office . . ." she continued.

"Yeah, I don't mean to disturb you, but I'm a little worried about the confusion. Your friend put 'second try' on this one and I'm hoping nobody on that end did anything to stop it."

"You think somebody from my office could have sabotaged Brad sending it? Like if Brad walked away from the fax machine for a second?" Claris ventured. "You're concerned about Nathan?"

"Not really," Philip answered, reconsidering. "If that were the case, he'd have absconded with the evidence altogether. Not just keeping the first attempt at faxing it out from messing up. It could simply be the thing jammed. But it doesn't sit right somehow. Anyway, I've looked these records over and it's rather obvious what's been going on. Nathan is pretty slick."

"Right. But if you saw it, and I saw it, somebody's going to catch on soon."

"But we're forearmed now. When do you want to make the trip to meet with the company president? This week? This weekend at the latest?"

"Does it have to be that soon?"

"Yes, Claris. Otherwise, I think you'll be pushing your luck. You've got to jump on this before Nathan gets wind of your plans. As it is, he thinks you're gone for good. He's still at your old office. I have a feeling from his methods here that he'll milk it for all it's worth before leaving for greener pastures," Philip answered, studying the papers again. "But he won't stay forever. And if he thinks you'll come back and do the right thing, he'll set you up even more and escape unscathed, leaving you holding the bag."

"Are you going with me?" she questioned.

"Yes."

"Then when can you get away? This weekend?"

"I suppose that's the most convenient for both of us. I just hope we're not making a mistake in holding off. I could get some time away from work, and you could too, even though you just started."

"This weekend's soon enough for me. I've got other things to tend to. In fact, I've got to meet someone in about twenty minutes. I've really gotta go."

"What? Don't tell me I have competition already?" Philip asked.

Claris noted the broad smile that widened on his face. He knew better than to think that. Not after the weekend they'd shared, the confidences they'd exchanged.

"Actually, it's a surprise. But it's nothing for you to be concerned about. And if it works out, I'll tell you about it this weekend," she promised.

* * *

When Claris pulled up to the rental property she knew this was the right place. The small house, close to the park and filled with tall, old oak trees, spoke of the quiet new beginning she longed for after such an ordeal. Besides that, the price was right. A tall middle-age man with angular features met her in the driveway as soon as she cut the motor.

"How'd you do? Miss Pemberton?"

"Right. You're the owner?"

"Yes, ma'am. This is a fine house you're getting," he promised, walking toward the front door. "That is, if you do take it," he laughed.

Claris strode inside and could already see herself ensconced in this setting. The cozy rooms, the warmth that emanated from the very structure, and the promise of better things to come . . .

"Well, I'll certainly say you've kept it up and in fine shape," Claris said as the man stood patiently by and let her make her own tour without exerting any pressure.

"I believe in taking care of what's important. Like this house, for instance. But I'll have to admit I owe much of that to my renters. I only rent to fine folks I can trust," he told her.

Claris turned around to face him.

"How can you tell that about me? I'm a stranger to this town."

"That's right. What you told me on the phone. But I've got a knack for spotting good character. My intuition hasn't let me down yet," he explained.

"Well, I can't give you any rental history records. I've owned my house for some time. Just relocating and I'm not sure where I'll end up living here permanently—in housing that is."

"I'll tell you what I'll do. I know where you work. That's enough for me. You give me a small deposit and I'll let you have it on a month-to-month basis like I did from my last renter."

"Oh. That's a great idea with my plans being so up in the air," she put in. "You normally rent a nice house like this month-to-month?"

"No," he answered, rubbing his smooth jaw and looking around. "Guess you can say I did it last time in the name of true love."

Claris had to laugh. "What on earth do you mean?"

"Why, the last renter was a woman who'd never been married but had a decision to make about going down that road. She was an older woman, never found true love until she moved back here from long ago. Anyway, she didn't want to rush right into answering about the marriage so I let her bide her time here. Month-to-month until she decided," he explained.

Claris stood waiting for him to finish his story. Instead he just stared at her.

"Well? Did she marry him?"

"Yes! Yes, indeedy. Took her only three month-to-month's to make up her mind," he said laughing. "She's now moved into his house and living happily-ever-after, it seems. Now do you want to take it or not?" he asked. "Marilyn's got my supper on by now and I'd best not keep her waiting. She gets pretty riled if I don't show up on time," he laughed.

Claris pulled out the deposit money she knew would be necessary and exchanged it for a key. The utilities were included in the rent and all was falling into place.

After the owner pulled away, Claris slid down the living room wall and sat on the hardwood floor. She took in a deep breath and wondered how something so horrible could have lead her to something so marvelous as meeting and falling in love with Phil. This house cinched the deal for her. It was a good sign, she believed, that the man offered the month-to-month arrangement and the background of the last tenant was a positive, too. Claris also wondered if her romance with Phil would end up in the same way as the previous woman who'd never married either. Would she be so lucky? she wondered. The only thing Claris knew for sure, was that it probably wouldn't take her all of three months to decide if Phil actually proposed marriage to her. She only had to get this dark cloud hanging over her head out of the way. Then things would be perfect.

* * *

Philip worked hard all week so he'd feel comfortable leaving town for the weekend again. Normally he brought work home with him, but not this time. He wouldn't have a moment to spare with traveling with Claris back to St. Louis to spill the beans to her previous boss as to what had gone down with Nathan. Things seemed to be falling into place, he decided, having hired his private detective friend from Chicago to look into the matter. He'd promised Philip that he'd get back to him by Friday, mid-afternoon, and it was now 10 a.m. The shrill ring of the phone brought him out of his deep thoughts.

When he discovered his detective friend on the other end of the line, he felt the timing couldn't have been better. However, his optimism was quickly deflated when he heard his friend's report. The news about this character, Nathan Beecham, was worse than he'd figured. He had a record, all right, and small crimes and white collar crimes were only a sampling of what he'd done in the past. Only it could never be proven. It seemed he was especially fond of women who helped him get away with his money schemes. Many of them disappeared without a trace just before Nathan would leave town for good.

The assumptions were that they'd left town too, for it looked as though they had been in on the schemes as well. At least that's what it looked like. This had taken place all over the country. The detective agreed with Philip that Claris might be his next victim if her whereabouts were noted, and especially if she came back to report him. The detective agreed to send the report as an e-mail attachment to Philip, and would also give the local authorities a call so when Philip and Claris arrived, they'd have police protection on their side.

Claris had come by first thing that morning, telling him she had some life-changing news but couldn't tell him there at work. It'd have to wait until later. When they were alone, she'd said. She seemed upbeat about it, so it must have been something good she'd found out from home about the office problems at hand. Something she didn't want to talk about in front of anyone who might overhear her dilemma, he imagined.

Phil then busied himself with the reports in front of him, trying hard to focus on the work that he needed to get out of the way before he left town. He was then aware that Chad had come in while he'd been so preoccupied and was now standing in front of his desk.

"Hello, Son. Any reason you're sneaking up on me like that?"

"No. I just didn't want to disturb you. You've been so hard at it and tied up all week. Haven't had time to talk at all," Chad explained.

Philip put down his silver pen and laid his hands on top of his thick report.

"I didn't mean to be inaccessible. Was there something you wanted to talk about?"

"Yeah," he confessed sheepishly. "But you're not gonna want to hear it."

"The Mason account fell through?" Philip ventured.

"No. That's on track. I've straightened out that little misunderstanding."

"Good. I knew you'd be a pro at this thing. I didn't send you to the best schools for nothing," he added.

"Right, Dad," he answered, taking a seat.

"You look upset. If it's not about the Mason people, what's got you in such a slump? Nothing's wrong with Sadie or the pregnancy?" he guessed, getting a little worried.

Chad shook his head. "No, nothing like that," he said, supplying nothing more. Philip glanced at his desk clock. The manager's meeting which would take up the majority of the rest of the day was due to begin immediately. He turned to his son as he continued to sit in silence.

"Chad, look, I hope you don't take this the wrong way, but whatever it is, please cough it out. I've got a meeting in exactly five minutes. After that, I'll be leaving for the weekend, so I'm sorry, but I don't want you to have to keep this news to yourself any longer. I know I've been rather hard to reach this week. So, if there's a business snafu this is a great time to fill me in before the weekly meeting," he explained rising and shifting a few reports and folders into a stack.

"Dad, it's not business. It's about Claris. You're not going away with her again this weekend are you?" he asked slowly.

"Yes, as a matter of fact I am. It's an important trip for the both of us, so don't try to stop me. Besides that, I don't know why you've got such a bad feeling about her. She's the best thing that's ever happened to me."

"Dad, I promise you, you don't know her. Don't let yourself get hurt by the likes of her."

Philip shoved the files for his meeting under his arm. He felt the blood rise to his face, anger about to overtake him. Claris had enough going against her for the moment. Adding Chad, his own son and her immediate boss, to the list was like adding insult to injury.

"Okay, Chad. I'm going to say this one more time. She's a wonderful woman who I intend to keep in my life—permanently. If you've got a problem with her, handle it. Soon you'll see her true colors and you'll be so ashamed of this attitude you've taken."

"So you're determined to go away with her again?" Chad asked rising to meet his father's stance.

"Yes. I am. I'm a grown man and your father. I don't see why I need your permission. I'm meeting her at Penny's Diner for a quick dinner directly after work, then we're taking off. So. There you have it. Deal with it."

"Dad, you're wrong about her. And I know you'll thank me later for wising up to her before she does any more damage to this family," he said. "We've gone through enough as it is, and I won't let you get hurt again," he promised.

Philip gave his son a warning look, then huffed out of his office, leaving Chad behind. The last thing he needed was a confrontation today of all days. Besides, he needed to get business taken care of and not focus on this other. Claris needed him more now than they ever, and it looked like help would arrive just in time.

* * *

Claris arrived at Penny's and took a quick look around. Fred, the man who'd suggested she stayed and not rush back out into the night when she'd first arrived was on shift. He ushered her over to a booth next to the window. Claris figured that was a good spot. That way she could watch for Phil.

She sat waiting for a good five minutes before finally getting a little antsy. He simply had more business to tend to before leaving town, she assured herself as an unexplained feeling of dread and nervousness overtook her.

Glancing around, she noticed Fred had his back turned, clearly busy with preparing an order at the grill, and the other waitress on duty was busy in the corner with an elderly couple. Still no Phil, she thought, checking her watch. He was only ten minutes late, she reminded herself, then looked around again.

When her eyes met the back of the man's head in the booth two down from her, she had an awful feeling in the pit of her stomach. He then rose and turned, coming down the isle in her direction. Reality then hit, as Nathan sidled up next to her, bent down, and plunged a revolver against her ribs. His raspy whisper in her ear let her know he meant business, and they both disappeared out the glass door without the slightest detection from anyone inside.

Chapter Ten

Claris' mind raced. Nathan put the hand gun in his jacket pocket, on the opposite side from her. There'd be no way to reach across him in front of the steering wheel and into his pocket to wrestle the weapon out of his possession. She quickly decided instead to act as though they were simply having a quarrel like in a dating situation. It seems they never got along very well in that relationship anyway. She decided to play it this way, hoping her intense fear of him would not show.

"I knew this was too good to be true. To be rid of you and start a new life," Claris spat as Nathan drove along a long narrow dirt road into the most remotest of places. He found a small widening place in the road and pulled over.

"Give me that duffel bag," he demanded, as he pulled her small luggage she'd brought along for the trip back home into the front seat.

"What do you want with me, Nathan? I left town. I didn't spill the beans on your little con."

The overly handsome man flashed her a grin, then plowed through Claris' personal items. He twirled a skimpy pair of panties on his finger, giving her a look that sent shivers down her spine. Surely he didn't mean to do that to her, here in the middle of nowhere, forcing her to give him what she'd never shared before in their short dating period.

"Is that what you want, Nathan? Your male pride was hurt in my disappearing?"

He let out a long, luxurious laugh, stuffing the strewn about items back in the bag.

"You flatter yourself, Claris. If that's what I'd wanted in our little fling, I would've gotten it."

"Now who's flattering themselves," she hissed. "I was simply having a good time with you, Nathan. Nothing romantic, and certainly nothing sexual."

"Give me your purse," he said as though speaking to a child.

"Why? What are you looking for, Nathan. I don't get it? Why come back for me?"

"Well, now. Let's see. Why would I need to come back for you," he began as he started fishing through her purse. "For one thing, somebody's gotten nosy. Too nosy. You've made it impossible for me to stay at my safe little job and continue as I have."

"Brad," she said softly. "Did he tell you where I was?" she asked incredulously. How could my best friends turn on me, she thought. Brad and Nancy were the only ones who knew of her whereabouts.

"Brad? Oh, so *that's* who was behind this pitiful scheme of yours."

"That's how you found me, right?"

"It's coming together now," he said, slamming her purse onto the seat. "So that's who faxed information about me to your boss, is it? I might just have to fix him too," he said, staring out over an open field.

The remoteness of the area, along with the shorter day time of the fall season meant the sun was beginning to go down. Claris didn't like this at all. She didn't know what else Nathan was capable of, and if he got mad enough, she thought, she might be in real danger. She decided she'd have to play this the best way she could to keep alive. The fact that she'd wanted to do the right thing now made her think twice. She was no match for Nathan, but who'd turned on her? If not Brad, then Phil? The idea horrified her, bringing a sinking feeling in the pit of her stomach.

"Whatever you think I have, Nathan, clearly I don't. Why don't you take me back. I'm not going to do anything to you. You've already set me up so that it'd look like I was behind it anyway. That's why I left. I can't fight you. Just take me back to Penny's, please," she found herself gritting out the words, hoping she could reason with a deceitful man with no morals. Her life depended on it.

"Where are the papers, Claris?" he asked, turning in his seat.

Claris held her breath as he tenderly trailed his long fingers along her jaw line, massaging the back of her neck, then fastening shut on her vulnerable neck. She felt the blood gathering, pulsing hard in her head. She could hardly breathe. She reached up to free herself of his grip, clawing at his hand, which only made him tighten his stronghold.

Her life then began to flash before her, knowing this might very well be the end. It was certainly possible. She thought about her past, her family, her relationships, her best friends, who would miss her, what she'd accomplished, what she wished she had done by now, the triumphs then regrets, and then Phil. She'd been set free by his love, his attentions, and his offer to help. For the first time in her life she'd felt she'd found her home as she'd never known it. They had just started out. A new beginning. One she'd have treasured and cherished. As her world began to fade and her field of vision narrow in a tunnel of darkness creeping in on the far edges of her sight, he suddenly released her then settled comfortably back in his seat, just as though nothing of significance had just transpired.

Claris heard crackling in her ears as dizziness began to dispel and her vision cleared. She gasped for breath, drinking in the air, holding onto her throat. She bent over, feeling the tears surfacing. She then fell back against her seat and turned to stare at the man who'd almost taken her life in a most casual way.

When Claris found her voice again, she could no longer hide her fear. After all, he'd forced her away by gun point, and almost strangled her to death in an instant.

"What do you want, Nathan? What are you going to do with me? Make me disappear without a trace?" she asked, fearing the worst.

"Haven't decided. That's easy enough, you know. It's been done before," he added.

"You mean you've killed before? Some poor person who got in your way?"

"Did I say that?" he questioned in a taunting way. "Now, look, cutie-pie. If you hand over what you had faxed to your new office, then I might call it even. Otherwise, I'll have to take care of any other loose ends you've managed to create."

"I don't have the papers, Nathan. What makes you think I do?" she asked, determined to find out if Phil put the call into him or if Brad or someone from her office had done so—somehow letting on what was taking place. Perhaps the new secretary? she wondered.

"Your boss put in a call to me. Told me where you were and where to find you at a little after 5:15 p.m. Yes, that's right. Do you think I'd fly down here and mess up a perfectly good weekend to go to some restaurant called 'Penny's Diner' for fun? Nope, I was tipped off so that I could stop you from ruining both our lives."

"You've already done that, Nathan. I won't say anything," she promised, though knowing in her heart she would now do whatever it took to put this man behind bars—that is if she lived to do so. She'd be the last of his victims, not to mention the end of his illegal schemes with company funds. Nathan just smiled at her. Claris feared he could see through her denial of turning him in.

"You don't believe me."

"Why should I?"

"Obviously my boss has the papers I had faxed. Okay, so I was considering turning you in. But since I have no evidence, and since I was going back without it, what does that say?"

Nathan rubbed his chin and glanced around at the fading sunlight. He heaved out a deep sigh, then started the car. He then did a U-turn in the small road and headed back toward civilization.

"It means the papers are somewhere and until I get my hands on them so nobody puts anything together, then you and I are a team. You go nowhere and I don't let you out of my sight. Got that, Babe?"

Claris shuddered as he barreled down the dirt road, pitching rocks and dirt everywhere. She didn't know if she or her little car either could take this kind of abuse without falling apart. What was worse, she wondered why Phil had turned on her as he had. He was the only one who knew about the faxed material, and certainly about their meeting time. She thought sadly of the good news she'd intended on telling him that night as well—that she'd moved out of the hotel and into the nice house which would show him she was serious about him and making a life with him. Nathan couldn't exactly be trusted, but she had to consider his words. Had Phil actually called Nathan? Told him where to find her there at Penny's? Was that why he hadn't shown up? He wasn't going to? He'd just left her to fend for herself? How is that possible? she asked herself.

Though in her heart she couldn't believe Phil was capable of such a thing, perhaps he'd felt she needed to deal with it and Nathan all alone. The facts of everything did add up, she had to admit as fresh tears flowed down her cheeks. She then realized the pain of that betrayal was greater than any torture Nathan could ever inflict on her.

* * *

Philip sat at the booth at Penny's racking his brain. Wherever could she be? Doesn't she know it'll take all the time they had to drive the distance to make it half-way that evening, then to start early the next day to make the appointment they'd set with the company president?

After a while, he'd imagined she may have forgotten something and gone across the street to her hotel room to retrieve it and that was the reason for her absence. After too much time had passed though, he'd gone over there after her. Claris' car was nowhere in sight, and after there being no answer at her door, the hotel manager explained that she'd checked out. He wouldn't give Philip any exact information about when, but that she was no longer a guest at the hotel.

He now found himself waiting at Penny's for the next hour, getting more and more confused. The truth finally dawned on him. As much as he thought Claris was into their relationship, that it was one that could last and become permanent, something he'd waited for, hoped for, maybe she hadn't shared the same feelings. As he glanced around one last time, searching inside and out for Claris, he told himself he'd have to accept the inevitable. Chad was right. He must not have known Claris at all if she was willing to pull up stakes and leave without him. He didn't even hold any hope that she'd felt she could do it on her own and would return after it was all straightened out. No, Claris was gone for good. Of that he was sure.

He placed a few bills on the table for the cups of coffee he'd ordered while he waited, opting not to eat at all that night. He'd lost his appetite. As he walked out the door of Penny's Diner, sadness overtook him, as though the weight of the world rested on his shoulders.

* * *

"Okay, so now we go to your house," Nathan explained calmly.

"I've been living at the hotel. I've checked out, though," she answered. Now that they were at least in the main section of town, Claris thought she may still have a chance to get away. Perhaps jump out the door at the next traffic light. However, as soon as that idea came into her head and instinctively leaned forward and toward the door, it was as though Nathan became immediately aware of it.

"Remember, if you try something stupid, I mean, another something stupid, like thinking you can get out of this car, think again. I've got a gun and I'm not afraid to use it. You know that, Claris."

She then sank back against the cushions, the fight in her beginning to wane. So now where do you take me, Nathan? I'm surprised you didn't get it over with and dump my body before now."

"It occurred to me. But it also occurred to me that your boss may have given you the fax, giving you false hope, then turned around to warn me."

"I can't believe Phil would be capable of such a thing," she mumbled

"Who's Phil? I talked to your boss, Chad."

"Oh. I just figured Phil did this," she answered carefully. The facts now becoming more clear. "I've got several people I answer to," she explained softly.

Nathan jerked the car into the parking lot of an abandoned, out-of-business restaurant. He put the car in park, then leaned dangerously over to Claris. She could feel his breath on her face and it made her sick to her stomach.

"Now you tell me where you live and let me take a look around. If I don't find the fax, then maybe I'll be satisfied that this Chad person threw it away. He obviously thought you were the one behind skimming company funds. He wants you out of that office, so he probably threw it away. Unless you got your hands on another set. That's what I'm here to make sure you don't have. I've already fixed the evidence at the office, so you're the last loose end I need to take care of before hitting the road. Onto a new situation. The world's full of 'em out there. So, now, Claris. What's it gonna be? Are you going to be a nice little girl and tell your old sweetheart where you lay that pretty head of yours now? Or do I quietly end your life in the back of this restaurant and feed you to that dumpster? Since it's closed, nobody would even think to look in it for months," he said in a deadly serious tone.

Claris instinctively brought her hand up to her neck, still sore from his last effort to crush the life out of her.

"Turn at the next light then down three blocks. I live down there," she informed him. Claris didn't want to give Nathan the upper hand, but if he were bent and determined to kill her, he could do that anywhere. At least if he did it in her home, the landlord would follow up and find her body. She just wished Philip knew where she lived. She'd waited to tell him the good news about her renting the nice house till that night and of her plans to stay. It was supposed to be a surprise to let him know how serious she was about their relationship.

Thoughts of a life with Phil brought fresh tears to her eyes. She'd finally found her man, only to have it snatched away by Nathan—and Chad. Perhaps it would've never worked, she thought wearily as they pulled into her driveway. Not if Chad would turn her over to a madman to do whatever he sought to do to her.

As they eased into the house, Claris searched the neighboring yards and street, wishing someone would be out to notice. If they were, she could scream for help. Anything. But all were safely inside, probably enjoying a nice meal with their families—while their new neighbor was in grave danger of never seeing the outside again.

"Okay, Missy. This won't take long. Got no furnishings at all except a kitchen table and chairs—oh, and a big bed, I see. Guess that tells me a lot about what you've been up to."

"That isn't funny, Nathan. Have your look around and then leave me in peace. I won't turn you in. I can see you've covered your tracks and set me up. I just want you out of my life for good."

Nathan chuckled as he caught her chin in his hand. "That is if I leave with you a life to live," he answered.

As he turned and began sorting through the first cardboard box in the corner, Claris had one last hope. She eyed the door, waited for Nathan to become engrossed in a stack of papers, then bolted for the outside world.

Reaching for the doorknob, she felt the excruciating pain of Nathan's strong arms squeezing around her, pulling her back and downward. She bumped her head on the hardwood floor and moaned in pain.

"No, no, no. This will just never do," Nathan said in a sing-song voice. He pulled her up and into a straight chair at the kitchen table. He then took off his belt and drew her ankles together, then found some twine she'd used to tie a bundle of shoe boxes together and tied her wrists behind the rungs of the chair. The thin rope cut into her flesh, but she was determined she would not let him know the extent of the pain he continued to inflict upon her.

"Now, isn't this a pretty picture," he said, admiring his handiwork. He then turned away. Claris felt she was finally beaten. There really was no hope. Phil probably thought she'd stood him up, and he hadn't a clue that she'd put down roots here and moved in. If she had just told him earlier, there would be someone who might come and rescue her. As it was, her fate would be up to a madman determined to make sure he got away with his creative accounting schemes, of which he was certainly a master. It's like he 'gets away with murder' over and over again. The wording of the cliché hit her like a ton of bricks. Murder. Again. The thought brought her eyelids slowly shut. She now had little hope that she'd ever come out of there alive.

* * *

Philip stared at the television with no interest. The football game he'd found did nothing to take his mind off Claris. How could she have left him without a word, he continued to ask himself. Would she be back at work on Monday? And if so, how could he continue the relationship if she'd had such little regard for his feelings as to do such a thing as take off without a word? Her car was gone. She'd checked out of the hotel. She was not at the designated meeting place.

He now wondered if his being late had anything to do with it. Had she even been there? He had a renewed anger at his son, Chad, for detaining him with business questions that could clearly have waited until Monday. But no, he insisted on just a few more minutes, he'd said.

Chad knew he was meeting Claris and had plans to go off with her that weekend, and Philip believed that his son was intentionally trying to make him late. Perhaps even thinking it would make Claris angry. Perhaps enough to cancel the trip.

Phil snapped up the remote control, searching the airwaves for something, anything, that would take his mind off the woman he'd grown to love. The one he believed would finally treat him and a relationship together with trust, honesty, respect. She'd turned his head, all right, but again, he had to face the facts. If she'd felt the same way about him, she'd have never left him.

One last thought plagued him. It was the fact that Claris had mentioned that she had something to tell him that night. Something life-changing, and no, she would not let him in on her news until they were alone. He'd first thought it had to do with the office problems back in St. Louis, but now he wondered if it had to do with her plans on leaving without him. That she was checking out of the hotel and leaving town for good. Did she go back home to straighten out this mess alone? Or was she too scared of Nathan to do that? Or perhaps too scared of a relationship with the depth and intensity he thought they'd shared?

Anger rose within him. He felt he'd just experienced the same thing his ex-wife had put him through—but even more unexpectedly. He pushed the "power off" button to the television then sat in silence.

Moments later a rap at the back door brought him to his feet. Claris! His heart swelled with relief as he rushed to the back of the house. When he swung open the door, he exhaled his excited breath. Chad stood waiting on the threshold. Philip turned away, walking slowly back to the den, saying nothing. Chad followed on his heels.

"Well, it's good to see you too, Dad," he said defensively.

"I thought it was Claris."

"Oh. Sorry about that. Will your own flesh and blood do?"

"Yes, yes. Take a seat. I was just watching your old alma matter get clobbered in football. Or at least I was making an effort to follow it."

"That why you turned it off?"

"I guess."

The two men sat in silence a moment, awkwardly staring at each other. Chad shifted nervously on the sofa.

"So, Claris isn't here, huh?"

"No. She's gone off on her own, I guess."

"Oh. Sorry to hear that, Dad."

"I'll bet," his father answered with sarcasm.

"No, really. She give you the cold shoulder or something?" he asked a little too cheerfully for his father's mood.

"You have to at least see the person in question for them to give you the 'cold shoulder.' I haven't seen her tonight, and given the fact that it's coming upon eight o'clock, I imagine I won't be."

Chad said nothing for a moment. He shifted again.

"Want to talk about it?"

"What's to say? There are more women out there like your mother than I ever imagined. This time I won't be so willing to give my heart to a woman. Maybe ever again."

"Oh, now let's not get carried away, Dad. Claris isn't worth your throwing away your love life forever. It might hurt a little now, but you'll get over it."

"That's just it, Son. I'm not sure I will."

"You didn't think you'd get over Mom's leaving us either, but you did. Same with this Claris person. Somebody else will come along and you'll be ready again."

"That's the sad part. Claris was different. It was as if we had always been together, but separated. Like she was always out there. I felt an immediate bond with her. We got along so well. We understood each other so well. It was so comfortable, and yet, so exciting to be with her. So, will I ever find that again? Would I trust it again? I don't think so. In fact, I know I won't. I've lived long enough, had enough experience to tell you that that kind of relationship is rare."

"But she left, right? So, she wasn't what you imagined her to be. That's all. She's really not your type, Dad. And she's not who you think she is. Trust me."

Philip took in his son's words, then slowly the obvious questions began to surface.

"Why do you keep saying that? That she's not who I think she is. Do you know something I don't?"

Chad came to his feet and began pacing the room. He wouldn't face his father, which made warning bells sound even louder.

"Chad? Answer me," he ground out.

"See, I knew you wouldn't like this."

"Like what?"

Chad paused, then took his seat again, facing his father.

"I did a little investigative work on Claris. It seems she isn't trustworthy. She's in on some pretty big financial scams, Dad."

"What makes you think that? Who've you been talking to?"

"Well, I've always had my doubts, but, forgive me, but I took a fax that came through your office. I knew it had to do with Claris since there was a note to her scribbled on it."

"So that's what happened. You took the fax. Chad, you had no right . . ." Philip began.

"Just let me finish. I studied the papers, read between the lines, then had to find out on my own."

"Chad! How could you . . ."

"Because you're my Dad! I couldn't let you be involved with a hustler. You must have just been vulnerable. I know she's appealing. Especially since she's younger than you, and she is a good worker, but . . ."

"Wait a minute," Philip began rising to his feet. "Why are you here? I told you I was going off for the weekend. Out of town with Claris. What made you think I would be at home? Leaving your pregnant wife on a Friday night to just 'drop by?'"

Chad's face reddened. "I, um, well, . . ."

"You knew I was meeting Claris at Penny's?"

"Sure, you told me that much, but . . ."

"Who did you call, Chad? Did you tip off her old employer of her whereabouts?"

"I'm her boss," he confessed. "I had the right to know if she was skimming money off the top at her old company. I had to call, Dad. I had to!"

"And what did you say when you called?" he asked, anger evident in his tone.

"That I was her new employer and asked for a reference. You see, she wouldn't give one before. You hired her on face value, and now that she'd done this with the papers as evidence . . . well, all I can say is her old boss was extremely grateful to me for letting him know where she'd gone. They've been looking for her and I think they might press charges, Dad. I guess they'll straighten that out. He said he'd give her the benefit of the doubt before doing so—that is if he could only talk to her first."

"Did he call Claris after that? Perhaps that would explain her taking off without a word," he ventured.

"Oh, no. He wanted to meet with her in person. That's why I told him he could reach her either at the hotel or at Penny's around 5:15 this afternoon or so. I think he was planning to catch the next plane. So, forgive me, Dad, but it's all for the best."

"So you knew I'd be here. That Claris would be tied up trying to explain her innocence to her old boss," he spat. "This is a despicable thing you've done, Son. You see, Claris is innocent. We've talked about this. We had a plan. That's what we were going to do this weekend. Go back and show her previous employer that this man was behind this, not Claris. He's got a record for it. I have a detective friend of mine who's been working on it, and this guy she worked for is a nasty character, Chad."

"Look, Dad, I think Claris has been feeding you a line. Because if she'd actually set up a meeting with her old boss, why was he so surprised to get my call? Why would he be planning to catch a plane if the two of you were planning on seeing him this weekend?" he argued.

Philip began to pace. "I don't know," he admitted. "But something doesn't feel right, and I'm so mad at you, Chad. Can't you see what you've done? Claris doesn't stand a chance now. She was going back on her own. Now it looks like they had to catch her—right there at Penny's Diner. Embarrassing her."

"Well, her boss seemed kinda cool about it. He didn't seem the type to cause a scene. She probably went quietly," he added.

Philip turned on his heels, a slow dread building in his stomach. "Oh, no. Please, no."

"What, Dad?"

"Who did you speak to? The man's name?" he asked, the words catching in his throat.

"Um. Nathan somebody. Wait. Nathan Beecham. That's it. The one whose name was on the expense account reports. He's the one. He was her boss," Chad explained.

Philip grabbed up his jacket and stormed toward the back door.

"Where are you going now?" Chad called after him.

"I don't know. But I'd better find Claris somewhere or I'm afraid I'll lose her forever. We all will," he answered.

Chapter Eleven

Philip tore into Penny's Diner glancing around frantically.

"What in tarnation is after you?" Fred, the night manager chuckled.

"Fred!" Philip said, swiveling around to face him. "You've got to help me. Have you seen Claris? Claris Pemberton? You know, the woman who you met here in the middle of the night and got to stay 'till morning, only she stayed longer?"

"I know, I know," he answered, reaching back to brace his arm on the counter. "She was in here."

"She was? When?"

"Earlier. Round 'bout 5:15 p.m. Maybe a little later. Didn't order anything much, though. Cup of coffee. Like she did the first time she came in—at 3 a.m. the first time," he answered with a smile.

"That's right. What are you doing here so early? Don't you usually come in around eleven?"

"See you got my schedule memorized. Yes, sir, I normally don't, but I'm doing my pal, Robert, a favor. He likes to spend the dinner hour on Friday nights with his bride, Dora. We're doing a little shifting around so he can be a good husband, you know. Me, now, I'm footloose and fancy free. But guess where he takes her on his night out? Right here."

"That's nice, Fred, and I apologize for cutting you short, but I've got to find Claris and right away."

"Not any trouble, I hope," he said, a frown overtaking his face.

"I don't know. Where was she sitting? Perhaps she left some clue behind. A note, maybe?"

"Can't say as I found a thing. In fact, the little lady forgot to pay for the cup of coffee, but then, it's just a cup, I guess. She was probably not thinking when she left."

"Did you see her leave?"

"Nope."

"Well, where?"

"Where? Where what?"

"Where was she sitting, Fred?" Philip put in impatiently.

"Why, that booth right by the door. Where Robert and Dora are sitting. Just went and spoke to them and I can't say I found anything at the table left behind.

Philip left Fred in mid-sentence to check the booth. He hated that Fred hadn't seen Claris leave. It would have given him some idea of what was going on.

"Excuse me," Philip said, standing before the cheerful, older couple. "I apologize for this imposition, but did you happen to see a note or anything left at the table when you sat down?"

"Why, no," Robert answered, raising his eyebrows to his wife.

"Nor I," Dora replied.

"I don't guess you'd let me look under the table, would you. It's very important," he explained.

The couple rose from their seats, allowing Philip to crawl below.

"Lose your wallet or something?" Robert asked.

Philip found nothing under the table, realizing it was a long shot. Still, what else did he have to go on? he thought frantically.

"No, sir. Not a wallet. Just looking for a friend of mine who was supposed to meet me here. Thought she left something behind," he said.

"Oh, I see," Robert replied. His wife scooted back into the seat, but the tall man extended his hand to Philip. "By the way, I'm Robert O'Grady. I've seen you come in with your son a time or two. And Sadie is your daughter-in-law, isn't she?"

"Yes, as a matter of fact," Philip answered, glancing out at the parking lot in hopes that he could spot Claris' car. Instead, he noticed a dark sedan with rental plates. He looked around. Although he'd been in town only a short while, he felt all the faces were familiar.

"I'll be right back," Philip promised Robert. The man continued to stand as Philip tried to get Fred's attention. Instead, he was busy with two dinner specials just coming out. He balanced the tray and headed for Robert and Dora. "Fred, can you do me a favor? Please?" he urged as he walked over with the tray. "Sure, Philip, but let me serve these nice folks."

Robert took his seat and Fred placed the piping hot food before them, then turned to Philip.

"What's the favor?"

"Who does the rental car belong to?"

"Oh, that. Some fella, a stranger you know, who was in here earlier. He left a twenty behind for a little ole vanilla malt, then disappeared. Don't have any idea where, though, since his car is still here and all."

"Could you call the police, Fred? Get them to check the plates and see who rented it. It could be important," he stressed.

Fred rushed off while Philip stepped back over to the couple.

"I'm terribly sorry for interrupting your dinner, Mr. O'Grady."

"Robert," he corrected. "And this is my Dora."

"Glad to meet you," he said, feeling the undercurrent of tension building. Any moment now he'd find out if Claris had been forced to leave with Nathan. Please, no, he thought to himself.

"By the way," Dora put in. "I don't mean to pry, but did I hear you ask Fred about a woman named Claris?"

"Yes," Philip answered in surprised. "Do you know anything about her whereabouts?"

"No, not exactly. Only that she moved into the same little house I rented while I made up my mind whether to settle down and marry this hunk of a man. Took a lot of stubborn pride for me to make that move, but anyway, that's beside the point. I just hope she comes to the same conclusion I did—about getting married. Are those your intentions, Philip, or are you really just friends?"

"Excuse me? Did you say you know where she's moved to somewhere around here?"

"Yes! 492 Cheshire, just off Main. Cute little house set off the road a bit. Private. Nice."

Fred rushed back to Philip's side, scratching his head and carrying a scrap of paper.

"The sheriff's on the line. Says the car is rented in the name of Nathan Beecham. Ring any bells to you?"

"You betcha. Is he still on the line?"

"Yes."

Philip raced to the phone. "Sheriff, meet me at 492 Cheshire. It's the new address for Claris Pemberton, and this Nathan Beecham may have her held hostage and wait, here's Fred again. I'm giving him the name and number of someone you need to contact, a detective friend of mine. He'll fill in the blanks for everything else," Philip said. He quickly wrote down the information on Fred's order pad then took off into the night. He just hoped it wasn't too late.

* * *

"So you think you're pretty smart, huh? There's no sign of any faxed information that implicates me and you've probably put it in some safety deposit box, right? Mailed it to somebody?"

"Really, Nathan, I've got nothing on you. Except maybe kidnapping and attempted murder."

Nathan chuckled, sounding amused like he hadn't a care in the world.

"Maybe you *are* telling the truth. Maybe you're smarter than you let on. You got some big ideas, but you didn't really have a leg to stand on, so to speak," he added, kicking the chair leg where her ankles were bound and secured. "And you knew you couldn't win. Just what am I to do with you now? Hmmm?"

Nathan leaned in closer, running his hand up and down her arm. Claris squeezed her eyes shut.

"Don't be so nervous," he said, suddenly moving away and pacing the floor. The hollow sound on the hardwood floor of the mostly empty room echoed through the house. She was aware of her rapid heartbeat and labored breathing. How long can this go on, she wondered.

Nathan then brought out the gun stashed in his jacket pocket, swinging it about in a playful, threatening way. It was just like Nathan, she thought, as he dangled her life in front of her. She closed her eyes again, not willing to watch him anymore.

"Yes, maybe you're right," he said in amusement. She cracked one eye open to find Nathan loosening his tie.

"What are you doing?"

"You shouldn't see this," he explained, wrapping the tie around her head, covering her eyes in a blindfold. She then gave one last blind struggle and fight, making it difficult for him, she hoped, then the sudden, ear-piercing sound of shattering wood and glass broke into the quiet space, followed by the loud succession of gunshots she'd dreaded ever since Nathan had forced her from Penny's.

Her ears were the only clue, for she soon discovered she felt no pain.

"Geesh, that's smarts," she heard Nathan grumble, followed by a string of expletives.

"That's right, and you're lucky you're still alive, seeing as you were trying to do us all in," she heard a strange man's voice answer.

"What's going on?" Claris called out, jerking her head back and forth, wishing she could see something through the blindfold of the tie that blocked her vision. She then felt the warmth of hands encircling the tie, pulling it loose from her head. First she saw two police officers grabbing Nathan in a stronghold, then the man who'd loosened the tie came from around the back of the chair into her line of vision—Phil. Dear, sweet, wonderful, Phil. She had no idea how he'd found her, but he was the best sight she'd ever seen in her entire life.

Chapter Twelve

"And I apologize profusely for all the trouble I caused you, Claris."

"Well, I don't know," Claris trailed off, turning her nose up and waltzing away. "I've got to see to the hamburgers on the grill now," she said, not giving an inch.

"How many times must I do this, Dad?" Chad questioned. "It's been six months and I'm still apologizing."

"You've still got some work to do to gain her trust, Son. That's all I've got to say," Phil added with a laugh.

The two men glanced out the patio doors where Claris peaked under the lid of the grill and then turned to Sadie, relieving her of Chad's infant son, Harris.

"She sure is good to Sadie and my little boy. Wish she'd give me some slack," he added. "She makes me pay at the office *and* at home. Seems like since that guy is behind bars and she's fully cleared of any wrongdoing she'd lighten up." Phil turned to get the ketchup and other condiments out of the refrigerator and the salad and put them on the already set table. He then noticed Chad was still watching his wife, son, and Claris on the patio laughing and carrying on in an easy exchange.

"Sadie likes her, doesn't she?" Phil asked softly.

"Oh, man! She's like a second mother to her, since she lost her own several years ago. I guess Claris and Millie share that job.

We can't leave out Millie over at Penny's, the one who helped get us together."

"No, of course not," he added with a smile.

"Here we are," Claris announced as she strolled in with the finished hamburgers. She put the platter of sizzling burgers on the counter then turned to wrap one arm around Philip and encircled Sadie who was now hoisting the baby in her arms. The three of them stood opposite of Chad as though it were three against one.

"Yeah, that's right, Claris. Be nice to everybody but me."

"Chad," his father began, starting to say something, then breaking into a chuckle. To this, Sadie fell in form and began laughing under her breath. Only Claris stood unmoved as she stared proudly back.

"What? What's so funny, you guys? You got some secret joke or something?"

"Well, Chad," his father started again. "I'm afraid the joke's on you. You're in big trouble. Really, really big trouble."

"How's that?" Chad began. "Because not only does Claris have it over me at work, making me pay dearly for my calling that guy, and here at your house when we have dinners together, and now what? Sadie's on your side too? Like I'm going to get it there as well? Is that it?"

"Even worse. You see, you know I told you Claris and I were going away to that cabin I finally bought?"

"Yeah."

"Well, that was only half of it," Philip told him. "You see, you're really in hot water now, because Claris Pemberton, is now Claris Barnett. Your new stepmother," he announced.

Chad covered his face with his hands, making a big play at tossing and turning around the room. "Oh, no! Now she's my stepmother too? I'll never live this down, will I?" he asked, swiveling around to face Claris.

"Sorry, but nope. Not in a million years," Claris answered, then smiled.

THE END